# The Black Stiletto

### Black & White

# The Black Stiletto
## Black & White

The Second Diary—1959

A Novel

## Raymond Benson

Oceanview Publishing
Longboat Key, Florida

For My Mother

# ACKNOWLEDGMENTS

The author wishes to thank the following individuals for their help: Will Arrington, Austin Camacho, John Douglas, John F. Fox, James McMahon, Pat, Bob, Frank, David, and everyone at Oceanview Publishing; and Peter Miller and the good folks at PMA Literary & Film Management, Inc.

A very special thank you goes to Athena Stamos for her splendid promotional help on *The Black Stiletto*.

Follow the Black Stiletto at www.theblackstiletto.net

# AUTHOR'S NOTE

While every attempt has been made to ensure the accuracy of 1950s New York City, the Second Avenue Gym, Shapes, and the East Side Diner are fictitious.

The
Black
Stiletto
Black &
White

# I
# *Martin*
## The Present

The vintage 8mm projector whirred, the reels rotated, and the brand-new bulb cast a flickering image on the bare wall. The film was over fifty years old, so the quality wasn't great. It was in black and-white, of course.

The scene was a room, something like a photographer's studio, for artificial lighting bounced off a backdrop that hung down the far wall. A tall woman in a black costume stepped into the frame. The camera was far enough away so you could see her full body and the width of the room. A male mannequin dressed in street clothes stood across from her. She assumed a position, prepared herself, and then leapt into the air, kicked her right boot forward, and struck the mannequin square in the chest. The "opponent" toppled backward and crashed to the floor. The woman landed lightly on both feet and looked at the camera. The mask covered the top half of her head and face. The filmmaker zoomed in for a close-up. The woman's dark eyes sparkled through the holes in the black leather, and her lipstick-covered mouth formed a sweet smile. She said something to the man behind the camera; but as this was a silent film, I didn't under-stand it.

There she was. The Black Stiletto. Unbelievable.

After a cut, the woman had repositioned herself on the studio floor and the mannequin was back in place. This time, she drew the knife from the sheath strapped to her right thigh—a stiletto, of course—and performed a lightning-fast maneuver to switch her grasp from the hilt to the blade. She then threw the weapon across the room. The knife penetrated the middle of the mannequin's throat. Once again, she looked at the camera, smirked, and then laughed at something the unseen filmmaker said.

It was simply amazing. Despite the bizarre getup—the snug, black leather jacket and belt, tight leather pants, knee-high boots, small backpack, and half-hood mask—she was really *cute*! Her bubbly personality simply radiated from behind the disguise. She had charisma in spades.

And she was my mother.

Still is.

And I'm beginning to wonder if I'm not the only one who knows.

The old small reel of 8mm film was one of several trinkets my mother had kept in a strongbox along with a letter to me that revealed her identity as the Black Stiletto. The film can was marked "March 1959," so I have to assume that's when the footage was shot. There's no indication of who was behind the camera.

Fascinated, I continued to watch the approximately five minutes of footage. It's really difficult finding an 8mm projector in this age of digital photography, but I managed to get one at a thrift shop in Palatine. I set it up in the privacy of my house in Buffalo Grove.

While there existed a few vintage candid films of the Black Stiletto, most of them were shot by amateurs on the street—fleeting glimpses of her running or climbing. This was the first real, close-up, somewhat professionally staged footage of the famous crime fighter that I'd ever seen. Maybe it was the *only* footage.

It was just a few months ago when I received the surprise of my life. My mother's attorney, Uncle Thomas—he isn't really my uncle, but I've always called him that; I've known him since I was a kid—had held the strongbox in safekeeping until which time she became incapacitated. And that she definitely is. My mom has Alzheimer's and currently resides in Woodlands North, a nursing home in Riverwoods, Illinois. She doesn't really know who I am anymore, although she recognizes me as someone she loves. She's seventy-three now. I'm almost forty-nine.

My name is Martin Talbot. My mother's name is Judy Talbot, née Cooper. Unbeknownst to anyone but me—that I know of—she was the legendary and notorious costumed vigilante known as the Black Stiletto, who operated in New York City and Los Angeles between 1958 and 1963 or so. After she seemingly vanished, the Stiletto became the stuff of myths and pop-culture mystique. No one knew her true identity or what happened to her, despite the deluge of Black Stiletto "products" that appeared in the eighties and since—comic books, action figures, Halloween costumes, and even a movie in the nineties starring a young Angelina Jolie.

Uncle Thomas didn't know the contents of the strongbox he handed over to me just a short while ago. You can imagine the shock when I learned my mom was the Black Stiletto. At first I didn't believe it. It was completely crazy. But then I started exploring our old house in Arlington Heights—which is still up for sale—and found her costume and a series of diaries in a secret closet in the basement. I've managed to read the first diary, marked "1958," and learned how fourteen-year-old Judy Cooper ran away from her mother, brothers, and an abusive stepfather in Odessa, Texas, back in 1953. She ended up in New York alone and penniless. There, she was befriended by Freddie Barnes, the owner of a gym in East Greenwich Village, and moved into a room above the facility. She worked as the gym's cleaning woman, but after hours Freddie taught her how to box. A Japanese trainer named Soichiro instructed her in martial arts before stuff like *judo* and *karate* were in the public consciousness. It was her first serious boyfriend, a Mafia soldier named Fiorello, who taught her how to use a knife. After Fiorello's murder, she became the Black Stiletto and took it upon herself to fight crime in the city. Law enforcement didn't like it. Soon she was wanted by the police and the FBI. Nevertheless, throughout 1958, the Stiletto fought petty criminals, the Mafia, and Communist spies. Late in

the year she managed to take a trip back to Odessa, find her abusive
stepfather—a man named Douglas Bates—and exact her revenge.

My mother's activities even reached across the span of decades
to bite us in the here and now. Roberto Ranelli, a Mafia hit man, was
released from prison; somehow he knew my mother was the Black
Stiletto, and he tracked her to the Chicago suburbs. Luckily, he was
old and unwell. Although he murdered my real estate agent and attempted to kill my mom, some latent memory in my Alzheimer's-
stricken mother kicked in—literally—and she miraculously disabled
the killer right there in the nursing home. But it was his heart that
killed him.

I'm still discovering my mother's story, but I've been terribly
busy. I'm currently jobless and I've had to spend time over the summer looking for employment. I also had to deal with my daughter
Gina's move to New York to attend Juilliard. I'm a divorced dad.
Gina's mother, Carol, still lives in the area and I suppose you can say
we get along all right. I wasn't terribly happy about Gina going to
New York to study acting and dance, but she finally convinced me
that she had to follow her own heart and not mine.

Anyway, I haven't had a spare moment to delve into my mother's
remaining diaries. I just now finally got the 8mm projector to view
that mysterious film.

Back to the images on the wall. The Black Stiletto "sparred" with
the mannequin, showing off her fighting ability. That poor mannequin took quite a beating. At one point she chopped the guy's
shoulder with a flat spear-hand, *karate*-style, and the arm fell right
off. She put a hand to her lips and giggled, turned to the camera and
mouthed, "I'm sorry." There was a cut and the arm was back on the
mannequin. My mother kept laughing. She was obviously having a
good time, but you could also tell she found the experience silly. She
rolled her eyes whenever the cameraman gave her direction. I assume they were the only two people in the studio.

After a couple more setups in which the Stiletto punched and
kicked and stabbed the mannequin, there was a cut and suddenly

we were outside on a Manhattan street corner. It was nighttime, the only illumination provided by a streetlight and some kind of spotlight the filmmaker had aimed at the side of a building and its fire escape. Due to the poor lighting, the picture was grainier than before. The Black Stiletto entered the frame, threw a rope and some kind of grappling hook to the bottom of the fire escape ladder. The hook caught, and she pulled the ladder down to street level. She then swiftly coiled the rope, attached it to her belt, and climbed the ladder to the second-floor landing. The filmmaker stayed on the ground and tilted the camera to follow her. She glided up the steps to the third floor and then the fourth. Her speed was uncanny. She moved like a cat, graceful and lithe. After reaching the fifth floor, she climbed the extra few feet to the roof, swung a leg over, and hopped up. Now she was a tiny black figure against the even darker sky. You could barely see her; nevertheless, it was obvious that she waved at the camera before darting out of view.

The film ended. The rest of the roll appeared to be blank feeder.

I was stunned. I was in possession of a gold mine. Who wouldn't pay big bucks for this footage? But then, of course, I'd have to reveal how I got the film. I'm not sure I can do that while Mom's still alive.

I was about to stop the projector, rewind the film, and watch it again—but suddenly there was another scene at the very end of the roll. This time, the Stiletto sat in a small room in front of a mirror surrounded by bright lightbulbs. Makeup supplies sat on the counter. A dressing room. She stared into the mirror, applied more lipstick, and adjusted her mask. Unlike in the previous footage, she didn't acknowledge the camera. In fact, she ignored it. I was certain she didn't know she was being filmed at this particular moment. She leaned forward, dissatisfied with something, and then she pulled off the hood/mask. Judy Cooper revealed herself to the mirror.

My mother. Age twenty-one. My God, she was beautiful. Her long black hair, which had been bundled up inside the hood, fell to her shoulders. She applied some mascara to her eyelashes, examined her handiwork, and then swept up her hair with one hand while she slipped the hood over her head with the other. After she tucked her hair inside, the Stiletto positioned the mask properly on her face and stood.

Cut.

The film truly ended and ran out of the projector.

This was an astonishing artifact of history. The Black Stiletto in action, up close and personal. It was both exhilarating and disturbing. I was excited to have an authentic recording of the woman in action. What bothered me, though, was that last scene. It caught her with the mask off, her full face revealed. She must have known about the footage, since the reel was in her safekeeping; but I'm convinced she was unaware of being filmed in the dressing room when the guy was doing it.

I rethreaded the film and viewed the whole thing again, trying to pick up clues as to where the thing was shot and who the cameraman might have been. There were no indicators to identify the building other than it was a typical five-story New York brownstone that sat on a corner. The street signs were out of the frame, so it could be anywhere in Manhattan.

When it was over, I was left with more questions. Did this mean there were more people who knew the Black Stiletto's true identity? Who was the cameraman? Why was the film shot? There had to be a story behind it.

Obviously I had to read the second diary—the one from 1959—to find out what it was.

# 2
# Judy's Diary
## 1959

JANUARY 9, 1959

I'm still a little shaken by what happened last night, dear diary. The Black Stiletto made her first appearance of '59 and it was an eventful one. I didn't sleep at all once I got back to my room.

But before I try to gather my thoughts about it, first let me bring you up to date. I haven't written since New Year's and I'm starting a new diary.

After the big annual party we had on New Year's Eve, I took it easy for a few days; just worked at the gym and stayed out of trouble, ha ha. A lot of stuff is happening in the world. Alaska became a new state this week, so I guess they have to make a whole new American flag with another star on it. Also, Fidel Castro just took control of Cuba. I knew it was coming and I told you so, dear diary. I was hoping my work last year taking out that Cuban spy might have done some good, but I suppose it didn't. There's a lot of talk in the papers speculating where Castro's allegiances are going to lie. America or Russia? Since he's a Socialist, he's probably going to side with the Communists. That worries a lot of people, Cuba being so close to us and all.

Anyway, I suddenly got stir crazy yesterday and decided to go out. I think it was hearing that silly Chipmunks Christmas song on the radio for the millionth time. I thought it was cute a couple of

weeks ago, but ever since it got to be number one, they've been playing it to death on the radio. Now I'd like to *strangle* those chipmunks! Thank goodness the new song by the Platters is climbing
the charts—"Smoke Gets in Your Eyes," and ain't that the truth?
It's too bad Elvis is in the army. I miss hearing new songs by him.
They keep putting out pieces he recorded a while back, like "One
Night" and "I Got Stung." More and more rock-and-roll acts are
giving him some competition, and I like a lot of it. Buddy Holly, the
Everly Brothers, Ritchie Valens. There're a lot of new popular
singers that aren't as wild, too, like Frankie Avalon and Bobby
Darin. They're all right, but I think they're a little too "safe"—that's
the only way I can describe them. I'm even listening to Frank Sinatra and Dean Martin a lot more than I used to. The other night Freddie put on a record by a jazz musician named Miles Davis. He plays
a horn. I liked it all right, it was different. It's interesting how most
of the jazz musicians are Negroes. Not too many white men play
jazz. Why is that? And that brings me to last night, for the first part
of this story has to do with Negroes.

It's been cold and wet outside, being January and all, so I dressed
in my warm Stiletto outfit and took to the streets. I guess I went
looking for a crime in progress, since that's what I do, but I can't say
I was hoping to find one. I mean, I really don't want crime to occur
at all. Wouldn't it be nice if people everywhere were always safe
from criminals? But I know that's never going to happen in a million years, so there I was, racing across the rooftops and down to the
shadows of the street to stalk the night.

It was around 11:30 or so and I was in the West Village. I hadn't
seen anything out of the ordinary, so I decided to go home and get
out of the cold. I was poised in-between buildings on 7th Avenue,
out of the streetlights, waiting for the traffic to ease a bit so I could
dart across and head east. Close by there's a jazz club called the Village Vanguard—apparently it's famous, a New York institution.
Anyway, a Negro couple came out, a young man and woman. I guess
they were in their 20s. Not much older than me. He had his arm

around her and they were laughing. They looked cute, obviously out on a date. Must have just heard some music in the club, but nobody else was coming out. I was maybe fifteen or twenty feet away from them, so my acute hearing picked up their voices. He said something like, "If we can get a cab, I'll make sure you're home on time." And she replied, "My daddy'll kill us if I ain't." They must've left the show early 'cause she had a deadline.

So the young man stood at the curb with his arm up, you know, like he was hailing a taxi. Several empty cabs drove by, but none of them stopped. I felt bad for them. Since living in New York I've become much more aware of the prejudice that exists against Negroes.

When I was growing up in Odessa, I didn't really think about it. Down in the south, we called them "colored." I've been training myself to say "Negroes" because that's more polite. The Negroes in Odessa all lived south of the tracks, not that far from where we lived, so I was used to seeing them. I knew a lot of white people in Texas didn't care for colored people and I sometimes heard my brothers saying "nigger this" and "nigger that" but I never used that word. I knew it wasn't nice. I've heard white people use that word here in New York and talk about Negroes as if they were less than human.

Thank God Freddie's not that way. He lets Negroes come to the gym. When I first came to New York, I was under the impression that most gyms were as segregated as anyplace else. But a lot of boxers are Negroes, so I guess it's not so unusual. In fact, all races come to the Second Avenue Gym. Whites, Negroes, Mexicans, and Latin fellas from Cuba or Puerto Rico. So I'm used to being around all sorts of skin colors. They're all just people.

Anyway, as I watched that poor couple wait for a cab, I remembered everything I'd been reading in the papers lately concerning the civil rights speeches made by a Negro preacher named Martin Luther King, Jr. He's always getting in trouble with white people. Actually, it's the other way around. White people are always making trouble *for* him. I still remember last fall when he was here in New York promoting his book, *Strive Toward Freedom*—which I read, by the way—and he was stabbed in the chest at a department store in Harlem. The irony is that it was a colored woman who did it. They said she was a mentally imbalanced homeless vagrant. I understand she was committed to a state mental hospital. Dr. King survived, thank goodness. Anyway, there's racial tension in all the cities, powder kegs ready to explode. I don't blame the Negroes at all for the unrest. They've had a hard time all these years. All they want is to be treated equally. I understand it. Why doesn't everyone else?

So I stood there in the shadows feeling sorry for those two young people, and then, from up the street, these three white men came walking. They were in their late 20s or early 30s, I guess. They looked like they were drunk or something, because they were talking loud and laughing, pushing each other, you know, acting tough. They saw the colored couple standing on the sidewalk and one of the men called out, "Hey, look at the niggers! Trying to get a taxi! Good luck, niggers!" I hate that word and don't like writing it down, but that's what they said. The men laughed like it was the funniest thing they'd ever heard. The boyfriend tried to ignore them, but I could see the young lady was getting nervous as the white men approached. She pulled on her date's arm and said, "Come on, let's get the subway." He saw the wisdom in her suggestion and nodded. So they started walking toward me, heading for the 7th Avenue subway entrance. But then the three troublemakers got in front of them.

"What you doing down here, *boy?*" one asked. "*Harlem*'s a long way away!" He said it like Harlem was some kind of ugly place. Unfortunately, because of the cold weather the avenue was deserted. There wasn't anyone else around to stand up for the couple. The three men continued to taunt the pair, forcing them back against the building. One guy shoved the colored man. That's when I couldn't take it anymore. I stepped out of the darkness and revealed myself.

"Stop it," I said. "Leave them alone!"

The three thugs whirled around and, boy, were they surprised.

"Look, it's her!"

"The Black Stiletto!"

They didn't know whether to be excited about seeing me in the flesh or if they should be angry that I'd interrupted their fun.

"Why don't you fellas run along and leave this nice couple in peace?" I said.

As for the young man and woman, they stood there wide-eyed and mouths open, half in fear and half in awe.

"Go on," I prompted. "Get out of here."

That's when the leader of the trio took a step in my direction. "What are you, some kind of nigger lover?" he snarled.

Well, I didn't like that one bit. I lost my temper. I moved in quickly and slapped the man across the face before he could react. I really hadn't meant to start a fight, I just wanted to teach the guy a lesson, you know, like a teacher scolding an unruly pupil.

"Now turn around and go away!"

The man hadn't expected that and his eyes turned red. "Why, you bitch!" he shouted, and he went at me, fists flying. I blocked the blows easily enough and then let him have a strong right hook on the jaw. He fell to the pavement.

Then one of the other guys produced a switchblade and flicked it open. He waved it menacingly at me, ready to attack.

I drew my stiletto, which, of course, was bigger and scarier. "You really want to play knives with me?" I asked him.

That didn't intimidate him. He swished the blade back and forth and came at me without much finesse, so I effortlessly kicked the weapon out of his hand. He yelped in pain and jumped back before I could stab him. I wouldn't have done it, but that's what he thought.

The third guy must have been the smartest one, for he said to his humiliated comrades, "Come on, let's get out of here."

"I'm not gonna let some *freak* get the better of me!" the man blubbered. He charged recklessly. These punks were all bravado. They talked big and acted tough, but they had no discipline or training. I sidestepped the raging bulldog and he missed me. He rushed at me again, and this time my knee met his stomach. *Oomph.* Knocked the breath right out of him. He staggered for a moment and fell back into the arms of the third guy, who implored, "Come on, Wayne, let's go!" Now he and the second guy were scared. They helped their gasping friend move away, and the trio disappeared down the avenue with their tails between their legs.

I turned to the couple, who stood shivering from fright or the cold, I don't know which.

"Are you two all right?"

The young man nodded. "Thank you, miss."

The woman also spoke. "Yes. Thank you. Are you really the Black Stiletto?"

I shrugged. "What time you supposed to be home?" I asked her.

"Midnight. In about ten minutes!"

"Wait here." I stepped out to the curb, raised my arm, and whistled as loud as I could. A taxi stopped right away. The driver's jaw dropped, and he stared at me like I was some kind of ghost. I reached into my backpack and pulled out some cash that I carry with me. Twenty dollars. That was more than enough. I waved the couple over and opened the back door for them. I gave the twenty to the driver and asked, "You don't have a problem with taking these nice folks up to Harlem, do you?"

"No, ma'am!" he replied.

"Good. And be quick about it. I've got your cab number and I'll know if they come to any harm. You understand me?"

The driver nodded, his jaw still hanging open.

The pair got inside and thanked me again. I shut the door and slapped the back of the car as if it was a horse. The driver pulled out into traffic and off they went.

That felt really good. Best twenty dollars I ever spent.

But that's not what shook me up and caused my sleepless night. That came next, when I was on my way back to the gym.

It happened at Washington Square Park. There were a few people walking here and there, but mostly the place was deserted. It suddenly started to snow, and it was gorgeous. I'm not crazy about winters in New York, but when it snows something magical happens. I was feeling good after helping that couple, so I walked out into the middle of the park and let the snow fall around me. I wanted to dance and sing and twirl around, so I did. Some pedestrians stopped to watch and point. Yep, a Black Stiletto sighting! And what was she doing? Dancing with an invisible partner in the snowfall. They must have thought I was nuts. I laughed aloud and waved. Some waved back.

And then there was a gunshot.

I felt the heat of the bullet whiz past my left side, too close for comfort. I immediately hit the pavement and lay flat, my eyes scanning the park's perimeter for the shooter. A man in a heavy coat started walking toward me from underneath the arch. His arm was outstretched; in his hand was a gun pointed straight at me. As he moved forward, he fired again. The round splintered the cement near my head, spraying tiny chips of concrete across my face.

I got up and ran.

I didn't know if he was alone or if he had friends with him. I wasn't taking any chances. Although he missed me twice, I could tell he had experience with the gun. The weapon was some kind of semiautomatic.

Another shot hit a park bench just in front of me. I crossed 4th Street and dashed to Thompson Street. With buildings east and west of me, I was safer. I slipped over to an unlit closed storefront, crouched in the darkness, and watched my pursuer. He reached the south edge of the park and prepared to cross 4th. He was alone. Although he was too far away for me to know for certain, I was pretty sure I'd never seen him before. There was something about his demeanor, though, that said "gangster." I had been around enough of those Mafia types when I was with Fiorello, I could spot them a mile away. I can't describe it—it's an attitude, along with the way they dress. And who else would walk around New York carrying a piece if he wasn't an undercover cop or a mobster? This guy was no undercover cop.

As soon as he reached the T-intersection of 4th and Thompson, he halted. He peered down the street but didn't see me. I was safely tucked in the shadows behind a line of garbage cans—and then my heart nearly stopped. I saw my footprints in the freshly fallen snow. The street and sidewalks were covered with a light dusting; my trail was in plain sight, leading right to where I squatted.

The gunman spotted the prints, too. From where he stood, he raised the firearm and shot three rounds—hitting one of the trash cans twice and shattering a storefront window pane behind me with the third. Shards of glass showered me. He continued walking toward my position with the gun pointed right at me. There was no place to run. I couldn't attack *him* unless he was closer. If he kept his distance, he could take potshots at me forever, or at least until his ammo ran out. Seeing that he had a semiautomatic and probably packed spare magazines in his pocket, the odds were pretty good that he'd hit me sooner rather than later.

Well, I wasn't going to be a sitting duck. I picked up one of the trash cans—it was full of smelly garbage—and I threw it at him. It made a terrible racket as it banged and bounced on the street. He shot at it reflexively, providing a diversion so I could stand, draw my stiletto, and throw it. It was a distance of thirty to forty feet, but I had practiced with targets at that range numerous times.

The blade struck him in the shoulder.

The man yelped. His gun arm jerked upward and he fired a wild shot, hitting the building behind me. He didn't drop his weapon, though. I bolted to the side, for the creep immediately regained his aim and let loose a salvo of bullets. The shadows saved my life, for I rolled back and dropped into the dark basement entrance of a brownstone next to the storefront. There, I stooped and kept my head below street level. The gunman stopped shooting; I knew he was trying to see if he'd hit me. After a few seconds of nerve-racking silence, I heard his footsteps approaching. He stepped onto the sidewalk and stopped. I imagined his confusion—where was she? She was just here!

Then someone inside the building turned on a light. The illumination cast a glow over the entire sidewalk—and me, too.

All that time I spent in gymnastics paid off. I placed my hands on the sidewalk above my head, pushed off with my feet and propelled my body up and over, just as I had done years before on the uneven parallel bars. He was standing right there, his body perpendicular to mine. Keeping my hands flat on the sidewalk, I swung my legs at him, parallel to the pavement, and collided with his shin. He shouted in pain and fell, the gun discharging aimlessly one more time before he dropped it. I think I broke his leg.

I quickly got to my feet, kicked the gun several feet away, and stood over him. He rolled and writhed, holding his lower left leg, his face grimacing in agony. The hilt of my stiletto still stuck out the front of his right shoulder. Blood covered his coat.

The sound of approaching sirens filled the air. I guess all that gunfire attracted the cops. I didn't have a lot of time. When they arrived, I wanted to be long gone. The city police would like nothing better than to capture the masked vigilante who they thought was such a menace. Never mind that she was one of the good guys.

I placed the sole of my boot on the man's chest and put my weight on him.

"Who are you?" I growled through my teeth. His eyes were now full of fear. He knew he had lost the battle. "Why were you shooting at me? *Answer me!*" I dug the heel of the boot into his sternum. He winced and grunted.

The sirens grew louder. They'd arrive any second.

"There's a contract . . . on you," he muttered between gasps. "Big . . . reward."

"A contract on me? From who? Why?"

There was a hint of a smile on his face. "DeLuca. For killing . . . his brother."

Then it made sense. The new Mafia don, Franco DeLuca, wanted revenge for the death of his brother, Don Giorgio. But I didn't kill him! Okay, dear diary, I *wanted* to kill him for giving the order to whack Fiorello, but the fat bastard went and broke his neck before I could do it. He was going to shoot me, and I disarmed him. I couldn't help it if the don lost his balance, fell, and hit his head on a table. I even called for the ambulance. But I got the credit for his death.

My ears twitched underneath my hood. The sirens were *really* loud now. The patrol cars were just around the corner.

I pulled my stiletto out of the guy's shoulder. He screamed. Sorry, mister. I then stepped off of him and started to run. I looked up— several pedestrians from the park stood on the north side of 4th Street and stared at me. Plenty of witnesses. Couldn't be helped.

At that moment, two cop cars pulled around the corner, lights flashing and sirens blasting. I hightailed it south on Thompson and took a left on 3rd Street. I don't think they saw me because no one chased after me. The cops were probably more interested in the guy lying in the street with a broken leg and knife wound.

I kept to the shadows, took my time, and slowly made my way east to Second Avenue and 2nd Street and the warmth and safety of my room above the gym. That didn't mean I could sleep, though. I laid in bed the rest of the night, tossing and turning, and reliving the events of the evening.

Sometimes this crime-fighting business isn't as fun as it's supposed to be.

# 3
# *Judy's Diary*
## 1959

### JANUARY 11, 1959

I thought I'd write a little this morning before I go to work in the gym.

Last night I went over to Lucy's apartment to watch TV with her. I've been doing that a lot lately since she moved out of my room and got her own place. She's doing much better now. Her injuries have healed nicely. She's still a little emotionally fragile and she doesn't want to testify at Sam's trial, but the D.A. says there's no case against him if she doesn't. I told her she has to do it. She can't let guys like Sam Duncan get away with beating up women.

She finally went back to work at the diner just last week. Manny put her on a part-time schedule for as long as she needs it, but she seems to be doing fine. I bet she insists on full-time work before the end of the month.

The good thing is that she's been seeing a lot of that lawyer, Peter Gaskin. At the New Year's Eve party she told me he might ask her to marry him but he hasn't yet. I told her not to rush into anything. I know from my experience (very *limited* experience, ha ha) that the first month or two of a new relationship is pretty intense. Well, heck, she knows that. She's been around the block more times than me. After all, she's six years older.

So I've been going over to watch TV with her. We like most of the same shows, although she's not as big a fan of *Alfred Hitchcock Presents* as I am. We like the comedies like *I Love Lucy* and *Milton Berle*. Oh, and *Candid Camera* leaves us in stitches. The other night we watched a new western show that premiered called *Rawhide*. *Ed Sullivan* is still a staple, and I enjoy seeing the musical acts he has on his program. I usually watch that at home with Freddie.

Last night we were watching *What's My Line*. During the commercial I picked up the *Daily News* and noticed that tired old police sketch of the Black Stiletto on one of the inner pages. The article said I was involved in all sorts of crimes in the city—burglary, assaulting people on the street, and even murder—all of which, of course, are lies. I felt my blood start to boil as I read that nonsense. The police commissioner was once again quoted as saying I was a "menace" and "dangerous." The entire force had orders to catch me and, if they had to, shoot me on sight.

Gee whiz, the cops are after me, the FBI is after me, the Mafia is after me. I guess I'm not the most popular girl at the dance, ha ha.

"Crime's getting a lot worse in the city," Lucy said. She must have noticed what I was reading.

"I guess so," I replied.

"Do you think she really helps or not?"

"Who?"

"The Black Stiletto."

"Of course she does. I don't believe a word of this. She doesn't commit crimes, she stops them."

"Are you so sure? Why would they print that if it isn't true?"

I put down the paper. "Lucy, don't tell me you believe everything you read in the newspaper."

"Well, it's supposed to be true, isn't it? Why would the newspaper lie?"

"Come on, the Black Stiletto caught your ex-boyfriend, remember? The guy who beat you and left you for dead. She brought him to justice. How can you say that about her?"

"Maybe she was just after publicity."

I was shocked. I couldn't believe Lucy was talking that way about the woman who avenged her. *Me*. But I couldn't say that.

"I'm surprised at you, Lucy. I thought you liked the Black Stiletto. You once told me you admired her. How can you be so ungrateful?"

She looked at me funny. "What's wrong with you? Why are you defending her?"

"'Cause I think she's brave and she's doing the city a service. What's wrong with *you*?"

"Nothing! I'm just saying maybe she's not as good as I thought."

I knew I was getting hot under the collar and had to calm down. I certainly didn't want her to get suspicious.

"I have to go," I said. I started gathering up my purse and stuff.

"Judy, what's wrong? What are you mad about?"

"I'm not mad. I just realized I need to do something back at the gym."

"You're ticked off about something. Wait, the show's not over yet."

"That's all right. I'll talk to you later."

So without much discussion, I left. Yes, I *was* mad at her. She was bad-mouthing *me* right in front of my face, but I know she didn't realize that. I'll apologize the next time I see her, but at that moment I wanted to shake her. It's like she's in denial about what happened to her. If the Stiletto hadn't nabbed Sam, there's no telling who else he might have hurt. He probably would've come back to finish the job on her so she wouldn't talk.

Once again I stewed in my room, unable to sleep well. All kinds of things were going through my head and I couldn't settle down. I felt blue. After the other night, when that gangster tried to kill me and I found out Franco DeLuca wants me dead, and then reading that article in the paper about how I'm as bad as the common criminals, I started questioning what I was doing. Does the Black Stiletto really do any good? Why don't I get more support from the public? It didn't make any sense. You'd think the police would want someone like me helping them catch the bad guys. Gosh, Superman sure doesn't have that problem in the comic books! The people love Superman and Batman! But they don't exist. I guess people can't accept a crime fighter who wears a disguise but has no "super powers." Sure, I can hear, smell, and see better than most people, and I know how to fight, but I'm normal. I'm a person. But according to the *Daily News*, I'm no better than a common thief.

So I'm wondering—if everyone really does hate me, why should I bother? Should the Black Stiletto hang up her disguise and disappear?

I have to go to work. Freddie's calling me.

LATER

I still have that FBI guy's phone number. Richardson. I still don't know his first name. Ever since we had those few short conversations on the phone, I've thought about him sometimes. He sounded like a nice guy. He also seemed to indicate he didn't think what I was doing was such a bad thing. But he's an FBI agent, so what do I know? He probably wants to catch me, too.

After work, I went out to a pay phone and called him. I never make calls from the gym as the Stiletto, you know. They have ways of tracing phone calls. I don't know how it works, but I've read about it. Anyway, since I have the direct phone number to his office, I figured I'd wish him Happy New Year.

It wasn't 5:00 yet, so I hoped he'd still be at work. He was.

"Special Agent Richardson," he answered.

"Happy New Year, Special Agent Richardson," I said sweetly. "I didn't know you were a *Special* Agent. What makes you so special?"

It took him a moment. "Stiletto? Is that you?"

"It's me. How are you? Did you have a nice holiday?"

I heard him chuckle. "I'm surprised to hear from you. It's been a while."

"I haven't talked to you in a year, Mr. Richardson! It was 1958 when we last spoke."

"That it was."

"What's your first name, anyway?"

"John."

"John Richardson." I said it a couple of times. "That's a nice name, John Richardson."

"Are you going to tell me your name?"

"Ha ha, nice try, John. I tell you what, you can call me Eloise."

"Eloise? You've used that alias before."

"You FBI fellas know everything, don't you?"

I couldn't believe I was flirting with a federal agent. I didn't even know him. I tried to picture what he looked like and envisioned a handsome, clean-cut man in a suit. Probably physically fit and in his thirties. I could go for a man like that. I really could. If only he wasn't working for the law.

"Can I help you with something, Eloise?" he asked. There was playfulness in his voice now too.

"Oh, no, not really. I just wanted to say hello and wish you a Happy New Year and all. You keeping out of trouble, John?"

"I am. I can see you're not, though. I just read about you in the paper."

"Yeah, and it's all lies, John. You know that. Don't you? I'm no criminal."

"But you are, Eloise. Vigilantism is against the law. The police are after you. So is the FBI, I'm afraid."

I laughed. "I'm more worried about Franco DeLuca's goons taking me out before any of you nice fellas do."

"Franco DeLuca? Why? What do you know about Don DeLuca?"

"He has a contract out on me. Blames me for the death of his brother. You know, Don Giorgio."

"And were you responsible?"

"No."

"Those are very dangerous people, Eloise. They're involved in some serious criminal activities. I hope you'll stay away from them."

"It's not like I'm gonna ring their doorbell and try to sell 'em Girl Scout cookies."

"You know what I mean."

"John, you know I'm not a bad person. Why do I get all this bad press? Why do they make up lies about me? I've never robbed anyone in my life. I don't attack innocent people on the street. I've never hurt anyone who didn't deserve it. I'm not a murderer."

As soon as I said it, I felt funny. It was a lie and I knew it. I *had* killed. Two men who definitely had it coming. A Mafia hit man who probably murdered dozens of people, and my evil stepfather who abused me when I was younger and drove my mother to her grave.

"You didn't kill Vittorio Ranelli?" John asked.

I played dumb. "You mean that mobster who was an enforcer for the DeLuca Family? Had a twin brother who went to prison?"

"That's the one."

"Weren't those two on your Most Wanted list? For murder, extortion, racketeering, and other crimes?"

"Yes, they were."

"Then what's the problem?"

John paused and then said, "The media paints you out to be just as bad as the criminals for a reason, Eloise. You're breaking the law. It's that simple."

"I don't understand why they don't report the good things I do."

"They have in the past. You've received credit for some of it. But you have to understand, what you do makes the police look bad."

"How?"

"When they can't catch some criminal, but you can, then of course they're not going to like you. I imagine they have connections with all the papers, so they want to perpetuate their side of the story."

I thought about that a second. "Does the FBI also have those kinds of connections?"

"Sure."

"So what would it take for you to use *your* connections with the papers to get a positive story about me printed?"

He laughed. "I don't know, Eloise. How about let's meet and talk about it."

"That's what you said before. You know I can't meet you in person. You'd arrest me, unmask me, and then I'd really get some bad press."

"I'm not so sure about that," he said. "Maybe I just really want to meet you. I like—I like your voice."

That surprised me. Now he was flirting with *me*.

"Well, what's that expression? Quid pro quo? If you do something about all this bad press, then maybe I'll consider meeting you. As long as you promise not to arrest me."

He was silent a moment and then he said, "I'll see what I can do, Eloise."

I thanked him and told him it was nice talking to him. He asked me when I would call him again, and I just told him, "Soon."

I had butterflies in my stomach as I walked back to the gym.

# 4
## John
### Home Dictaphone Recording

Today is January 11, 1959.

This and subsequent recordings are personal supplements to my submitted written reports to Special Agent in Charge Don Haggerty. I'm making the recordings at home on the new Dictaphone I got for Christmas.

I was surprised to receive another phone call from the Black Stiletto this afternoon. I haven't spoken to her since last fall.

She's an interesting case. The woman sounds so normal over the phone, just an ordinary girl with a Southern accent. She's definitely not a native New Yorker. I place her from somewhere like Oklahoma or Texas. When I asked her for her real name, she coyly told me it was Eloise, which I know isn't true. She's used that name before in dealing with the police and FBI. Yeah, the more I think about it, the more she sounds like a Texas girl.

I'll have to report this to Haggerty tomorrow. He'd already left the office when I got off the phone with her. Ever since he learned she gives me a call every now and then, he's been hounding me to catch her. I told him all she does is call and chat. Haggerty wants me to lure her in. When I asked him what he meant by that, he winked and laughed in that vulgar way he does. I told him I didn't think the FBI had any reason to arrest her. It's a New York City Police matter. Haggerty snapped at me. He said the fact that she was involved with the capture of a Cuban spy made her the Bureau's business. He also said she's obviously mixed up with the mob, too, and that's the Bureau's business, too. I couldn't argue with him. He wants the usual written reports on my progress. I just typed a scathing report about her that I'll give to him, and keep a copy for my files, of course.

I suggested to Haggerty that we should be concentrating more on the narcotics traffic in New York instead of chasing after a female vigilante who so far has done nothing but help the police— and us. He asked me if I could chew gum and walk at the same time. In other words, I'm supposed to handle multiple tasks at once. Work the narcotics cases and catch the Black Stiletto.

Still, I think she's right about something she said on the phone. The Black Stiletto doesn't get the credit she deserves.

Special Agent in Charge Don Haggerty. What a piece of work. Between you and me and the four walls of my apartment, I think the man is a bag of hot air. I don't know how he got to be one of the SACs in New York. Frankly, I think I could do the job. That said, I don't believe I'd want to be Assistant Director, the top dog in the field office. Haggerty reports to him. But Haggerty's always playing politics instead of doing his job. He's always "out to lunch" with NYPD Chief Bruen in Manhattan—they're bosom buddies—or he's with the mayor, or the governor, or this judge or that judge. Seems like he delegates all the administrative work and hands out cases to me and the other Special Agents. That means we're doing the overtime.

A lot of the other SAs in the New York office are working on Communist cases, looking into the civil rights unrest, or the racketeering pestilence. I keep saying in the weekly meetings that narcotics trafficking is about to explode and be bigger than anything. They don't listen, which is why I'm on the lower priority cases.

Speaking of my own cases, there was another heroin bust in Harlem. The police raided a convenience store that's a front for Purdy's operation. Allegedly a front, I should say. The city police may have bungled the arrests. The three men they took into custody were later released. Carl Purdy has his fingers in a lot of pockets in this city. He's as bad as the Italian mobsters. But, hey, if the Negroes want to be hopped up on narcotics, then they will be. Purdy will meet that demand. It's a scourge. I'm convinced he's the man in charge in Harlem, although I have no hard evidence yet. Added to that are more and more mobland killings. The Negro gangsters are battling the Italian gangsters for control of the narcotics business. Every other week there's another body or two on both sides. I think this is going to become a much bigger problem, not only in New York City, but all over the country. We've always had illegal narcotics, but nothing like we're seeing now. It's only going to get worse.

[Long pause on the Dictabelt.] I wonder when she'll call me again.

# 5
# *Martin*

## The Present

I went to see Mom at the nursing home today. Since I've been unemployed, I try to spend more time with her. I do have a job interview later today, though, and I must say it's about time. I was out of work over the summer and what money I had in reserve is quickly depleting. Eric, my headhunter, has sent out my CV to a number of firms that are looking for a corporate accountant and auditor of my caliber. Unfortunately, all the good nibbles have been outside the Chicago area. I can't move while my mother is in a nursing home, so that severely limits the job possibilities.

You'd never think the Judy Talbot of today was the Black Stiletto. She is rail thin, has white hair, and no longer has that spark of life I once knew so well. Alzheimer's is such a cruel, horrible disease. It's taken her very soul away and left a living, frail shell that's slowly dying. I try to be upbeat when I see her, but it's terribly depressing. Nursing homes are depressing anyway, but when it's your own mother who's in one, then it's a hell of a lot worse.

She doesn't really know who I am anymore. When I walk into her room, her eyes brighten a little. She knows I'm someone she loves and who loves her, so that's good. I don't think she understands what our relationship is anymore. I'm not sure she remembers she has a son, even though on her dresser there are pictures of me at various ages. In many of them we're together. I remind her sometimes that I'm her boy, and she nods; but I'm pretty sure the concept flies right over her head.

There's still no new roommate. Since she was admitted to Woodlands, she's gone through a few of them; however she seems to outlive them all. I certainly prefer it that way. I don't know if it makes any difference to her, but I enjoy the privacy it gives us. I can put on music she likes, read to her, and show her old photographs. Come to think of it, these are all the old photographs we own. They were taken after we settled in Illinois. She says I was born in California, but I was too young to remember being there. I do have fleeting memories of traveling in a car, stopping in lots of hotels, living in apartments here and there, and finally coming to Arlington Heights. I was still preschool age at the time. We moved into our house—that's still up for sale—when I was in second grade.

I wish she had photos of her life as Judy Cooper. I'd love to see what her brothers look like. I have no idea if my Uncle John and Uncle Frank are still alive. So far I haven't attempted to find them. I'm afraid it would open up a can of worms if I did. I'd have to explain how come I waited until now to contact them—I didn't know they existed until I read Mom's first diary!—and there would be all sorts of questions I couldn't answer. Maybe someday I'll take the chance.

When I walked into her room, Mom was sitting in a rocking chair I'd bought her for Mother's Day. She enjoys it, I can tell, but whatever's going through her mind is a mystery. She just rocks and stares blankly out the window.

"Hi, Mom!" I try to be as cheerful as I can.

She looked over at me and produced a smile. "Hi!" she said. She's always glad to see me.

"How are you doing, Mom?"

"Okay." She's a woman of few words these days.

"Hey, guess what, I have a letter from Gina I can read to you. You know Gina, your granddaughter?"

There was a flicker of recognition in her eyes. She continued to smile. "That's nice," she replied. I really don't think she made the connection, so I pointed to Gina's high school graduation photo, which also sat in a frame on the dresser. "That's Gina."

Mom smiled wider. I still wasn't sure if it clicked, but I do know she always responded well to Gina when my daughter visited. It was almost as if they shared some kind of secret language. Gina was always good in sports and gymnastics when she was young. Before she got sick my mom always watched her granddaughter with interest. Then Gina became more interested in acting and dance, and now she's at Juilliard.

I pulled out the letter and read it aloud. Gina had addressed it to both me and "Grandma Judy."

Gina began her freshman year less than a month ago. She wrote how she loves Juilliard. Her classes are intense and she's working very hard. She's at school from 8:00 a.m. to 11:00 p.m. every weekday with classes, private lessons, and rehearsals. She says she's making tons of friends and everything is great. Gina lives in the Meredith Willson Residence Hall, which is named after the guy who wrote *The Music Man*, and shares a suite with seven other students.

At the end, Gina wrote, "Give Grandma a kiss for me and tell her I'll see her at Christmas." So I leaned over and kissed Mom on the cheek. That made her smile again, and I swear I thought her eyes welled up slightly. Maybe she comprehends more than I think. I just don't know.

I wish I could show Mom that reel of 8mm film and see if it loosens any memories buried in those dark recesses of her gray matter. But I know from experience that mentioning the Black Stiletto elicits an unfavorable reaction. The last time I did, Mom became very anxious. It's impossible to know if she still has any inkling she was the Stiletto. With Alzheimer's, the memories are there, it's just that the brain can't access them. I do believe the Stiletto resides somewhere in her mind's hard drive, but any mention of her provokes an emotional response that is obviously painful. So I've let it go and stopped trying to talk to her about it.

After Mom had lunch, there was a knock at her door. A woman I'd never seen before stuck her head in. "Hello, am I interrupting?"

"No, come on in."

She was younger than me, probably in her early forties, and she wore a white lab coat and a stethoscope around her neck. Brunette, my height, and the largest and brightest blue eyes I'd ever seen. I swear. My first thought?—this was a very attractive woman.

"I'm Dr. McDaniel. Margaret McDaniel."

"Martin Talbot." Then I processed who she was and quickly stood. "Oh, you're my mom's new doctor." I'd heard that Woodlands was bringing in someone new. She wasn't my mom's primary-care physician—just someone who made the rounds at the nursing home and made "recommendations."

"That's right." A nurse walked in behind her, obviously prepared to help the doctor do something. Dr. McDaniel shook my hand and then addressed my mom. "Hi, Judy! How are we doing today?"

"Okay."

"I've just come to take your blood pressure and take a look at that bedsore."

I was surprised. "Bedsore?"

Dr. McDaniel nodded. "They didn't tell you? Your mom has a bedsore on her posterior. It's nothing too serious. I discovered it during our last exam. It's very minor, just the beginning of one, Mr. Talbot, nothing to worry about."

No one at the nursing home had said anything. I didn't appreciate that. "Okay," was all I could think of to say.

"You're her son, right?"

"Yes."

"I'm glad you're here. I'd like to have a word with you after the examination. Do you have time to wait?"

"I have an appointment in a little while, but I don't have to leave for a half hour."

"This will only take five minutes. Could you wait outside? I'll come find you when we're done."

So I left and waited in the common room, where patients sat and vacantly watched television or stared into space. It wasn't a pleasant place, and I tried to spend as little time as possible in areas other than my mother's room. A soap opera was on TV, which made it all the more excruciating. Finally, though, Dr. McDaniel appeared.

"Let's go over here where we can talk," she said, indicating a vacant round table in the corner. I followed her over and sat.

"How's the bedsore?" I asked.

"Much improved. I caught it before it had developed into anything serious. I'll send a report to her primary-care physician. It would help if she walked more, got some exercise. Was your mother once athletic?"

I nodded. "I think so. Not in my lifetime, but she liked to work out in our basement. She had a punching bag she'd whale on."

The doctor smiled. "I believe it. Despite her thinness, she still has fabulous muscle tone. It would be nice if we could put some weight back on her."

"How's she doing otherwise? I mean, mentally."

The woman pursed her lips. "Her condition is stable. The Alzheimer's symptoms are no better and no worse. She seems to have hit a plateau. The onset of the illness was sudden, wasn't it?"

"Yes. Within two years she went from normalcy to what you see today. Her doctor said that was uncommon but not unusual. The disease hits people differently."

"That's correct."

"So you don't know how long it will be before she gets worse?"

"I'm afraid not. We'll just have to keep her mind stimulated. I'm sure it helps that you visit her a lot."

I shrugged. "I do what I can. She's my mom."

"Of course. Now, what I really wanted to talk to you about are all those scars she has on her body."

"Scars?"

The doctor nodded. "She's got several. They're very old—fifty years or more—but for a woman, well, they're very unusual. Was she in the armed services?"

I never saw my mother naked, so I was unaware of this stuff. "No. She wasn't." Of course, I had a good idea how she got the scars, I just couldn't say.

"More disturbing are the two old gunshot wounds."

"What?"

"Your mother was shot twice. I know, because I'm a former army doctor. I know gunshot wounds when I see them. She has one on the left shoulder and one on the left side of her abdomen. There's also a long scar on her right shoulder that I suspect was done with a sharp blade, like a knife. How did she get them?"

I did my best to feign surprise and shock. "My God, I have no idea!" I knew how she got the shoulder bullet wound—I read about that one in her first diary. Douglas Bates had shot her. The long scar on her right shoulder I had seen; and it was indeed caused by a knife injury that Freddie Barnes crudely stitched up. But I didn't know about the shot to the abdomen. I suppose I'd learn its history in a future diary. "There's a lot I don't know about my mother's life before I was born," I said. "I knew she had the scar on her right shoulder. She always said it was from a car accident."

The doctor looked skeptical. "It was a poor suturing job, something a professional wouldn't do." She glanced sideways at me. "No other doctor has ever asked you about this?"

"No. This is the first I've heard of it."

I don't think she believed me. I'm not a very good liar. My mom always caught me when I fibbed to her. Come to think of it, Gina and my ex-wife Carol are good at seeing through me, too. My poker face sucks.

"All right," the doctor said. "I thought you might know something. I was certain she'd been in combat."

"Nope. Gosh, not that I know of."

"Very well." She stood and held out her hand. "It was nice to meet you, Martin. I'm sure I'll see you again soon."

I shook her hand and thanked her.

As I drove on the crowded expressway toward Chicago, I thought about what Dr. McDaniel had discovered. How did my mom get that second gunshot wound? Was it the reason she eventually abandoned the Black Stiletto?

Once again I considered the big secret I was sitting on. How much would it be worth to sell my mother's story to the media? I'd probably never have to work again.

God, it's tempting.

# 6
# Judy's Diary
## 1959

FEBRUARY 5, 1959

Oh, dear diary, I can't believe Buddy Holly's dead! And Ritchie Valens and the Big Bopper, too. They were in a plane crash a couple of days ago. It's horrible. The radio's been playing Buddy's music nonstop. I've had his tunes going through my head ever since it happened. What a tragedy.

There were more stories about it in this morning's paper. I was reading one of them when Freddie said, "Did you see the notice from the Hollywood movie producer?" I didn't know what he was talking about, so he showed me. The headline was—HOLLY-WOOD WANTS BLACK STILETTO.

What?

Apparently a movie producer named Albert Franz wants the Black Stiletto in his next movie. He paid for an ad to contact her and asked that she call his New York office. There was a number printed. The ad said, "There could be good money in it for her."

I told Freddie it was a load of bull. He laughed but said I should consider it. Money never hurts. I personally don't see how the Black Stiletto can make a movie and keep her identity a secret. I told Freddie to forget it. Nevertheless, he tore out the ad and stuck it on the refrigerator with a piece of tape. He said, "You might change your mind."

"Fat chance," I said.

It's time to go to work. Freddie has me training some of the men now. More and more of them want me to train them instead of Freddie. I wonder why? Surely it can't be because I'm a young woman with a splendid figure (if I do say so myself, ha ha)?

LATER

I saw Tony the Tank today!

Toward the end of the workday, he came into the gym. I last saw him at the New Year's Eve party. He asked me if I had a chance to talk, and I told him I'd meet him at the East Side Diner at 5:15. When I finished with work, I went up the street and sat with him at a booth. Lucy wasn't working. "Sixteen Candles" by the Crests was playing on the jukebox.

After some small talk, he said, "I bet you know why I wanted to see you."

I replied, "Because I broke one of your guys' legs?"

He nodded. "Don DeLuca—Franco—he's pretty upset about it. The family is really out to get you."

I acknowledged the guy told me about the contract on my head. "What can I do about it, Tony? I had to defend myself. He was shooting at me."

He said the don has offered some kind of reward to anyone who kills me. What that means in Mafia terms, I don't know.

"Tony," I asked, "does anyone besides you know I'm the Black Stiletto?"

He shook his head. "If the don or anyone in the family knew I was talking to you, I'd be a dead man."

"Well, then, I can take care of myself as long as you keep it a secret. How are they going to find me unless someone gets lucky on the street, like that guy last month."

Tony shrugged and said, "I'm just warning you. Maybe it's not such a good idea for the Black Stiletto to show her face anymore. Er, I mean, her mask."

"Let me worry about that. I appreciate you telling me."

He had a piece of pie while I drank some coffee. The record on the jukebox switched to "My Happiness" by Connie Francis. Tony started talking about how difficult it was for the family these days. He said the mob was thrown out of Cuba by the new regime, so all the Italian "businesses" were hurting. They had invested in casinos and hotels in Havana, just like they had in Las Vegas, and Castro shut them out. The federal government was also cracking down on organized crime. Ever since the Senate hearings earlier in the decade, the heat on the mob has been intense. He said there are new crime organizations coming in and vying for territory. The narcotics business is especially a sore spot. The heroin comes in from France and Southeast Asia, and there are different groups importing and distributing it. Tony's family works with one of these groups, but he didn't tell me who they were. He said Negro gangsters in Harlem are trying to take it over and it's getting ugly. There's a war going on between them, and Tony doesn't like it. He named a couple of guys I'd met who were killed recently. Gunned down on the street.

"A lot of the old-timers in the family were completely against getting in on drug trafficking," Tony said. "Don Giorgio didn't like it, but Franco does. He says all the big money from now on will be in narcotics."

When I was dating Fiorello, I was really naïve about the Mafia. Or maybe I was in denial. I knew what they were doing was illegal, but I ignored it. Love is blind. I was so crazy about Fiorello that I didn't want to know about all the bad things with which he was involved. But ever since he died, I've come to realize how evil those people really are. I thought they ran only stuff like gambling and bookmaking, but now I know they operate prostitution houses, protection rackets, blackmail schemes, drug trafficking, and they murder people. At first I was sucked in by their loyalty to each other and the familial atmosphere around them. Now it makes me sick to think I was going to their parties and fraternizing with Fiorello and his friends. Tony is the same way, and I wonder if I'm being a hypocrite for staying friends with him. But he's so lovable and nice that I just don't think of Tony as a killer. I trust him.

"So you're going along with it, Tony?" I asked. "Drugs are bad. They ruin lives."

He shrugged again. "What can I do? I follow orders."

"Why don't you get out? Just leave."

He laughed wryly. "You can't get out. Once you're in, they don't let you leave. Not alive, anyway."

FEBRUARY 14, 1959

It's Valentine's Day and I don't have a valentine. I suppose there's Freddie and there's Soichiro, but they're not really boyfriends. I thought about calling John Richardson just to flirt but decided I'd better not. Besides, I didn't have time because I was late for my lesson with Soichiro. Anyway now it's after 5:00 and I'm sure John's gone from the office. Oh well.

In *karate* class I'm working on the higher levels of Black Belt. I'm already at the first level, which is called 1st *dan*, or *Shodan*. Soichiro explained to me that I won't be able to reach the higher levels until I'm older because the ranks have minimum age and time requirements. For example, I won't be able to attain 2nd *dan*, or *Nidan*, until two years after I get my Black Belt (1st *dan*). The minimum age to be a 2nd *dan* is 20, so that part's not a problem. But you have to be 25 and wait 3 years since getting 2nd *dan* to get a 3rd *dan*. You have to be 35 years old to get a 5th *dan*! Additionally, the levels above 5th *dan* are reserved only for extremely special *sensei* who become great teachers, start important martial arts schools, and such. Soichiro says he's never met an 8th *dan* or higher, as they're only in Japan. Soichiro himself is only a 4th *dan*. Another important factor in obtaining higher ranks is competing in tournaments. I really don't want to do that. I want to keep my ability in *karate* and *judo* private. I never want anyone to see me compete and put two and two together and think, *maybe she's the Black Stiletto*! So if I only reach 2nd *dan*, I'll be happy. Most students never obtain a Black Belt, so I've already hit a major milestone.

Since then, I no longer train with a class full of students. It's just me and Soichiro, one-on-one. I like it that way. Lately he's been having me practice moves while wearing a blindfold. I asked him what the purpose was, and he said it's to develop my other senses other than sight. He said I should *hear* and *feel* an attack coming. I can already do that, but Soichiro doesn't know about my heightened sensory abilities. I figure it's still good training, though, so I put on the blindfold and we had a match. At first Soichiro was very gentle. He moved slowly and telegraphed his strikes so I could ward off his blows easily. I stopped and told him to do it for real.

Ouch.

I heard his arm and *seiken*—*karate* fist—whishing through the air at me. I felt it coming, but I was still too late to block the blow. He hit me right on the sternum—not hard enough to do serious damage, but it hurt like the dickens. He could see I was in distress, so he asked me if I was all right. I told him, "Yes," and to keep going. Then I concentrated harder. Everything was pitch-black with the blindfold on, but I sensed him moving around me. I could faintly hear his bare feet on the mat, something I'm sure no one else could do. He came at me—and I swear I heard one foot leave the mat, so I knew he was going to kick me. I immediately blocked it and reciprocated with a *mae geri*, a front kick, to his stomach. It surprised him. This time it was my turn to ask if *he* was all right!

This went on for ten minutes. Back and forth, give and take. Sometimes he'd trick me and get a strike in. Most of the time I was able to block him and deliver a *tsuki te*—hand attack—or kick back at him. At the end, he instructed me to remove the blindfold. We bowed and then he said, "Good." I was pleased.

He went into his little office while I went to the ladies' room to splash some water on my face and wipe some of the sweat off my body. I usually take a shower back at the gym, although if I wanted to I could do it there at Studio Tokyo.

When I went back in to say goodbye, I saw Soichiro sitting in his chair and holding a framed photograph. He had the most curious expression on his face, like something was deeply troubling him. In fact, as I think about it now, after the fact, I've noticed that in the past couple of weeks, Soichiro has seemed distracted. That's not like him. From what I know of Japanese people, they don't get distracted easily.

I said, "Goodbye, Soichiro-san."

This startled him. He quickly slammed the photo facedown on his desk and composed himself. He bowed his head slightly, the usual nonexpression on his face, and said, "Until next time."

There was an awkward moment that passed between us, as if I'd caught him doing something private. I asked, "Is anything wrong, Soichiro-san?"

Ever the stoic Japanese, he simply said, "No. Nothing wrong. Until next time."

Well, dear diary, you know me. I knew he was lying. I could tell, like I can always discern when people lie to me. Something was bothering him. But I also knew he was too proud to ever display emotion or reveal any personal problems to me. It was his nature.

There was nothing else to do but leave. I'm a little concerned about him, but I suppose he can take care of whatever it is that's worrying him.

But I was determined to find out whose picture he was looking at.

FEBRUARY 18, 1959

Something happened at the gym today. I was busy cleaning the wall pulleys and rowing machines, a task I do once a week, when a Negro man came in and greeted Freddie like a long-lost friend. They shook hands, smiled, and laughed. The man looked to be around Freddie's age, somewhere in his mid-40s. He was tall and built, as if he worked out a lot. Had grayish curly short hair.

Curious, I went over to them on the pretense of grabbing a dry rag from the front counter, and Freddie said, "Judy, I want to introduce you to someone."

The man's name is Mike Washington. Freddie said they'd known each other since they were teenagers. They were boxers together in the '30s. Apparently Mike will start coming to the gym on a regular basis.

Dear diary, you know I have what they call a sixth sense about people. I can usually tell within a few minutes of meeting someone whether they're a good person or a bad person. Everyone releases a "vibration" that I pick up on. That's the only way I can describe it. Ever since I went through puberty, I was able to do it, you know that. If someone doesn't have a kind heart, then I feel it. I realize it's some kind of gift I have, 'cause I've found no one else who can do it.

Anyway, Mike Washington immediately made me feel uncomfortable. He barely looked at me, but he was friendly enough and shook my hand—it was a strong, firm grip, too!—but I knew this man had secrets. He looked like he could be a mean, scary guy if he wanted. Maybe that comes with the territory of being a boxer, which it does, but I don't know. It was weird.

"Do you still box?" I asked him.

Mike shook his head. "Not professionally. I just try to keep up with the training. Now that I'm out of—er, now that I'm here in New York, it's nice to see Freddie again and find a nice place where I can work out."

Freddie added, "You know, Judy, you'd be surprised by the number of private gyms that don't allow Negroes, unless the gym is associated with professional boxing. They usually have to go to one of those 'coloreds only' gyms, but not here. Everyone is welcome at the Second Avenue Gym, regardless of race or creed."

"I don't see any other *women* here, Freddie," I said.

Both Freddie and Mike laughed. "Judy, that's different!" Freddie replied. "We'd really get in trouble if we started mixing genders in a gym. You're the exception, of course. You work here!" He turned to Mike. "Judy's quite a boxer herself. You should see her."

"I never seen a woman boxing, much less working in a gym before," Mike said. He still wouldn't look me in the eye.

I told him it was nice to meet him and then I went back to my tasks. I watched the two of them; everything seemed okay. Freddie eventually shook Mike's hand and the man left.

A little bit later I was able to get Freddie alone. "Tell me about Mike," I said.

Freddie was honest. Mike Washington's an ex-con. He just got out of prison. I asked what he was in prison for.

"Manslaughter," Freddie said.

So maybe that was why I sensed something not quite right about him.

Freddie went on to say, "He pulled 15 years of a 20-year sentence for killing a crooked manager associated with the mob. The guy was white, so the jury gave Mike a tough sentence."

"What were the circumstances? Why manslaughter and not murder?"

"It was complicated. The manager wanted Mike to throw a fight. Mike didn't want to do it. So the manager had Mike drugged before the match. Mike still doesn't know how he did it. He thinks it was heroin or something like that. So Mike was in no condition to win a fight. He went down in the first round. It was humiliating for him. The next day Mike went to the manager's office and beat the crap out of him. He left the guy alive, though. The manager had to go to the hospital and he was there several days—but he died of heart failure or a stroke, I can't remember which. The D.A. decided to charge Mike with murder, but it got whittled down to manslaughter. All the time Mike was worried the mob would come after him, too. But then it turned out the manager was ripping off the mob, so they left him alone."

"So Mike spent 15 years in prison?"

"He did. Poor guy. I'm sure it was rough."

"Prison can turn a man's soul very dark, Freddie. Are you sure you trust this guy to come around here?" I had to ask it.

"He was my friend, Judy. We haven't seen each other in 20 years, but yeah, I trust him. We lost touch for about 5 years before he went to prison. Our paths went in different directions when I joined the army. By the time I was discharged in '45, he was already in jail."

"Well, I have to tell you, Freddie, I get a bad feeling from him. I don't know why. He seems nice enough, but—I don't know. I can't explain it."

"Mike's been through a lot, Judy. I'm gonna give him the benefit of the doubt." He then gestured toward the clock. "We need to finish the cleaning before we close unless you want to stay late."

*We?* Ever since I started working at the gym, Freddie never lifted a finger to clean stuff.

"Okay, boss," I said, doing a little kowtowing bow. "I'll get right on it, sir!"

That made him laugh.

As I went back to work, I decided it wouldn't hurt to keep my eye on Mike Washington.

# 7
## John

Today is February 18, 1959.

I'm even more convinced that Carl Purdy is the new narcotics kingpin in New York City. For the past several years the Bureau was concentrating on the Italians and the French—the Corsicans, to be exact. It's no secret the Corsicans are the leaders in smuggling heroin into the United States. But once it gets into the country, they don't get involved in the distribution. That's where Purdy comes in. Purdy and his network of Negro gangsters are single-handedly spreading this poison all over the city and beyond. The Italians certainly have their hands dirty, too, but it's getting to where they're number three on the food chain. Mob families like the DeLucas have lost a lot of clout. They want in on the distribution racket badly, and it's caused a lot of trouble. Dead bodies everywhere you look.

I don't understand Purdy's mentality. The Negroes are all complaining about civil rights and equality, and yet Purdy sells that junk to his own people. He makes addicts out of everyone in Harlem, and what does that do? It's a vicious cycle. Drug addiction breeds poverty and disease and death. It's no wonder Harlem is becoming a ghetto. Once upon a time, Harlem was jumping. It was a place to be seen, to go out and hit the nightclubs. Now, no sensible white person would set foot up there. And whose fault is that? Carl Purdy's, among other low-life gangsters.

We now know Purdy uses profits from brothels in Harlem to

fund his distribution machine. These brothels are scattered all over the city, even below Harlem. They also serve as heroin dens. Purdy's men get the prostitutes addicted to the heroin, and then they keep the women under control by dangling the drugs over their heads. It's a despicable business. He also runs bookmaking, protection rackets, and the so-called policy racket, which is a gambling scheme similar to a lottery. It's also called the Numbers Game, or *bolita* in Spanish Harlem. It's played illegally from countless locations. I'm positive Purdy makes millions off the Numbers Game, which also funds his narcotics operations.

Finally, after months of preparation, I've finally authorized the placing of an undercover informant within Purdy's organization. He will report directly to me. Haggerty is skeptical, of course. He's never on board with anything I come up with. Haggerty puts me in charge of the narcotics task force in Harlem and then gives me crap about the cost of paying, regulating, and protecting the informant. What the hell does he want me to do? You'd think Haggerty was on Purdy's side. Well, tough. The informant starts work tomorrow.

Haggerty's also still hounding me about the Black Stiletto. Have I heard from her? What's her name? Where does she live? When are you going to find out? I told him I haven't heard from her since January. He told me it should be my top priority to catch her. Really? Top priority? How about catching Carl Purdy and the villains who are wrecking the lives of innocent Negro families? And probably the lives of a lot of white people too.

The last time I talked to the Stiletto, she told me she might agree to meet me if I did something about the negative press she's been getting. I do have a contact at the *New York Daily News*. Maybe I should give Doyle a call. He owes me a favor. If I word it right, maybe she'll ring me up to thank me. It's worth a try.

# 8
## Judy's Diary
### 1959

FEBRUARY 20, 1959

Yesterday I had another session with Soichiro. We did blindfold practice again, and I'm getting better at it. This time he used a club, what he called a "blackjack," that thugs and hoodlums sometimes use on the street to beat people. The object for me was to ward off his blows and disarm him if I could. Luckily, the blackjack was made of rubber, for he hit me several times before I got the hang of it. If it had been the real thing, I'd have a few broken bones and a concussion!

Soichiro is very graceful and can be extremely silent when he wants to be. He said if I could pass the exercise with him, then in a real-life situation I probably wouldn't have any trouble. Most opponents aren't as quiet. Men often make a lot of noise when they fight. But what if there is more than one attacker? If they're coming at you from all sides, the sounds get all mixed up. Soichiro said he was teaching me to isolate noises in the darkness—to listen in "slow motion." I suppose I've always been able to do this, I just never honed the capability with any strict discipline. By the end of the session, I was able to block his attacks and knock the club out of his hand. On a couple of tries, I actually got hold of the blackjack and took it away from him! He invited me to come to one of the lower-level classes so I could try my skill with several students at once. I told him I'd be up for it.

Despite all that, I still sensed that he's worried about something. Before class started, I found him sitting in his office, staring at the wall. At first I thought he was asleep with his eyes open, if that's possible, but then he turned and acknowledged my presence. Usually when I arrive, he's already on the mat doing stretches or something.

"Are you all right, Soichiro-san?" I asked him.

"I am fine," he replied bluntly. Again, I knew he wasn't telling the truth.

Anyway, we had class without any other indication of his troubles. But then afterward he retired to his office without saying a word. Usually there's a little bit of small talk between us. I know I'm one of his favorite students, even though he's never actually said so. Soichiro keeps things close to his chest, which is a very Japanese thing to do. I went back in and said, "Soichiro-san, I can tell something is bothering you. I'm your friend as well as your student. You can trust me. Won't you tell me what's wrong?"

He actually got mad and snapped at me. "Nothing wrong! See you next time!"

I said, "Okay, okay," and I left. But I was determined to find out more.

That night, the Black Stiletto made her way over to Christopher Street where Studio Tokyo is located. It's still winter and pretty cold outside, but not as bad as it was in January. It's risky crossing the wide north/south avenues in full regalia, so I simply put on a coat over my disguise and left off my mask. Then I'm just a normal New York woman walking from east to west. When I got to the West Village, I removed and folded the coat, put it in my backpack, slipped the mask on, and I was ready.

The studio is on the second floor of a plain old building. There's a pizzeria on the ground floor and apartments above it. I could see the lights were off. Normally students had to be buzzed in the front door on the street; as it was late and the pizzeria was closed, I used a lockpick to get inside. The door to the studio was a tougher challenge—it took five tries with different-sized picks to get it open. There was no alarm.

Dear diary, I hope you don't think I'm being a snoop. I told myself I was doing the right thing. If Soichiro wasn't going to let me help him, then I had to help him anyway—that's the way I look at it. So I crept into Soichiro's office, flicked on my little flashlight, and sat at his desk. I didn't see the framed photograph, so I figured it must be in one of the drawers. They were locked. The lockpicks came in handy once again, and I found some very interesting items.

First of all, the framed photo. It was a family portrait of a younger Soichiro with a Japanese woman and an infant. Soichiro looked like he was in his late 20s or early 30s, and he was wearing a Japanese military uniform. I'm pretty sure it was taken in Japan, too. The woman was wearing a kimono, a formal one for dressing up. My gosh, I didn't know Soichiro was married, if the woman was his wife. After all this time I thought he was a bachelor who lived alone.

There was one more picture tucked away in the desk. It was an unframed, wallet-sized school photo of a young Japanese girl. It was more recent, probably taken in the last five or six years. It's hard for me to tell the age of Japanese people, but I would guess she was about 11 or 12. On the back was some Japanese characters scribbled in ink and the number 12. Maybe that was her name in Japanese and her age, as I suspected. I decided to open the back of the frame of the family photo to see if anything was written on the back. Sure enough, there were more Japanese characters. I didn't know how to read Japanese, but there's a guy who comes to the gym named Harry McBain. He reads and speaks Japanese. I could ask him what they said. So I looked around for a pen and some scrap paper, and I copied the characters as best I could. I then replaced the photo in the frame and put it and the school picture back in the drawer.

On top of the desk was a basket full of mail. I glanced at what was there; it consisted mostly of bills addressed to Soichiro Tachikawa. There were several from a realty company and I was pretty sure it was the one that leased the studio space to Soichiro. I opened up the most recent one.

It said Soichiro was three months late on rent and if the total was not paid by the end of February, he would be evicted.

That's what Soichiro is worried about! He's having serious money problems.

I carefully examined the other bills, did some calculations, and found that he owed something like $10,000 in rent and utilities. No wonder he's not himself these days.

Rummaging through the desk again, I found a checkbook with a ledger. A lot of the notations inside were written in Japanese, but the numbers were readable and I could easily determine which column indicated payments and which one showed deposits. The money was flying out the door with very little coming in. Most curious of all was a payment of $5,000 at the beginning of the month. I went back to the previous month and found that he'd paid $5,000 in January, too. And again in December. I couldn't read to whom it was paid, so I also copied those characters on my scrap paper. Who could this be? $5,000 a month? He couldn't possibly afford it with all the bills and overdue rent.

There wasn't much else in the desk that meant anything. However, I did find a public library card that had Soichiro's home address on it. He lives on Charles Street, which isn't very far away. I never knew that.

I carefully put everything back the way I found it, slipped out of the studio, made sure the door was locked, and left the building. Without my mask on and in my coat, I walked over to Charles Street. By now it was midnight, but there were still quite a few people out and about along Bleecker Street. New York is the city that never sleeps. It was dark and quiet on Charles, though, so I felt fairly incognito. I located Soichiro's building, a brownstone of five floors, four apartments on each floor. Throwing caution to the wind, I stepped into the inner foyer where the mailboxes and call buttons were.

I found his box—marked "S. Tachikawa, I. Tachikawa"—it was apartment 10. That meant it was on the third floor.

Who was "I. Tachikawa"? His wife? His daughter? Another member of his family?

I stepped back outside and crossed the street so I could get a full view of the building. A fire escape structure adorned the front façade, so I figured there was another one in the back. Buildings in Manhattan are so close together. To tell the truth, I didn't even know how to get back there. There must be a teeny-tiny alley and a gate somewhere, or you had to get to it from Bleecker or 4th. Then, again, I could just use my lockpicks if I had to get inside his apartment.

Before I made things too complicated for myself, who do you think turned up walking down the street toward the building? Soichiro himself. He was all bundled up in a coat and hat, but I immediately recognized him. I ducked into a doorway and stood in the shadows so he wouldn't see me.

What was he doing out so late? Midnight in Manhattan is only for criminals, barflies, and Black Stilettos!

It took him a minute to get to the front door. After he unlocked it and went inside, I waited another minute or two—and just my luck—a light came on in a third floor window! His apartment faced the street.

This was my chance to see who "I. Tachikawa" was. Once again I removed my coat, stuffed it in the backpack, put on my mask, and crossed the street. Since my last appearance as the Stiletto, I'd picked up a pulley hook at a hardware shop—not as big as a grappling hook, but large enough to fit on a pole the size of a ladder rung. I quickly tied it on the end of the rope I always carry and then stood beneath the fire escape ladder that was attached to the second-floor grated landing. Normally from that level you would slide it down a track to the sidewalk. I needed a way to lower the ladder to me, and the rope and hook did the trick. It took me three tries, flinging it up to catch the bottom rung, but I finally got it.

I felt very exposed there on the street, but luckily it was late and

I didn't see anyone on the sidewalk. I quickly climbed the ladder and made my way up to the third floor. Then, as quietly as I could, I crept over to Soichiro's window to peer inside.

It was a bedroom, but it wasn't his. It was too feminine, as if a teenaged girl lived there. There was a high school pennant on the wall, a lot of Japanese decorations, and a Western-style American bed with some stuffed animals on it. I wasn't sure if Soichiro slept on a Japanese mat or not, but whoever lived in that room certainly didn't.

It was very clean and tidy. In fact, it looked to me as if no one had been using it for a while.

The bedroom door was open; by crouching lower I could see across the room and into a hallway. At one point, Soichiro passed by the open door. I quickly shot back out of view. After a few seconds passed, I looked again.

I studied the bedroom some more and came to a conclusion. I could be wrong, dear diary, but I have a feeling the room once belonged to Soichiro's teenaged daughter and that his wife was no longer with us. I don't know why or how I suspect that, it's just my crazy intuition. It was also obvious the daughter was not around. Soichiro was in the apartment alone. I don't know how long he had lived this way, but the bedroom was just too tidy to indicate any recent habitation.

Soichiro suddenly entered. I froze, for if I had darted away I'm sure he would have seen the movement. He was carrying one of those miniature Japanese trees, what do you call them? A bonsai? He placed it on his daughter's dresser and stared at it reverently for a moment.

And then he turned toward the window. I ducked out of view, but he had seen me. I scrambled down the fire escape as he opened the window and looked out!

"Hey!" he shouted.

I kept going. By then I was at the bottom landing and started to descend the ladder.

"I call police!"

Great, Soichiro. You do that.

I dropped to the sidewalk, landed on both feet, and shot out of there at a run. Once I got to 7th Avenue, I stopped to put on my coat and take off my mask. Then I hailed a taxi to take me back to the gym. On the way I pondered what I'd learned. Soichiro was once married, but not anymore. He has a daughter who no longer lives with him. He owes a lot of money to his landlord. He's paying someone big bucks each month instead of using it for rent.

Of course, I could be mistaken about all this. Those are big assumptions. I should probably investigate a little more before I do anything stupid. But one thing's for sure—I have to help Soichiro.

# 9
# Martin

## The Present

The job interview went really well, to say the least. I was hired on the spot! That's a first. I start next week. I guess I was fortunate the firm acquired a client-in-crisis mode and they need someone with my experience immediately. Bob Konnors, the guy who'll be my boss, checked my references then and there while I waited outside his office. Within the hour I was talking to Human Resources.

That put me in a great mood, so I drove back from the city straight to Woodlands North. I was well aware my mother wouldn't comprehend my news, but I wanted to tell her anyway. She'd pick up on my vibe and do that empathy thing she does. Perhaps she'd feel as happy as me.

It was nearly dinnertime when I arrived. The common room was full of patients and orderlies running about with trays of food.

Mom usually got sleepy after she ate so I wasn't going to stay long. I found her in bed but awake. She must've sensed she was about to be fed. Her appetite, I think, is still pretty good, so I don't know why she's so thin, although I can't imagine eating the stuff that's placed in front of her. It's always looked really, really horrible, but she seems to like it.

"Mom, guess what? I got a new job and I start next week!"

Her eyes brightened slightly and she smiled at me. "That's wonderful," she said sweetly.

That felt good. She knew I was excited about something and had the right response, whether she understood what I was talking about or not. I feared the day when she was no longer able to draw upon her menu of appropriate reactions.

Her food arrived a few seconds later. I watched her eat—she could still manage by herself—as I talked for a few more minutes. I said good night and kissed her on the forehead before she was finished with the cakelike dessert, the only thing on her tray that looked truly edible.

As I was walking out, Dr. McDaniel was also leaving for the day. We simultaneously crossed the common room on our way toward the exit. The white lab coat was gone. Again, I was struck by her hotness, but now I was wary. There had been a hint of accusation in the doctor's voice when she asked me about mom's injuries, and I didn't like it.

"Oh, Mr. Talbot, hello," she said, forcing us to stop.

"Dr. McDaniel, leaving for the day?" I asked. I was in such a jubilant mood I damn near bounced.

"I'm glad I ran into you. I'd like to ask you something if you don't mind. Since our conversation earlier, another question arose and I found myself thinking about it."

"What is it?"

She pulled me conspiratorially to the side of the room, where no one could listen.

"Am I correct that your father has been gone a long time?"

Her question surprised me. People rarely ask me about my father and, if they do, I always give the same answer.

"He died in Vietnam. I never knew him."

This seemed to frustrate her and she shook her head. "Then I suppose you wouldn't know."

"Know what?"

"Whether or not your father abused your mother."

I was stunned by her bluntness. "What?"

Dr. McDaniel shrugged. "It was just a possibility. Mr. Talbot, I must tell you I am deeply concerned about the wounds on your mother's body."

I didn't see the relevance those ancient scars had on Mom's current treatment and I said so. Perhaps too defensively.

"There are some studies that suggest abuse occurred in some cases of Alzheimer's. At any rate, I don't believe a woman would sustain gunshot wounds in a case of family abuse. Mr. Talbot, I'm wondering if your mother might have been a victim of a crime during her younger years."

The response I gave was probably not a wise one. Half jokingly, I said, "What are you gonna do, call the police?"

"I might have to."

Again, her answer was a slap in the face. "What?"

"It may be my duty to report this."

I didn't think she had the right to do that. Her idea was absurd, but I simply asked, "What for?"

"It just concerns me, Mr. Talbot. We can talk another time. Your mother is doing fine; I looked in on her just a while ago."

This woman was strictly business, and for my money, somewhat presumptuous. I was a little angry.

"Okay, thanks," I said.

She nodded and walked toward the exit.

The nerve! I mean, really! Why was this good-looking woman such a bitch? Was I overreacting?

I waited a few moments to let her find her car and drive away before I went out there, too; otherwise I might have strangled her in the parking lot.


Back at my house, I began the evening ritual of making what served as my dinner. I'm no cook. Since the divorce, I've whipped up a lot of frozen dinners. Take-out and delivery are frequent options, but that gets expensive. I didn't feel very energetic, so I heated up a

Tombstone pizza. I'd been so ecstatic earlier, but now I was in a funk.

The TV is usually on during dinner. I listen to the news if that's still on; second choice is some dumb time waster that fills a gap. I don't like too much silence in my home. If it gets too quiet, I'm reminded of the fact that I'm a man approaching fifty, living alone in a small house with no girlfriend. I used to add "and no job" to that list, so maybe I should add "with a cat." Not that I want one. Dogs are more fun, but I don't particularly need the burden of taking care of an animal right now. Maybe after Mom—but I don't like to think about that.

That tacky but addicting show *World Entertainment Television* came on while I ate my pizza and drank a Coors Light—I need to lose some weight and I think a lot of it was caused by indulging in chic European beers with funny names. I wasn't really watching the program; from my little dining table near the kitchen, I can't see around the corner into the living room. But I heard the usual celebrity gossip stories and behind-the-scenes looks at current movies. Then, just as I was stuffing the last bite of crust in my mouth, I heard the female newscaster say, "And now a story on the Black Stiletto. Remember her?"

I nearly fell out of my seat getting up so quickly. I rushed to the TV and saw a cute, well-dressed Asian woman. A caption identified her as "Sandy Lee." Behind her was one of those fake screens they use for pictures, videos, and text. It displayed a photo of my mother in costume. It was a familiar picture, one that's been used by the press for decades.

Sandy Lee continued. "You would have to have lived on the moon for the last fifty years not to have heard of the Black Stiletto. Although the costumed vigilante was active only for a few years in the late nineteen fifties and early sixties, her image—and legend— has been duly exploited by the media."

Other often-used vintage photographs appeared full frame on the TV.

"The Black Stiletto tackled common crooks, the Mafia, and Communist spies, often resulting in the capture and arrest of these criminals," Sandy said in a voice-over. "But, in fact, *she* was also wanted by the police and the FBI for taking the law into her own hands."

It was the same old stuff, but I was curious why they had a story on the Stiletto. This was all household knowledge.

Then Sandy Lee said, "*World Entertainment Television* has obtained exclusive vintage film footage of the Black Stiletto, up close and personal. This material has never been seen before."

That got my attention. The visuals then changed to a heavy guy with gray, longish hair and nervous eyes. The man was probably in his sixties, but I couldn't be sure. Fifties at least. He wore a white shirt unbuttoned too low, exposing a hairy chest and a ridiculous amount of gold necklaces.

"Johnny Munroe of New York City discovered a reel of 8mm film in a safety deposit box owned by his father, Jerry Munroe, who once worked as a photographer in Manhattan during the fifties."

Sandy Lee continued, asking him questions in an interview setting.

"Mr. Munroe, isn't it true you found the small reel of film after your father's death?"

"That's correct," Munroe answered. He had a thick New York accent. To me he sounded like a wise guy, a fella trying to act tough even though he was edgy in front of a camera. He wouldn't have been out of place on *The Sopranos* or in *GoodFellas*. "My father lived to the ripe old age of ninety-two. He passed away last year, may he rest in peace."

"And isn't it also true he was an ex-convict for most of his later life?"

"Yeah, that's true. He got out of prison in nineteen eighty-three, having served nearly a twenty-five-year sentence. He was completely rehabilitated, I might add."

"Why was he in prison?"

The guy rolled his eyes, as if he was a little embarrassed. "Uh, it was for distributing obscene materials. But, hey, what was considered obscene in the fifties looks tame by today's standards." He held up his right hand as if he was swearing an oath. "All of that stuff was destroyed when he was convicted, I can tell you that. The only thing I found in the safety deposit box was the Black Stiletto film. I believe my father shot it in the late fifties."

Then they cut to the film itself.

My jaw dropped. I felt my heart start to race.

It was the exact same footage I had found in Mom's strongbox. Black-and-white. The cameraman's studio. Fake fights with the mannequin. The climb up the fire escape at the end.

Then I was struck by sheer terror. Was the additional scene in the dressing room going to be seen by millions of viewers? Was my mom about to remove her mask on national television?

The show cut back to Sandy Lee. A still shot of the Stiletto adorned the screen behind the anchorwoman.

"What was the Black Stiletto doing, posing and clowning around for Jerry Munroe? Was it some kind of promotional film? Even Mr. Munroe's son, Johnny, doesn't know. Tell me, Johnny, are you sure the film is the only Black Stiletto item your father left behind?"

Back to Munroe, whose expression indicated he was uncomfortable with the question. He shrugged and answered with, "I may have some other material, but I need to verify that it's authentic before I make it public, you know?"

"What would you say to her if you met her today, Mr. Munroe?"

"I don't know. I just hope she's still alive. Regardless of whether she is or isn't, maybe somebody out there knows somethin' about her."

Back to Sandy. "When we asked Mr. Munroe about this 'other material,' he remained coy. But he did offer this hint."

Munroe. "If it's real, then it'll blow the lid off the Black Stiletto legend for good."

And back to Sandy. "Thank you, Mr. Munroe. This is Sandy Lee for *World Entertainment Television*. We'll be right back."

The segment ended and the show went to a commercial.

I couldn't believe it. It was only days since I had finally got hold of a projector and watched the film myself. And now, there it was on national television. Incredible.

And what the hell was Johnny Munroe talking about? What "other material" did he have? Was it the extra footage of my mother unmasking herself? That had to be it. Why else would his father keep a copy of the film in his safety deposit box?

I had to find Johnny Munroe and stop him from distributing that footage.

# 10
# *Judy's Diary*
## 1959

I'm in my bedroom and it's almost midnight. I can't seem to fall asleep, although I'm pretty tired. I worked out hard today and had double-training sessions with clients because Freddie wasn't feeling well. The good thing about the double-training was that I got to work with Harry McBain and ask him about the Japanese writing on Soichiro's photos.

Harry's a World War II veteran who got wounded in the war. His right leg took the brunt of a grenade on Guadalcanal and he's gone through several surgeries. Miraculously, he didn't lose the leg, but it's all messed up inside. He's forced to a life of rehabilitation, three times a week. The doctors told him he had to keep working the muscles in that leg or the circulation could go haywire. He's got a sense of humor about it, though. He calls it his "Gumby Leg" because it wiggles and bends weirdly when he walks.

Anyway, Harry lived in Japan for six years in the late forties and early fifties. He had some military desk job over there. So I showed him the scrap of paper I scribbled the Japanese characters on. My handwriting wasn't the best, but he figured it out.

On the back of the school photo was written "Isuzu, age 12," and on the back of the family portrait was "Soichiro, Machiko, and Isuzu, Hiroshima, 1944." The notation in the checkbook regarding the $5,000 monthly payments was to "Akuma." I asked Harry what that meant, and he replied, "That's the Japanese word for devil."

Oh my gosh, dear diary, the mystery thickens! Soichiro is paying $5,000 a month to a *devil*? And Hiroshima—that was the city we dropped the atom bomb on! Isuzu is obviously Soichiro's daughter. I wonder what happened to Machiko, most assuredly the woman who was his wife and Isuzu's mother.

During my lunch break, I went upstairs to find Freddie at the kitchen table reading the paper. The radio was on, and I heard my dreamboat Elvis singing a song I hadn't heard before.

Thrilled, I asked, "What's that?"

Freddie didn't care much for Elvis Presley. "I think they said it was the preview of a new song that's gonna come out in a week or two."

"What's the name of it?"

"I don't know!"

It had a good beat and a typical Elvis melodic hook. When it was over, the DJ said it was called "I Need Your Love Tonight." I can't wait to buy the record! I think I might also have to buy a new copy of *Elvis' Golden Records*, an album with a bunch of his hits on it. I've played it to death and there's an awful scratch on side two. It skips right in the middle of "Love Me Tender." He sings, "Love Me Ten—Love Me Ten—Love Me Ten" over and over. It drives Freddie nuts.

Anyway, I had to grab a quick bite and get back downstairs. As I got some tuna fish salad out of the fridge, Freddie said, "Look at this." He pointed to the *Daily News*.

My mouth fell open. The article's headline was BLACK STILETTO NOT ALL BAD?

For once it was a positive article. An "anonymous source" in the New York City Police Department said the street cops "secretly admire the Black Stiletto and hope she's never caught." The chief of police, Patrick Bruen, commented that if he ever found out who said that, the officer would be put on unpaid leave. But John Richardson, Special Agent of the FBI, was quoted as saying, "The Black

Stiletto does a great service for the city. People shouldn't believe everything they read about her in the newspapers." Oh, my gosh! He came through! John did what he said he would!

I can't tell you, dear diary, how excited I was—and still am.

Well, after I read the article, I took a few minutes to run outside to a pay phone. I called John at his office. The exchange went like this:

Him: "Special Agent Richardson."

Me: "Public Menace Stiletto."

Him: "Well, hello there."

Me: "Hi. How are you?"

Him: "I'm doing well."

Me: "Did you happen to see the *Daily News* today?"

Him: (Laughs) "I sure did. Did you?"

Me: "Yep. I'm guessing you had something to do with it since you're quoted."

Him: "I have friends in high places. Unfortunately my boss wasn't very pleased. He'd still like to get you in handcuffs."

Me: "I hope you didn't get in too much trouble."

Him: "It's nothing I can't handle."

Me: "Listen, I can't really talk. Can I call you at home? Wouldn't that be more private? You know, you're at the FBI and all that. You could be recording this."

Him: "I assure you I'm not. But it's probably a good idea. I'll give you my unlisted home phone number."

And he did! I had to memorize it 'cause I didn't bring pen and paper with me.

Him: "I want you to know I normally don't give out my number to strange women."

Me: "I believe you, but just tell me one thing."

Him: "What?"

Me: "Are you married?"

Him: "No."

For some reason, dear diary, I felt a little tingle when he said that, ha ha. I couldn't think of anything else to say, so I told him I'd call him this evening and hung up. I ran back to the gym all flustered and excited. I didn't care if I had to do double-training; I was in such a good mood!

And then Mike Washington showed up. He's been coming to the gym twice a week since I met him. Once again, my invisible antennae went on high alert. It was as if an electrical current was switched on in my spine. This guy simply oozes danger and deception. For one thing, he's very quiet. He barely says hello to anyone except Freddie. He stands apart from the other fellas and trains on his own. He never asks for someone to spot him. Another thing is he doesn't look me in the eye, and I don't trust anyone who won't do that.

At one point he was pounding the speed ball in a professional, steady rhythm. The look on his face was so intense, as if all his enemies were stuffed inside that punching bag. I wasn't far away; I was spotting Jimmy on bench presses, but I couldn't take my eyes off Mike.

He caught me watching him and stopped hitting the speed ball. "What are you looking at?" he asked, glaring at me.

"Nothing," I said, but I know I probably sounded guilty. I made up something to add. "You're pretty good at that."

He muttered under his breath and continued to punch the bag. I averted my eyes, focused on Jimmy, and tried not to pay any attention to Mike Washington for the rest of the day.

I can't be imagining this, can I? What if I'm wrong? If Freddie likes him and trusts him, who am I to say otherwise?

Heck, I can't help it if he gives me the willies. I just don't like the guy.

In direct contrast to Washington, there's Clark. He's a Negro teenager who also recently started coming to the gym for boxing lessons. Freddie asked me to be Clark's coach. At first I think Clark wasn't too happy about having a girl teach him boxing, but after a couple of lessons he realized I knew my stuff. He's slowly coming to respect me. He's a very nice young man. Says he lives on Avenue C near the East River. Apparently it's an ethnically diverse neighborhood, but with very few Negroes. Clark wants to learn how to defend himself against white teenagers who give him trouble on the street. I told him that fighting is not always the best solution in a case like that; if someone got hurt, the police would automatically blame him because he's a Negro, whether or not he started it. Clark said he didn't care. He was tired of being picked on. He's a small fella, so I can see how he'd be an easy target for white racist bullies.

Work finally ended for me around 7:00. I showered, changed clothes, and had some supper with Freddie. He was feeling better and promised he'd be back to work tomorrow. When I was done, I put on a coat and told him I'd be back in a little while. I went up the street to the East Side Diner so I could use the pay phone inside. Lucy was working and she was glad to see me. It was slow so we chatted a minute. I felt like I had to order something—I couldn't just come into the diner and say I wanted to use the phone. She'd ask me why I didn't just use my own phone at home. So I sat at the counter and had a piece of blueberry pie and a Coke. When she went to wait on a customer, I got off the stool and went to the phone booth.

John's phone number was easy to remember. I dialed it and he answered after three rings. This time he just answered with, "Hello."

I lowered my voice and did a terrible impersonation of Joe Friday. "I'm looking for Special Agent Richardson."

John laughed. "Oh, my. Is the story I'm about to hear really true? Have the names been changed to protect the innocent—or the *guilty?*"

That made me laugh, too. "I hope you don't think it's wrong of me to call you."

"What do you mean?"

"You know, a woman calling a man."

"Not at all. Emily Post may object, but I certainly don't. I'm glad you did."

"Thank you again for the story in the paper. I'm gonna cut it out and put it in a scrapbook."

"You will? Do you really keep a scrapbook?"

"Nah. But maybe I should start one. What do you think?"

"It might be worth something someday."

"Maybe. I do keep a diary."

Lucy stopped in front of the phone booth. Through the glass I saw her give me a questioning look. I just smiled and waved her away. She shrugged and went on.

"A diary, huh? That's where you keep all your secrets?" he asked.

"I don't have any secrets," I replied. "Well, not many."

"I know your name really isn't Eloise."

"How do you know?"

"Come on. I'm an FBI agent."

"Okay, so what if it isn't my real name?"

"I'd like to know your real name."

"Why?"

"So I can call you that. It sounds funny for me to say, 'Well, hello, Black Stiletto!' 'Good night, Black Stiletto.' 'I'll talk to you later, Black Stiletto.' I guess I could shorten it to just 'B.S.'"

I like a guy who can make me laugh. "Ha ha, very funny. I'm afraid you're just gonna have to use Eloise for now, John."

"It's not very fair, is it? You know my name but I don't know yours."

"Nuh uh. I can't forget you're an FBI agent. We're not playing that game."

"So what about our deal?" he asked.

"Our deal?"

"Didn't we have a deal? I get you some good press and then you'd agree to meet me in person."

Oh, gee whiz. Did he have to bring that up?

"I'm gonna have to think about that, John. I still don't trust you. For all I know, you want to make up to your boss and really put me in handcuffs."

"Come on, *Eloise*. I assure you I'll play nice."

"Look, I'll tell you what. I like your voice and I like talking to you. I'll call you more often, how'll that be?"

"I'd like that."

"And then, maybe after I get to know you better, who knows?"

He went "Tsk, tsk, tsk," and said, "You're playing hard to get, you know."

"Isn't that what a respectable woman's supposed to do? I have my reputation to think of."

He laughed.

"What's so funny?"

"The Black Stiletto is worried about her reputation."

"Yeah, I guess it's a bit ironic." Lucy passed by the booth and gave me a funny look again. At that moment, the operator asked me to deposit another dime. "Hey, I gotta go. But I'll call you again soon, okay?"

"You have to go already?"

"I'm at a pay phone, John. Next time I'll bring more money."

"Okay, *Eloise*. I'll talk to you soon?"

"Soon."

"Goodbye, Black Stiletto."

I laughed again. "*Goodbye*, Special Agent Richardson!" And I hung up.

When I came out of the booth, Lucy was standing at the counter adding up a check. I returned to my stool to finish my pie.

"Who were you talking to?" she asked, of course.

"Oh, just a guy," I said with fake nonchalance.

She raised an eyebrow. "Oh, really?"

"Yeah."

"Who?"

"Just someone. I don't really know him. Yet."

"You called him from here?"

"Yeah."

"Why?"

I shrugged. "Just felt like it. Mmm, this sure is good pie."

"Judy! What are you not telling me?"

"Nothing, Lucy. Really. It's a guy I've never even met."

"But you call him on the phone?"

I shrugged again. "So what? I can do that if I want."

She smiled, shook her head, and took the check to the customer. I quickly finished the rest of the pie and Coke, left some money on the counter, and waved goodbye. "See ya, Lucy!" She looked at me like she wanted to talk to me some more, but I was already out the door.

So now I'm back home trying to go to sleep. Yep, it was a pretty good day. But now I'm gonna turn out the light.

# 11
## *John*
### HOME DICTAPHONE RECORDING

Today is February 21, 1959, and it's about ten thirty p.m.

The Black Stiletto called me tonight and we had an interesting conversation. She's a very flirtatious woman.

Doyle at the *Daily News* did a great job with the article I asked him to print. It wasn't a hard sell to his editor; they love material on the Black Stiletto. It ran in this morning's paper and it quoted me as I instructed. I don't know where he got the quote from the alleged anonymous New York cop, but Doyle must have phoned Chief Bruen's office to get a comment from him.

As expected, I caught hell from Haggerty about it. He about blew through the roof when he saw I'd been quoted. I let him chew me out for a full minute—how the Bureau is determined to catch the Stiletto and here I am telling her she's got nothing to worry about. He went on and on, threatening to demote me and all that, and then I said, "Don, hold on a minute. Think about this. You wanted me to lure her in, right? Those were your words. She hadn't contacted me in a while, so this is the only way I knew how to get her attention. And it worked. She called me at lunchtime."

He looked surprised. "She did?"

"Yes, my plan worked," I told him. "And we've made a date to talk again on the phone."

Haggerty then rubbed his chin and said, "You know, maybe

giving her false confidence is a good thing. She'll start to trust you and then you can get closer to her. Good work, Richardson." Then he laughed about Chief Bruen's comment. "I'll bet Pat about shit his pants when he saw that one of his own men defended the bitch."

I gave him my written report outlining my plan to "lure her in." He went back to his office and I returned to mine. Business as usual. What a jackass. Unfortunately, he's the boss and I have to do what he says.

She called me at home and we talked for nearly five minutes. I'm going to check with our surveillance guy tomorrow and see about getting something installed on my phone so we can trace calls. If I can keep her on the phone long enough, I can find out where she's calling from.

I didn't expect her to agree to meet me right away after the deal we made last month. I don't blame her, I guess. I'd be suspicious, too. But I can tell she enjoys talking to me. Like I said before, she's flirtatious. I flirted right back at her. She promised she'd call me again soon. Haggerty's right. Getting the Black Stiletto to trust me is the first step toward luring her in. And I made some progress tonight.

In other news, my informant has succeeded in penetrating Carl Purdy's inner circle. He knows it's a dangerous job, but he's willing to do it. I've asked that he find out the dates and locations of up-coming drug deliveries. The Corsicans bring the stuff over by boat, but how it's smuggled in we don't know. If we can kill off both arms of the beast, we'll make a large dent in the illegal narcotics trade in this city. Probably the whole country.

The Italians are restless. The police busted a protection racket in the South Street seaport area. There was a shootout and two men were killed. No cops were injured. The mob is getting desperate if their soldiers fight for their lives over a protection racket. Times must be hard. They're losing the race to control the narcotics business and they don't like it. I fear there will be more bloodshed before all this is over.

[Pause.] The Black Stiletto has a terrific figure, from what I've seen in the few photos that are circulating. Sexy voice, too. I wonder what she looks like under her mask.

# 12
## Judy's Diary
### 1959

MARCH 1, 1959

More tension with Mike Washington today.

It was my day off from the gym. Since it was also the day of the month when Soichiro pays $5,000 to the "devil," I had some time to look into the matter. But before I left, I decided to ask Freddie about some equipment repairs we needed. I could pick up some parts at the hardware store while I was out.

I didn't see Freddie anywhere, but I did find Mike Washington behind the counter where the cash register is. In fact, the register was open, and he had his hands in the till!

"Hey! What are you doing?" I snapped as I rushed over to him. Everyone in the gym stopped what they were doing and watched.

Mike didn't react as I expected. I thought he would quickly slam the register drawer shut and try to cover up his actions. Instead, he stood there and continued to take money out and count it.

"I asked you what you're doing!" I growled.

He looked at me and said, "Freddie asked me to get some petty cash to buy some parts at the hardware store. You weren't here and he wanted to fix some stuff."

I studied the man's face and determined that he wasn't lying.

"Where's Freddie now?"

"I don't know. In the locker room?"

At that moment, Freddie indeed came out of the locker room and saw us. He must've sensed the friction so he came over to the counter.

"Something wrong?" he asked.

"Freddie," Mike said, "Judy here thinks I'm stealing."

I responded with, "Look, I came down and saw him with his hand in the drawer, that's all. You gave him permission to do that?"

Freddie nodded. "It's your day off, isn't it?"

"Yeah, but I just came down to ask you if you wanted *me* to get the parts while I was out."

"Enjoy your day off, Judy. Mike can do it. I don't mind. He says he can get parts cheaper in Harlem."

I looked at him. "That's where you live?"

He almost sneered. "'Course that's where I live. Where'd you think I live? On fucking Fifth Avenue and Central Park?"

That took the breath out of me. Even Freddie reacted. "Mike, there's no call for that kind of language."

Mike dropped his head and looked sheepish for the first time. "I'm sorry. I'm sorry, Miss Judy. It's just that—well, I'm having a lot of personal trouble right now. My nerves are on edge."

He still wouldn't look me in the eye. "What kind of trouble?" I asked.

Freddie jumped in. "I think that's Mike's business, Judy. Why don't you go on, Mike. You got what you need?"

He nodded and shut the register drawer. "I'll be back this afternoon."

"Okay, Mike, see you later."

"I'm sorry, Mike," I said, but he didn't turn around to acknowledge my apology.

When he was gone, Freddie turned to me. "What's wrong with you?"

"What's wrong with me? What's wrong with you! Did you see how he acted? Did you hear what he said? You're letting him take money out of the cash register? He's not an employee, Freddie."

"He didn't want to say anything in front of you, 'cause he thinks you don't know he just got out of prison. But apparently he's having a hard time integrating back into society. Until recently he couldn't find work or a place to live. I actually offered to give him some part-time work, but he refused. Don't get upset, but I let him come to the gym for free. That's why he makes the trek down here all the way from Harlem. Mike says he has a job now, but I don't know what. His parole officer is giving him crap about being around known criminals in Harlem, which violates his parole. Mike can't help it if the only place he found to live in is a dump where there's a lot of crime. You know, narcotics and stuff."

I wasn't convinced. "I get a bad feeling from him, Freddie. Maybe he just doesn't like girls or something. He sure isn't very nice to me."

"You gotta remember, Judy, he was in prison for fifteen years. He never saw any women during that time. He probably feels intimidated around women now, especially a beautiful white woman like you. He knows very well there are people who wouldn't take kindly to him being in the same room with you, seeing that you dress in leotards when you're training. In the south, Negroes are lynched for just looking at a white woman."

"I can't believe he's that intimidated. He's not shy around me, he's belligerent. He doesn't like me for some reason."

Freddie shrugged. "I don't know what to tell you, Judy. He needs a friend right now and I guess I'm it. I hope you two can be friends, too. You don't seem to have any trouble with the other Negroes who come in here. You're friends with Jimmy, aren't you?"

"Sure, I love Jimmy! And I'd like to adopt Clark. He's a sweetheart. Freddie, I'm not prejudiced or anything like that. You know I'm not. I get along with everyone."

Freddie pursed his lips and thought for a second. Then he said, "Well, try to let it go for now. Let's see how it shapes up. If after another week or two and he still bothers you, I'll do something about it."

"Thanks."

"Now get out of here. It's your day off."

So I did. First I went to my regular *karate* class at Studio Tokyo. Soichiro was even more solemn and quiet. At one point he seemed to drift into a daydream during the lesson, which is totally out of character. This money problem he's got is weighing heavily on him.

Where could his daughter Isuzu be? Trying to do the math in my head—if she was an infant in 1944 when that family portrait was taken, then she'd be a teenager now, like 16 or 17. That's too young to leave home, isn't it? Of course, I left home at 14, but I'm different, ha ha. Is she at boarding school somewhere?

Anyway, after class was over, Soichiro avoided me and hid in his office. The poor guy. I really feel sorry for him. I love him like a third father—my real father is number one, Freddie is number two, and Soichiro is number three. I can't imagine him losing the studio. I have to try and help him, but first I want to know where that $5,000 is going each month.

I happen to know Soichiro's teaching schedule. All the classes were in the morning today, so I killed time in the West Village until noon, when his last session was finished. I discreetly positioned myself across from the studio on Christopher Street—in civilian clothes, of course—and waited. Thank goodness the weather had warmed up a little, but it was still chilly. After a half hour, I was ready to find a diner and get a hot cup of coffee—when suddenly Soichiro stepped out the front door of the building and started walking east. After he was a good half block away, I set out following him. He carried a briefcase, which was also atypical of Soichiro. I had a feeling I was going to find out some answers.

When he reached 7th Avenue, he turned north and went inside a bank. That figured. He was probably withdrawing that $5,000. I knew from looking at his ledger that he didn't have a whole lot of money left to withdraw—those payments couldn't go on much longer.

I waited for ten minutes or so and pretended to window shop, even though there aren't many stores along that section of 7th. Finally, Soichiro emerged from the bank, briefcase in hand, and started walking north again. I continued to trail him, but then he made a quick right turn onto 10th Street and headed east. I did the same. But when he crossed Waverly Place, I thought I lost him. A lot of people were on the street, it being lunchtime and all, and Soichiro's not the tallest man in the world. A sea of heads moved along the street in both directions so I just kept going. I crossed Greenwich Ave. and still hadn't spotted him. I felt frustrated and angry. And then—there he was, still walking ahead of me on 10th toward 6th Avenue. Breathing a sigh of relief, I kept my distance but stayed in pursuit.

Then, as soon as he reached 6th, he raised his arm to hail a taxi. I stopped walking for fear that he'd see me. Lucky him—a cab pulled right up and he got inside. Darn! As soon as it pulled away, I ran to the avenue and raised my hand, too. I wasn't as fortunate— several taxis went by that were already occupied. I stomped my foot and muttered, "Come on, come on!" But after a minute had passed, I knew it was too late to follow Soichiro's cab. It was long gone, headed uptown.

I was very disappointed. All I could do was go home, so I did.

MARCH 2, 1959

This has been an action-packed day, and I never once put on my Black Stiletto disguise.

First, I worked until 3:00. Then I went to my *karate* lesson at Soichiro's. Boy, that was tough. All during the lesson, Soichiro acted like he was mad at me but was doing his best to hold it in. He was particularly rough during the exercises and practice matches. At one point he actually hurt my forearm with a hard blow. I went, "Ow, Soichiro!" He stopped, stood rigid, and then bowed. "I am sorry," he said.

"What's got into you?" I asked.

His eyes narrowed and he whispered, "Why you follow me yesterday?"

Oh, dear diary, I felt a shiver run up my spine. You know that feeling when you get caught with your hand in the cookie jar?

"You . . . you saw me?"

"Of course I see you! I know when I am followed!"

He was very angry.

"Look, Soichiro-san, you're my *sensei* and you're my friend. I know you're having some money troubles and I want to help you."

As soon as I said that, his eyes grew livid. "You know nothing about it!"

"Soichiro-san, please, don't be mad at me. Don't you understand? You can trust me! You can tell me. You need to tell someone. You're in some kind of trouble. You owe a lot of money, I know that."

Cutting through his stoic façade, I could see he was conflicted. He wanted to tell me but his pride wouldn't let him.

"You owe a lot of money and you will lose the studio if you don't pay, isn't that right?" I asked gently.

Finally, he nodded.

"Listen, don't you worry. I know a way I can get some money for you. Big money. I will help you."

Soichiro shook his head. "No. You must not do that. Stop interfering!"

I could tell he was actually afraid of something. So I bowed and said, "Soichiro-san, with all due respect, sometimes you must graciously accept the generosity of your friends. I need to go home and make a phone call. I'll get back to you."

So I hustled back to the gym, went straight to the kitchen, and took the Hollywood producer's newspaper ad that was still stuck to the refrigerator. I then went back outside to a pay phone 'cause I don't like to make calls as the Stiletto from my home phone. If the offer is really legitimate, then I can demand a lot of money to make this movie or whatever it was, right? Well, it would be my pleasure to give it all to Soichiro. So I phoned Albert Franz's New York office and a female receptionist answered.

"Franz Productions, how may I help you?"

I was nervous! I started to talk and it came out in a croak, so I cleared my throat and spoke again. "Um, I know it's been a few weeks since that ad was put in the paper, but the producer Albert Franz wants the Black Stiletto to contact him about a movie deal."

"Yes?"

"Well, that's me."

"I beg your pardon?"

"I'm the Black Stiletto."

I thought I heard her snicker. "Of course you are."

"No, I really am the Black Stiletto. Is this a legitimate offer or not?"

"It's a legitimate offer, ma'am, but you have to prove you're the Black Stiletto. Since that ad ran, we've received hundreds of phone calls from women claiming to be the Black Stiletto."

*Oh geez.*

"Well, how do I prove it? You want me to come to your office in my disguise?"

"Anyone can put on a silly costume, ma'am. We've had a few dozen of those come in, too."

This woman was starting to tick me off. "Then what do you suggest I do?"

"We're asking all applicants who want to be taken seriously to send us a screen test."

"A what?"

"A screen test. Some film footage of you in action, so to speak."

"How do I do that?"

"If you don't have access to a professional studio, find yourself an amateur camera bug who shoots 8mm film. Get him to do it. That's what other applicants are doing."

I had no idea what she was talking about. "What's supposed to be on it? How long should it be?"

"A few minutes are sufficient, but we need to see that there's no question it's really the Black Stiletto in the film. Do you have our office address? That's where you would send it along with a head shot and résumé."

*Head shot and résumé?*

"Uh, okay, thanks." I hung up.

This was going to be more difficult than I thought.

I went back to the gym and found someone who might be able to advise me. "Hey, Freddie, if I wanted to find a camera bug who shoots 8mm film, where would I go?"

He looked at me funny. "What for?"

I shrugged and rolled my eyes. "Just wondering."

"You mean someone who shoots movies?"

"Yeah, homemade movies."

He rubbed his chin and thought about it. "There's a place on 14th Street called Movie Star News. They have what you call camera clubs, where amateur and professional photographers go to find models and such. Is that what you mean?"

"Yeah, I think so."

He laughed. "Those camera clubs shoot a lot of cheesecake pictures, Judy." I had no idea what that meant. Freddie saw my confusion and laughed again. "You know—pin-ups! Girls in bathing suits, nightgowns, or maybe even nothing at all."

I must have turned a thousand shades of red. "Really?"

"You asked, Judy."

We were in the gym and some of the guys were close by working out, so I lowered my voice to a whisper. "What if I wanted just some 8mm film shot of *her*?"

Now he was confused. He whispered back, "Who?"

"Freddie! The Black Stiletto!"

He furrowed his brow and looked at me sideways. "Why do you want to do that, Judy?"

"That's my business, Freddie. Come on, help me out here."

"Yeah, I suppose you could find someone there who'll do it. I suggest you be careful, though. The guy who runs the place got in trouble with the government for sending pornography in the mail, or something like that. Could be some shady characters around there."

I'm not sure what to think of that, but I don't have any other options. Soichiro needs that money now.

Freddie told me exactly where on 14th Street the place is, so I went there. Movie Star News is a dusty and dank little place that specializes in selling photographs of movie stars to collectors. They also have movie posters and other memorabilia. I didn't know there was a market for stuff like that. Anyway, there was a woman working there. When I told her what I was looking for, she pointed me to a bulletin board. "All the guys post notices up there if you're looking for work."

"Work? No, I'm not looking for work. I'm looking to hire someone to shoot some, um, custom film."

She still nodded at the board. "Take your pick. Most of those guys'll be glad to take your money."

I went over and studied the bulletin board, which was covered in business cards and handwritten index cards. Most of them had a guy's name, a phone number, and a comment like, "Looking for open-minded model," or "Glamour photography." Some offered to shoot bar mitzvahs and weddings. Some of the photographers indicated they were members of a camera club. Several notices had pull-off tabs with the phone numbers written on them. I took a few of the ones that sounded promising, and then I went back to the lady behind the counter.

"Can you recommend any of them?"

She shrugged as if she wasn't much interested, but she glanced at the handful of names and numbers I'd taken. "All of those fellas are pretty talented. You can't go wrong with any of 'em."

"Are they nice men?"

Then she really looked at me like I was crazy. "Sure. They're nice. We wouldn't associate with them if they weren't nice. Most of the guys who post on that board are professionals. Not all of 'em are amateurs."

I thanked her and started to leave—but then I noticed a black-and-white photo of Elvis Presley on the wall.

"You have pictures of Elvis?" I realize now how dumb I sounded.

"Yes, we do."

"Can I see them?"

She got up, opened a drawer in a filing cabinet, and pulled out three huge folders full of photos. "Take your pick," she said as she slapped them down on the counter in front of me.

My gosh, I was in heaven looking at those pictures! Some were in color, too. I wanted all of them. I asked how much they were, and decided to splurge and get a couple. I stood there for ten minutes trying to decide which two to buy—there were so many good ones. I finally got one of him in his army uniform, and one of him on stage with a guitar.

Then I went home. At first I thought I should go out and use the pay phone to call these guys, but I finally figured there wouldn't be any harm in using the home phone. These were photographers, not policemen. So I started calling them, one by one. I can't believe it, but I told each fella I was the Black Stiletto and was looking for a cameraman to shoot three to four minutes of me in action. Most of them didn't believe me. One guy said he'd do it for free if I'd pose for some seminude photographs. I hung up on that one. The nerve! Finally there was a guy named Jerry Munroe who sounded nice. When I told him who I was, he was thrilled. He started making suggestions of how we could go about it. He said he could set up a mannequin in his studio and I could use it as an "opponent," you know, I could perform moves on it. He also said there's a fire escape outside his studio if I wanted to use that for any outdoor stuff. I was impressed. I told him it would have to be done at night, and he replied that wouldn't be a problem. All in all, he seemed to be professional and willing.

He wanted $300 for the work, which included a reel of finished, developed film. I told him that was fine, but we had to do it as soon as possible.

We made a date to shoot tomorrow night.

After I hung up, I put my pictures of Elvis on the wall. I feel like some teenaged fan, but now he looks at me from just about anywhere I stand in the room.

Gosh, I'm nervous! I'm gonna be in the movies!

# 13
# Judy's Diary
## 1959

MARCH 3, 1959

I can't get my heart to slow down, dear diary. There was an "incident" tonight.

The mob tried to kill me again.

I should start at the beginning.

Jerry Munroe's photography studio is at the corner of East 29th St. and Park Avenue South. There's not a storefront or anything, it's just a commercial building and he occupies the entire second floor in a loft space. I showed up for my film shoot at 8:00 p.m. as scheduled. It was a little strange standing at the front door in my disguise and ringing his buzzer. A few people were walking on Park Ave. South; they pointed and stared. I remember hoping none of them get the bright idea to call the police.

Jerry is a well-dressed little man about 5 feet, 5 inches tall, very thin, and he had dark, slicked-back hair, a tiny mustache, and a ruddy complexion. There was a cigarette permanently hanging from his mouth. At first I thought he might be Latin, but he had a thick Bronx accent. I figured he must have some Italian blood or something in him; he definitely had a Mediterranean look.

He was pleased to see me. "I can't believe the Black Stiletto is in my studio! Man, oh, man, wait until the guys hear about this!" he said.

I told him, "Mr. Munroe, you can't tell anyone. You have to keep it a secret. That's part of the deal. This film is between you and me, and what I do with it is my business. Otherwise we can't proceed."

He looked a little disappointed, but he finally nodded and said, "Okay." I studied his expressions and mannerisms to see if my instincts picked up anything fishy about him. So far he seemed okay. I didn't get a sense that he was dishonest or anything, but I did pick up on something that wasn't quite right. He carried himself confidently but somewhat abrasively, as if he was a "know-it-all." I've heard of something that short men sometimes have called a "Napoleon complex," in which they think more of themselves than they really are. Maybe that's what was bothering me, but I really don't know. For the time being, I tried to put any doubts out of my mind and get on with the shoot. That was the most important thing.

The studio was set up like you'd expect. Lighting equipment was situated all around a space in front of a dark background drop that hung down one wall. A male mannequin stood in the center. At one end of the studio was a small kitchen. Off to the side was a little dressing room and bathroom. I didn't see a bedroom, so I figured Jerry lived somewhere else.

Oh, and the place reeked of tobacco smoke. There were several ashtrays in different areas of the space—all filled to the brim with cigarette butts and ashes.

Before we started, Jerry looked at me and asked, "You're not wearing any makeup, are you?"

I shook my head. I didn't think it was necessary since I had on a mask.

"You'll want to put on makeup so your eyes will show up better. Some lipstick will define your mouth more. I have some stuff there in the dressing room you can use. Why don't you take a few moments to make yourself beautiful?"

I thought—what the heck. Why not? I went into the dressing room and shut the door. There was a mirror with those lightbulbs around it like you see in the movies. A bag of makeup supplies was on the counter. I sat down in front of the mirror and studied my face beneath the mask. First I put on some lipstick. I wouldn't be able to get to my eyes without removing the mask, so I looked back at the door to make sure it was closed. I took off the mask and let my hair fall to my shoulders. I then applied some eye shadow and mascara just like Lucy once showed me how to do. I then bundled up my hair with one hand, pulled on the mask with the other one, and stuffed my hair into the back of the hood. I've gotten to where I can do it quickly, like in two seconds! I have it down to a science, ha ha! After a quick adjustment of the mask/hood, I stood and left the dressing room.

A film camera sat on a tripod. Jerry told me to stand in front of the backdrop so he could check the lighting with some kind of meter. I felt pretty silly standing there while he waved that thing around me. It was also pretty warm under all those lights. When he was ready, he told me to attack the mannequin as if it was a bad guy. I laughed. I couldn't help it. I felt ridiculous. Jerry told me to relax and "put myself in the moment." He started talking some mumbo jumbo about "method acting," a technique used by Marlon Brando and James Dean where they rely on memories that might be relevant to the situation. So I tried to think of the mannequin as Douglas, my horrid stepfather. Even though Douglas is no longer with us (ha ha), I did my best to pretend that life-sized fake body was him.

I jumped and performed a *tobi geri*—a jump kick—and knocked the mannequin to the floor.

Jerry's mouth would have dropped if he hadn't been smoking a cigarette. I guess I just proved I was the real McCoy, for he said, "You really *are* her!"

"You had doubts?" I asked.

"Hey, some lady comes in here in a costume and says she's the Black Stiletto, you gotta admit it's a little out of the ordinary. I had to see it to believe it. No offense."

"None taken."

He set the mannequin back up.

And so it went. I tried all sorts of setups, different types of *karate* kicks and punches. At one point, the mannequin's arm fell off! I started laughing 'cause it was pretty funny. I told him I was sorry, I didn't mean to break it. Jerry said not to worry about it; he snapped it back on the torso and kept shooting. After punishing that poor mannequin for fifteen minutes, Jerry told me to use my knife. I asked him if it was okay to stab the mannequin, and he said to go ahead. So I stood some feet away from it and threw the stiletto. It plunged directly into the mannequin's neck. Bull's-eye. Jerry captured a few more shots like that, and then he told me to stand in front of the mannequin and puncture it a few times. So I did.

Then he asked, "You want to go outside?"

I wasn't too comfortable about appearing on the street, but it was night. He suggested that perhaps we'd look like a movie crew and no one would suspect I'm the real Black Stiletto. I shrugged and said, "Okay."

We went out to the corner of 29th and Park Ave. South. The building's fire escape was on the 29th Street side, so he set up the tripod there. He had a portable spotlight but most of the illumination came from a streetlight on the corner. It took him fifteen minutes to set up, and then we were ready. What was I going to do? I figured I could climb the fire escape to the roof of the building. Jerry said he'd probably lose me in the darkness as I got higher, but that was as good a suggestion as any.

So I used my hook and rope, repeating the trick I'd done at Soichiro's apartment building. Amazingly, I caught the ladder's bottom rung on the first try, pulled it down, and scampered to the second-floor landing. Then up the steps to the third floor. And so on, until I reached the roof. I swung a leg over the edge, pushed myself up, and I was there. I looked down at Jerry and waved.

As they say in Hollywood, "That's a wrap."

We went back inside, upstairs to the studio. Then Jerry did something I didn't like. And maybe this had to do with what I sensed about him that I couldn't put my finger on earlier.

"You want this as a rush job, right?" he asked.

"Yes, please."

"How fast?"

"As soon as you can do it."

"I have to develop the film and edit it down to three minutes; that could take a while."

"When do you think you'll have it?"

"Give me two days. But since it's a rush job, I have to charge you another hundred."

I thought that was kind of sleazy. "You told me it would be $300."

"That was for the normal delivery. Developing and editing usually takes about a week. If you can wait that long—"

"No, go ahead. I just have $300 with me tonight, though."

"You can pay me the other $100 when you pick up the film."

So I dug into my backpack, found the cash, and gave it to him. "So what do I do, just come back here in two days?"

"That should do it."

"Same time?"

"I'll be here."

"Thanks, Jerry."

"You'll be pleased with the results. What do I call you, anyway?"

"Call me Eloise."

"Is that your real name?"

"What do you think?"

He smiled. "Okay, okay, I got you." He held out his hand and I shook it, but he didn't look me in the eye.

I left the studio, went down the stairs to the first floor, opened the front door, and stepped outside to the sidewalk. I started to go left and east on 29th Street, but two men wearing hats and heavy coats rounded the corner with purpose. They were ten feet away from me. Both of them carried guns.

My senses went haywire.

Just as gunshots filled the air, I leaped to the right between two parked cars at the curb. The men moved forward to shoot me between the vehicles, so I slipped beneath the car to my left. My body lay prone beneath the dirty underbelly. Not stopping for a second, I then rolled out toward the street—not too far, I didn't want to get run over by passing traffic! As soon as I was clear of the car, I jumped to my feet and scurried up the side of the vehicle to its roof. It happened so quickly, the men were just starting to stoop and shoot beneath the car. One of them looked up and saw me—I kicked him hard in the face with my right boot. His gun—a revolver, from the looks of it—flew out of his hand. He staggered back to the building behind him until he tripped over his own foot. By this time the other guy was rising with his gun aimed at me. I kicked the revolver out of his hand with my left boot, drew my stiletto, and jumped on top of him. We both fell to the pavement, me straddling his chest and my blade against his left cheek.

The first guy quickly recovered from my blow and was back on his feet, mad as heck. He rushed me, so I sliced the cheek of the fella below me just to keep him occupied. He yelped and I hopped off of him, ready to face the first guy. With my stiletto in hand, blood dripping off the tip, I crouched in a fighting position.

"Come on," I spat. "You want more?"

The man hesitated. His pal writhed on the ground, his hands covering his face and blood oozing between his fingers. My opponent eyed one of the revolvers on the pavement, just a couple of feet away—closer to him than to me.

No one moved.

I then noticed we had attracted an audience. Pedestrians stood watching, but they kept their distance. I heard someone say, "It's the Black Stiletto!" And another person shouted, "Call the cops! Quick!"

I couldn't waste any more time. Instead of cutting the guy, I performed a *mawashi geri*—a roundhouse kick—in which I twisted my hips in a circular motion so that the ball of my left foot swung inward, allowing me thrust my right leg up and out. I struck him in the sternum so hard that he collapsed.

That was my cue to scram.

I sheathed the knife and ran around the corner, heading east on 29th. I didn't stop until I reached Lexington Avenue. Looking both ways, I darted out into traffic, timing my crossing to barely avoid several vehicles headed downtown. Once I was on the other side, I kept running along 29th to 3rd.

It wasn't until I got to 2nd Avenue that I halted, found a dark doorway, crouched, and caught my breath.

That was close, dear diary. Those two men—I'm sure they were gangsters, probably working for Franco DeLuca—it was as if they'd been waiting for me to come out of the building. How did they know I was there? Had someone in the mob seen me during the film shoot at the side of the building and called them? That must be it. But I was inside the studio after that for only a few minutes. How were the hitmen able to show up in such a short time? Maybe someone saw me earlier, when I first arrived at Jerry's building.

Then I got to thinking about what it was that bothered me about Jerry.

He looked and acted like a gangster. Yes, he was short, but he was cocky and full of himself, just like the wise guys I'd met before. He was one of them. I'd bet my life on it—in fact, I almost did.

# 14
# *Martin*

## THE PRESENT

After reading some of Mom's diary, I knew who Jerry Munroe was. I now understood why my mom made a film with him. I'd have to read more of it to see if there was further mention of Munroe in the diary, but instead I spent the next day trying to locate contact information for his son Johnny in New York City. From Buffalo Grove, Illinois, that turned out to be harder than I'd expected.

The Internet was no help. There are a billion Munroes in New York and it seemed the first initial for half of them was a J. I went to the *World Entertainment Television* website for contact information, and was presented with several e-mail addresses, depending on which department you wanted to reach, and a corporate address and phone number. I tried calling first.

It was inane. The recorded voice went on and on with a menu of choices that had nothing to do with what I wanted. Did I want the WET Fan Club or the WET Online Store or the WET Comment Line? The remote possibility of talking to a live person was never offered.

So I studied the e-mail addresses on the WET website. Everything was WET-something. I'm sure they all laughed real hard in the conference room when they realized they could create licensed products like a WET beach ball, a WET blanket, and a WET noodle. I'm not kidding.

There was a General Questions address, one for Employment,

one for Submitting News, and a few others that were just as useless. For a moment I considered sending an e-mail to General Questions, but then I figured it's answered by flunkies and would never be seen by the right people.

I clicked back through the various pages on the WET website until I came upon anchorwoman Sandy Lee's "personal page." Apparently, she's a lot more popular than I realized. After skimming her bio and admiring the several head shots, I noticed the hyperlink: Contact Sandy!

Surely the woman didn't answer the e-mails herself. No way. Some assistant to an assistant handled the job. I'd bet Sandy Lee knows nothing about what comes in.

Nevertheless, I clicked on the link and a new window addressed to SandyLee@WETOnline.com popped up. What was the worst that could happen? The recipient would think I'm a crackpot. Big deal. So I wrote: "Dear Ms. Lee: I enjoyed your segment on the Black Stiletto. I would be very interested in contacting your guest, Johnny Munroe, for I may be able to help him with whatever he needs authenticating." I signed it Martin but left out my last name.

I never expected a response.

At the end of the workday my in-box displayed an e-mail from Sandy Lee. I had to assume it was *the* Sandy Lee, for it was short and sweet.

"Dear Martin, I, too found the segment exciting! The gentleman you seek can be reached at—" and she provided a phone number. Just like that. I was amazed. Apparently the WET people don't care too much about their guests' privacy.

I made the call. Voice mail picked up, and it sounded like him. Same hard-core New York accent and tough-guy demeanor.

"You reached Johnny Munroe. Leave a message and how I can contact you, and maybe I will."

Beep.

I was suddenly struck dumb. I hadn't planned on leaving a message. What could I say? That this was the Black Stiletto's son calling and I wanted to talk?

"Uh, Mr. Munroe, my name is Martin Talbot."

Shit! I didn't mean to use my real full name. That flustered me even more, and a few seconds of awkward silence went by. But then I somehow managed to collect myself and say, "Regarding your appearance on *World Entertainment Television*, I may be able to authenticate whatever it is you have on the Black Stiletto." I left my cell phone number and hung up.

Did I come off as a crank? Would he believe me? How many other similar calls would he receive?

I shrugged and fixed dinner. Scrambled eggs and toast. No bacon. That's right, breakfast for dinner.

As I sat at the table to eat, I glanced at the clock. Gina would probably be finished with school for the day. An hour later in New York would make it late evening for her. I dialed her cell phone number and got the voice mail, which was unusual for Gina. She could be in the middle of a funeral and she'd answer her cell phone if it rang.

"Hi, honey, this is dad, but you already know that 'cause I know you check the caller ID every time you get a call. I just wanted to see how you are. Haven't talked to you in over a week. Call me back when you can. Love you."

A couple of hours later, I went to bed and struggled to go to sleep. Dozens of invented conversations and situations raced through my head. Would I really hear from Johnny Munroe? Was he as slimy as I thought he was? Why was I slightly concerned about Gina not answering her phone? I told myself she's a grown college student and it was only 9:00 in New York when I called. She was probably still at school. Maybe she'd finally learned that using a cell phone in certain public situations was rude. How many e-mails did Sandy Lee normally receive? Did she ever get suggestive ones? And how cool was it that I actually got a real e-mail from Sandy Lee?

I think that was my last thought before I finally drifted away.

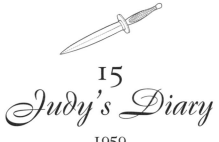

# 15
## Judy's Diary
### 1959

MARCH 5, 1959

Well, dear diary, I'm a movie star, ha ha.

Dressed as the Stiletto, I went over to Jerry Munroe's studio tonight to pick up the film. I was a little wary after what happened the other night. I have no idea if Jerry had anything to do with the attempted hit on me, so I planned to look hard at the man and see if I could detect anything other than the fact that he thinks he's a little tough guy and is a serious chain-smoker.

As I stood outside the building, I noticed the windows of Jerry's studio had metal gates on them. They could be unlocked from the inside in case he had to get to the fire escape, but they would certainly make it difficult for burglars to gain access. If he was located on the ground floor, I could sort of understand the need for them; but on the second? After he buzzed me in and I went up the stairs, I caught that the steel door to the studio was reinforced with not one but two deadbolts. Why in the world would a photographer need so much security? Was he just paranoid?

"Hello, Stiletto," he said as he shut and locked the door behind me. The cigarette still dangled from his mouth.

I asked him flat out, "Why do you need so many locks on your door?"

He shrugged. "You can't be too careful. Lots of crime these days." He didn't look me in the eye, which is always a bad sign.

"Like what happened outside the building when I was leaving the other night?"

Then he looked at me. "I heard about that. Are you all right?"

"Of course." I studied his face. He blinked a couple of times. He was less confident and cocky than he was the last time I was there. Nervous, in fact. "You don't happen to know who those guys were?"

Jerry made a face. "No. Why should I? The police said they were professional hitmen with the mob. Is that true?"

"I just know they tried to kill me outside your building. How did they know I was here?"

"I have no idea." He immediately turned away and nodded toward a film projector he'd set up. There was also a portable screen on the far side of the room. "You want to see your movie?"

*He knew something about the hit*. I was sure of it.

"Okay," I said.

There were two chairs by the projector. I sat in one, but he chose to stand by the machine. He turned it on, then walked to the wall and switched off the lights. The film started. There was no sound, just the black-and-white images on the screen.

He had cut together several of the various "fights" with the mannequin. Some of the in-between banter between me and the camera—laughing and rolling my eyes—was included. I asked him why he didn't edit that out.

"I thought it made you more real, you know, more human," he answered.

After about three minutes of the indoor footage, there was a cut to the street. The images were darker and grainier, due to the lack of adequate lighting. Nevertheless, you could still see me as I climbed the fire escape all the way to the top of the building. Once I was up there, I was just a tiny dark figure moving around. I waved at the camera and the film ended.

"That's it," he said as the film ran through the projector and flapped around the reel. He shut it off. "What do you think?"

Frankly, I didn't think much of it, but it would do. "Fine," I said. "I appreciate it."

"Just 'fine'?"

"Hey, you're not Cecil B. DeMille, okay? It will do for what I need. It's fine, Jerry."

"Okay." He threaded the end of the film to the empty reel and rewound it. When it was done, he put it in a small film canister and handed it to me. I gave him the balance of his fee.

"Thanks," he said. "Listen, how can I get in touch with you?"

"Why?"

"I have friends—you know, other photographers in the camera clubs—they'd pay you to pose for them."

"Did you tell anyone you were shooting me?"

"No! I'm just saying, I think you could make some money doing this."

"Then why am I paying you? Never mind, just kidding. I don't know, Jerry, I'm not thrilled about fraternizing with the public, you know what I mean? I'm wanted by the police, I guess you know that."

"And apparently by the mob, too."

"That's right. Do you know anything about that, Jerry?"

Again, he averted his eyes. "No, of course not."

Then I hit him with the question, out of the blue. "Jerry, are you up to anything illegal?"

His reaction was almost palpable. I swear he turned pale for a second and turned away. "What are you talking about?" he blustered. "I'm just a photographer." Then he laughed.

He was lying, dear diary. But there was nothing I could do. I put the film can in my backpack and headed for the door. "Okay, Jerry, thanks a lot."

"Wait. What about my photographer friends? Will you think about it? How can I contact you if I wanted?"

This time when he said it, I detected something different in his voice. The guy really wanted to contact me again. Could it have something to do with the mob hit? Did he have information that might lead me to some answers if I followed through with his request?

"All right, Jerry," I said. "I read the *Daily News*. Put an ad in the classified section—'To Film Star from Munroe.' You might need to run it a few times. I can't guarantee I'll see it, but if I do, I'll call you."

That was good enough for him. "Okay. Thanks."

I held out my gloved hand. He hesitated a second and then shook it.

"Nice doing business with you," I said.

Again, he wouldn't look at me as he answered, "My pleasure."

I heard him bolt the door twice when I left the studio. Downstairs, I cautiously opened the front door, looked both ways, and determined there were no additional Mafia hitmen waiting for me. A few pedestrians did double takes as I stepped out to the sidewalk.

Then I dashed east on 29th into the darkness.

MARCH 6, 1959

I'm writing this at 10:00 p.m., for the Black Stiletto is ready to go out and do something risky. So, dear diary, if I don't come back, you'll know why.

This morning I planned to drop the film can off at Albert Franz's office, which was located Midtown near the theatre district. But first I had a lesson with Soichiro. When I was on my way to Christopher Street, I realized I couldn't just walk in to Franz's office, unmasked and in civilian clothes, and hand them the film. I figured it would be best to mail it, but that would take up time. Soichiro needed that money immediately. So the plan was to stake out the office and see if there was a way to surreptitiously deliver it with no one seeing me.

That never happened.

When I got to Studio Tokyo, there was a sign on the door that said, "Class Canceled." I rang the buzzer anyway, but Soichiro didn't answer. I had a bad feeling about it.

I went to the pay phone on the corner and dialed the studio's number; no one picked up. Thinking I'd get the subway to Times Square, I started walking north on 7th Avenue—but as soon as I came to Soichiro's bank, I saw him coming out! I quickly ducked into a storefront entryway and watched him. Again, he carried that briefcase, and as before, he started walking east toward Avenue of the Americas, or what we New Yorkers simply call 6th Avenue.

This time I made sure he didn't see me. I backtracked to Christopher Street and ran east. People must have thought I was a madwoman, rushing through clumps of pedestrians shouting, "Excuse me, excuse me!" I made it to 6th Avenue and was in luck—a passenger was just getting out of a cab at the curb.

"Taxi!" I shouted.

The driver motioned me inside. I got in the backseat, closed the door, and said, "Just pull up to 10th Street and wait a second. I'm gonna have you follow another cab." I handed him a twenty dollar bill. "This will get you started."

"Okay, lady," he said, and he did what he was told. We waited about a minute and, sure enough, Soichiro appeared coming out of 10th with his arm raised to hail a cab. I ducked down and said, "If that Japanese man asks if you're free or not, wave him away. Don't let him come near."

"He just got a cab."

I raised my head and looked. Another taxi had pulled up and he was climbing in.

"Okay, follow them, please."

We drove up 6th Avenue, past 14th Street, past 34th and 42nd, and all the way to 59th, where Central Park begins. Soichiro's cab then crossed 59th and entered the park on what they call the East

Drive. My taxi did the same. We drove past the zoo, on up toward the boathouse and ponds, and eventually behind the Metropolitan Museum of Art. The driver went around the reservoir and up into parts of the park where I'd never been before.

We were headed to Harlem.

The road emptied out at 110th Street, the top of the park. Soichiro's cab went through a yellow light and crossed the street before we could. They went straight into Lenox Avenue, still headed north.

"Try not to lose them!"

The driver must've considered it a challenge. He kept his eyes peeled on the back of the cab until the traffic light changed to green. He sped across 110th and zoomed ahead, finally catching up with Soichiro's cab at 120th. I wondered where the heck Soichiro was going!

Finally, his cab turned right on 128th Street. My driver was good—he did the same but kept his distance. Hopefully the other driver didn't suspect anything.

Then Soichiro's cab pulled over to the curb.

"Wait, stop!"

My driver smoothly swerved over and halted. We were five car lengths behind.

"Okay, let's wait here for a bit." The meter was running up but I didn't care.

Soichiro got out, leaned in to speak to the driver, and then shut the door. Apparently the driver was going to wait for him. Carrying the briefcase, Soichiro turned and went into a bar called Good Spirits. How original. It looked like a dive. I couldn't imagine who Soichiro was meeting in there. He was paying $5,000 a month to a Negro? What was going on?

My gosh, dear diary, I didn't see one white person on the street. Everywhere you looked there were Negroes. A few stared at us as they walked past the cab. The driver, who was also white, and I must have stuck out like full moons in a clear night sky. For a moment I thought about that cute couple I met coming out of the Village Vanguard a couple of months ago, and I wondered—what are they doing now? Are they in love? Do they live close by? Harlem is a big place, of course. I understand it was once a vibrant community, full of music and nightlife and history. Now it seems pretty run-down, the big city equivalent of the shantytown that was across the tracks back in Odessa. Most white people are afraid to come up to Harlem now. They think the Negroes are all crooks and killers. I know that's not true. It's like that Dr. King has been saying, the Negroes were handed a raw deal and it's no wonder they've had such a hard time. Of course there's inequality in this country! If there's crime in Harlem, it's because of the poverty, and if there's poverty, it's because of the inequality.

Anyway, a few minutes passed and Soichiro came out of Good Spirits. He went straight to the waiting taxi and got inside.

"Okay, we can go now," I told my driver.

"You want me to continue following him?"

"Nah, but you can take me to back down to the Village. Christopher Street and 7th Avenue. I won't be surprised if they take the same route."

So that was my first venture into Harlem.

After I paid the driver, I got out of the cab and walked back to Studio Tokyo. I caught Soichiro just as he was unlocking the front door.

"Soichiro-san."

He turned and showed no emotion at seeing me. "Sorry. Class canceled."

"I know. Can I talk to you?" I asked.

Soichiro hesitated for a moment and then nodded sharply. I followed him inside and up the stairs to the studio. Once we were inside, we took off our jackets.

"You want tea?" he asked.

"No, thank you. Soichiro-san, I have something to say and I know you won't like me saying it, but I'm gonna say it anyway." I knew that sounded dumb as soon as it came out of my mouth.

He folded his arms and sat, Japanese-style, on the mat in the studio. I followed suit.

"I know you need money. I know you're paying an exorbitant amount to someone in Harlem." His eyes flickered with anger. I held up my hand. "Let me finish before you berate me." He didn't say anything, so I continued. "Look, I know someone who is willing to give me a lot of money to help you, and I will do this, especially if Isuzu is involved in something bad."

His mouth dropped.

"Isuzu is your daughter, right, Soichiro-san?" I could swear his eyes welled up, just a little. He was seriously hurting. "Please tell me what's going on. Believe it or not, I can help. I am your friend."

After a long silence, he finally opened up and started to speak. "Isuzu just child when we come to America. Her mother—her mother dead."

I kind of figured that, but it still took my breath away. "I'm so sorry, Soichiro. What happened to her?"

He answered with a heavy sigh. "Hiroshima."

Oh my gosh. The bomb. "She was there?" I asked.

He nodded. "Isuzu and me—we in Tokyo to visit my parents. I was trainer in army, and was summoned to special recruiting center in Tokyo. Machiko couldn't go on journey, she pregnant with second child. Tokyo being bombed, too, I thought it too dangerous for Machiko. I brought Isuzu to stay with grandparents outside city for few days while I worked. Then atomic bomb dropped."

He was silent for a while. I didn't know what to say. Eventually he continued.

"I took Isuzu to America when she turned eleven. We settle here. I have cousins in New York. They come here in '30s, before war. Now Isuzu fifteen. Sixteen in May."

He still hadn't answered my first question. "So is she in some kind of trouble?" Soichiro wouldn't answer. Finally, I said, "Well, I know it has something to do with that bar in Harlem. Good Spirits. I'm going up there myself."

Soichiro's eyes widened. "No! Judy! Very dangerous! They—they kill you—or worse!"

I almost laughed. "What could be worse than killing me? Who are they, Soichiro-san? Tell me."

Then it all came out.

Dear diary, it's horrible. Isuzu somehow got involved with narcotics. Soichiro doesn't know how it happened. Some black gangsters from Harlem are responsible. Once she was hooked, she started sneaking up to Harlem after school to buy drugs. Then one day she didn't come home. For weeks, Soichiro didn't know where she was. He reported her missing to the police, but they were no help. Finally, two Negro men came to visit him at the studio. They told him Isuzu was "safe" in Harlem. One of the men said she would continue to be safe as long as Soichiro paid $5,000 a month for six months—and then they would see to it that she came home. Soichiro had no choice but to deal with him. Then, in a new development, the gangster changed the terms a few days ago. Now Soichiro has to pay $10,000 for three more months before Isuzu can come home.

I was shocked. "Soichiro-san, that's kidnapping and extortion! Why don't you go to the police?"

He said Isuzu would die if he went to the cops. The gangster made that clear.

"Do you know where they're keeping her?"

He shook his head. All he knew was that he had to deliver the payments to the man at that bar.

"What's this crook's name?" I asked.

"Purdy," Soichiro answered. "Carl Purdy."

I got up and said, "Don't worry, *sensei*. My friend will take care of this. Isuzu will be home before long. I promise."

This time Soichiro didn't say or do anything to stop me. It was clear he was at his wit's end.

I left him there and went back home.

Gee whiz, dear diary, I didn't need to shoot that stupid film after all. I don't need to be in a Hollywood movie to get a bunch of money for Soichiro. I just have to send the Black Stiletto up to Harlem and find this Carl Purdy character.

So that's what I'm about to do now. Wish me luck.

# 16
## Judy's Diary
### 1959

MARCH 7, 1959

It's early on the 7th, 2:00 in the morning. I just got back home from my excursion to Harlem.

I waited until 10:30 p.m. to go out. I took the 3rd Avenue bus uptown wearing my jacket over my disguise, my mask in the backpack. It's a long way to Harlem from the East Village, and I figured the less time I had to appear on the street as the Stiletto, the better. You never know when an ambitious cop or a cocky mobster might decide to try and pick me off.

The bus let me off at 128th Street. I felt cold and alone. The streets were dark, wet, and nearly deserted. There didn't appear to be many pedestrians out this late in Harlem. I saw a few Negroes here and there, especially farther west toward the center of the community. I hid in the shadows to don my mask and stuff my jacket in the backpack. Then I flitted from one dark entryway to the next, making my way west to Good Spirits. Crossing Park Avenue was no problem, but near Madison there was a group of young Negroes—male teenagers—loitering in front of a brownstone. I tried to avoid them, but they saw me and shouted.

"Hey, who the fuck are you? Where you goin', lady? Why you wearin' that mask?" Things like that. What, hadn't they heard of the Black Stiletto? I tried to keep moving but they stood in my way, acting tough.

Then one of them said, "Hey, she white." Then another one finally realized who I was. "That's the Stiletto! The Black Stiletto!" Some of them hadn't heard of me. I guess Harlem is its own little world, separated from the news coming out of the rest of the city.

"Look, she got a knife!" One pointed to the sheath on my thigh.

"You lookin' for trouble, lady? You in Harlem now," the big-talking leader said menacingly. He wasn't much older than Clark, my protégé at the gym.

"Just let me pass," I said. "I'm on a mission."

"A mission? She on a mission!" He growled at me, "Not on our turf you ain't."

The rest laughed. One guy said, "Tell her, Sonny."

Then "Sonny" produced a switchblade and flicked it open.

I didn't want to get into a fight, certainly not before I'd accomplished what I came to Harlem to do, and absolutely not with these teenagers. I reckoned they were no older than seventeen.

"You don't want to do that," I said, but the group was already starting to surround me. The leader moved closer, the blade carelessly balanced in his hand. It was obvious they thought they were the neighborhood watchdogs, but they had no discipline or training for a real fight. Still, that didn't mean they weren't dangerous.

When Sonny least expected it, I kicked the switchblade out of his hand. With the speed of a snake, I drew my stiletto, grabbed him by the shirt, pulled him toward me, whirled his body around to face his gang, and placed the tip of my blade against his neck.

The others gasped audibly.

"Now you nice fellas listen real close," I said. "I'm gonna forget you drew a knife on me. You're gonna let me pass and I'm gonna go about my business." I looked at the kid who had recognized me as the Stiletto. "You had best tell your friends who I am." I then addressed Sonny, who was trying his best to appear unafraid. I gave him a tiny poke with the knife, pricking the skin a little. "And you.

Do we understand each other?" I asked. "Am I gonna have any more trouble from you? You're a brave and handsome young man. I'd really hate to have to hurt you. Your name is Sonny?"

He didn't say anything.

"Answer me!"

It took another little poke of the knife to get him to speak, albeit defiantly. "Yeah. Sonny," he spat.

"Well, Sonny, you may not believe this, but I like you. I respect the fact that you and your friends protect your neighborhood. But I'm not here to make trouble for you. So you're gonna let me pass and we're gonna forget all about this, right?"

After a moment of glaring at me, Sonny nodded. I released him.

"You fellas are doing a fine job," I said. "Keep up the good work." And then I sprinted through them and crossed Madison Avenue. I looked back to see them still standing there, watching. I gave them a little wave and kept going.

Oh my gosh, my heart was beating a mile a minute! I hadn't realized how scared I was until I was a good distance away. I had to stop in a rotted-out building façade and catch my breath. Standing there in the shadows, I breathed deeply and waited until my heart rate finally slowed. I was ready to move again, but then I heard a rustling behind me. It frightened the dickens out of me! A colored man was lying on cardboard, wrapped in stinky blankets. I can't believe I didn't sense his presence at first. Then I noticed there were two or three others next to him. Squatters. Homeless people.

"Gimme a dollar," the first man said. "C'mon, gimme a dollar." He reached a gnarly black hand out to me.

I took off. I don't know why, dear diary, but that disturbed me more than the encounter with the young toughs. I know New York can be a rough place for some people, especially if you don't have money; but I'd never been face-to-face with homeless people in the vicinity of their squalor. I didn't like it.

Shaken but alert, I crossed 5th Avenue and was now on the block where Good Spirits was located. Its neon sign shone brightly in the darkness, telling one and all that they were open for business. Well, I knew I couldn't just walk in the front door. There had to be an entrance in the back, but like on most streets in New York, the buildings butted up against each other, side by side. About a quarter of the way down the block I found an opening to the alley between 128th and 127th. Back in Texas, alleys behind houses were big. In New York, they're tiny little passages between the backs of buildings. I don't think people call them alleys here. Anyway, I slipped through the space and found myself in a dark, dirty, narrow pathway full of tall foliage, garbage, and junk. And rats. Yes, rats. They scurried out of my way as I moved forward. It was repulsive.

I reached the back of the bar, and sure enough, there was a door—and it was ajar. I heard jazz music inside, some of that crazy saxophone stuff that Negroes listen to. It wasn't like the jazz Freddie played for me. This stuff sounded like the musicians were hopped up on those drugs they take.

Anyway, I crept to the door and listened carefully for any signs of movement. All I heard was the music, so I dared to peek in. It was a storage room, full of cartons of booze and other bar supplies. A door on the far side of the space was open, leading to the rest of the establishment. I stepped inside and slowly moved forward. When I got to the other door, I saw a small office to the left. The music was coming from there. The light was on, but it was empty. I slipped in and shut the door.

There was a desk and chair, a phone, a filing cabinet, and lots of paperwork in baskets. The walls were covered with framed photos of well-dressed colored men smiling for the camera. A couple of the same ones appeared in several pictures, possibly the proprietors with important customers. The source of the music was a record player that sat on a small table in the corner. A album sleeve stood upright on the floor against the table. It was *Something Else!!!! The Music of Ornette Coleman*. I'd never heard of him. The sounds coming out of that hi-fi were weird.

I started looking through the stuff on the desk. One thing that stuck out was a little tray full of business cards. They said, "Harlem Delight," with an address on 131st Street and phone number, along with a silhouette of a woman's body. I may be naïve, dear diary, but I was pretty sure it was an advertisement for a house of ill repute. You know—a brothel. I took one and put it in my pocket.

Before I had time to do anything else, I heard footsteps outside the office door. I froze.

Someone knocked. "Who's in there?"

I quickly moved to the wall so that I'd be behind the door it if it opened.

What do you know!—it did. I held my breath.

The man on the other side of the door muttered, "What the hell, man—?" Then he came all the way in and went to the desk. I noticed a handgun sticking out of the back of his trousers. I knew as soon as he turned around to leave, he'd see me. I had to act, so I shut the door and stepped out from the wall. The man whirled around and nearly screamed when he saw me.

I drew my stiletto for emphasis. "Hush! Don't say a word!"

That didn't work. The man reached behind his back and pulled out the gun—a revolver. He squeezed the trigger just as I attempted an *uraken*—a back-fist blow—with which I hoped to knock the gun out of the man's hand. Unfortunately, I managed only to jar his gun hand slightly to the right. The bullet discharged and hit the wall behind me. As he pulled the revolver back toward me, I released a *mae geri*—front kick—to that vulnerable spot between a man's legs. Soichiro's old trick he'd taught me worked again. The man's expression suggested he'd just been kicked in the balls—which he had. He dropped the gun and fell to his knees, groaning and heaving in pain. I sheathed my knife.

More knocks on the door. "Hey! Rascal? Rascal, you in there?" It swung open and a second fella barged in. Before he could register what was going on, I twirled out of position and punched him hard in the stomach. He bent over with an "Ooompf!" I then clasped my hands together and clobbered him on the back of the neck. He dropped flat on the floor, out for the count.

Then all was quiet except for the music and the first guy's moaning. He didn't look like he was going anywhere, so I stepped out of the office and carefully snuck around the corner to peek at the interior of the bar. There were maybe five or six customers—older colored men—sitting with their eyes closed in front of half-finished drinks. They appeared to be so drunk they weren't aware of what was going on. No one stood behind the bar. It must have been the bartender I'd knocked out.

I went back to the office, shut the door, and drew the stiletto. My first victim had just thrown up all over the floor. Gross. I kneeled beside him, careful not to step in it, and put the blade to his face. It was then that I recognized him. He was one of the regular subjects in the photos on the wall.

"What's your name?" I asked.

He just groaned some more.

I placed the blade across his neck. That got his attention.

"What's your name?"

"Rascal."

"Rascal what?"

"Rascal Jenkins."

"Are you the manager?"

He nodded.

"I'm looking for Carl Purdy. Do you know him?" That got a reaction. His eyes grew big and he almost forgot his pain. "I take it that's a yes. Where can I find him?"

Suddenly the man was scared, very much so.

"Do you know who I am?" I asked. He nodded. "So where do I find Purdy?"

He gave me an address and said that Purdy lived in a "big, nice house." I looked up at the photos. "Is that him with you in a lot of those pictures?"

Rascal nodded again. Now I know what Purdy looks like. He's in his 30s, I guess. Tall and handsome. Black as night. Has a three-inch scar at the left corner of his mouth that slides down his lower cheek and beneath his chin. His hair was straightened in the "conk" style that so many Negro men were doing, especially the musicians like Chuck Berry and Little Richard. In short, he looks like any of my old Italian gangster friends, only he's a Negro.

I showed Rascal the business card I took off the desk. "What's this place?"

He wouldn't answer me. I had to prod him with the stiletto again.

"A place to meet girls."

Just as I thought. "It's a whorehouse?"

He nodded.

Then, as much as I hated to think it, a thought occurred to me. "Are there any Japanese girls there?" That question threw him. He furrowed his brow. "Well? Are there?"

He nodded. "One."

It was all I needed to know, but I continued to ask more questions. "What's this bar to Purdy?"

"He owns it."

"Does he come in here?"

Rascal nodded again.

"It's his office?"

"He uses it sometimes for business meetings."

I understood. "So it's a base for all of his activities? Narcotics, prostitution, extortion, theft, that kind of stuff?"

The guy was too scared to lie. He nodded once more. "It's one of the places he uses. He has lots of places, all over Harlem."

"Okay. You tell him the Black Stiletto is coming for him." I picked up Rascal's revolver and sheathed my knife. "Best not get up for a few minutes. I wouldn't want you to be sick again."

I left the office, walked back through the storeroom, and out to the alley. When I got to the street, I dropped the revolver in a drain and then ran east. It took another hour for me to get home, but I made it without incident. I figured it was too late to find the brothel tonight.

This calls for a solid plan of action. I need to scope out the territory and gather more information. I can't just waltz into one of Purdy's businesses without knowing what I'm doing. Of course, I did that tonight, ha ha, and that wasn't so bad. Still, I imagine he's got armed men stationed at the brothel.

I wonder if my friend John Richardson might be able to help. Surely he knows something about Carl Purdy. From what I gather, this Purdy must be a major player in Harlem. I bet the FBI has a file on him. Besides, I haven't spoken to John in a while.

It was an eventful night, but the one thing that makes the most noise in my head is what Rascal said about the brothel.

I'd bet my left little toe that the Japanese girl there is Isuzu.

# 17
# *John*

## Home Dictaphone Recording

Today is March 7, 1959.

It's been a couple of weeks, but I finally heard from the Black Stiletto again today. She called me at the office, so I immediately signaled my assistant, Tom, to try and trace the call.

At first she was apologetic about not being in touch. She said she's been busy. I asked her if she meant she was busy in her personal life or busy as the Stiletto. She answered, "Both." I wanted to keep her on the phone as long as possible, so I told her I hadn't seen anything in the news about the Stiletto. She told me to wait and see, there might be something soon.

Then she asked me a surprising question.

"What do you know about a Negro gangster in Harlem named Carl Purdy?"

That floored me. Very few people out of law enforcement know who he is. I asked her how she knew about him. She wouldn't say, but she wanted to know how big his organization is, how many men he has, what kind of protection he has, and what businesses he owns in the city.

I told her she's playing with fire. I was honest and told her Carl Purdy is a very dangerous individual and that he's the heroin kingpin in Harlem, although the Bureau and the city police have no concrete evidence against him that justified an arrest. The Negro mob is run similarly to the Italian mob—no one in the lower ranks will talk if he's caught. Additionally, the Negro gangsters also bribe judges, politicians, and police, just like the Cosa Nostra. It's difficult to make charges stick to Purdy's soldiers. In answer to her questions, I said Purdy is most likely well protected, is armed, and never goes anywhere without bodyguards. His home is an upscale brownstone and is guarded. We know he owns a restaurant, a couple of bars, and several other residential and commercial buildings in Harlem. He is a very wealthy colored man.

I asked her what she was planning to do. She wouldn't say; only that it had to do with a prostitution racket that Purdy was running. That made sense. Purdy has his hands in all kinds of illegal activities—gambling, bookmaking, prostitution. All that stuff funds the narcotics distribution operation.

There's no question she's walking into a serious situation. I tried to warn her.

By then, Tom held up a finger and mouthed the words, "East Greenwich Village." I needed to keep her on the line a few more seconds to get the exact location.

I asked the Stiletto once again if we were going to meet in person. She asked me, "When and where, and how do I know it's not a trap to arrest me?" My answer was, "Anytime, anywhere, and you have my word you'll be safe."

She hesitated a moment and then said, "I'll see you at the East Side Diner at Second Avenue and 4th Street for lunch tomorrow at noon."

Talk about a surprise! I asked, "In or out of costume?" She laughed and asked how she'd know me. I said I'd be wearing a brown suit and hat—the traditional Hoover "uniform"—and then she hung up.

I looked at Tom—the expression on his face said it all. The connection was broken too soon. All we know is that she used a pay phone in the East Village. Given the address of the lunch date, that clicked. Could it be she lives around there?

After glancing at my calendar, I cleared the way for me to have lunch downtown tomorrow. How will I know her? Is she leading me on? It's probably not a bad idea to have Tom accompany me undercover and take photos of all the customers at the diner. Maybe it's a place she frequents.

It's interesting the Stiletto is looking into Carl Purdy. I've been telling Haggerty pretty soon that guy's name will be all over the papers. Purdy will take a wrong step sooner or later and his little fiefdom in Harlem is going to crumble down around him. Haggerty, of course, scoffs and claims Purdy has nowhere near the power I think he does. He's more interested in catching the Stiletto instead of the biggest narcotics lord in the city.

Whatever.

I typed another written report for Haggerty on how I plan to catch the Stiletto.

# 18
## Judy's Diary
### 1959

MARCH 8, 1959

Oh my gosh, dear diary, I can't believe what I did today! I saw John Richardson in the flesh, and he's *gorgeous*! I did a bad thing, though. I didn't reveal myself to him. It was probably a dirty trick, and I wouldn't have been surprised if he didn't ever talk to me again—but he did.

So here's what happened.

I got him to come to the East Side Diner for a lunch date, but I stood him up. Well, not really. I was there, but he didn't know it. I felt bad that I had to deceive him, but I thought I needed to get a good look at him before I do something as risky as meeting him in person for real. I had to get a sense of who he was, what he's like. You know, if I detected he was a bad person, I would have stopped calling him.

The good news is he seems to be a nice guy, from what I could observe.

The whole thing started when I called him at his office yesterday to find out some information about Carl Purdy. He was surprisingly candid and revealed some helpful stuff. I plan on visiting that brothel tonight, and now I feel better prepared. Then he hit me with the same old question of when I was going to meet him, so I thought—why not? I told him I'd see him at the diner for lunch today. Those were my exact words. "I'll see you at the diner for lunch." I didn't say I'd *meet* him. But I did *see* him.

After we hung up, I called Lucy 'cause I knew today was her day off. I asked if she and Peter wanted to go to the diner for lunch. That way, there'd be three of us in a booth and if John showed up, he wouldn't suspect anything. I'd just be one of a threesome. He said he'd be wearing a brown suit and hat; even though a few business-men might go to the diner for lunch, I figured I could tell if a guy sitting alone was him or not.

Lucy and Peter were already there when I showed up, thank goodness. I knew Lucy likes to sit in a particular booth if it's not taken; it's against the back wall where there's a mirror. She usually sits on the side facing the front window, so she can look out on the street. That's good for me, 'cause if I sit across from her, I can see the entire diner by looking at the mirror to my left. And that's how it was.

From the clientele already seated, it didn't appear John was there yet. I didn't see one single man in a business suit. There were a couple of men by themselves, but they weren't dressed in suits. The clock on the wall said it was five minutes until noon, so it was still early. While I waited, Lucy, Peter, and I talked and ordered some food.

Someone put money in the jukebox and played Ritchie Valens's song "Donna" and that new Frankie Avalon tune, "Venus." I like Ritchie's records, but I'm not too crazy about Frankie Avalon. He's too much of a teen idol, more of a pretty boy than a rock-and-roll singer. I wouldn't call what he sings rock-and-roll at all. He's just like Fabian and Bobby Darin, they're interchangeable! I miss Elvis.

Peter's a terrific guy. Lucy's lucky to have him. It's so obvious that he dotes on her. He's two or three years older and already established in a law firm of some renown. I hadn't heard any more talk of marriage since New Year's, but that sure changed today!

"Notice anything different about me?" Lucy asked. She was sitting with her elbows on the table with her forearms upright and the back of her hands toward me. At first I didn't know what she was talking about. She looked exactly the same as the last time I saw her. Then the light hit the enormous rock on her finger and nearly blinded me, ha ha!

"Oh my gosh, Lucy! You're engaged!" I squealed like a little girl. I grabbed her hand and pulled it closer so I could examine the huge diamond ring. "That's beautiful!" I looked at Peter and said, "You did good, honey." He blushed. "When did you pop the question?"

Lucy answered for him. "Last night. He actually got down on one knee. It was so romantic. I almost died when I opened the box."

"So when's the big day?"

Peter replied, "We're talking about it. Maybe a year from now. We'd like to spend at least a few months engaged. I like the word 'fiancée,' and want to use it as much as possible."

At that point I saw a man wearing a fashionable brown suit and hat enter the diner. He was tall, appeared to be in his thirties, and was very handsome. He scanned the restaurant as if he was searching for someone. I immediately knew he was John Richardson. I watched him in the mirror while Lucy started gabbing about the romantic dinner she and Peter had last night and how he had proposed. It went in one ear and out the other while I studied John. He took an empty booth by the window, scanned the diner once more, and then studied the menu. I felt bad. I wanted to slide out of my seat, run over to him, and say, "Here I am! I'm the one you're looking for!" But I didn't. I couldn't.

Sally, one of the waitresses, tried to take his order. I heard his voice and confirmed it was him. He was polite and said he was meeting someone, but he'd have some water while he waited. Every now and then he'd look out the window and watch the people on the street. He glanced at his watch. According to the clock on the wall it was five after.

When it got to be 12:10, I could see he was becoming a little concerned. He started making faces and drumming his fingers on the tabletop. Lucy and Peter kept talking about mundane stuff like where they might want to live once they got married. Right now they have separate apartments that are too small for the both of them. Our food arrived and we started eating, but I kept watching John in the mirror.

At 12:15, he finally placed an order. I heard the words, "I guess she isn't coming, so I'll have—"

It bothered me more than I thought it would. I realized then it was a mean thing I'd done. It was selfish. I wanted to know as much about him as possible without giving him anything in return.

All this put me off my food. Lucy asked me if anything was wrong. "Oh, I'm not that hungry, I guess," I answered. I ate what I could, but I hated knowing I'd disappointed John.

Twenty minutes passed. We finished our meal and Lucy and Peter lit cigarettes. Apparently John was done with his lunch, too, for he asked Sally for the check. I watched him leave a tip on the table, and then he got up with the bill and paid for his meal at the cash register. Then he walked toward the washrooms, which are located on the other side of the place, next to the phone booth. As soon as he'd gone into the men's, I said, "Excuse me a second, I gotta go to the ladies'." I slipped out of the seat and took my time walking across the diner. I stopped to talk to Sally for a second, hoping John would be coming out just as I got over there.

Sure enough, I timed it perfectly. He opened the men's door and stepped out as I was moving past. We bumped into each other!

"Oh, excuse me!" I said. "Excuse *me*," he countered. We practically said it simultaneously. He smiled at me—most men do—and I smiled back. I took that very brief moment for my senses to detect anything about him that might raise red flags. There was nothing, but admittedly I didn't have much of a chance to make a thorough evaluation. I couldn't linger or he might get suspicious. So I went on into the ladies' room.

When I came out, he was gone. It was terrible. I felt so guilty. I wanted to make it up to him. He had kept his end of the bargain, and I'd given him the brush-off. The three of us sat and talked a while longer and then Peter said he had to get back to work. After saying goodbye to my friends—dear Peter paid for my lunch despite my protests—I went to the pay phone at 2nd Street and called John at the office.

"Special Agent Richardson."

"I'm sorry," I said. "Did you just get back?"

He was quiet a moment and then asked, "What happened? I was there and waited for you."

"I know. I was there, too."

"You were?"

"I couldn't bring myself to do it, John. I just couldn't. Please understand."

"But I didn't see—oh, well, there were several women in the diner, they just weren't sitting by themselves. You were one of them?"

"Yes."

"So now you know what I look like, but I don't know what you look like."

"I think you're very handsome. And you're a sharp dresser."

"Thank you. The Bureau insists we wear suits. And hats."

"I feel bad about this. You have to understand I had to be sure about you. I have to trust you. Thank you for coming alone and keeping your end of the deal."

"I understand."

"You're not angry?"

"No. I had a nice lunch."

"John?"

"Yes?"

"Next time. I promise. We'll meet. I have to figure out how it'll work, but now I know I want to go through with it."

There was a pause. "Next time, then."

"So I can call you?"

"You're in control, Stiletto. Eloise. Whatever your name is."

I laughed. "Okay, John. I'll talk to you soon."

"I hope so."

Then we hung up. The phone call made me feel better. I suppose he's not really angry. Perhaps a little perturbed, and I don't blame him. So, next time!

But now the Stiletto needs to make another journey to Harlem.

## 19
## Martin

### THE PRESENT

I received a phone call from Johnny Munroe the day after I left that message on his voice mail. He was brusque and pushy. It's understandable, I suppose. He told me he'd already received thirty-eight calls, all from crackpots.

"I assure you I'm on the level," I told him. "I may be able to help you."

"How?" he asked. "Your name is Martin Talbot and you live in Chicago. What qualifications could you possibly have? Unless you have firsthand knowledge of the Black Stiletto and her whereabouts, you can't help me."

"Okay, it's obvious you have some information you want to keep close to the chest. I, too, have things I don't want to reveal. We're going to have to meet halfway."

"Then you tell me what you got and maybe I'll tell you what I got."

I contemplated this one-sided proposal. There was no way he was going to give up anything without me providing a motivation for him to do so.

"All right," I said. "I have a copy of the film footage you showed on *World Entertainment Television*."

There was a moment of silence. Then: "You do?"

"Yep. The whole thing. The entire roll."

"All of it?"

"That's right. Now let me ask you something, Mr. Munroe. Does your copy of the film have an additional scene at the end, one that wasn't shown on the TV show?"

Again he was quiet. Then: "Yeah. It does."

"There you go. Now do you believe me?"

After a moment's hesitation, he asked, "Who are you?"

"That's not important. I'm calling because we need to come to an understanding. That extra film footage must never be seen. It should be destroyed."

This time he laughed. Softly at first, but then it grew into a belly laugh, as if I'd just told him the funniest joke in the world. When he caught his breath, he said, "You gotta be kidding. What for?"

"Because I represent the Black Stiletto's interests." I couldn't think of anything better to say.

"Oh, do you now? And how can that be? Is she alive? Are you related? You gotta tell me more, Talbot."

"Maybe I can. Perhaps we need to meet in person. Can you come to Chicago?"

Again the belly laugh. "Me? Come to Chicago? Or should I say Buffalo Grove, wherever the fuck that is. Yeah, that's right. I checked you out before I called. There are so many wonderful tools on the Internet these days. Hell, I'm looking at your house right now on Google Maps street view. Now listen to me, Talbot. I don't go anywhere for you. You gotta come to me. Why don't you come to New York? I'd be happy to meet with you here."

I knew that wasn't possible. I'd be starting my new job on Monday and, frankly, I couldn't afford such a trip right now. I told him I couldn't do it.

"Well, then, I guess I'll have to take *World Entertainment*'s offer of half a million bucks for any additional Black Stiletto material I might have, especially anything that might reveal her identity. The fact that you've got another copy of the footage validates it, wouldn't you say? I can't believe my father would make only one print from the negative."

*Holy shit.* This guy was serious. "Does the negative exist?" I asked, trying my best to keep the nervousness out of my voice.

"Maybe it does, maybe it doesn't. I tell you what, though. Since you represent the Black Stiletto's interests, as you say, I'll make you a deal. Sounds to me like you really want to keep the rest of my film from going public, am I right?"

I didn't expect any deal from him to be fair, but I said, "Yeah. That's the idea."

"All right, I'll sell you the film for a million bucks. Then *World Entertainment* won't get it."

"Isn't that extortion?"

"Nah. It's a friendly business offer between two individuals. I'm givin' you first refusal. One million bucks."

"You're crazy."

He laughed again. I didn't like the guy at all.

"Why don't you take the weekend to think about it? I'll give you a call on Monday and we can talk again. How'd that be?"

I hung up. I was so angry I couldn't think straight. What began as an innocent, fact-finding phone call on my part had led to a million-dollar extortion threat.

Damn. What was I going to do?

I jumped in the car and drove to Woodlands to see Mom. This was serious. I was faced with making a choice between the lesser of two evils. On the one hand, if I let Munroe do what he wanted, my mother's youthful face would be exposed to the world. On the other hand, if I legally attempted to stop the guy, I'd be forced to reveal my mother's identity and present evidence that she's the real deal. The latter was definitely the worst that could happen. If the un-masking scene was shown on television, the odds were against the possibility that someone would recognize my mom when she was twenty-something. We could still probably remain anonymous.

Still, it was my duty to do everything in my power to prevent that bastard from displaying Mom's face to the world. How was I going to stop him without compromising my mother, not as the

Stiletto, but as she is today? Trying to come up with an answer to that just made me angrier. It all had to do with that damned film and its invasion of her privacy.

Mom was in her room, sitting in her rocker and listening to a CD of Elvis's greatest hits. I gave it to her a while back. One of the staff must have put it in for her. It's true that she responds well to Elvis music. It definitely changes her mood for the better. As she listens, a smile of pleasure breaks through the wall of hurt, confusion, and depression that is Alzheimer's. She even sways in her chair a little. Gina is sometimes successful at getting her grandmother up to dance.

I hated to spoil the party.

"Mom, I have to talk to you."

She looked up and grinned at me. "Oh, hi."

I remember my mother as a lively and talkative lady; now she was a woman of very few words.

"Hi. Listen to me a second, Mom, okay? I have to ask you something." I sat on her bed across from her, reached over to the dresser, and turned the volume down a bit.

Mom turned her head toward the player and asked, "Oh, is it over?"

"I just turned it down, Mom, so we could hear each other. Look at me, Mom." I took her hands and held them. She seemed to like that. "Mom, I know this might be hard for you to remember. You probably won't know what the hell I'm talking about. But I have to ask. Do you remember the film you made in New York? With Jerry Munroe? A film, Mom, you left it for me. It's footage of you in costume." I knew from experience the words "Black Stiletto" triggered an unpleasant emotional response from my mother, so I avoided them at all costs.

Something—I swear—something lit up behind those sad greenish-brown eyes. Then she gasped slightly and her expression became one of mental struggle. There was a memory lodged in there and she knew it. She just couldn't reach it.

And then, out of the blue, she said, "Not a costume."

I blinked. "What?"

"Disguise. It was my disguise."

Christ Almighty, it was the first time my mother had ever ac-knowledged anything to do with the Black Stiletto. In the past, she'd just become agitated and upset if I mentioned her.

"Do you remember the film, Mom?" I held up and cupped my hands to form a small circle. "This was how big it was. A reel of film. Black-and-white film. Of you. Jerry Munroe shot it in New York. Do you remember?"

For a moment I thought I'd mined some dormant remembrance. Her face hardened and she squinted. It was a great effort for her, but she found a way to reach back into the past. For a second.

"Jerry Munroe," she said, as if the name was something that tasted bad.

"Yeah, that's him, Mom. Do you remember? Well, you know the ending, right? The part he secretly filmed and you didn't know about it? You were in a dressing room and—" I mimed the action. "—you pulled off your mask."

She gasped again and then it was gone. Her face changed. It was as if the dark vision in her brain had suddenly departed. After a few seconds of stillness, she resumed her role as the unhappily compla-cent Alzheimer's patient.

"Mom? Is there anything you can remember about it?"

And then her eyes rolled upward and she fainted.

"Mom?" I got up and went to her. Mom's head lolled to the side and her body drooped beneath it. "Mom!"

First I made sure she wouldn't slide out of the rocking chair. Her limp body appeared to be safe from falling, so I leaped for the call button that hung by her bed. I pushed it frantically, then jumped up and ran to the door. One of the nurses was already on her way, so I darted out to greet her.

"My mother's fainted, I think," I huffed. The woman hurried with me back to the room. Mom was beginning to stir. She moaned lightly.

"Let's put her on the bed," the nurse said. "Can you get under her arms? I'll grab her legs."

I nodded and reached behind my mom. "Hey, Mom," I said to her, "we're going for a ride." She was as light as a pancake.

Once she was stretched out on her bed, the nurse began checking vital signs. Dr. McDaniel walked in a moment later.

"What is it?"

"Judy fainted," the nurse said to the patient. "But we're better now, aren't we?"

"I'm glad I was still here," the doctor said. "Let me take a look."

I stood near the door as Dr. McDaniel and the nurse poked and prodded my mom. I was struck again during one of those male mo ments of how good the doc looked, even after working all day. She murmured some instructions to the nurse, who moved swiftly out of the room, and then turned to me and said, "Mr. Talbot, I'm sending your mother to the hospital for some tests. This may have been a mild stroke."

"*Stroke?*" You could have stabbed me with an ice pick and it wouldn't have stung more.

She held up a hand. "Wait until after the tests before coming to any conclusions. It's possible it's not serious at all. Her blood pressure is lower than normal and her heart rate is increased. Was she upset about something?"

And once again, after an initial attraction on my part, I thought the woman's bedside manner was cold and abrupt. "I beg your pardon?"

"Was she upset about anything?"

Uh-oh. She'd caught me. "Not that I know of. She was listening to music." I pointed to the CD player—Elvis was still lightly rocking in the background. "I turned it down when I came in." I went over, stopped the music, and approached Mom. Her eyes were closed and she looked rather peaceful, all things considered.

"I suggest you follow the ambulance to the hospital," Dr. Mc-Daniel said. "You'll want to take care of the bureaucracy."

"I hope we don't have to keep her in very long," I said. "Hospitals are hell for Alzheimer's patients. They don't understand why they're there and why they're being poked and pricked and confined to bed."

Dr. McDaniel shook her head. "We try to keep the nursing staff aware and properly trained in handling Alzheimer's patients. Unfortunately, that doesn't always happen."

With those comforting words, she left the room, so I sat with my mom until the paramedics arrived with the gurney. Then I drove my own car behind the blaring ambulance to Highland Park Hospital.

The day had definitely gone from bad to worse.

# 20
## Judy's Diary
### 1959

EARLY MORNING, MARCH 9, 1959

I'm in my room wrapping my left knee 'cause I got hurt tonight. I'm gonna be walking with a limp for a while. Nothing's broken, thank goodness, it's probably just sprained. How it happened is quite a story, so here goes.

I took a cab up to Harlem around 9:30 p.m. Had my trench coat on over my disguise, my mask in the backpack. The driver almost refused to take me to Harlem—he was a white guy—but I said I'd report him to the taxi company if he didn't. I even gave him a little speech about prejudice, which I'm sure he didn't appreciate. Nevertheless, I tipped him good and that satisfied him. He let me off on 131st Street, where the Harlem Delight brothel is located.

It was a rundown brownstone. Even though the exterior looked as if it was abandoned, there were lights on in some windows. Still, it wasn't a very inviting place. By now it was around 10:00 p.m., so dressed as the Stiletto, I waited across the street in the shadows of a quiet building entryway, hoping no one would come in or out. I watched the bordello for twenty minutes and saw two colored men enter the place; a little bit later I watched a different guy leave. Customers.

I wasn't getting any younger, so it was time to act. I crossed the street and moved along the row of buildings until I found an egress to the narrow alley between 131st and 132nd. It was a tight squeeze and just as filthy and disgusting as the one between 127th and 128th. I didn't see any rats this time, but I bet if I looked hard enough, I'd find them!

The rear fire escape on the building was in disrepair. Some of the metal stairs were broken in parts, but the landings appeared to be intact. Getting up to the first landing was a challenge, though, because the lower ladder was missing. After two throws, I managed to catch the edge of the grated platform with the homemade grappling hook on my rope. I tested it to see if it would hold my weight without tearing down the fire escape, and then I shimmied up the rope just like I used to do in gym class back in school. I was on the landing in seconds; I coiled the rope and attached it to my belt. I figured the higher I went, the less likely I'd run into bad guys, so I climbed the rickety stairs to the fifth-floor landing. Half of the bolts securing the fire escape to the building were loose. The whole thing wobbled. It was a disaster waiting to happen—the assembly held my weight fine, but I was certain it would collapse if more than two people climbed on it.

There was no light in the window at this level. I carefully peered through the dirty pane and determined it was an empty bedroom, or so I thought. Luckily, the window wasn't locked. It was stuck, though, and I had to use old-fashioned elbow grease to raise the thing. It squeaked and creaked a little too loudly for my comfort level, but there was nothing I could do about it. Once I'd lifted it far enough, I slipped inside.

Imagine my surprise when I saw two colored women lying together on top of the sheets of an unmade twin bed. They wore nightgowns. One was snoring and the other breathed heavily. At first I thought they were just asleep, but then I saw the drug paraphernalia on a nightstand by the bed. A hypodermic needle. A rubber hose. A cigarette lighter and a crusty spoon. I may be naïve about a lot of stuff, but I knew those things were tools for heroin use. Upon closer examination, I saw that the two women were really young girls—

teenagers, I think. Maybe sixteen or seventeen. Drugged up and oblivious to the world.

I shook the one that was breathing heavily. "Hey," I said. "Wake up. Are you all right?"

She stirred and moaned. I persisted, shaking her and even giving her a little slap on the cheek. "Come on, I need to ask you something. Can you open your eyes?"

I expected her to scream or something when she saw me. I imagine waking up to the sight of me in my disguise could be pretty frightening, but this girl was so doped up she barely registered what she was looking at. Her eyes blinked a few times and they had a glaze over them.

"Who you?" she hoarsely asked.

"The Black Stiletto. Don't be frightened, I'm here to help. You heard of me?"

She almost passed out into her heroin daze again, but I shook her to keep her cognizant.

"What's your name?" I asked. She whispered something I couldn't understand. "What? Try to speak louder, honey. I'm here to help you."

"Ruby."

"Ruby, can you hear me all right? Who's your friend here?"

She looked very confused. Ruby turned her head and realized she was next to another person.

"Oh, that's Angela."

"Can you tell me if there's a Japanese girl here?" I asked.

Again, she furrowed her brow. She put a weak hand to her forehead and rubbed it. Clearly, she was not on this planet.

"Ruby. Is there a Japanese girl here?"

A faint nod, followed by a whisper.

"What?"

"Lotus."

"That's her name?"

Again a nod. "Lotus Flower."

"Where is she? What floor is she on? Do you know?"

I also wanted to ask her how many men were in the building, but it was hopeless. I couldn't talk to that girl. I'm surprised she was alive. She and Angela looked terrible. They were skinny and had dark circles under their eyes. Their arms were black-and-blue where they'd been shooting up. I don't understand how *anyone* could do that. For someone who's withstood being cut by knives before, I sure hate needles.

A cold breeze blew through the open window, so I shut it. No use giving the poor girls pneumonia while they lay there. Nothing else to do but stealthily explore the building until I found Isuzu. "Lotus Flower" had to be her.

I quietly opened the bedroom door and looked out into an empty, dark hallway. There was a bathroom and a door, presumably leading to another bedroom across the way. The floor was hardwood, but it was rotted and noisy. Pieces were missing here and there. Someone could get a serious splinter walking barefoot. Unless someone was behind that closed bedroom door, I was alone up there with Ruby and Angela. I heard male and female voices below, coming from different parts of the building. Laughing, talking, and sounds of sex. I also detected the faint strains of music, probably originating from a record player way down on the ground floor. It was Negro blues, something I don't really listen to, but it's related to the jazz that Freddie sometimes plays on our hi-fi.

To my ears, that blues music just sounds sad, as if all the hardships in the world are bundled inside the musicians' souls. I thought it was very fitting for such an unhappy place. I could practically touch the emotions in the air. My instincts were going haywire. I felt nothing but despair, sorrow, and pain.

I crept into the hallway and went to the stairs. Leaning over the railing, I saw lights on the fourth floor and heard a door slam shut. Then a man's heavy footsteps on the creaky wooden slats grew louder. I saw the top of his head as he moved to the stairs. He was coming up! I quickly slipped into the dark bathroom and stood as still as a statue. A large, burly Negro came into view; he obviously acted as muscle for the brothel. I don't think I'd ever faced a guy as big as him.

He reached the fifth floor and headed toward Ruby and Angela's room.

"Psst. Hey," I said.

The man turned, not expecting anyone to be behind him. I let him have it with a swift front kick to his belly and followed through with an *ippon ken*, or single-point fist attack, in which my middle finger is bent to protrude beyond the rest of the fist to form a striking point. I got him right in the Adam's apple. I didn't want to kill the guy, so I had to pull my punch a bit; nevertheless, the one-two strike completely stunned him. He fell to his knees, at which point I gave him an old-fashioned right hook. He plummeted sideways and was out. Miraculously, I hadn't made much noise. I waited and listened to see if anyone down below had heard the scuffle, but nothing happened.

I dragged the big guy into the bathroom and shut the door. He was breathing, so I know I didn't crush his windpipe. He was lucky, if you ask me. After seeing the condition of those poor girls in the bedroom, I was angry. I wanted to teach the pimps a lesson they wouldn't forget.

The stairs creaked as I went down to the fourth floor. No bathroom there, but there were three doors, all closed. I listened at one and heard, well, you know what I heard. A man and a woman. The second door was quiet, so I opened it. Empty. The third room was also silent, so I opened that door, too.

Oh my gosh, dear diary, I couldn't believe my luck. A young Japanese girl sat on the bed, still and expressionless. Dressed in a nightgown, she stared straight ahead at nothing. I stepped inside and shut the door.

"Isuzu?" I asked.

She slowly turned her head to me. Her red, glassy eyes widened a little.

"Don't be frightened! I'm a friend of your father's."

Her mouth opened to speak, but she couldn't. I could see she was doped up like Ruby and Angela, just not as comatose. The poor girl looked undernourished and she had a thick wound on her lower lip, as if someone had recently hit her. I went and sat beside her.

"Isuzu, I am a friend. I've come to get you out of here. Do you understand me?"

She just looked at me with incredulity.

"I'm not going to hurt you. I'm here to help you. Can you hear me? Nod if you understand."

Isuzu started to whimper.

"It's okay, dear, it's okay." I put my arm around her and gave her a hug. "This will all be over soon. Trust me. Will you do that?"

She didn't know whether to nod, cry, or scream.

"Can you walk?"

No response, just tears. This was going to be harder than I thought.

"All right, you wait here. Okay? Wait right here. Don't go anywhere. I'm coming right back. Do you hear? I'm coming right back."

I got up, listened at the door, and opened it. Before leaving I looked back at her. She had her face in her hands.

Then I went down to the third floor, where there were more bedrooms and a bathroom, the door of which was open. A young colored girl in a nightgown stood in front of the sink, looking into a cloudy mirror and putting on lipstick. Knowing she'd probably make a lot of noise if she saw me, I quickly rushed into the bathroom and shut the door.

"Don't scream, I'm a friend!" I whispered. She still yelped and backed away from me. "No, no, it's all right! Hush, I'm not here to hurt you!"

She wasn't drugged, but she had that same look of undernourishment. Perhaps she was new to the premises and wasn't a total junkie yet. She started trembling and asked, "Are you . . .?"

"The Black Stiletto? Yes, I am."

"Whatchu want?"

"How many men are here?"

She looked too scared to answer me.

"I won't let them hurt you. Please tell me how many are in the building."

"Three."

"Is one of them a big guy?" I raised my hand to indicate his height. She nodded. That meant there were only two men left. I could deal with those odds. "Are they armed?"

"Huh?"

"Do they have guns?"

"Oh. Yeah."

"What's your name?"

"Sheila."

"Well, Sheila, you're not going to make any noise, are you? I'm going down there to beat the crap out of those guys. You're not going to stop me, are you?"

She shook her head.

"Good girl. Just stay put. The police might be coming soon. I don't want you to get arrested, but if you are, you just tell them you were being kept prisoner here. Will you do that?"

She nodded.

"That's true, isn't it? They won't let you leave?"

"I can leave," she said. "I just—I don't really want to."

"Why not?" I pointed to her nightgown. "You like doing what you're doing?"

She didn't answer, but I'm pretty sure I understood the problem. The girl didn't think she had many other options in life. There was a roof over her head, and the drugs were a powerful incentive to stay put.

"Never mind, Sheila. You just stay quiet, okay?"

She nodded again.

I went out the door and down the stairs to the second floor. A girl and a customer—both Negroes—were just coming out of a bedroom. She screamed. The man was in his forties, I think, and looked like an ordinary guy on the street. He was scared, too. Not playing nice anymore, I drew my stiletto, pointed it at them, and pushed them back into the room.

"Quiet!" Then I addressed the man. "I'm not going to have any trouble from you, am I?"

He raised his hands as if it was a stickup. "No, ma'am!"

"Stay here and shut the door, both of you." I left, but by then one of the men who ran the place was coming up the stairs. He had heard the scream.

"Gloria? You all right up there?" he called.

I sheathed the knife, crossed the hall, and flattened against the opposite wall. I hoped that when the man reached the top of the stairs he'd be gazing toward Gloria's bedroom door, away from me. The footsteps on the stairs grew louder. He was almost there. Sure enough, he was focused on the couple's door. When he stepped on the landing, I performed a *fumikomi*, a stamp-in kick, which is a type of side thrust used mainly against an opponent's knee, thigh, or instep to break his posture. I aimed for the knee and probably shattered it. He crumpled in place and then started screaming like all get-out. The man fumbled with trying to draw a revolver from a holster strapped to his calf. I stopped him and shut him up by kicking him squarely in the face. Out like a light. For good measure, I took the gun and tossed it down the hall into a dark corner.

That's when the one remaining guy downstairs started shooting at me. He was at the foot of the stairs, gun in hand. I felt the bullets burn the air near my shoulder, so I immediately hit the floor, then rolled to the side, out of view. A bedroom door flung open; another colored girl saw me and screamed.

"Get back inside and shut the door!" I shouted.

I heard the man climbing the steps at a run. Couldn't let him reach the landing; even though I'd practiced the heck out of disarming opponents, there was always a risk when a gun was involved. The odds were always in favor of the man who held a firearm. So I quickly drew the stiletto, flipped it, and grasped it by the blade with the maneuver I'd rehearsed hundreds of times. I then raised my arm, stepped into the space at the top of the stairs, and flung the knife at the charging gunman. Not waiting to see if it hit, I bolted to the right as he fired the gun again, barely missing me. But I heard him gasp; this was followed by a thundering crash on the wooden stairs. I risked looking. The man was rolling down to the bottom; he'd dropped the handgun midway. I quickly descended the steps to meet him on the ground floor. My stiletto had penetrated his right pectoral, just beneath the collarbone. I pulled it out and he screamed in pain. After wiping the blood on his shirt, I stuck the point under his chin.

"You tell Carl Purdy I'm coming for him," I hissed.

I then cut a piece of rope from my coil, grabbed his wrists, and tied them together and to a post on the stairs.

Time to grab Isuzu and get the heck out of there. I ran back up the stairs, past the sleeping beauty with the broken knee, and onward to the third floor. That's when my right boot crashed through a weak point in one of the steps. I went down hard, striking my own left knee against the edge of the step just above the hole. Man, oh man, it hurt! There I was, clumsily splayed on the stairs with my leg dangling underneath the boards.

"You all right?"

It was Sheila. She stood above me—and she had a gun in her hand.

"You're not going to shoot me, are you, Sheila?" I asked, wincing with pain.

"I called the police."

"Can you help me up? I promise you I'm just gonna get my friend and leave."

"Your friend?"

"Isu—er, Lotus Flower."

"She's your friend?"

"Are you gonna help me, or what?"

By then, more frightened girls had emerged from bedrooms to see what all the racket was about. A couple of male customers, too. When they saw me, they skedaddled down the stairs, not stopping to reveal their faces. Sheila and another girl finally had the decency to get me out of my predicament. Once I was on my feet, I put weight on my injured leg and almost cried in anguish. I tested the knee by feeling and poking it; it hurt like the dickens but I was sure I didn't break anything. I limped to the fourth floor and back to Isuzu's room. She was standing in the doorway, looking a little more coherent.

"Can you walk with me?" I asked her. "I'm taking you home."

Unfortunately, she was still too drugged to think straight.

"Aw, geez, Isuzu," I said. "Come on, let's go." With that, I put an arm behind her legs, the other around her back, and lifted her off her feet. She was as light as a feather, thank God. The strain on my knee wasn't so easy, though.

I carried that poor, frightened girl all the way down to the first floor. The other women in the building stood and watched me. They were either too scared or too brainwashed to move. Sirens grew louder. The cops were just outside the building, so I turned to speak to those young Negro girls.

"Tell the cops what's been going on here. Tell them that you are victims, do you understand? You're victims. Those men did this to you. I'm sorry I can't help you all."

With Isuzu still in my arms, I then turned to the front door and managed to unlock and open it with one hand. Two police cars were out front, their red-and-blue lights blazing. Several uniformed men immediately took positions and aimed guns at me.

"Holy shit, it's the Black Stiletto!" one shouted.

"Put your hands up and don't move!" another ordered.

"Can't you see I'm carrying someone?" I yelled back. "This girl needs urgent medical attention. She's a kidnapping victim and she's been forcibly drugged by the gangsters who run this bordello! I'm asking you to allow me to approach."

The cops hesitated. They couldn't very well shoot me with Isuzu in my arms. I continued to limp forward, one step at a time.

"I came here to rescue this girl. Her name is Isuzu Tachikawa. I've disabled three men—criminals—who ran this house of prostitution and narcotics. There are several innocent girls inside. They're victims and drug addicts. They all need medical help. But please, call an ambulance. Help Isuzu first. I beg you."

The cops' leader kept his gun trained on me. "Lay her on the sidewalk."

"You won't shoot me?"

"You're wanted by the police," he said. "We have to arrest you."

I heard more sirens in the distance. Backup was on the way, so I addressed all four cops.

"I know you nice fellas are just doing your jobs. But I'm not the bad guy here. There is plenty of evidence inside the building that'll bring down some serious gangsters. They're involved not only with prostitution, but with narcotics and racketeering and who knows what else. I'm asking you to let me put this girl down and walk away. You know it's the right thing to do."

The leader said, "You're a material witness. Place the girl on the sidewalk. Now."

So I did. I gently laid Isuzu on the cold pavement. She was unconscious now, having fainted or passed out from the drugs. I then raised my hands and stood straight.

"Remember her name," I said. "Isuzu Tachikawa. Her father runs a martial arts school on Christopher Street called Studio Tokyo. Please let him know she's safe." The guns were still aimed at me. I swallowed. Dear diary, I've never been so scared in my life. "Now I'm going to walk away from here and you're not going to arrest me or shoot me in the back. I know you won't. You're going to tell your superiors that you saw me, but I got away. That's the truth, too. I got away. I know you'll do the decent thing. I trust you."

And then, dear diary, I swear I did either the bravest or the dumbest thing I've ever done. I turned and walked east—limped, rather—with my hands still raised. I fully expected the policemen to rush after me and put me in handcuffs. Or gun me down. But they didn't.

*They didn't.*

I'd made it twenty or thirty feet along the street when I dared look back. The cops had already rushed into the building. Not a single one remained on the street to see what I did.

The Black Stiletto vanished into the night. And now here I am, nursing my knee.

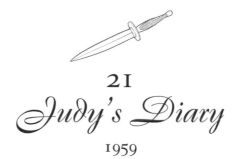

# 21
## Judy's Diary
### 1959

It's still March 9, 1959, but now it's evening. I'm exhausted and about to go to bed.

After a few hours of fitful sleep this morning, I got up at the usual time to work in the gym. My leg still hurt like all get-out, but I did my best to plunge ahead. Over breakfast, Freddie slid the newspaper across the table. There was a surprisingly accurate story about the Black Stiletto on the front page.

The headline was BLACK STILETTO BUSTS NARCOTICS DEN. The article related how the police raided a Harlem "narcotics den and brothel" last night after the Black Stiletto made its existence known to the authorities. The "crime fighter"—I think calling me that is a first!—apparently discovered the illegal enterprise, infiltrated it, and disarmed three men who were arrested and charged with a number of crimes. Two of the men were admitted to a hospital for "injuries." It didn't say what kind. Several women were also arrested on charges of prostitution, but District Attorney Barney Wilcox was weighing evidence of the women's culpability. There was no mention of Isuzu.

I thought of Ruby and Sheila and the other colored women I'd seen there. I hope they're all right. I wish I could have rescued all of them. Maybe this experience will motivate them to stay off the drugs and get help. I don't know a lot about those narcotics, but apparently it's very difficult to kick the habit once you're addicted. If they don't kill you, they damage you for life.

The article went on to say the narcotics den was part of a network of criminal enterprises allegedly owned by Carl Purdy, a Harlem man who has been arrested and charged for a number of crimes in the past, but he's never been convicted of anything since he served five years in the early 50s for armed robbery. Purdy has been linked to several murders, drug trafficking, prostitution, protection rackets, and other gang-style crimes in Harlem, but according to D.A. Wilcox, the police have never found hard evidence against the man. However, Purdy was arrested at his home early this morning after the brothel raid. D.A. Wilcox said there was now "sufficient evidence" that Purdy was involved in last night's operation. John had told me no one but the FBI and the police knew about Purdy. Well, the public is aware of him now!

At the end of the article, Chief of Police Bruen said the Stiletto was a "criminal as bad as the gangsters" by taking the law into her hands, although one New York City police officer was quoted as saying, "The Black Stiletto isn't the villain the press sometimes makes her out to be. Tackling these Harlem gangsters took a lot of courage."

So, once again, the Stiletto got some good press. I'm on a roll, ha ha!

During work today, Mike Washington came to the gym to work out. I hadn't seen him in a while and actually hadn't missed him until he walked in. He looked like he'd recently been in a fight. There were bruises on his face and he had a busted lip. As usual, he was in a grumpy mood. I asked him what happened to him, and he replied that he got into a bar fight. I knew he was lying. He may have been in a fight, but it wasn't in a bar.

While Washington was using the rope pulleys, Freddie came down and saw him. Washington stopped to talk and the two men smiled and laughed as Washington told his story. I couldn't hear everything, but he explained to Freddie how the fight went. He demonstrated some of the action by miming some punches. At the end, Freddie slapped his friend on the back and went on. Washington continued working on the pulleys.

Okay, maybe he's telling the truth. I could be wrong, but I trust my instincts. My "lie detector" is pretty reliable. Whether or not he's fibbing about the bar fight, I still think Washington is hiding something.

I must say it's a pleasure working with young Clark, the colored teenager I mentioned before. He's making good strides in the boxing ring. I've taught him stances and how to move around an opponent, which is really one of the first things you need to know before learning how to punch. Clark's starting to share more of his personal life with me. He says he loves books and reads a lot. That made sense—I took him to be a studious type of guy rather than a typical male who was interested only in sports. He says he's learned how to avoid the bullies on his block, mainly by taking alternate routes to and from his apartment building. Unfortunately, once he's on his street there's no other way around them. He came in the gym with a busted lip recently and I felt so sorry for him. One of these days he'll be able to defend himself. I hope. The Black Stiletto is tempted to go over to Avenue C and teach those white boys a lesson!

After work I went to my *karate* class. I was very curious to see if Soichiro was any different after last night.

It was very frustrating because he didn't indicate that anything had changed. However, during the lesson he was back to the old Soichiro—no nonsense, emotionless, and focused. Well, *that* was different. It was the way he always was before Isuzu got in trouble. So I took that as a good sign. Still, I wanted him to acknowledge that she was safe.

We went through the hour-long class without any talk of last night, although he did note my injured leg. He asked what was wrong and I told him I'd hurt it at the gym. He nodded with understanding and didn't mention it again. As the lesson continued, though, he exhibited no inclination to go easy on that leg. Talk about pain! Then, at the end of the session, as I was about to go change into my street clothes, Soichiro offhandedly mentioned his daughter. He was standing next to me and looking in another direction, almost as if he wasn't addressing me in particular.

"Isuzu safe now," he said. "In hospital. Need doctor attention for a while."

"Oh, that's good news, Soichiro-san!" I replied. "When did this happen?"

"Last night. Police found her. Brought her to hospital. They call me."

"That's great. I knew it would work out. Did you tell them about Carl Purdy?"

He hesitated and then nodded abruptly. "*Hai!*" he said in that forceful way that Japanese do.

Then he turned to me and our eyes met.

"Thank you, Judy-san," he said.

I swear there was a moment between us—an instant of understanding. It was then that I realized Soichiro is aware of who I am. He put two and two together. Or maybe he's known all along. Whatever—Soichiro knows the Black Stiletto is Judy Cooper.

I'm not sure how I felt about that at the time, but now as I sit in my bedroom writing this, dear diary, I am very pleased and comforted. The two men who mean the most to me—Freddie and Soichiro—both know my secret. As I wrote before, they are like surrogate fathers to me.

Isuzu is safe. And Carl Purdy is behind bars. Life is good.

## 22
## *John*
### HOME DICTAPHONE RECORDING

Today is March 10, 1959.

The Black Stiletto made the news again yesterday, and I didn't have a thing to do with it. I knew something was up when she asked me about Carl Purdy the other day. On the night of the eighth, she broke into one of Purdy's whorehouses in Harlem. She incapacitated three very tough men—broke one guy's knee and stabbed another one—and she rescued a fifteen-year-old Asian girl. The girl's name is Isuzu Tachikawa, a Japanese immigrant. It's a mystery why the Stiletto brought that particular girl out of the brothel. Perhaps she is someone the Stiletto knows?

I made some calls, cashed in a few favors, and got pretty much everything the police have. They found out the girl's father is a martial arts instructor, also a Japanese immigrant, who has a studio in Greenwich Village. That's very interesting. I wonder if the Stiletto knows him instead of the daughter. I figure the police are smart enough to follow up on that. I learned the cops woke the Jap in the middle of the night to inform him his daughter was at Roosevelt Hospital. She's severely malnourished and apparently a heroin junkie, but otherwise doing well. She will have to go through a rough withdrawal, of course. Police believe she was either kidnapped or lured into the prostitution business with promises of narcotics. The same is probably true with the other girls who were taken from the premises. They were mostly Negroes, but there were also a couple of Latin girls. They were all arrested on prostitution charges, but today the D.A. dropped them. They're all being sent to medical facilities to help them with drug rehabilitation. Nearly all of them are runaways or were reported missing months ago. It's all pretty incredible. As for Isuzu Tachikawa, her father told police he was paying extortion money to Carl Purdy, who was also arrested around five in the morning yesterday. I'll bet that was a sight to see, waking him and his family up at that hour.

Well, I thought that was going to be the end of Purdy's Harlem empire, but I was astounded this afternoon when all charges against Purdy were dropped and the bastard was released after being held just a little over twenty-four hours. I found that hard to accept. The guy owns the building where the prostitution and drug dealing was going on. Wasn't he caught red-handed? And then Chief of Police Bruen and the D.A. had a press conference and announced that evidence against Purdy was obtained illegally and there wasn't enough to prosecute him. D.A. Wilcox looked pretty pissed off about it, as if it was Bruen's fault. Bruen, on the other hand, seemed pretty smug about the whole thing. It's the same old story. Purdy gets arrested for something, but then he's free the next day.

The reason I bring all this up is that today during the lunch hour, I left our offices at Sixty-Ninth Street and walked south on Third Avenue to get some fresh air and exercise. It was a cool but pleasant day. I found a busy pizza joint and decided to grab a couple of slices. As I stood at the front counter, I saw none other than Haggerty and Chief Bruen sitting at a table in the back of the restaurant. They, too, were having lunch, but they also appeared to be having a deep discussion. It looked to me like Haggerty was angry about something and Bruen was trying to calm him down. If you ask me, Haggerty's always angry about something. I knew the two men were friends; there's a photo in Haggerty's office that features Haggerty, Bruen, and two other guys on a golf course. I suppose it's good for the FBI to know what the police are doing, and vice versa. I got out of there before they spotted me.

Then, two hours later, Chief Bruen and the D.A. held that press conference, and now Purdy is a free man.

I must say I'm surprised.

After the press conference, Haggerty was in a foul mood. He sniped at me again about the Stiletto and asked me about the progress of catching her. I told him I'd have a report ready at the end of the day, which I did. In it, I reiterated what I've said over and over in previous reports. I was trying to befriend her and get her to trust me. Eventually she could very well reveal her identity to me. Once that is accomplished, we could move in and arrest her. I dutifully turned in the report and filed one carbon copy at the office and one here at home in a personal file I've marked "Stiletto." I've started compiling everything I have on her, and I keep these Dictabelts in a separate space.

I pulled out the photographs Tom shot at the East Side Diner two days ago. She'd made me pretty angry not showing up for our lunch date, but Tom had been positioned at the front of the diner with a briefcase camera. He got pictures of everyone in the place. She called me later to apologize, but she claimed she was there. Once again she was flirtatious and sweet, so it was difficult to stay mad at her.

I laid the photos out on the table in front of me and studied all the women that were in the diner. It was easy to eliminate the ones I thought were too old to be the Stiletto; there were only four other women in the place who were probably in their twenties. That's excluding the waitresses, which I suppose is a possibility, but I kinda doubt it. Anyway, I studied the pictures of the four women. I remember one of them bumping into me outside the bathroom. She was tall, had dark hair—almost black—brown-green eyes, and was quite attractive. Very fit, too. Could that have been her? Was bumping into me her way of making contact?

One other girl in the diner could be a suspect, too, but I'm leaning toward the one with dark hair. Maybe that's her. Now I'm trying to place her voice when she spoke to me. Was it the same voice on the phone? Possibly.

Damn, she's gorgeous.

Even though it's pretty far downtown from the Bureau's offices at Sixty-Ninth and Third, I may try to make it a point to shadow the diner when I can get away. If it's a place she frequents, then there's a good chance she'll bump into me again.

# 23
# Judy's Diary

1959

APRIL 4, 1959

Sorry, dear diary, I've been busy and haven't written in nearly a month. Well, busy isn't the right word. "Lazy" is probably more like it. I just haven't felt like writing, mainly because I've been reading a couple of books—*Breakfast at Tiffany's* by Truman Capote, and *The Dharma Bums* by Jack Kerouac. The first one came out last year and was a best-seller, and since it takes place in New York I wanted to read it. Actually it's a collection of four stories. I'm not sure what I think about the main character in the first one, Holly Golightly. Like me, she's really a country girl and she comes to the big city; but *unlike* me, she becomes a rather shallow society gal. Still, it's very interesting. Peter Gaskin recommended the second book to me. Jack Kerouac is one of those "beat poets" you hear about. I already read *On the Road* and enjoyed it very much. *Dharma Bums* is his newest book, and I'm not crazy about it. Too much stuff about Buddhism, but I do like the outdoor travel sequences.

I've also been reading more about Dr. Martin Luther King. He went to India during February and March and has been preaching about his experiences there. The papers here in New York don't cover his talks much since he's from the south; most of his activities take place down there. But the *New York Times* occasionally reports on what he's doing and saying. Apparently a small book containing two of his sermons, called *The Measure of a Man*, will be published this month. I plan to read it. I don't know why, but everything that man says touches me deeply. Is it because I grew up so close to the Negroes in Odessa? Is it because lately I've been involved with a number of the problems the Negroes here in New York are facing? Who knows? It doesn't matter. I just admire the man. He's very brave to be so outspoken on civil rights for Negroes. There're a lot of white people who'd like to see him silenced.

I saw the funniest movie last night with Lucy and Peter. It was called *Some Like It Hot* and it starred Marilyn Monroe, Jack Lemmon, and Tony Curtis. It was also pretty dirty! I was actually shocked by some of it, but it was still hilarious. Seeing two men dressed up like women was so silly. And I *love* Marilyn Monroe. What a beautiful and sexy woman. I've been told I can do a pretty good imitation, dear diary, but you know that already.

There's a debate going on in my head whether or not to phone John Richardson. I haven't spoken to him in weeks. Am I leading him on? Is he leading me on? Can I trust him? He's so handsome and looks so sharp in that suit of his. I must like him or else I wouldn't keep thinking about him. I suppose I'll get up my nerve pretty soon and give him a call. Otherwise he'll throw me over for his secretary, ha ha!

APRIL 11, 1959

I have a bad sore throat. I don't know how I got it but I've had it for three days. I hate being sick. Freddie keeps saying I should go to a doctor and get some medicine, but I keep telling him it's just a cold and it'll go away. I have real low energy and actually had to take off work today. It hurts to talk, too. Freddie felt my neck under my jawbone and said my glands are swollen. He wants me to stay away from him so he won't get it.

There were two interesting stories in the paper today. The first was a really big one, something that could be very important. NASA, that organization that launches rockets into space, has announced the selection of seven military pilots who will become the first American astronauts. They're called the "Mercury Seven," because the name of the space program is called Mercury. Very soon, NASA will start sending a man up in a space capsule to orbit the earth. I think that is so amazing. It's like all those silly science-fiction movies we've been watching are coming true. I wonder if they'll ever send a man to the moon. Freddie has his doubts, but I think anything is possible. Scientists keep coming up with new advancements all the time. A hundred years ago, whoever thought man could fly in a plane? Or fight infection with penicillin?

I think it'd be fun to go into space. I'd love to see the earth from above. I flew in those two airplanes to Texas in December, and I thought that was incredible. I can't imagine being higher in the sky than those planes. There's something romantic about the idea of astronauts. The newspaper had all the Mercury Seven's pictures, and every one of them is handsome. I wouldn't mind dating an astronaut! Unfortunately, I think they're all married.

The second item in the paper had to do with Carl Purdy. There was another big gangland gunfight, this time in Little Italy. Apparently it was between the Italian mob and the Negro mob. Four men died—all Italians. Franco DeLuca was quoted, "This is the work of Carl Purdy. He's a menace to this city." Right. As if DeLuca isn't. Anyway, the gunfight had to do with narcotics. The Italians were about to receive a shipment of heroin from overseas and the Negroes intercepted it.

Why can't Carl Purdy and his gang listen to Dr. King? Why is there all this violence and crime? It's no wonder the Negroes aren't treated with respect. White people just think they're criminals, lazy, or dumb. I know that's not true. Look at some of those musicians like Nat King Cole or Ella Fitzgerald. They're wonderful! And in my opinion Dr. King is one of the smartest men in America. If he was white, he could be president someday, but I guess since he's not that'll never happen. There's been a lot of talk in the news that a

Catholic might be running for president next year—Senator Kennedy. I don't understand why a person's race or religion should make a difference in whether or not he could make a good president, but apparently it does. I've heard people on the street bad-mouth Kennedy and Dr. King for those very reasons.

I'm rambling, dear diary. I must have a fever. I just lie here in bed and listen to the radio or play records. I wish Elvis would put out a new song. I've worn out my copy of "I Need Your Love Tonight." Actually, I like the other side of the record even better. It's called "(Now and Then There's) A Fool Such as I." I may be wrong but I think it rose higher in the charts than "I Need Your Love Tonight."

Ugh, I feel awful. I'm gonna try to sleep.

APRIL 12, 1959

Freddie talked me in to seeing a doctor this morning. You know, I've never seen a doctor since I came to New York. The few times I've been hurt, it was always Freddie who patched me up. The scar on my right shoulder that Freddie stitched up might look better if a professional had sewn it, but I think a wound like that would have aroused suspicion. So I have to live with a pretty ugly scar there for the rest of my life. Oh, well. And that bullet wound I got in Odessa—my Mexican friends' doctor fixed that. I still don't know if he was a real doctor or not. Luis told me he helped illegal immigrants, so he probably wasn't.

Anyway, this afternoon I saw this nice man named Dr. Goldstein. He was about fifty years old, I guess. Curly grayish hair, glasses, and kind eyes. I told him I'd had a sore throat for several days. He looked in my mouth, had me say, "Ah," peeked in my ears with that funny instrument doctors use, listened to me breathe through a stethoscope, and took my temperature. I had 100.9 degrees! He said I had tonsillitis and an ear infection. Then he asked me when I'd last had a gynecological exam. (I had to look up the word to know how to spell it!) I said I didn't know what that was.

Dr. Goldstein was surprised. He told me what it was and I was shocked! It's when a doctor looks up a woman's—down there! I couldn't imagine having someone do that. I never had it done when I was growing up in Odessa—maybe I was too young. And I certainly haven't done it since I came to New York. Dr. Goldstein said it was something a woman should do at least once a year. There are apparently a lot of diseases and problems that could occur, like cancer or abnormal periods.

So I let him do it.

Oh my gosh, dear diary, I felt so embarrassed! I had to undress and put on a flimsy smocklike thing. A good part of my shoulder was visible, and he saw the scar. He asked, "My Lord, how did you get that?"

I told him I was in a car accident when I was younger. He took a longer look at the scar and said, "It's not very old, is it?"

Doctors must be able to tell the age of a scar, so I didn't lie. "It was last year."

"Did a doctor stitch you?"

Then I did lie. "Of course."

"Well, I'm sorry to say, he did a terrible job. Where was this?"

"Look, Dr. Goldstein, could we just get on with the exam?"

He realized I didn't want to talk about it, so he had me lie down and put my feet in cold metal stirrups with my legs spread apart. The next thing I knew, he was touching me down there, spreading me apart, looking inside with cold instruments. I hated it!

When it was all over he told me I could get dressed. While he made notes at a table, I went behind the screen and did so. After that I sat down so he could talk to me.

"Judy," he said, "I suggest you should have your tonsils out as soon as this infection clears up. They're awfully swollen, so it's a bit difficult to tell for sure, but I believe there's an abnormality on the right one. It's probably benign, but I'd like to make sure." He wrote out a prescription for me and also the name and number of a surgeon who did tonsillectomies. (I looked up that word, too.) Then he said,

"I hope you'll make it a point to come see me every twelve months. It's very important for a woman your age to have regular gynecological exams."

"Okay." What else could I say?

He wanted to see me again in a week but to go ahead and make the appointment with the tonsil doctor in two weeks' time.

After I paid and left the office, which was on East 33rd Street between 3rd and 2nd Avenues, I went to a pay phone. I don't know why, but I had a sudden compulsion to call John. So I did.

He was at the FBI office, so I didn't want to talk long. A secretary answered this time and I told her "Eloise" wanted to speak to him. She asked me what it was regarding. I replied that it was personal.

John picked up after a few seconds' pause.

"Hello there," he said.

"Hi, John."

"Er, Eloise?" He sounded confused.

"Yeah, it's me."

"You don't sound like yourself."

"I've got a bad cold. And tonsillitis."

"Oh dear. You need to take care of yourself. It must be from all that running around at night you do. Oh, and by the way, congratulations on that business up in Harlem last month. I haven't talked to you since then."

"Thanks. John, I have to get my tonsils taken out. I may not be able to talk for a while."

He laughed. "You'll still be able to talk. It just hurts for a few days. And you'll get to eat a lot of ice cream. Although in my opinion that ice cream thing is a myth. It actually produces more mucus in your throat, coats it with milky stuff that isn't too good for the wounds. I'd suggest just drinking a lot of ice water."

"Thanks. Hey, I want to ask you something."

"What's that?"

"Why was Carl Purdy released? He was in jail for what, a day?

What he was doing at that place was horrible. Those poor girls. The men were making them use heroin and sell their bodies."

"I know. I don't understand it either. Obviously, Purdy has connections. A lot of these mobsters do. They pay bribes to public officials. That kind of thing has been going on since the beginning of time. Don't quote me on that, though. I really have no idea how it happened."

"It's not fair," I said. "Purdy needs to pay for what he did to them."

"I agree with you. But you need to stay away from Purdy and his organization. They are very, very dangerous. They're too big for the Black Stiletto."

"Oh, I doubt that." I coughed and sneezed.

"You'd better get home; you sound terrible. But one more thing before you go."

"What?"

"What's your connection to the Japanese girl you rescued?"

I was afraid he'd ask me that someday. I lied. "Nothing. She was in bad shape and seemed way too young to be in a place like that. And she was different from the other girls. She was the only Asian, I think. I just picked her up and took her outside."

John said, "I see. My boss wanted me to have a talk with the girl's father a couple of weeks ago. Do you know him?"

*Oh my gosh! Soichiro!* "Uh, no," I replied.

"He teaches Asian fighting techniques. Did you know that?"

"I don't know him."

"I was just wondering, seeing as how you seem to know how to do that stuff. *Karate. Judo.* There aren't a lot of people in this country who practice that."

"I learned mine somewhere else, John."

"Okay, if you say so."

I couldn't help but ask. "So what did her father say? Was he grateful for what I did?"

"I think he was. I asked him if he knew you, and he said he

didn't. He couldn't imagine why you would rescue his daughter. It's just as much a mystery to him as it is to the law enforcement people. Did you know Carl Purdy was extorting him for a lot of money?"

"Ye—uhm, wasn't that in the paper?"

"No, it wasn't."

*Darn, he almost caught me!* "Then I guess I didn't know that. Are the police going to do anything about it? Or the FBI?"

"The man can't prove it. He paid Purdy in cash. We can see he made withdrawals from his bank, but there's no way we can link it to Purdy. However, the man can try a civil suit, the burden of proof isn't as challenging. I just hope Purdy doesn't come after him in an act of revenge."

I felt a shiver when he said that. "Does Purdy do that kind of thing?"

"Yes, he does. Sometimes it can be weeks, maybe months later, but he often gets even with his enemies. Usually before the trial date."

Soichiro would have to be warned. *Then I forgot John could trace the call from his office!* "Listen, John, I feel terrible, so I'm gonna hang up now. I'll call you soon." And I did. I didn't let him say goodbye.

I took a bus downtown, filled my prescription, and went home to bed.

APRIL 28, 1959

Dear diary, I have "tons-holes," ha ha.

Yep, yesterday I had my tonsils taken out. I was admitted to Bellevue Hospital on the evening of the 26th and had to spend the night. I couldn't eat or drink anything after midnight. My tonsillitis had cleared up a week earlier, so Dr. Goldstein okay'd me for the surgery. The doctor who did the procedure was another nice Jewish man named Dr. Weinblatt. Yesterday morning they wheeled me into the operating room. Then the nurse put a mask over my mouth and nose and I had to breathe a sweet-smelling gas. I fell fast asleep! The next thing I knew, I woke up real groggy and woozy. My throat hurt like the dickens. The nurse gave me some ice water to drink, which made it feel better temporarily, but I knew this wasn't going to be a walk in the park like everyone had been saying.

The doctor let me go home yesterday afternoon. I felt like dog poo-poo, forgive my language. Freddie was real sweet and took care of me, though. He'd actually come to the hospital yesterday morning and sat in the waiting room while I had the surgery. He brought me one of those new Barbie dolls as a present! I love her! I never played with dolls much when I was a kid, but there's something truly special about this Barbie. Freddie made me some oatmeal—which I couldn't swallow—but then I had a popsicle. That felt good on my throat. Dr. Weinblatt said it might be difficult to swallow food for a day or two. He wants to see me in five days to check how I'm doing and take the stitches out.

Last night I kinda wished John was able to call me. It would have been nice to hear him say some comforting words.

Gee, I sound like a wimpy girl!

APRIL 30, 1959

I feel much better. I'm able to swallow food, although it needs to be pretty soft. I'm surviving on soups and oatmeal and spaghetti. I'm gonna go in to work tomorrow. My "tons-holes" are still sore, but it's nothing compared to what it was three days ago.

To celebrate my reemergence into the workforce, this evening I went outside to a pay phone and called John at home. I always surprise him when I call. He asked how I was, and I told him about the tonsils and all that. He told me he would've come to visit me in the hospital if he'd known about it. And if he'd known my name. I laughed at that. I told him he was sweet and asked why he manages to be so romantic when he doesn't even know me. John said he's "falling in love with my voice," if you can believe that, dear diary! Well, for what it's worth it made me feel good.

"When are we going to meet for real?" he asked for the millionth time. "I promise no law enforcement action. I just want to talk to you."

I think he's broken through my defenses, dear diary, 'cause it didn't take me long to answer, "Okay. I'll do it. But you have to wait until my throat is all better. Another week or two."

He said that'd be fine.

"Where are we gonna meet?" I asked.

"That diner?"

I thought about that, but then I realized I really didn't want him to know my identity. I'd meet him as the Stiletto. "No, it has to be a secret location. I'll meet you in my disguise."

"All right. How about my car? I could park somewhere in a discreet and private place, and you can approach it at an agreed-upon time. No one will know. No one will see."

I had to ask. "How do I know it won't be a setup, John?"

"Come on, Stiletto, we've been through this a dozen times. I assure you it won't be a set-up. You have my word."

"As a gentleman?"

He chuckled. "I've never thought of myself as a gentleman, but sure, you have my word as a gentleman."

It was at that point I knew I had to meet him in person. "Okay, John. I'll call you and we'll set up a time and place. As soon as my throat is better."

"Whatever you say, sweetheart."

*Sweetheart?* He called me *sweetheart!*

"You take care of yourself and get well," he said.

After I hung up, I felt my heart beating hard in my chest. That man does something to me! I'm already nervous about meeting him. I could always back out of it, but somehow I knew this time I'd go through with it.

I wanted to sing as I walked back to the gym, but instead I hummed to myself because that was easier on the throat. The tune was that new hit song by The Fleetwoods, "Come Softly to Me."

Don't ask me if that means anything significant!

# 24
# Judy's Diary
## 1959

I met John Richardson tonight.

I can't believe I'm writing this about an FBI agent, dear diary, but he's a dreamboat!

It happened like this. Last night I called him at home. He asked me if I'd recovered from having my tonsils out, and I told him I had. Right on cue, he wanted to know if I was ready to meet him. I said *yes*.

He suggested we meet in the Meatpacking District in lower Manhattan, specifically West 13th Street just west of 9th Avenue, north of Gansevoort Street. During the day it's probably a very busy place—I'd never been there—but after dark it's kind of a creepy, deserted area. John said he'd park his car, a black 4-door Ford sedan, in front of the Garibaldi Meat Company building at 10:00 p.m. tonight. He said the car would glaringly stand out to the criminally minded as a police or Fed car, ha ha.

So I donned the Black Stiletto disguise, slipped out my bedroom window, ran across the roofs to the telephone pole I always climb down to the street, and made my way across town. During the winter I'd gotten used to wearing my trench coat over my outfit, without a mask, and then walking on the streets like any normal pedestrian. But now the weather was too warm for a coat. The

Stiletto had to take her chances not being seen, just like in the early days! Moving any distance while sticking only to shadows takes some time, so I left the gym early enough to allow for delays. Crossing the wide avenues is always a challenge. I can't use the intersections and crosswalks; that would be like a big neon sign pointing at my head saying, "Black Stiletto HERE!" Instead, I cross mid-avenue, between intersections, and take my chances by darting into the traffic and rushing to the other side. To anyone who notices me, hopefully, I'm just a flash in the night. Was she there or not?

I reached the Meatpacking District at 9:45. First I went up and down the street and checked for other cars. There were a couple here and there, but they were empty and locked. I checked the roofs and windows for any signs of light or other indications of a surveillance team. Then I perched alone in the darkness of a doorway across from the Garibaldi building and waited. Yes, I was nervous. Butterflies bounced around inside my stomach. I've never been to a prom or school dance, but I imagine that's how I would have felt if I had.

At 9:55, a black Ford sedan pulled onto the street and parked in front of the building. The headlights against the building provided a momentary backlight, allowing me to discern the silhouette of the driver, the only person in the car. It was him. I recognized the outline of the hat. He turned off the car and doused the lights. I watched him for a few moments and saw the flick of a match and the ember of a cigarette. He rolled down the window and flicked ashes out the side of the car.

It was now or never.

I crossed 13th, approached the passenger side of John's car, and tapped on the window. He reached over and opened the door, and I got in.

Oh my gosh, I was sitting in the front seat of a car with an FBI agent. "Hi," I said. Talk about being at a loss for words!

"Hello. I'm glad you made it," he said.

"Did you think I wouldn't?"

He shrugged. "You've stood me up before."

"I have to be careful." I looked around the car, although I don't know what I thought I'd see.

"I'm alone," he said. "Don't worry. Try to relax." He held out his hand. "I'm John."

I removed my glove and shook his hand. Was it my imagination, but did I feel an electric charge when the skin of his palm touched mine?

"I'm the Black Stiletto," I said, and then I laughed. He did, too. It was obvious we both felt a little awkward. He offered me a cigarette, but I shook my head.

"You gonna tell me your name?" he asked.

"You know I can't, John. I have to admit it's very difficult to trust you. The law is after me. The police want to draw and quarter me. I'm on the FBI's Most Wanted list. You're one of *them*, John."

"I'm not going to turn you in. I have no intention of hurting you or getting you in trouble."

"I appreciate that. You'll have to give me some time. Maybe we can meet like this again. After all, this is our first date." I laughed. "You don't expect a girl to reveal everything on the first date, do you?"

He smiled. "I suppose not," he answered. It was a wonderful smile, by the way.

"So tell me about yourself, John. Where are you from? What do you like to do?"

He shrugged. "I'm from Poughkeepsie. I'm an only child. My father is a lawyer and my mother is a housewife. They live in Florida now. I've lived in Manhattan since I was twenty-six. I started working for the Bureau when I was twenty-seven."

I wanted to ask him how old he was. He must have sensed it, for he added, "I'm thirty now."

"What do you do for the FBI?"

"I'm a Special Agent in the New York City Field Office. It's located on East Sixty-Ninth Street and Third Avenue. Our offices occupy the sixth through the fourteenth floors, as well as the penthouse. I'm on the seventh floor. I'm one of many agents. We report to Special Agents in Charge, and there are a few of them in our office. Some field offices around the country have only one SAC, but because New York encompasses a large population and territory, we have several."

"Do you carry a gun?"

"Of course. Standard issue Model ten Smith & Wesson six shot thirty-eight-caliber with a four inch barrel."

I giggled. I really didn't need that much information. "Do you have it with you?"

He nodded. "Mind you, I don't do a lot of field work. I'm mostly an administrator. I'm given a number of assignments to oversee. If the case warrants it, I'll go out with other agents to make arrests and all that. I've never been in a firefight. I hope that never happens."

"Have you ever arrested anyone?"

"Many times. But our jurisdiction is for federal crimes. If I saw someone breaking into a liquor store, for example, I couldn't arrest him. That's a job for the police. But if he was stealing the liquor and transporting it across state lines, then I could."

"Then why is the FBI after me?" I asked.

"Because you've been involved with organized crime and Communists."

"Huh?"

"You've been involved with the Cosa Nostra. My boss thinks that makes you an accessory to federal crimes. And there was that business last year with the Cuban spy. That's federal stuff."

"For heaven's sake, I'm on your side!"

He held up his hands. "You're preaching to the choir. If it was up to me, I'd tell the Bureau to lay off. The city police, on the other hand, they have a right to find you and arrest you."

"Do you think I deserve it?"

He thought a moment. "I don't condone vigilantism. It's dangerous and it could get innocent bystanders hurt. That said, I think you're doing a marvelous job. You're a brave girl. And from what I can see of your face, you're beautiful, too."

Oh, gosh, that did it! I felt myself blush and looked down. I don't know how he could tell, though. My mask covers half my face—only the bottom of my nose, my mouth, and my chin are exposed, and of course my eyes are visible through the holes.

"Flattery's not gonna get you anywhere," I said. "But thanks."

"You're welcome. Where did you learn all your fighting skills? Not to mention your ability to sneak around and break into places. What were you in a former life, a cat burglar?"

I laughed. "Nope. Just an ordinary gymnastics student in school."

"You had to have taken lessons in those Japanese fighting techniques."

"Yes, I have."

"Most people haven't heard of that stuff. How did you come across it?"

"That's a long story," I said. "And personal. I think I'd rather not talk about me."

"At least tell me where you're from. Oklahoma? Texas? Arkansas?"

"How could you tell? Is my accent that bad?"

He chuckled. "Well, you don't sound like your average New Yorker."

"I'm from Texas. But I've been in New York since I was fourteen."

"Do you have family?"

I held up my finger and wagged it. "Too personal."

Our conversation went on like that for about ten minutes. It covered mostly mundane stuff like New York sights, books we'd read, and movies we'd seen.

We spent a total of twenty minutes in the front seat of his car, just talking, flirting a little, and him smoking a couple of cigarettes.

He mentioned he should have thought about bringing something for us to drink and that next time he would. He asked what I like, and I told him I wasn't particular.

Finally, I felt it was time to say good night. I said I'd had a nice time and that I'd meet him again this way. We shook once more and he put his other palm on top of my hand. It was nice to be touched by a man again. It's been quite some time since Fiorello, you know. Well, there was that Cuban, Rafael Pulgarón, but he doesn't count, does he? I had a burning desire to kiss John, but I wasn't going to be so forward. It wasn't ladylike. Or Stiletto-like, ha ha. I think I was a little disappointed that he didn't try it himself. Maybe next time? Anyway, I let him hold my hand for a few moments and then it was time to go.

I got out of the car—and as soon as I did, a NYPD patrol car slowly rounded the corner on 9th Avenue. Its headlights hit me straight on and I froze. The car stopped and I saw there were two patrolmen in the front seat. My first thought was that they had been waiting all along to ambush me, but I could tell by their slow reaction they were just as surprised to see me as I was them. It took a second for me to snap out of it, and then I bolted around John's car and ran west on 13th. The patrol car's red-and-blue lights flashed on and it tore out after me. There weren't too many places for me to hide. The buildings butted against each other, and I saw no accesses between them. The only thing I could do was run. I reached the Washington Street intersection and turned north. That was a mistake. Up ahead was 14th Street, and there were always cars there, no matter what time it was. To compensate, I moved as close as possible to the buildings on the east side of Washington, where I found a dark gap next to a loading dock. Just as I slipped into it, the police car rounded the corner. I didn't know if they saw me, so I stayed perfectly still and prayed for them to drive on by.

They didn't. The car stopped right in front of the loading dock. They *had* seen me!

Both police officers jumped out of the car, guns drawn. One of them moved the little spotlight attached to the car toward me and bathed me in bright illumination. I was trapped, simple as that. Nowhere to go.

"Freeze!" one shouted.

I raised my hands.

"Walk out slowly. Keep your hands up."

I did. Once I was out in full view, one of them said, "Look here, we've got ourselves the Black Stiletto."

"Is it really her?" the other asked.

The first cop had a flashlight in his other hand. He focused it on me and asked, "Are you her?"

"You're asking *me*?" I replied.

The first officer ordered his partner to cuff me. As the guy started moving closer and unhooking the handcuffs from his belt, John came running around the corner from 13th Street.

"FBI! Stop right there! FBI!" he shouted.

The first officer swung his flashlight over to catch John, who was holding up his badge as he ran. The policemen obviously didn't know what to do. When John caught up to us, he let them study the badge.

"I'm FBI Special Agent John Richardson. This is a federal matter and the city police have no jurisdiction here. Let her go. I'm handling this."

The first cop said, "What are you talkin' about? What's a federal matter?"

"The Black Stiletto and the FBI are involved in an undercover operation. I suggest you two officers leave the scene immediately. If the operation is compromised in any way, the Bureau will be very unhappy with the NYPD." He leaned in to examine the cop's badge. "Officer McCauley, I have your badge number. Are you going to cooperate?"

The two policemen looked at each other.

"He's telling the truth," I said.

John added, "The clock is ticking. The Stiletto and I need to be

in our positions in less than ten minutes. You're impeding our operation. You must leave this instant!"

Finally, the first cop said, "Let's go, Pat."

"I shouldn't cuff her?"

"No. Let's go. Get in the car."

McCauley switched off the flashlight and went around to the driver's side of the patrol car. His partner eventually acquiesced and got
in the passenger side. In a moment they were gone.

John asked, "Are you all right?"

"Yeah. Thanks."

"You're welcome. You'd better get out of here."

"I will."

"I'm probably gonna catch hell for this if those cops talk."

"Let's hope they don't."

He nodded. "See you soon." With that, he turned and walked
back toward 13th and turned the corner.

Now I'm back home and it's nearly midnight. All I can think
about is how John saved me from being arrested. I suppose I *can* trust
him.

Wow. I think I'm smitten.

# 25
# John

Today is May 14, 1959.

I thought the Stiletto would call me since our meeting the other night, but she hasn't. I find her terribly intriguing. I wanna know what makes her tick. Why would a young woman who is obviously beautiful put on a costume and become a vigilante? What's in it for her?

The morning after our "date" I studied Tom's photos from the diner again. I'm convinced the black-haired girl is her. She has the same eyes. If she's indeed the Stiletto, then she's one of the most attractive women I've ever seen. A knockout, really. Those brownish-green eyes are simply mesmerizing. Tom asked me if I thought any of the women in the diner that day was the Stiletto. I told him, "No," and that the diner lead was a dead end. I don't want him sniffing around.

On my lunch hour yesterday, I went downtown again. It was my fourth trip to the diner since that day the Stiletto stood me up, but so far the black-haired girl hasn't come in. However, in the photo she was sitting with a couple, a man and woman. The woman is blonde and also fairly attractive. On a couple of occasions when I showed up for lunch, the blonde was working as a waitress. She's obviously friends with the Stiletto, so yesterday I made it a point to note that her name tag said, "Lucy."

It was just my luck that the man from the photo was in the diner at the same time. Lucy waited on him, and I could tell by their body language they are a couple. It's apparent in the photograph, too. They're either married or engaged, 'cause Lucy wears a big diamond ring on her left hand. He was well dressed in a suit, so I figure he's a banker or a lawyer who works nearby. At one point, I overheard Lucy call the man "Peter."

After a while, Peter went to the men's room. I got up, paid my bill, and then followed him inside. He had just finished his business at the urinal and was washing his hands. I stood at the urinal and asked, "Hey, Peter, how are you doing?"

He turned and said, "Fine, thanks." He didn't know me, of course.

"Say, who's that gorgeous girl I've seen you and Lucy with—you know, the one with dark hair and brown eyes, tall, long legs—"

Peter furrowed his brow. "Do I know you?"

I zipped up and used the sink while he dried his hands. "Sure, we met a while back, gosh, last year sometime. I guess you don't remember me, I'm Larry Turkin." I told him I worked for one of the big law firms in the city. "We met at one of those soirees we always have to go to." I dried my hands and shook his hand.

"Oh, right," he said. "Was it one of the City Bar dinners?"

"Yep, sure was. Say, I couldn't help but notice you and Lucy are still together." I nodded my head toward the door, indicating the diner.

"Yeah, we're going to get married, but we haven't set a date yet."

"Congratulations!" I slapped him on the arm as if I was an old war buddy. "So you gonna help me out? Is that girl single? You know, the one with the dark hair? It's almost black, you know who I mean?"

"Judy? She's the only girl I know with black hair."

"She's one of Lucy's good friends, isn't she?"

"Yeah. Judy Cooper. And yes, she's single."

"You wouldn't know her phone number, would you?"

He pursed his lips. "Nope, sorry. But Lucy does. Should I ask her?"

I didn't want Lucy to tell the Stiletto a man was asking about her. Since I had her name, I could find out her number at the office. There was always the chance Peter would mention it to Lucy, but I'd be long gone.

"That's okay," I said. "Don't worry about it. Hey, Peter, it's good to see you. Maybe I'll see you at another City Bar dinner."

"Sure, um, Larry," he said. "Nice to see you again."

I left the men's room ahead of him and went straight out to the street.

So now I know her name. Judy Cooper.

Haggerty continues to press me about catching her. I don't understand why he has a bug up his rear about her. At any rate, in yesterday's report, I revealed I'd met the Stiletto and pretty much told the truth about our rendezvous on 13th Street. Those two NYPD officers must've kept quiet, officially at least, for I haven't heard anything about our encounter. I was almost certain Haggerty would find out that Special Agent Richardson had told two city cops the Stiletto was in an undercover operation with the Bureau. Hadn't happened, though. So far, so good.

This morning Haggerty was ecstatic about the report. He asked me all kinds of questions. What did she look like? What's her name? What did she say? I told him if she agrees to meet me again, I'd find out a little more. He wants to set a trap and catch her next time, but I said she's too careful. It would never work on that deserted street. She can *smell* it if someone else is there. I told Haggerty that the more confident she becomes, the easier it will be to lure her to a secluded spot from which she'd have no escape.

Now I'm going to see what I can find out about Judy Cooper.

## 26
## *Martin*
### THE PRESENT

As expected, my mom was a difficult patient in the hospital. She had no idea where she was and couldn't understand why she had to stay in bed. She belligerently and constantly challenged the nurses and doctors. I had to stay with her each day just to keep her somewhat calm. Despite the struggles, though, the tests went well, and she was released after the weekend.

Mom had not suffered a stroke. The way it was explained to me was that she most likely went through a "vasovagal syncope," which is the fancy term for simply fainting for no apparent reason. Actually, what caused her to lose consciousness momentarily was a sudden rush of adrenaline and her heart no longer having the strength to keep up with the demand for increased pumping action. Once again, I had to fudge the truth and tell the doctors I had no idea what had upset her.

I guess that taught me not to bring up anything related to the Black Stiletto to my mom ever again. At least over the weekend I got to catch up on reading her diary during the infrequent times she fell asleep. I'm learning more and more about her every time I pick up one of those books.

Because Mom was released on Monday, I had to call Konnors at Chicago Audit, my new employer, and say I couldn't make it in. He understood and expressed his concern for my mother, but I detected a tad bit of annoyance in his voice. I knew he needed an auditor to start with his new client as soon as possible, but hopefully one more day wouldn't make a difference.

It took a little while, but Mom seemed happy to be back at Woodlands. At first, though, she was very confused. I'm not sure where she thought she was supposed to be, but the room wasn't "home" to her. Perhaps she remembered our old house in Arlington Heights as being her home. Maybe it was Los Angeles. Or New York. I have no idea. But after an hour, she settled into her old routine. The nightmare visit to the hospital was completely forgotten. And the best part will come next. While insurance and Medicare usually takes care of Mom's bills, I know I'll be stuck with a portion of them. There's no such thing as 100% coverage.

It was only after I got home that I remembered I hadn't heard from Gina. Usually she's pretty good about calling her dad back. I removed my cell phone from my pocket and checked the "missed calls." There wasn't one from Gina, but there was another New York 212 area code number listed. Whoever had called had left a voice message. I don't know why I didn't hear it ring. Maybe I was in that no signal zone of the rural two-lane road through Riverwoods that stretched between Woodlands and the interstate entrance. Anyway, I dialed my voice mail and listened. It was the heavy New York accent of Johnny Munroe.

"Talbot, have you thought over what we talked about? Give me a call. You have my number. If I don't hear from you in forty-eight hours, *World Entertainment Television*'s gonna have a new segment to air."

Great. I had no idea what I was going to do about that. I hadn't had any time to think about it over the weekend. Should I confide in Uncle Thomas, my mom's lawyer? Perhaps he could give me some advice. We'd have a client confidentiality thing, wouldn't we? Uncle Thomas couldn't—and wouldn't—reveal my mom's secret. Still, it's a tough decision. At least while she's alive, I want to keep my mom safe from the firestorm that would explode if the world learned who the Black Stiletto really was.

Before I could contemplate the problem further, my cell phone rang. Caller ID indicated it was my ex-wife.

I answered and said, "Hi, Carol."

"Martin!" She was sobbing.

"Carol? What's wrong?"

"It's . . . it's Gina! She's hurt!"

"What?"

"She's in the hospital!" She started going off in the middle of the story, not making any sense.

"Wait! Slow down! Carol, please," I pleaded. "Take a breath and start from the beginning."

I heard her sob again, but she did her best to collect herself. "I got a call from a New York police detective just a little while ago. Gina—she was attacked last night in a park. Martin, she was assaulted."

"Oh, my God!"

"She's hurt pretty bad. I don't have all the details. She's in St. Luke's-Roosevelt Hospital."

"Carol, God, what do we do?"

"I've got a flight booked in the morning. I'm going out there."

"I'm going, too. I'll go online right now and book a flight. What airline are you on?"

"United." She told me the flight number and time.

"Maybe I can get on the same flight. I'll try. Jesus, what else do you know?"

"Only that they weren't sure who she was for the last twenty-four hours. Whoever did this stole her purse, which of course contained her driver's license and IDs. She regained consciousness a few hours ago and told them to call me."

"And she was . . . she was raped?"

"I don't know! The detective said—"

"What's his name?"

"Uh, I wrote it down. Here it is. Detective Ken Jordan. I have his phone number, too."

"So what did he say?"

"He said she was physically assaulted. I think he said 'attempted rape,' but I was so frazzled I can't remember. She's in stable condition, but her jaw is broken. It had to be wired shut."

"Jesus!" My heart was pounding. I thought it was going to burst out of my chest. "Did they catch who did it?"

Carol sobbed again. "No. But a witness said he saw some black man running away from the scene."

That figured. New York City. Black man. Crime. Assault. Rape. I couldn't help it. It's how I always pictured New York. One of the first things I wanted to say was, "I *told* you not to let Gina go to Juilliard! New York's a dangerous place!" But I didn't. It wouldn't help. Carol was upset enough.

"Okay, I'm gonna try and get a flight," I said. "Try not to worry."

"Martin, she's our little girl!"

"I know, honey. And we'll be with her tomorrow. I'll call you back and let you know what I find out."

I suppose it's every father's nightmare. Daughters will always remain our little girls, no matter how old they are. It's our nature to protect them and love them. If anything bad happens to them, our instinct is to charge after the perpetrators and see that justice is done. I don't know what I'd be able to do, but I wasn't going to sit on my ass in Chicago.

I booked a seat on Carol's flight to LaGuardia.

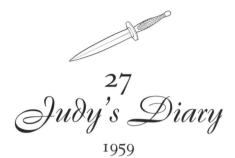

# 27
# *Judy's Diary*
## 1959

MAY 16, 1959

I had another car date with John tonight. Mmm, it was more fun this time 'cause we were a lot more relaxed.

I called him at home last night and suggested we meet again. He was all for it. Same time, same place. He said he'd bring food.

After the usual long day at work, I had just a light dinner with Freddie since I knew I'd be eating later. I prepared to go out as the Stiletto, when suddenly it started pouring outside. Well, the Black Stiletto doesn't travel with an umbrella, so I was gonna get wet. Luckily, my outfit's leather repels water to a certain extent. In anticipation of being uncomfortable, I brought along a couple of towels in my backpack.

Crossing over to the West Side was easy and difficult at the same time. The rain kept away people who didn't have to be on the streets, but traffic was worse. Therefore, running along the sidewalks was a breeze, but darting across the avenues between moving cars almost got me killed!

John's Ford was parked in the same spot in front of Garibaldi's. Just to be safe, I did a quick reconnaissance (another new word I learned and looked up in the dictionary so I could spell it!). The street was empty; we were alone. Hopefully no members of New York City's finest would bother us this time. Finally, I approached the car's passenger side and tapped on the window. He quickly opened the door and I got in.

"My God, you're soaked!" he said.

"Sorry. I don't want to get your car all wet." I pulled out the towels and laid them on the seat beneath me. "I came prepared, though."

"Don't worry about it. I'll run the heater for a bit to warm you up." He started the car and turned a knob on the dashboard. I know nothing about cars. I never got my driver's license. One of these days I'm gonna have to do that. After a few minutes, the inside of the car got pretty toasty. The heat also helped unfog the inside of the windows. I guess it was our breath that was clouding 'em up.

I smelled hot food. John opened a paper bag and removed some take-out cartons. "Hope you like Chinese," he said.

"Love it. That's very nice of you."

"It's from a place on the ground floor of my building. Of course, just about any Chinese place is good in New York City. It's like the pizza joints. You usually can't go wrong."

There was beef and broccoli, sweet and sour pork, and sautéed string beans. John also had a couple of bottles of Coke, which he opened with a thing on his key chain. "I would have brought beer or wine, but I didn't know if you drink alcohol," he said.

"Sure I do. Doesn't everyone?"

"Actually, I don't. I might have a glass of wine every now and then with dinner, but I don't normally drink socially. Hard liquor doesn't agree with me, and I've never developed the taste for beer. I know, I'm an oddball."

"That's okay," I said, indicating the cigarette in his hand. "You make up for it with tobacco."

"Oh, I'm sorry, is it too much smoke in here for you?"

"A little."

He lowered his window a bit and threw the butt out. "I shouldn't smoke and eat at the same time anyway." He handed me a plastic fork and napkin. "You sure you're not too wet?"

"I'm fine, but I'm gonna take off this jacket." I started to unzip it down the front and his eyes widened. I laughed and said, "Don't get too excited, I have a T-shirt on underneath." I laid the jacket on the floorboard and sat there in my leather pants and white T-shirt. What I didn't anticipate was what happened to my nipples! Oh my gosh, dear diary, they perked right up and I'm sure he could see them poking through my T-shirt. I wasn't wearing a bra because my jacket is tight-fitting and supports my breasts quite well. As soon as I realized what was happening, I was really embarrassed, but I tried not to let it show. I considered putting the jacket back on, but I figured that would just call attention to the problem. So I just concentrated on the food and tried to forget about those vivacious nipples. Sheesh!

After a while it got too warm in the car with the heater on, so he shut it off and we rolled down the windows a bit more. "We have heaters in the company cars, but no air conditioners," John said. "J. Edgar Hoover has 'em taken out. He thinks it costs too much money to run the air conditioner in a car. One of these days I hope he'll learn it costs more to take out the A/C than it does to run them!"

The rain lessened, and it became quite pleasant sitting there. We finished the meal and he tucked away the garbage in the backseat. Then we talked for a while, just like last time. On this occasion I revealed that I'd run away from home and ended up in New York when I was 14. I didn't want to give him too much information, but I said I'd met some people who took me under their wings and helped me get on my feet. John told me he was in the army for two years after he graduated from high school. He was finished his service just before the Korean War started, thank goodness, and then he went to college at Cornell in Ithaca, where he got a degree in government.

"At first I thought I wanted to be a politician," John said, "but then I got the idea to join the FBI. I applied, got accepted, went through the training, and here I am."

He told me a little how the FBI works and what his duties are. Apparently he doesn't like his boss very much.

After spending about forty-five minutes in the car, I figured it was time for me to go. I thanked him for the food and his company.

"This is like a drive-in movie," I said, "only without the movie!"

"I suppose we could do that sometime," he said. "We'd have to leave Manhattan, though. I know a wonderful drive-in theater that has the biggest screen you can imagine, and in the summertime you can sit on the grass outside your car to watch the movie and have a picnic if you want."

"That sounds fun! Where is it?"

"Poughkeepsie. You ever been there?"

"Nope. Isn't that where you said you're from?"

"That's right. The Overlook Drive-In opened in, gosh, was it nineteen forty-eight or forty-nine? I was just out of high school. When I'd come home from college for the summers, my friends and I would take dates to the Overlook. We'd pile as many people in the car as possible—sometimes in the trunk!"

"And the drive-in is still there?"

"Yep."

"Gosh, let's do it! Is it a long drive?"

"A little over two hours."

I laughed. "Maybe we should find one closer."

And then he did something that took me completely by surprise. Even though I was wearing my mask, he leaned over, put a hand behind my neck, pulled me closer, and kissed me on the mouth. It was just a little, light kiss, nothing too fiery, just enough to be sweet and tender. Oh my gosh, my heart nearly jumped out of my chest. Then he stayed where he was, our faces just a few inches from each other. It was a little weird, me having the mask on and all, but he didn't seem to mind. He looked deeply into my eyes, and I could tell he wanted to kiss me again. So I let him.

This time we opened our mouths and *really* kissed.

Wow. He's a good kisser, dear diary.

We moved back to our respective places in the front seat. No one said anything for a few moments. It was a whole lot warmer in the car, let me tell you!

Then I put my jacket back on, took my towels off the seat, and said, "Okay, John, I gotta go. I'll call you!" I got out of there fast. I felt awkward. I'd never kissed anyone while wearing the Stiletto mask. It was strange.

Happily, the rain had stopped. I waved goodbye and took off into the night.

MAY 18, 1959

I spent last night stalking the city looking for some action. After the winter and my illness in April, I was fed up with being indoors. Going out to meet John those two times got me yearning to do some real Black Stiletto work. You know—catch some crooks in the act of committing crimes or help some little old ladies cross the street, ha ha. Well, I didn't find one crook or one little old lady. A few pedestrians spotted me, though. One group cheered as I ran by, but I heard at least one boo. I guess you can't please everyone.

Just to be daring, I scouted Little Italy to see if any of Franco DeLuca's goons might try to kill me again. Many of his soldiers operated out of there. All I saw were tourists eating at tables outside the Italian restaurants. Made me hungry. I was tempted to stop, sit at a table in full costume, and order some pasta and wine. Maybe that would have brought out the hit men. Then I could have had a rumble right there on Mulberry Street. Oh, well.

Today I worked at the gym, as usual. Clark continues to improve in his lessons. He's such a sweet kid. When we're not in the ring, we talk about books. He recently read *Invisible Man* by Ralph Ellison. I hadn't read it but had heard about it. It sounded interesting, and seeing that it was about how the Negro is alienated in America, I thought it would be something I'd enjoy. We also talked about the movie *The Defiant Ones*, and how much Clark admires the actor Sidney Poitier. Poitier was nominated for an Oscar this past year for his part, along with Tony Curtis, but neither won. I wonder if Poitier or any other colored actor will ever win an Oscar? Wait, that woman in *Gone with the Wind* won one, but I think she's the only Negro to ever achieve it. Clark says his father keeps telling him that people should stop referring to Negroes as "Negroes," and instead just call them black men and women or "African Americans." I wonder if that'll ever catch on.

Mike Washington showed up and I got bad tinglings from him, as usual. After my lesson with Clark, he said something to me I sure didn't like.

"You gonna get that boy in trouble."

"What do you mean?"

"I seen a black man lynched and burned alive for just lookin' funny at a white girl. And there you is being his friend. Some cracker'll find out and won't like it. That boy be dead meat."

I was too appalled to respond. I just walked away, shaking my head. What an angry, unhappy man. Freddie buddies up to him all the time. I want to like the guy, but it's obvious he doesn't like me or something. I don't trust him. You know what it really is? I think I finally figured it out. Washington reminds me of those gangsters up in Harlem. I get the same sense of danger from him as I did from them. Could he be involved with those guys? After all, he does live in Harlem.

This afternoon I went for my *karate* lesson. Soichiro has been in a much better mood lately. Apparently Isuzu is back, living with him in their apartment on Charles Street. She was in a rehabilitation facility for two months, but Soichiro didn't say where it was located. From what I understand, she had a very difficult time going through the heroin withdrawal. I hear it makes people crazy for a while. It's supposed to be very painful, both physically and mentally. I can't imagine it. I'll never do any of those narcotics. I don't need them and have no desire to try them. There's been a lot of talk about marijuana lately. The "beatniks" who go to the coffee shops these days—guys like that author Jack Kerouac and the poet Allen Ginsburg, and some musicians—apparently they all smoke marijuana. Supposedly it's not as bad as doing heroin, but I still don't want to know what it does.

That reminds me. Lucy, Peter, and I were at a poetry reading at a place called Café Wha? on Macdougal Street last week. Some guy played bongos while a few people stood and read original poetry, one at a time. I smelled something strange and Lucy told me it was marijuana. Several folks in the audience had been smoking it outside and they reeked of it. The poetry was really weird, too. I didn't understand it. Peter said it was "avant-garde" (once again, I had to look that up to spell it right). That means it was experimental. If you ask me, they need to stop experimenting and write something that makes sense. After the poetry, though, a folk singer named Pete Seeger performed. I enjoyed that a lot.

Back to Soichiro—we haven't talked about what happened in February. I thought perhaps he'd bring up the Black Stiletto at some point, but he never has. He must respect my privacy and sensitivity about keeping my identity secret. I know he still thinks about Carl Purdy, though. Soichiro has been talking to a lawyer and they filed a civil suit against Purdy that has yet to go to court. One day he mentioned offhandedly that he'd heard Purdy sometimes goes after and gets revenge on people who have done him wrong. I told Soichiro that he didn't do Purdy wrong, the Black Stiletto did. At any rate, I think Soichiro worries Purdy might come looking for Isuzu again.

MAY 31, 1959

It's 3:00 in the morning and I just got home from a date with John! And oh my gosh, this one was something else! It didn't end as well as I would have liked, but for the most part it was quite the adventure.

As this is Memorial Day weekend, I called John and asked if he wanted to get together again. He said he was hoping I'd call because he wanted to see me. John really wants a phone number where he can call me. But in order to give him a phone number, I'd have to reveal my name. Then everything would be spoiled. I think. I'm not sure anymore, dear diary! I really like him, and I *think* he likes me, too. The way he was acting in the car tonight, I know he sure likes *kissing* me, ha ha! Maybe I will divulge my identity to him. If only he wasn't an FBI agent!

Anyway, our date was tonight—well, now it's early Sunday morning—our date was Saturday night. He wanted me to meet him earlier, before nightfall, because he "had plans." So I crossed town without my mask and a light jacket covering my disguise. When I saw his car parked in the usual spot, I donned the mask before he could see me, and then I got in the car. He said, "We're going for a drive, Stiletto." That made me nervous and I told him so. He asked me to trust him and that we'd have a lot of fun. So I went with it. For all I knew, he could've driven me into an FBI trap and I'd be arrested, but he didn't.

John drove north through Manhattan and up into the Bronx. Before long, we were out of New York City altogether.

"Where are you taking me?" I asked.

"You'll see."

He got on U.S. Route 9 and then I knew what was going on. We talked about it the last time. He was taking me to Poughkeepsie, but I pretended I didn't know. I wanted to let him have his surprise.

Along the way we continued our small talks, getting to know each other better. One of the topics of conversation was the astronaut monkeys. NASA sent two monkeys up into space and they came back alive and well. Their names are Able and Miss Baker. The pictures in the papers were real cute. It was funny to see monkeys wearing space suits. We also listened to the radio. John isn't too much of a rock-and-roll fan, but he was tolerant of my excitement when they played an Elvis song. John rolled his eyes when they played "The Battle of New Orleans" by Johnny Horton. It's on its way to be number one and you hear it *everywhere*. John likes Frank Sinatra, Dean Martin, Tony Bennett, Perry Como, and—oh my gosh!—Doris Day.

It's very easy to talk to John. I have to be very careful what I say. Too much information might give him clues as to my identity. But seeing that he's an FBI agent, he could very well already have me pegged. I hope not. Not yet, anyway.

The drive took over two hours, just like he said. Before long, we were at the Overlook Drive-In Theater, which was just as impressive as John described. The screen was huge. We parked and put the speaker inside the window, and then he went to the snack bar to get us some food. He came back with hot dogs, sodas, and popcorn. I felt funny sitting there with my mask and outfit on. Once it got completely dark outside no one could see in.

It was a double feature. The first movie was a western called *Rio Bravo*, starring John Wayne and Dean Martin. It was great! I don't normally like westerns, but it was funny and exciting at the same time. The second feature was *Some Like It Hot*, which I'd already seen, but I was happy to watch it again. However, we didn't do much watching. By the time that movie started, we'd finished all our snacks and were ready to snuggle just like all the teenagers and other couples we saw in cars around us.

We started kissing and I swear we didn't stop for thirty minutes! Talk about "some like it hot!" After the first ten minutes, he casually pushed me back on the seat until I was lying down. Since my legs are so long, it was kinda clumsy. He got on top of me and we continued to kiss like that. Dear diary, I really wished I wasn't wearing that darn disguise! I yearned for a man's touch on my body again. Alas, the leather insulated me, so even when his hand moved up to my breast, I didn't feel it like I was supposed to. I knew his hand was there, and it was exciting and all that, but I guess it was like taking a shower with a raincoat on.

Then at one point he reached up to my mask and touched the bottom edges. "May I?" he asked.

He wanted to unmask me!

"No, John," I said. "Please. No." And that ruined the moment. I pushed him off of me and we sat up. "I'm sorry," I said. "I'm not ready for that yet."

Then he said, "You know how bizarre it is to kiss you with that mask on? Is it always going to be Halloween with us?"

That hurt my feelings. In any other circumstances it would have made me angry, but I was really starting to like him. Making out with him was wonderful, and I'd lost myself in his kisses.

"Maybe we should go back to the city," I said.

He nodded and started the car. We left before the movie was over. The drive back was kinda tense, but after an hour he finally said, "Look, I'm sorry. It wasn't a nice thing to say."

"It's all right. I understand what you mean." And I did. "It's weird for me, too. Maybe I'll take off my mask for you in the near future."

When we got to Manhattan, he asked if he should drive back to the Meatpacking District or if it would be more convenient if he dropped me somewhere else. I asked if he could let me off in the Village. He drove to Washington Square and pulled over to the curb.

"John, where's your apartment?" I asked.

"Why?"

"Maybe I should visit you there next time."

He gave me the address. It was a seven-floor building on East 21st Street, just east of 3rd Avenue. I asked if there was a fire escape that was easily accessible. He told me it was in the front of the building and that his apartment was on the 5th floor.

I said that was good to know. Before I got out of the car, I thanked him for the wonderful evening, leaned over, and kissed him.

I hope I didn't put him off with the mask thing. Gee whiz—most girls try to keep their panties on; I keep guys from taking off a stupid mask!

# 28
## Judy's Diary
### 1959

JUNE 7, 1959

Dear diary, do I have something to tell *you*!

Last night I went to see John at his apartment. I didn't leave until around 2:00 a.m.

I suppose you can guess what happened.

Since it was Saturday, I called him at home. There was no answer in the afternoon, but I tried a little later. Still no answer. After dinner I decided the Stiletto would pay him a surprise visit. I had no idea if he'd be home, but I figured I could get the lay of the land around his apartment building. It was just where he said, on East 21st between 2nd and 3rd. The fire escape was on the front. I suppose there was one in the back, too. The building was much bigger than Soichiro's brownstone in the West Village, and there was a doorman at a desk just inside the front door. That was going to make access a little tricky. I estimated it was approximately fifteen feet between the door and the fire escape. As long as the rung ladder wasn't squeaky when I pulled it down, I'd probably be okay.

It was nearly 10:00, so it was plenty dark. New York is the city that never sleeps, though, and there were many pedestrians around, even on 21st. I crouched in a dark alcove at the edge of the building, waited until there was little foot traffic nearby, and went for it. Once again using my homemade grappling hook at the end of a rope, I pulled down the ladder, made sure it was secured in place, and shimmied up to the fire escape's first landing. So as not to attract attention, I pulled the ladder up after me. I waited there for a moment to make sure the doorman didn't hear me and no one walking on the other side of the street saw me. As long as I stayed away from lit windows, I was okay. My outfit acted as camouflage against the night. I moved on up the steps to the second landing, and so on, until I reached the fifth.

The light was on inside John's apartment. Peering inside, I saw a bedroom. There wasn't much to speak of, just a double bed, chest of drawers, and a mirror. There was a closet on the far side of the room, where I imagined John kept his clothes. A door led off into a hallway. I assumed there'd be a bathroom and a living room/kitchen area and that was it. A modest one-bedroom bachelor apartment in Manhattan.

I tried to open the window but it was locked. So I tapped on it. Nothing happened. I tried again, a little louder. Finally I knocked as if it was the front door. Finally, John appeared. He was wearing trousers and an undershirt, was barefoot, and boy, did he look surprised! I laughed, and then a smile as big as the horizon spread across his face. He moved to the window, unlatched it, and pulled it up.

"What are you doing out there, you crazy girl?" he asked.

"Hello, sir, I'm selling Girl Scout cookies. Would you like to buy some?"

"Sure, but get inside before someone sees you!"

I crawled in over a radiator and stood next to him. "I don't think anyone spotted me. I was real careful. I hope I'm not disturbing you. Are you busy? You want company?"

"Of course! Let me grab a shirt, though," he said. "This is . . . this is quite extraordinary!"

I didn't mind seeing him in his undershirt. It kinda reminded me of Marlon Brando in *A Streetcar Named Desire*; but he felt self-conscious, so I didn't say anything. He grabbed a shirt out of the closet and then said, "Let's go in the living room. I'll give you the grand tour. This is my bedroom, obviously."

He showed the way into the hall and indicated the only bathroom, which was equipped with a real tub and shower fixture. I don't have a bathtub in my apartment. I miss reclining in a tub of hot water, casting off my problems and tensions in a sea of suds and rubber duckies.

The living room was more fleshed out, so to speak. There was a couch, a comfy chair, coffee table, a television, and a hi-fi on a stand containing a bunch of records. In another section of the room was a dining table with two chairs. A wall separated the kitchen from the rest. A desk, chair, and a small filing cabinet stood near the hi-fi. The hall went on to the front door of the apartment, next to which was another closet.

"Very nice, John! I didn't think bachelors could be so neat, but you are, apparently."

"FBI agents are very organized by nature," he said. He gestured to the desk. "I take my work home with me a lot." The desk had a phone, an in-box and out-box full of papers, and other stuff. There was also a machine with a microphone on it.

"What's this?"

"Oh, that's a Dictaphone. Besides the written reports I turn in at the office, I like to dictate my thoughts on these Dictabelts." He gestured to an open box on top of the filing cabinet, which was full of plastic "belts" coiled into individual smaller boxes.

"I've heard of Dictaphones but I've never played with one."

"You speak into the microphone and a stylus records the sounds by pressing a groove on the Dictabelt. Ten years ago or so, it used wax cylinders. I suspect someday they'll have magnetic tape for them, like a tape recorder." As he spoke he closed the box containing the plastic belts. I guess he didn't want me to see confidential subjects written on labels affixed to the smaller boxes. I didn't care. I wasn't about to invade his privacy, especially if it was FBI business.

"Would you like a drink?" he asked.

"Whadaya got?"

"Even though I don't drink alcohol, I do keep some in the apartment. I have vodka and bourbon, and stuff you might want to mix with it like orange juice or Coke. I also have some wine. I think I have some ginger ale, or I could make tea or coffee."

I asked for a screwdriver—just old-fashioned vodka and orange juice. He said he'd have a little, too, only he'd go easy on the vodka.

So we sat on the couch and had drinks. He'd made mine pretty strong, and I told him so. "You trying to take advantage of me, mister?" I asked in my best Marilyn Monroe imitation.

"No, I just want some of those Girl Scout cookies," he admitted, and then he leaned in and kissed me. And that was the program for the next ten minutes or so. Kiss, grope, kiss, grope. I could tell he was getting excited, for his breathing became heavier.

So I asked, "Can I really trust you?"

He stopped and looked me in the eyes. "Sure."

"I mean *really* trust you?"

"Yes. I promise."

I gently pushed him away and then I took off my mask. After that I shook my head and let my hair fall to my shoulders. I tossed the mask/hood on the floor.

"Better?" I asked.

You should have seen his face. His bottom jaw was practically on the floor. He wasn't expecting that!

"My God, you're beautiful," he said. "You really are."

"I bet you say that to all the Girl Scouts."

"Not on your life."

And he leaned over and we started kissing again.

Well, I figured since he knew what my face looked like, I might as well show him everything else. I took off my outfit, he undressed, and we ended up in his bed. He started to turn off the light by the bed but I told him not to. I wanted to see him as much as he wanted to see me.

Dear diary, it was bliss. We did it three times. I'm not gonna go into details, 'cause I'm turning red just writing this! Suffice it to say that John Richardson is a wonderful lover.

We fell asleep in each other's arms, but I woke up around 2:00. I told him I had to go. He asked me to stay until morning, but I shook my head.

"The only clothing I have is the Stiletto outfit," I said. "It's difficult to travel by daylight. In the winter I wear a long coat over my disguise and stuff my mask in my backpack. But in warm weather that doesn't work."

"I wish you'd stay. Another time?"

"Perhaps."

"What's your name?"

I put a finger to his lips. "One revelation at a time, darling."

"When will I see you again?"

"Soon."

He stayed in bed while I dressed. After a final long kiss, I put on my mask and slipped out the window. He got up to close it behind me. I went down the fire escape and jumped to the sidewalk from the first landing. No one saw me.

Could it be possible? Is Judy Cooper smitten again?

I think so, dear diary. I think so!

# 29
## *John*
### HOME DICTAPHONE RECORDING

Today is June 20, 1959.

Judy Cooper, the Black Stiletto, has been visiting me at my apartment for a couple of weeks now. So far we've had three such dates. She's not aware that I know her real name. She still insists I call her "Eloise."

Written reports on the subject have become problematic, to say the least. Haggerty wanted me to gain her confidence. I'm not sure this is what he meant, but I guess I've lured her in, all right. She trusts me well enough to remove her mask — and clothes. I must say she is quite an independent and vivacious girl.

At the office I've tried to find out as much as I can about Judy Cooper. Unfortunately, she has no history. Nothing. It's as if she doesn't exist. I'm beginning to wonder if that's her legal name. There's no driver's license registered to her. There are plenty of Social Security numbers assigned to Judys and Judiths Coopers all over the country. I've concentrated the search in Texas, but she's never told me what town she came from. There are a lot of Judy Coopers in Texas, too. The Manhattan telephone directory doesn't help. The three Judy Coopers with real phone numbers are two old ladies and a teenager.

At least once a week I go downtown for lunch at the diner. I've seen Lucy, the waitress, and she smiles at me as if I'm a regular customer. I'm hesitant to engage her in conversation about Judy. I haven't seen her boyfriend, Peter.

I have to be careful when Judy's with me. I'm afraid I'll accidentally call her by name. I'm not sure how she'll take it. She has a lot of affection for me, it seems, but I also get the feeling she could fly off the handle if she felt threatened or tricked in any way.

I'm really enjoying her company, and I'm not sure how to handle it.

On the narcotics cases, more and more Negro street hoods are being arrested for selling heroin. The buyers range in age from thirteen to sixty. It's incredible. None of them remain in jail very long. Someone always bails them out. The ones that go to trial get off with light sentences. No one fingers the higher-ups.

The police had one guy in custody who named Carl Purdy as the boss. He called Purdy the "Harlem Kingpin." He agreed to testify against Purdy for a reduced sentence. Then one day a colored lawyer came to visit the guy in jail. The next morning, the guy had hanged himself. No case.

My informant is now working close to Purdy's inner circle. He acts as muscle, a bodyguard of sorts, and is being paid to do so. He says Purdy is about to wage total war on his enemies, whoever they might be. The Italians? The police? The Bureau? In the meantime, I've asked the informant to get a handle on the supply channels for the heroin. We're pretty sure it comes from Corsica, but we need to know the direct routes.

[Pause on Dictabelt.] I've been thinking about Judy a lot. That's probably not a wise thing to do.

# 30
# *Judy's Diary*
## 1959

JULY 5, 1959

I am so mad I could spit.

That film I made with Jerry Munroe has come back to haunt me. I knew I shouldn't have trusted that slime bag. I suspected he might be involved with the mob and it turns out he is. He's a damned crook, pardon my language.

Since I ultimately never needed that roll of film to audition for the film producer, I'd forgotten all about Munroe. Then, on Friday, the 3rd, as I was having my breakfast before going into the gym, I happened to see his note to me in the classifieds section. Apparently he'd been trying to contact me for weeks with an ad in there every day since May. Must have cost him a small fortune.

"To Film Star from Munroe. Call Office."

Curious, I went outside to a pay phone and gave the guy a call. When he answered, I said, "It's the Stiletto. I saw your ad in the paper."

"Took you long enough," he grumbled.

"I'm not in the habit of scouring the classifieds."

Then he said, "You need to pick up a shoe box. You'll find it to the left of the loading door entrance on the Twenty-Ninth Street side of my building, taped under a street-level window sill, about two feet off the sidewalk. It's brown and it's taped up."

"Why? What's in it?"

"You'll see."

"Why the cloak-and-dagger stuff?"

"You'll see. Do you understand the location?"

"I think so."

"And Stiletto?"

"What?"

"It's in your best interest to pick it up as soon as possible."

Then he hung up. Well, dear diary, I got an extremely bad feeling about that call. My danger instincts went through the roof. I could tell by the tone of his voice that this wasn't friendly repartee. Munroe was up to something and it wasn't good.

I had to wait until dark, of course, to retrieve the shoe box. I couldn't very well go during the day as Judy Cooper—Munroe or someone else could've been watching. It might've been a trap for the mob to get me. Or the cops. Who knew?

I waited until 11:00. Moving cautiously through the shadows, I approached Park Avenue South on the south side of 29th from Lexington. I kept my eyes peeled for any signs of men sitting in parked cars and waiting for me to show up. When I was within thirty feet or so from the intersection, I grabbed the flashlight from my belt and shined it across the street to the area on the side of the building Munroe mentioned. Sure enough, I saw the small box underneath the windowsill. The average person on the street wouldn't notice it unless someone was actually looking for it. I flicked off the light, looked both ways, and then darted to the other side. The shoe box was taped securely, but I ripped it off easily with my stiletto. Not wishing to stick around longer than I had to, I ran with the box back toward Lexington. Incorporating my usual stop-move-stop-move system for traveling through the city streets, I made it over to 2nd Avenue and 18th Street before my curiosity got the best of me and I had to open the box. Only then did I see he had written, "To Film Star" on the top with a black marker. I sliced through the tape with my blade, and removed the lid.

Inside were six eight-by-ten black-and-white photos. The first four were still frames from the film he'd shot. Me fighting the mannequin, me laughing at the camera, and me climbing the fire escape. No surprise there. It was the fifth and sixth shots that took my breath away.

They were of me in his dressing room with my mask off. I was looking in the mirror and applying makeup. I remembered doing that, but I had no idea he was filming me! The frightening part was that my face was fully revealed in the mirror.

The creep had secretly unmasked me.

A note was beneath the photos. This is what it said—

Stiletto You will recognize some of these shots from your film. Each photo is from film footage I shot. I have the negative and a copy of the unedited, complete version of *The Black Stiletto Unmasked*. Nice title, huh? I have certain associates in the Italian olive oil and wine importing business. I think you've run across them in the past. They would pay a lot of money for this film. Unless I receive $10,000 from you within five days, I'm afraid I'll have to sell the film to these customers. Actually, perhaps the police would like to see it, too. Or the *Daily News* or *New York Times*. I think I could get rich with this film. But I'll give you the right of first refusal. You are to leave the money in this same shoe box, taped under the window sill as before no later than midnight July 6. That gives you all day Monday to gather the funds. I trust you won't let me down. Oh, are you thinking about calling the police? Are you sure you want to do that? That would certainly blow your identity, wouldn't it, Stiletto? I also warn you NOT to come to my studio. As you know, it is well secured; there is no way you can break in. And my Italian friends may be watching. I've also hired a serious bodyguard.

J.M.

That bastard. That conniving, sneaky, slimy, greaseball son of a bitch. I think you'll pardon the language, dear diary, given the circumstances.

I stuffed the box and its contents in my backpack, then went back to Park Avenue South. I was ready to shout up to his studio and tell him to come down and meet me face-to-face. Of course, I couldn't do that. But I did notice the lights were on in his second-floor studio. He was inside.

I tried to recall everything about his studio. There wasn't a bedroom—just the studio, a bathroom, a little kitchen, and that makeshift dressing room. *He slept elsewhere*. That meant he had to go home at some point.

Glancing across Park Avenue South, I noticed one of the buildings on the west side was under construction and covered in scaffolding. Great. It was a perfect spot from which to watch Munroe's place. At the right moment, I dashed across, climbed up the scaffolding to the second landing, and sat in the darkness on a large piece of plywood. I didn't know how long it would take, but I planned to sit there until Munroe showed his greasy self—and I was gonna follow him home.

Thank goodness I didn't have to wait long. The lights shut off on the second floor at 12:30. After a moment, the little creep came out of his building and started walking north. He was accompanied by a big guy. A mobster with a gun, no doubt. I was tempted to grab them right then and there, but I wasn't sure where he was keeping the film and negatives. I had to get my hands on those before I taught the bastard a lesson.

So I stalked them up Park Avenue South. Flitting in and out of shadows, I tailed the guys up to East 36th Street. They turned east. I waited a moment to let them get a ways ahead, and then I followed. At one point Munroe looked behind him, as if he'd felt someone's presence. I froze. My dark outfit blended in with a cluster of garbage cans on the sidewalk. He didn't see me, so he and his pal continued walking.

Munroe and Goonface crossed Lexington and stayed on 36th. I

ran against a red light, dodged a speeding taxicab, and then hugged the building at the corner of Lex and 36th. Munroe and his buddy headed toward 3rd. I slowly moved forward, passing some pedestrians who gawked at me. I put a finger to my lips and kept going. Then I saw Munroe stop at an apartment building on the north side of 36th, not quite at the end of the block. He shook hands with his escort and then went inside. The big guy walked on to 3rd Avenue and hailed a taxi. I quickly positioned myself across the street and kept my eyes on the windows of Munroe's building.

Third floor. A light turned on. And there was a fire escape on the front of the building, leading right to it.

I crossed the street and entered the front door. It was the usual setup for a non-doorman apartment building. The front door opened to a small inner foyer where the mailboxes were located. Beyond that was the security door, which was opened by a resident's key. I studied the mailboxes and there it was. J. Munroe—12. Figuring there were four apartments to a floor, that worked out right.

Now I knew where the blackmailer lived. And his apartment wasn't nearly as safe and secure as his photography studio.

With a plan forming in my mind, I went back to 29th Street, removed the shoe box and a pen from my backpack. I wrote on the inside bottom of the box: "Will comply. But I will need until Tuesday night." I kept the photos and his note.

I then used the tape to secure the box under the windowsill as before, only I made sure it was upside down. That way, if he checked to see if I'd gotten it, he'd know there was a message for him.

Then I went home.

I knew exactly what I was going to do.

# 31
## Martin

THE PRESENT

I visited New York a few times when I was in my twenties, so I wasn't unfamiliar with it. I never liked the city. Call me a wuss, but I find it intimidating. It's different from downtown Chicago. People say they can feel the energy of Manhattan and it's true. You're aware of it as soon as you step onto the streets. It's just that there's something about that energy I don't like. Never have. New York makes me feel edgy.

Carol and I shared a taxi and went straight from LaGuardia to St. Luke's-Roosevelt Hospital. We'd flown on the same plane, but didn't have seats together. That was fine with me. I like Carol, I still do, I really do, but I couldn't live with her again. And she feels the same way about me. The divorce wasn't nasty. Painful, sure, but we remained friends. Sort of. Hell, we have to.

We share a child.

When we saw our Gina, Carol started to cry and my heart nearly burst. I wanted to pound the wall and shout to the heavens, "Why did this happen?" Instead I simply held my daughter's hands and let her cry. She needed it.

Her jaw was wired shut, so she couldn't talk very well. Try talking without opening your mouth—you can speak by manipulating your tongue and lips—but it's very tiring business, not only for you but for the listener. She'll have to take her meals through a straw for over a month.

Her beautiful face was bruised. Not only by the large one cover-ing her left cheek, but also by the dark rings around her left eye.

Her body was also covered in cuts and abrasions.

She had apparently put up a vigorous fight.

That bastard.

If I could get my hands on him, I'd kill him. I really would. I'd beat his head in with a baseball bat. That always works.

The good thing, it turned out, was that she wasn't raped—but the guy had tried. The crime was interrupted before the deed was done. But that didn't make the ordeal any less traumatic for my dar-ling daughter.

We sat with Gina for an hour, and then she went to sleep. An In-dian doctor assured us that from a physical standpoint she'd be fine. He expected her to be released tomorrow or the following day. The jaw would heal in six to eight weeks and cause no permanent damage. With some physical therapy over the next few weeks, she'll be okay.

Her emotional wounds were a different story. Dr. Rahman out-lined a counseling and rehabilitation plan that Gina must follow. Ac-cording to him, many victims have found it extremely helpful. In time, he predicted, Gina would move on and put this terrible inci-dent behind her.

Bullshit. I knew better. Just look at my mom and how she re-acted to being sexually assaulted.

Then we met with NYPD Detective Ken Jordan in the hospital cafeteria. Carol and I hadn't eaten a thing and we were starving. Jor-dan, who wore plainclothes and a gun belt, had coffee. I was all set to berate him for not catching the black guy who was seen running away from my fallen daughter.

It turned out Detective Ken Jordan was black too.

The guy was in his late forties, I think. He started off explaining how the crime went down. It was Sunday night and Gina was out with some friends. It was a pleasant evening, so she decided to walk home along Riverside Park. It was 10:00 at night and normally this would have been a perfectly safe thing to do. A lot of people were still out and about. Still, wouldn't Gina have known better? What was she doing walking alone in the park at night?

The perpetrator simply approached her on the park sidewalk in the vicinity of West 75th Street and Riverside Drive. Gina said the man had a knife and forced her into the trees. There he beat her and started to do his business, but he was startled by two joggers who luckily appeared out of nowhere. The culprit grabbed her purse and ran. The joggers saw he'd left a white clump on the dark ground, went to investigate, found my daughter, and called the police.

"So you're personally gonna catch him, right?" I asked, pointing at the detective.

Jordan looked at me sideways. "I beg your pardon?"

"Well, he is black, right?"

"Sir, I'm not sure I know what that's supposed to mean. As a matter of fact, the perpetrator is white. Your daughter told me so."

Boy, did I feel foolish. I looked at Carol and back at him. "We were told a witness saw a black man running from the scene."

Jordan nodded. "The two joggers both thought he was black, and we were going on that until your daughter regained consciousness. She said he had a dark scarf covering his face. Perhaps that's why the witnesses thought he was black. She saw his eyes and the skin around it. He was definitely a white man."

"I see." I felt like crawling under the table. I hadn't meant anything racist by what I'd said, but I'm sure it came out that way.

"Do you have any leads?" Carol asked.

"Mr. and Mrs. Talbot—"

"We're not married," she said. "I'm Carol Wilton."

"We were married," I explained, but that was probably information I didn't need to add.

Jordan nodded. "Your daughter's case is very similar to some other assaults we're investigating. We believe it's the work of an individual who's done this more than once. What your daughter was able to tell me jibes with some of the details of the other cases. We think they're all related. In fact, your daughter knows one of the other victims—she attends Juilliard as well." He paused a second and then added, "In those crimes the sexual assault was completed. Gina was very lucky."

That didn't make me feel any better. "You're talking about a serial rapist."

He nodded. "Could be. We're not sure yet."

"So what do you want us to do?" I asked.

Jordan seemed surprised by that question. "Do? All you need to do is take care of your daughter. See her through this tough time."

Carol suppressed a sob and asked, "Should we plan to stay in New York for an extended period of time?"

"Not at all, depending on how Gina is cared for, that is. You two can go back to Chicago any time you want."

"Wait," I said, "you mean there's nothing we can do? I want this bastard caught."

"We do too, Mr. Talbot. And we'll catch him. Eventually he'll screw up and we'll get him."

It was mid-afternoon when Carol and I took a cab to our hotel, which was just a few blocks away. Hotel Empire on West 63rd Street was a decent two hundred dollar-a-night New York hotel, a reasonable rate for its prime location near Lincoln Center. Divested of bags, we could easily walk from the hotel to the hospital.

We checked in to separate rooms, of course.

Once I was alone, I found myself juggling an odd mixture of moods. I felt sorry for Gina and dreaded what she would have to go through to get better. I spent a few good minutes crying. The tears stopped when I realized how extremely angry I was. I was mad that it happened at all, mad at the bastard that did it, mad at the police for not catching him, and mad that I was helpless and couldn't do a thing about it.

I started to unpack and noticed my cell phone was still off. They made me turn it off on the airplane, and I didn't remember to turn it back on. I did so, and found a voice message waiting for me.

It was my new boss, Konnors. Oh, shit. I never told him I had to take an emergency trip to New York.

The call was short and sweet. Konnors said he'd already replaced me. He thanked me for wasting his time.

I phoned him back, waited a minute or two, and he answered. I explained what had happened to my daughter. He expressed sympathy, just as he had when I had to deal with Mom in the hospital. But he also said he had a job to do.

Konnors told me, "You seem like a nice guy and I'm sorry for all the bad stuff that's happening in your life, but I needed a guy last week. I can't afford to wait for you. Sorry, Mr. Talbot."

I told him he was insensitive, which was another example of me acting on impulse and saying the wrong thing without thinking first. I guess I burned that bridge.

Carol and I had planned to have some dinner together and then go see Gina again that evening. We could've gone back to the hospital after checking in, but a nurse suggested that Gina needed to rest. Too much excitement this soon was probably not a good idea. So there I was in my Manhattan hotel room and I had a couple of hours to kill.

And I thought—somewhere in the city was that shithead, Johnny Munroe.

If I only I knew someone in New York. A cop. A lawyer. Someone I could trust. I needed help if I was going to take on Munroe. I had very little money, so paying him was not only absurd, it was impossible. Should I go to the New York cops?

I sat and thought through the ramifications of doing so. I would have to tell them I was being extorted and then they'd want to know what Munroe was threatening to reveal. Cops don't have to keep anything secret. They can gab to their wives or friends. The media often sniffs out the sensational stories from talkative policemen. I rejected going down that avenue.

Then I glanced over at my open suitcase. My mom's 1959 diary was sitting in there, nestled between the folded clothes.

John Richardson. The FBI agent. Was he still alive? Was he still in New York? Would he remember my mother? If they were really sleeping together back then, then he'd be a total jerk if he'd forgotten about it.

On a whim, I called information and asked for the nonemergency number of the FBI's New York Field Office. Surprisingly, I got it. I dialed it, but didn't expect a live person to answer. A woman.

"FBI."

"Oh, hi, I'm trying to find the whereabouts of a former agent who used to work here in New York in the nineteen fifties. I'm a friend of the family."

"Hold on, please."

I was transferred to another department. Another woman answered. "Human Resources."

Again, I explained what I was after. She asked for the former employee's name, so I told her. I heard some typing and she said, "I'm not allowed to give out any contact information. If you would like to leave a message with us, we'll see to it that he gets it."

So he was alive.

After a moment's hesitation, I said it. "Tell him Judy Cooper's son called. My name is Martin Talbot." I gave her my cell phone number.

I hung up and picked up the diary. I suppose I should feel icky reading about my own mother's love life, but actually I found it fascinating. She was a very progressive young woman for her day.

When Mom mentioned the location of Richardson's apartment building, I wondered if there was any chance in hell that he still lived there. Most likely not. He could have gotten married, had kids, and moved to the suburbs or to Florida or to Timbuktu. It was a highly unlikely possibility that he was in New York.

I still wanted to see the building. In fact, I wanted to see all the locations my mother's mentioned in her diaries and walk in her footsteps. Were the East Side Diner and the Second Avenue Gym still there? Now that I didn't have to get back to Chicago by tomorrow,

I could stay a while. Carol had a job, so I could volunteer to hang around for Gina, and Carol could go on back. She probably wouldn't want to, but I could make the offer.

And then I'd find the time to explore Mom's haunts, as well as find a way to derail Johnny Munroe.

# 32
## Judy's Diary
### 1959

JULY 7, 1959

It's the wee early hours, around 2:00 a.m., and the Stiletto has struck back against the forces of greed, slimy blackmail, and revolting perversion!

Yesterday evening I went to 36th Street and 3rd Avenue, near Munroe's apartment building, dressed in civilian clothes. My Stiletto outfit was in my backpack and I looked like an ordinary college student trekking home from classes. I stopped at a pay phone and called Munroe's studio. He picked up and I immediately put the phone down. Good.

With lockpicks in hand, I stepped into the inner foyer of his building and easily gained entry through the security door. I went upstairs to the third floor and found the door marked "12." Luckily, no neighbors saw me. Once again, a lockpick got me in the door. He had a dead bolt on it along with the regular lock in the knob, so it took a little more time and effort to finally get inside. But I did.

Once I was there, I did a quick look around. The apartment reeked of tobacco smoke. The bedroom was a mess, clothes were scattered here and there, the bathroom was equally disgusting, and the living room appeared as if three bachelors lived there instead of one. The guy was a real slob at home.

I proceeded to make my preparations. First I closed all the window blinds. I straightened up the bedroom enough so I could walk around the bed. He had one of those barlike headboards, which would suit my purposes just fine. I laid out my tools—rope, a gag, and a pair of heavy wire cutters I'd borrowed from the gym. Then I donned my Stiletto outfit, mask and all, and waited. And waited. And waited.

It was around 11:30 p.m. when I heard Munroe's key in the door. I quickly moved to a position against the wall behind the door just as it opened. As soon as he was within reach, I grabbed the bastard by his greasy slick hair, pulled back his head, and pressed the stiletto against his neck.

"Don't make a sound, you creep," I said.

I scared the heck out of him. He immediately started shaking and whimpering, trying to say, "Don't hurt me, don't hurt me—"

"Shut up!" I said.

I kicked the door closed behind us, let go of his hair so that I could turn the dead bolt, and then marched him into the bedroom. As soon as we were in there, I whirled him around and gave him a solid right hook to the jaw. He fell back on the bed, dazed. In five minutes I had him securely tied down, his arms affixed to the headboard, his legs to the box springs.

The little guy wasn't so tough and cocky now.

"You took a lot of precautions to protect yourself at your studio, didn't you?" I said. "Big ol' bodyguard walking you to and from home. Plenty of metal gates on the windows and reinforced steel locks on the studio door. What is it you're hiding in there, Munroe? Why do you need so much security for a photography studio? Is it because you're a stinking, no-good blackmailer?"

Sweat was pouring from his forehead. "Look, I'm sorry. I didn't mean it. We can call the whole thing off. I—"

"Shut up, I'm not finished! Didn't you think someone like the Black Stiletto could find out where you live? Who do you think I am? Some loony girl who puts on a Halloween costume for fun and games? Are you really that stupid to think you could get away with blackmailing me? And where do you get the right to film me in private, in your dressing room, taking off my mask? I ought to slice off your nose right here just for doing that. Is that what you do to all your models? You secretly film them undressing? Are you some kind of pervert? What do you do with the pictures and film? Sell them? What, do you have a clientele of other perverts who buy that sort of thing?"

"Please . . . I . . ."

"Shut up!" I unbuckled his pants and pulled them down. He was wearing boxer shorts. Then I picked up the heavy-duty wire cutters.

"You think you're a real tough guy. Hanging out with the mob, blackmailing clients, strutting around like you're Napoleon."

"What are you gonna do with those?"

I worked the cutters in the air—snip, snip, snip—for effect. "Back on the ranch where I'm from, we'd take the troublesome bulls out of the pen and teach 'em a lesson." I was making this stuff up; I never lived on a ranch and had no experience with cattle or livestock. "My daddy taught me how to castrate 'em with a tool just like this. And believe me, them bulls are a lot bigger than what you have down there. So I figure these snippers will do the job nicely."

"*No!* What do you want? Please?"

He was terror stricken. Good. I had him where I wanted him.

Snip, snip, snip. I lowered the cutters down to his shorts, and then I made as if I was about to pull 'em down. I really hoped I wouldn't have to go that far! I had no desire to see that disgusting man's willy-willy.

"I'll do anything! What do you want, please?"

So I stopped and considered. "All right, for one thing, I want to know who has seen that film."

"No one! I swear!"

"You haven't shown it to your gangster buddies?"

"No!"

"Not your big fat bodyguard?"

"No!"

"You and I are the only ones who know the contents of that dressing room scene?"

"Yes. I swear. Please!"

Dear diary, you know how I can determine if someone is lying or not. He was too scared to lie. I believed him.

"Does anyone know it exists?"

He hesitated. Someone did.

"Who knows?"

"Franco DeLuca and a couple of his men. But they haven't seen it. I swear!"

"So you told him you have it and were negotiating a price for it?"

"Yeah, that's right."

"So you were gonna get ten grand from me, plus a lot of money from him? And maybe more from the media?"

He nodded furiously.

"How much was DeLuca gonna give you?"

"Ten grand."

"And you're absolutely positive no one has seen it? If you're lying, I can tell. I have super Black Stiletto powers that can see through liars. They're part of the special abilities I picked up when I came down from outer space."

His eyes grew wide then. I wanted to laugh, but I successfully stayed in character. I think he actually believed I was from Mars or something, ha ha.

"All right," I said. "I want all the copies of the film, any photos you developed from it, and the negatives. We're gonna make sure they're destroyed. Okay?"

He nodded. "Sure. But there's one thing."

"What?"

"I've already set a plan in motion. If anything happens to me, the film will automatically go to DeLuca—and the police."

I studied his eyes. The bastard was lying.

"Really?" I picked up the snippers again and pulled down his boxers. Ewww, his thing was all shriveled and ugly. I opened the cutters and placed the sharp edges right against his scrotum. It was sickening, but I tried not to let it show how gross it was for me. "Guess what. I can tell you're lying."

"No! Please no! Don't do it!"

I applied a little pressure. He could feel the blades.

He screamed.

"Shut up! Am I gonna have to gag you? Now, I'm gonna snip one off and see if you're willing to comply with my demands. If not, then, well, I'll have to snip off the other one."

"All right! I was lying! The film is safe at my studio!"

I pulled away the cutters. "There is no 'plan in motion' to send it to DeLuca or the police or anyone?"

"No!"

"Okay, now we're getting somewhere." I pulled up his boxer shorts and then his pants. "Right, so now you're gonna let me have the keys to your studio, and you're going to tell me exactly where all these things are kept. I'm gonna go over there while you rest nice and comfortable here. Once I find what I'm looking for, I'll come back and release you. Easy as that. You can live to shoot film another day."

At that moment I saw something dark cross his face. Something in his eyes.

*There was something at the studio he didn't want me to see.*

"Do we have a deal?" I asked.

He had no choice but to nod.

"Where are the keys?"

"Pants pocket."

I reached in and found them. There were a lot of keys on the ring. He explained that one opened the building door, and three were for locks on the studio door. Another key opened the steel window grates.

"And where are the negatives and film?"

He closed his eyes. He really, really didn't want to reveal this. "In . . . my safe."

"Where is it?"

"Under the desk in the office."

"Is it a combination safe?"

He nodded.

"Better give me the combination." I wrote it down as he recited it. "Okay, Jerry." I took the gag and tied it securely around his mouth. "Can you breathe all right? Comfy? Good. I'm gonna go over there now. Am I gonna run in to any of your gangster buddies?" He shook his head. "All right. You sit tight and I guess I'll be back in about an hour. Then we'll put this unfortunate business behind us, right?" He nodded. I patted his cheek, gathered my tools, and left his apartment. I was careful to lock the door on my way out.

By now it was after midnight. The streets had cleared of most pedestrians, but you know New York—there're always people out and about. Flitting from shadow to shadow, I made my way to Park Avenue South and 29th Street. I noticed the shoe box was no longer taped under the window sill. As nonchalantly as I could, I went to Munroe's building, unlocked the ground-floor door, and went inside. I'm pretty sure no one saw me. I went up the stairs to the second floor, and then proceeded to unlock the fortress that was his studio. I was in.

A single light was on near the desk, next to the phony dressing room.

The big man—the bodyguard who had walked with Munroe back to his apartment the other night—was sitting there. So much for Munroe telling the truth about running in to any of his gangster buddies. The bastard. The big guy was wearing trousers and an undershirt, rolls of fat protruding out of it like blubber.

The fella turned and his mouth dropped open. "What the—?" He must have thought I was Munroe coming in since I'd used the keys.

He stood and went for a gun holstered behind his back. By that time, the stiletto was in my hand and in throwing position. I let it go before he'd raised the pistol. The blade caught him in his upper arm, a little more to the left than I'd planned. Still, it did the trick. He yelped and dropped the gun. I quickly moved in and let him have a front kick to the face, which dropped him back on the desk. He actually broke the thing, crashing through the top, sending papers and envelopes and office supplies all over the place. He slammed on top of Munroe's safe, which, sure enough, was underneath. The fat guy rolled off and struggled to pull the stiletto out of his arm.

I helped him do it. Now the creep was bleeding like a slaughtered pig. He'd need medical attention soon, but he wouldn't die. It was a superficial wound.

However, I'd let down my guard. The guy wasn't a professional bodyguard for nothing. While on his back, he kicked my legs out from under me and I fell. The stiletto went flying and I didn't know where. For a guy his size, he moved fast. He was on his feet in no time, and he let loose with a monstrous kick to my abdomen. It took the breath right out of me. I saw twinkle spots as he kicked me again, this time in the rib cage. The pain was so bad I couldn't think. My reflexes must have gone on autopilot or whatever they call it, for I involuntarily rolled backward to avoid another blow.

The guy was a rhinoceros! He moved in, reached down and picked me up by my jacket collar. He pulled back a fist and let me have it, right in the face. I swear I thought he knocked some teeth out, but afterward I found he'd only busted my lip. Still dazed, I managed to wiggle out of his grasp. His hands were so big and my body so wiry that it was difficult for him to keep hold. This gave me time to back up, catch my breath, and think.

The animal rushed toward me, growling and huffing.

This is where Soichiro's training kicked in. I released an *ushiro geri*—a back kick—which struck the guy in the sternum. It would have disabled and possibly killed an ordinary man, but this fella was so fat and muscular that it barely fazed him. Still, he was surprised by my sudden rebound. I then performed a little hop to get in position for a powerful *mae geri*—front kick—which slammed him on the chin. This time he staggered. I kept going. One after another, I moved in with a series of serious *karate* moves—a roundhouse kick, a side kick, another front kick, and then got close enough to let him have three *seiken* fist attacks to the face. I broke his nose, demolished his front teeth, and darn near crushed his Adam's apple.

One final kick to the groin was the coup de grâce. It might be fighting a little dirty, but, hey, as Soichiro once said, in a real fight there are no rules.

Big Man collapsed like an imploded building. He lay on the floor like a beached whale, covered in blood and sweat. Yuck.

I tied his hands and legs and secured him to the sofa. If he woke up, he was probably strong enough to drag the sofa across the room, but there was no way he could walk with his legs hog-tied and arms behind his back. I did what I could to bandage the knife wound on his arm. He'd live. The parting touch was wrapping a gag around his mouth to keep him quiet. I found my stiletto way across the studio floor. I wiped the blood off on his trouser leg and then went to the bathroom to survey my own damage.

Dear diary, my stomach and side really hurt. I really prayed the bastard hadn't broken any ribs. I'd been through that before and it's not an amusement park ride. I looked in the mirror and gasped. Blood ran down my chin and out my nose. I washed my face to get a better look at the abrasions. They actually weren't too bad. My upper lip was split, but my teeth were intact and I'd have a beast of a bruise on my cheek. I found a washcloth and held it to my mouth for a few minutes to get the bleeding under control, and then I went back into the studio to focus on Munroe's safe. It was a big one.

At least he didn't lie about the combination. The safe opened right up and it was full of stuff—envelopes, little brown packages, and small film cans. The first thing I did was pull out the film cans. Each one was marked with a woman's name—"Mary," "Joanne," "Lisa," "Debbie." Curious, I opened one, took out the reel, and un-threaded a foot of film to look at the frames. They were 8mm, so it was tough to see what's on there. But in the rubble of the smashed desk there was a light box and a flat magnifying glass you could lay on top of it. Miraculously, they weren't broken. I switched on the light box, placed the film on it, and covered it with the magnifier.

It was footage of a woman with no clothes on. Of course it was!

I dug through the other cans until I finally found one marked, "B.S." Black Stiletto? I opened it, and there it was. My film footage. I recognized the opening scene when I laid it on the light box. I stuck it in my backpack and then rummaged through another set of cans with each girl's name and an additional "Neg." written on the labels. The negatives. I found mine, confirmed it was the correct one, and buried it in my pack. Just to make sure, I started going through the large flat envelopes, because they all contained eight-by-ten photographs.

Dear diary, I was shocked by what I found.

They were dirty pictures. I mean, *really* dirty. I'd seen my share of *Playboy* centerfolds and girlie magazines, but I had never ever seen anything like this. This was pornography, plain and simple. These were pictures of women doing things to themselves, men and women doing things, and women doing things to men. In explicit detail. They left nothing to the imagination.

I thought: wasn't this stuff illegal? I didn't know.

There was a ledger in the safe, so I pulled that out and looked at it. Inside Munroe had written names and mailing addresses of men all over the country. There were little code symbols by the names, probably indicating what kinds of pictures Munroe sent to them. Dollar figures were noted in columns by each customer, which I figured was what each buyer paid for Munroe's "products."

And then I found the worst. Oh my gosh, my dear, dear, diary, my heart stopped and I wanted to cry when I saw the pictures contained in a group of envelopes held together with a rubber band.

Children. Boys and girls, ages, I don't know—five or six all the way up to teenage. Doing horrible stuff with each other and with grown-ups.

This I knew was illegal. This was a crime against humanity. This was the lowest of the low.

Shaken, I sat in the chair by the desk. It took me a moment to calm down. I knew what I had to do. First I checked on Fat Guy to make sure he was still out cold. He was snoring heavily, so that was all right. Then I called John Richardson at home. Apparently I woke him up.

"Hello?"

"John, it's me."

He must have heard the tension in my voice. "Is . . . is something wrong?"

"Yes." I explained what I was doing, where I was, and what I'd found. When I told him about the ledger with the mailing addresses he said, "All right, that's a federal crime. He's mailing obscene material through the U.S. mail. The FBI can get involved in this."

"Are you gonna arrest Munroe?" I explained he was at his apartment, and that a bodyguard was tied up and unconscious on the floor of the studio.

"Unfortunately, it was breaking and entering," John said. "Everything you've found would be inadmissible in court."

"That's not right, John. There are children involved. This man needs to be put away for life!"

"I understand and I totally agree with you. But the law works the way it does. Let's think a minute."

"Hurry, John. I want to be out of here before Sleeping Beauty wakes up."

"Okay, listen to me carefully. Leave everything just as it is. Leave all the stuff from the safe out in the open, right there where you found it. The pictures, the films, everything."

"All right."

"But I want you to take two or three of the really bad photos— one or two with children and one with the adults—and take them back with you to Munroe's apartment."

"All right."

"When you leave the studio, just close the door and leave it unlocked. From a pay phone, I want you to call this number and report suspicion of transporting obscene materials through the mail, much of which involves exploitation of children." He gave me a phone number. "Got it?"

"Yeah."

"Then hurry back to Munroe. Leave the three photos you took from the studio somewhere visible near Munroe, out of his reach. Then, call the same number I told you and report that you've caught a pornographer who has been violating federal law by exploiting children and sending obscene material through the mail. He's tied up and ready for arrest. See, that way the feds will simply find all the evidence when they come to rescue your boy. Be sure to leave Munroe's apartment unlocked, too."

"I will. Can I tell 'em I'm the Black Stiletto?"

"Sure, I don't see why not."

"Might as well get a little credit for this, huh?"

"Yeah. That's quite a job you did."

"Thanks."

"Will I see you soon?"

"You betcha."

I hung up and did what I had to do. I stuck three of those horrible photos in my backpack and left the studio, making sure to keep the door slightly ajar. From a pay phone I made the first call. The operator wanted my name and all that, so I told her I was the Black Stiletto and hung up. It was another short trek the few blocks back to 36th Street. I used Munroe's key to get in downstairs, then ran up to the second-floor studio.

Munroe was where I'd left him. His eyes were wide with fear. He noticed my face and I could tell he knew how I'd received the fat lip.

"What's the matter, Jerry, are you surprised to see me? Did you think your friend Henry the Rhinoceros was gonna take care of me and save the day? Sorry, fella. It didn't work out that way. Okay, Jerry, I found the film and the negative. Are you sure this is all? These are the only copies?"

He nodded his head furiously.

"Good. Now I'm gonna make a phone call if you don't mind."

I picked up the receiver by his bed and dialed the FBI again. I gave the operator the news and location of Munroe's apartment. From the expression on Munroe's face, I could see he was upset that I wasn't keeping my end of our deal. After I hung up, I said, "Jerry, I'm not gonna let you go, not after seeing what I found in that safe of yours." I pulled out the repulsive photos and showed them to him. He started crying. I laid them on the edge of the bed.

"You're a bad, bad man, Jerry Munroe," I told him. "I trust I'll never hear from you again."

And then I left. I was home in a half hour.

Despite the fact that I found evidence of a truly vile crime, I feel good that I put an end to that vermin's so-called business.

Score another one for our side.

# 33
## *John*
### HOME DICTAPHONE RECORDING

Today is July 8, 1959.

It was in the news this morning how the Black Stiletto and the FBI busted a national mail-order pornography racket that included the exploitation of children. Very serious crimes. The pornographic photos and films of adults, well, we've seen all that before and it wouldn't have been a federal crime if the perpetrators hadn't sent it through the U.S. mail. It was the material with children that was disgusting. Jerry Munroe and his partner, "Big" Pete Romero, were arrested and held without bail. The pair has ties with the DeLuca crime family, and it's becoming clear the mob was behind the mail-order business. The Bureau is just now starting to look into whether DeLuca was aware of the child exploitation part of it. If so, it's possible we can bring down the entire house. The evidence is still coming in, but unfortunately it appears that Munroe and Romero were slipping in the child exploitation material with the other pornographic stuff of their own volition. In other words, they may have been using the mob's distribution channels for "straight" pornography to sell their own brand of sickness. The Bureau is bringing DeLuca in for questioning tomorrow.

Judy never told me how she got involved with Munroe. Perhaps she'll tell me the next time she pays a visit to my apartment.

Haggerty is angry that she's getting credit for the bust. He says it's the Bureau that made the arrests. He doesn't know she called me to report the crimes. I tried to tell him it was the Stiletto who alerted the Bureau about Munroe, but Haggerty won't hear of it. Once again, he asked me for a report on the progress of catching her. I'll tell him I've narrowed down the approximate geographical area of Manhattan where I believe the Stiletto resides—the East Village.

Judy still isn't aware that I know her name. I'm not sure how to proceed. She trusts me more and more every day, which is exactly what I want. I plan on visiting the diner again this week. In the meantime, I hope she comes by the apartment again soon.

# 34
# Judy's Diary
## 1959

JULY 13, 1959

I've been sore for days. It turns out I didn't have any broken ribs, thank goodness, but they were bruised like all get-out. Freddie made me wear one of those rib pad things you wrap around your torso. I'm still wearing it. I imagine it will take another week or so before the pain lessens. In the meantime I'll just rest and won't do anything too active, although supposedly exercise is good for it. As for my face, well, I've had busted lips before. That's healing fine, but the bruise on my face is nasty. I got a lot of comments about it from the guys at the gym. Some of 'em said they wanted to know who did it so they could go out and "beat his ass." Almost all the fellas at the gym love me. They know I'm pretty tough and can hold my own in the ring, but they still think of me as a helpless, defenseless girl. If they only knew, ha ha.

Of course, Mike Washington looked at me and grinned. "What happened to you?" he asked. I think it was the first time he ever smiled at me.

I gave him the same answer he gave me when I asked him about his face a while back. "Got into a bar fight."

He chuckled. "Guess you and me gotta stop drinkin'." Then he walked away.

Was that an olive branch? Was that his attempt at being nice for a change? I don't know. He still makes me uneasy.

Freddie put up one of the new American flags in the gym today. He's always had a flag on the wall, but they just made one with 49 stars on it—the new star is for Alaska. Now I hear they're going to admit Hawaii as a state, so they're just gonna have to turn around and make another flag with 50 stars. I guess that keeps all those Betsy Ross's busy.

Tonight Lucy and I are going to see *The Nun's Story* with Audrey Hepburn. But as soon as my ribs feel better, I'm paying John a visit. I miss his hands. And lips. And shoulders. And gosh, listen to me! I'm making myself blush.

JULY 19, 1959

Dear diary, I'm all flustered and angry and confused.

Today I went to the East Side Diner for lunch. Lucy was working, and I thought I'd just visit with her and have a sandwich or something. Well, when I got there, who do you think was sitting by himself in one of the booths?

John Richardson.

I froze in my tracks. Was this a coincidence? Or did he know?

Our eyes met and he silently acknowledged my entrance.

That answered my question. Well, I was furious. I turned around and walked out, not knowing what to think. I started back toward the gym with all sorts of thoughts running through my head. How did he find out who I was? He must know my name. Did he know where I live?

Before I'd gone a complete block, I turned around and went back. I decided to have it out with him. If he was going to play FBI agent with me, then we had some serious talking to do.

He was still sitting at the booth, calmly drinking a cup of coffee. A plate with the remains of his lunch sat in front of him. I sat across from him. "Sorry (I Ran All the Way Home)" by the Impalas was playing on the jukebox. I don't know why I remember dumb stuff like that.

"So you know," I said.

He nodded.

"What are you going to do?"

"Well, Judy—I can call you that now, can't I? I mean, it is your name." I didn't answer him. My eyes were burning holes through him. "Judy, don't be angry," he continued. "How could I go on seeing you the way we were? I didn't know your name. I didn't know anything about you. You were a woman wearing a mask who'd come into my apartment through the window. We'd make love and you'd leave. What kind of relationship is that?"

"You're an FBI agent. I had to be careful."

"You're right, and you know what? I'm supposed to have you arrested. It's one of my assignments. I'm supposed to track you down and put you behind bars. But I don't want to."

My heart was pounding in my chest. "Does anyone else know my name?"

"No. I haven't told a soul. Not yet, anyway."

"Not yet? You mean, you plan to?"

"Look, it's all I know. I don't even know where you live. Yet. And keep your voice down. You don't want to attract too much attention here, do you?"

I looked around the diner. No one was watching us, but Lucy saw me and came over to the table.

"Hey, honey, do you two know each other?"

"Um, yeah," I said. "John and I, we've been seeing a bit of each other."

"Really?" She was surprised. "How come you didn't say anything?" She addressed John and said, "No wonder you've been coming in here a lot."

Oh, so today wasn't the only time he'd come to the diner!

She asked me if I wanted anything to eat, but I was too upset to think about food. I asked for a cup of coffee and she went away, obviously sensing we were in the middle of a serious discussion. The record on the jukebox changed to "Dream Lover" by Bobby Darin. Oh geez!

"Look, Judy," he said, "maybe the Stiletto should just disappear."

"What?"

"You don't have to be her. She could just put away her costume and retire. It's a dangerous business anyway."

"What are you saying?"

"Well, then we could date each other. For real."

I was taken aback. "So in other words, you couldn't do that if I remain the Stiletto."

"I'm afraid I can't. I'm a federal agent. I have a responsibility to my job."

"Wait, is this some kind of ultimatum? If I give up the Stiletto, we can live happily ever after as lovers, but if I don't you'll have me arrested?"

"When you put it like that it sounds harsher than what I mean. I care about you, Judy. I don't want to see you in jail and I don't want to see you hurt. That bruise on your face—it's not becoming of a beautiful girl like you. If you stopped the vigilantism, I could tell my boss that I believe the Stiletto is either dead or left the city. And then you and me, well, we wouldn't have to hide."

I couldn't believe it. What kind of a choice was that? Give up the Black Stiletto and be his girlfriend, or don't give up the Stiletto and go to jail. And I thought I was starting to fall in love with this guy. Dear diary, I felt my heart tearing in two, right then and there.

"You would really have me arrested?" I asked. "Even after all we've—?"

He didn't answer. Instead he said, "I want to know the real Judy Cooper. And I'd keep your identity a secret for the rest of my life. No one would ever know."

I gritted my teeth. "How can you do this? This is some kind of blackmail or extortion, you know that, John? You're trying to use our shared intimacy against me. You think I'm gonna cave and fall for the strong, handsome government agent. If that's so, then you don't know the real Judy Cooper at all. You want to arrest me? Go ahead. Make the call right now. And I'll tell the world how you went to bed with me first. I'll say how you had no problem with that. Is that conduct becoming of an FBI agent? Are they gonna give you a medal for fucking the Black Stiletto and then putting her behind bars?"

He blinked. He was shocked by my use of the "F" word. I even shocked myself, but I was so mad I couldn't help it.

"Judy—"

"You want to arrest me? Then do it. Let's see if you're man enough." At that second, Lucy came back with my coffee. Before she put it down, I stood and walked out the door. I didn't look back. I'm sure there was an awkward moment between her and John. I didn't care. I'm sure Lucy will want to know all about it tomorrow and I'll find out what he said.

When I got back to the gym, I was ready for a fight. I needed to release some tension. I saw Mike Washington sparring with Jimmy in the ring. They both wore boxing gloves and face guards.

"Washington!" I shouted.

They looked up.

"You and me. Let's spar," I said. I went over to the bench, pulled off my shirt and trousers, revealing the leotard and tights I had on underneath. I grabbed a face mask and gloves, and climbed into the ring. I gave the gloves to Jimmy and told him to tie 'em on me. Washington's brow furrowed; he wasn't sure what this was all about. Jimmy removed his own gloves and did as I said. Then I was ready. I asked Jimmy to referee.

Washington shook his head. "I ain't gonna do this."

"What, are you a coward? I heard you were a big tough boxer. You went to prison for killing someone. You afraid to fight a girl?"

His eyes flared at the mention of prison.

"Weren't you part of the mob? Taking falls for the Mafia? I

wouldn't be surprised if you're involved in all that crime in Harlem. You know Carl Purdy? Is he a friend of yours?"

Something passed over his face when I said that. I'd hit a nerve. I don't know why I said it, it just came out. Whatever. It made him mad enough to go through with it.

Jimmy rang the bell. We came out dancing. I moved in quickly and struck him with a jab. He put up his hands to defend himself like a pro, but I managed to deliver an uppercut and another jab. He wasn't trying.

"Come on. Fight back!"

I hit him again and again, but Washington just took it or blocked my punches. This went on for a few minutes. I was the one getting the workout—he mostly stood in one place, only swiveling his body to face me when I danced around him. Finally, the bell rang.

"What's the matter, Washington?" I taunted. "Did prison kill your drive? Or are you up in Harlem shooting up heroin with Carl Purdy's gangsters?"

That did it. He raged across the ring at me and the bell hadn't rung for the second round. He slammed me with a roundhouse that knocked me to the floor. Everyone in the gym gasped. They couldn't believe what they'd seen.

Jimmy tried to step in. "Hey, let's calm down. Mike, that wasn't fair, man. I don't know what's going on here, but—"

By then I was on my feet. "Shut up, Jimmy. This is between him and me."

Washington and I started again, this time without the timing of a round. He jabbed, I crossed, he delivered a half uppercut, and I cross countered. Then it was a real fight. Anger drove us forward, but we were sufficiently trained to keep cool and box properly. Offense, defense, block, slip, a hook, a punch, cover-up, bob, weave, jab, jab, jab.

The blows became fiercer. I really wanted to knock the guy down. I could tell he wanted to hurt me.

Punch, duck, block, jab, uppercut, weave, jab, jab, jab.

Then a whistle blew loudly, echoing through the gym.

"Stop! Right now! Stop it!"

It was Freddie, of course. He climbed into the ring and got between Washington and me.

"What the hell is going on here? Mike? What's this all about?"

I answered for him. "I made him spar with me."

"It didn't look like sparring to me. What's the matter with you two?"

"Sorry, Freddie," Washington said, "I was just doin' what she wanted."

Freddie looked at me. I must have been a mess. There I was, half dressed, huffing and puffing, flushed with fury. He had rarely seen me in such a condition.

"Go shower, Judy," he said. "Cool off. Then stay upstairs. I'll talk to you later."

Great. Now Freddie was mad at me. I shoved my gloves at Jimmy, who untied them. I pulled off the face guard and dropped it at Freddie's feet. Then I stormed out of the ring and went to the stairwell. My shower wasn't in the regular locker room, which was for men only. I had to go upstairs to the apartment to "cool off."

It's now hours later and I've settled down. I don't know what came over me. When I was a child I had a nasty temper. I guess some of that boiled to the surface today. I've been avoiding Freddie, but eventually I'm sure he's going to sit down with me for a "fatherly" talk. Everything will be fine. I'll have to apologize to Washington and then we'll all go on as before.

But what about John? Will he really turn me in? And can I help it if I still have feelings for him? What if he's right? Should I retire the Stiletto? Could I live with myself?

He said he wanted to know the "real" Judy Cooper. I'm beginning to wonder if she exists.

# 35
# *Martin*

## THE PRESENT

Electing to stay with Gina as much as she could, Carol refused to go back to Chicago for the time being. I told her I'd be happy to stay— I didn't have a job waiting for me. Carol replied, "You can do what you want, Martin. I'm here for Gina."

I spent all of Tuesday morning at the hospital. Gina was in better spirits and it looked as if she would be released later in the day. We were waiting on her doctor to give her a final checkup and officially discharge her. I love my daughter dearly, and I would have stayed at her side as much as I could, but with Carol there fussing over her, I felt like a third wheel. I suppose it would have been different if Carol and I were still married. Or maybe not. So, when we heard Dr. Rahman would be delayed until nearly four o'clock, I asked the ladies if they'd mind if I went out. Through her wired jaw, Gina suggested I go to the Museum of Natural History. I'd been there before, but I replied that was a good idea. I promised to be back before she saw her doctor, and Carol had my cell phone number just in case. I think Carol was glad to be rid of me.

Needless to say, I didn't go to the museum. I was reasonably familiar with the subway system; buying a MetroCard and using public transportation would certainly save a fortune in cab rides. Armed with a handy MTA map, I could travel practically anywhere in the city quickly and efficiently. That was one good thing about New York.

Another improvement I noticed upon boarding the #1 train to Times Square, where I would transfer to the R train to go to the East Village, was that the trains were much newer and cleaner than they had been in the eighties when I last visited Manhattan. Back then it was downright creepy to ride the subway. At least it was for me, an out-of-towner. People who lived in the city didn't seem to mind what I thought was an intangible but ever-present atmosphere of impending violent crime. Call me a coward—I was uncomfortable with New York then, but I must say it seemed different now. With 42nd Street now the land of Disney and family entertainment instead of a mecca of porn shops and drug dealers, Manhattan was downright friendly.

Once I was downtown, I made my way to Second Avenue and 2nd Street. I didn't see the gym where my mom lived and worked— but in its place was Shapes, one of those chain gyms for women. I put my face up to the big plate-glass window to peer inside. Plenty of women were busy on treadmills and Nautilus equipment. Almost all of them gave me a dirty look. To them I was probably some pervert wanting a glimpse of hot babes in workout clothes. I moved away, somewhat disappointed. It would have been nice to see the place as it had been in the late fifties.

From there I walked north two blocks, and lo and behold, the East Side Diner was still there. I couldn't believe it. I'm sure it had had a facelift since the fifties; at least the signage was modern. The interior looked just as I imagined it, although it was possible the booths and counter stools had been reupholstered. A jukebox stood in the corner. I went to it and was convinced it was the same one my mother had loved. It sure looked like an antique. They had updated the playlist, of course; it had a bunch of songs not only from the fifties, but from the sixties and seventies, too. There was only one Elvis Presley single—"Heartbreak Hotel." Since the thing was all lit up, I figured it still worked; so I threw in a quarter and played the song in honor of my mother.

I sat in a booth, ordered a BLT on rye, and then called Woodlands to see how my mom was doing. She was unable to talk on the phone anymore, but I sure wish I could've told her where I was. The nurse I spoke to said she was doing fine. Mom was eating and sleeping well, and she seemed relatively calm and happy. Even though she wouldn't understand the message, I asked the nurse to tell my mom I was away, that I loved her, and that I'd see her soon.

As I ate my sandwich—which was darned good—I gazed at my surroundings. It was difficult to wrap my head around the fact that the diner was such a central part of Mom's life in New York. I wondered if Lucy was still alive. Should I try to look her up? Would anyone at the diner know? Would they remember Judy Cooper?

The two waitresses on duty were young. The cook behind the grill was black. I figured the odds weren't too good that I'd learn anything. Besides, it would be awkward to explain who I was. So I ate my lunch, paid, and went quietly on my way. Still, it was something of a transcendental experience to sit in a place so pivotal to the Black Stiletto's history. And no one knew about it but me.

And John Richardson.

If the FBI had indeed delivered my message to him, the man hadn't responded. There were no missed calls on my phone.

So I decided to take the bus up Third Avenue to 21st Street. That's where my mother had indicated his apartment building stood, if it was still there. From what I've read in the diary so far, it sounded like the relationship between Mom and Richardson didn't turn out too well. Nevertheless, I found myself drawn to check it out.

The building in question, between Second and Third, appeared to be pretty old, so I figured it was the same structure. Throwing caution to the wind, I went inside the inner foyer where the residents' mailboxes were located. One by one, I read the names until I came upon #502. And there it was: "J. Richardson."

*Holy mother of God!* What were the chances of that?

I pushed the call button for his apartment. After a moment, a voice came through the little speaker by the mailboxes.

"Yes? Who is it?"

His voice was raspy, like an old man's. "John Richardson?" I asked.

"Yes?"

"Are you the John Richardson who was with the FBI in the nineteen fifties?"

Hesitation.

"Mr. Richardson?"

"Yes. Yes, that's me."

"Mr. Richardson, my name is Martin Talbot. Did you get my message? I called the FBI's New York office yesterday. They were supposed to forward it to you."

Another pause. "Yes, I received it."

*Oh, wow. What now?*

"Well, what I said is true. I'm Judy Cooper's son. I'd like to talk to you. May I come up?"

Then there was an awfully long silence.

"Mr. Richardson?"

"Fifth floor." The inner door buzzed.

# 36
# *Judy's Diary*
## 1959

AUGUST 20, 1959

I've been in the dumps for a month, dear diary. The incident with John really gave me the blues. The only bright spot so far in the past couple of weeks is that a new Elvis record came out—"A Big Hunk o' Love." I love it, of course, but being heartsick and all kinda takes the thrill out of it. "Sea of Love" by Phil Phillips captures more of my mood, but the lyrics make me sad. "There Goes My Baby" by The Drifters is also right on target.

As you can see, I haven't been doing much but listening to the radio and playing records. Actually, you know what record hits my mood right on the button? Freddie bought a new album by the jazz artist Miles Davis. It's called *Kind of Blue* and it's the talk of the town. It's so melancholy and dreamy at the same time. What is it about Negro musicians that give them the ability to bring out that emotion so well? I've heard a lot of those jazz musicians use heroin. I don't know if it's true, but maybe that's why the music is so painfully beautiful. You can feel the hurt in it.

Other than sitting around and listening to music, I work in the gym, have lessons with Soichiro, and visit Lucy and Peter. They still haven't set the date for their wedding, but it'll probably be next spring. She asked me to be her maid of honor. I told her I'd treasure it, but deep down I'm kinda sad. I'd like to be in love and have a steady beau, but it just hasn't worked out that way so far, has it?

As expected, Lucy wanted to know all about John. I told her I'd met him at the diner one day when she wasn't working. I hate to tell fibs, but it's a little one. I said we went out a couple of times but we didn't hit it off. She couldn't understand why. "He's so handsome in that suit and hat of his," she said. That he is. "And he's an FBI agent! How romantic!" I guess that's true. Anyway, I told her to forget it. If it means anything, he hasn't come back to the diner since that day. And he hasn't sent any feds to arrest me. Maybe my outburst made him think twice about it. I don't know and I don't care.

Well, I do care, but I pretend not to.

I went out twice as the Black Stiletto. Maybe I was looking for trouble, but I didn't find any. It's been a hot summer, and I guess the crooks are trying to stay cool. I've been reading, however, that there are more heroin deaths occurring in the city, mostly in Harlem. I'm considering going after Carl Purdy and his organization. Even if it is too big for me, like John said, it would be worth a try. But then again, it'd be like going after DeLuca's family. An impossible task.

One thing I've done to augment my Stiletto activities is buy a camera. With that I can document crimes in progress or use it for surveillance. It's a new Kodak Brownie Starmatic and it's automatic. I can also adjust the exposure to compensate for poor lighting if I want to. The number 127 film is a little high priced, if you ask me, but I like the camera and it fits snugly in my backpack when I want to go places. So far I've taken pictures at the gym to test it out. A lot of the guys want copies for laughs.

Time to go see Soichiro.

LATER

Something terrible has happened, dear diary! Oh my sweet God, oh my Lord, Soichiro's dead! I can't believe it! I am just devastated!

I can't stop crying. I'm in my room with a bottle of bourbon and I'm slowly getting drunk. This is the most terrible day.

This afternoon I went to Studio Tokyo for my lesson, as planned. But Christopher Street was blocked by fire trucks and police cars. A building was on fire. A large crowd of people stood on the street and sidewalks, gawking behind sawhorse barricades. Black smoke billowed into the air, but at first I couldn't tell what building was aflame. Then I suddenly got one of my danger alerts that start at the base of the spine and shoot up to my neck. I knew that could mean only one thing. I feared the worst, so I forcefully made my way closer. After some pushing and shoving, I eventually got right up to the barricade.

Yes, it was the building where Studio Tokyo was located—and it appeared that it was only the second floor that was on fire. The pizzeria on the ground floor seemed okay, but of course there was going to be some damage to it. The apartments above the studio were also gonna be affected—but from the looks of it, Studio Tokyo was demolished.

I shouted to a nearby cop. "What happened? I go to school at that studio!" I don't think my words registered, 'cause all he said was, "Keep back, keep back."

"Where is Soichiro? Where is the owner?" I cried.

The policeman ignored me. A group of firemen held a hose and blasted water at the second-floor windows, which were broken out. A few brave firefighters went in the ground-floor door, prepared to battle the flames from the inside.

I felt someone tap my shoulder. I turned to see Isuzu beside me. Tears ran down her face.

"Isuzu! Where's your father?" I asked.

She could barely speak. I had to ask her again.

"Inside," she answered.

My heart burst. I felt so helpless standing outside. I wanted to rush in with the firemen and look for my *sensei*, my teacher, my friend.

"I heard you say you are a student there," Isuzu said.

"Yes, I am." I put my arm around her. "I know we've never met but I know who you are. My name is Judy."

She nodded. "My father spoke of you. He says you are his favorite—" And then she started bawling, her head buried in my chest. I don't think she knows I'm the Black Stiletto. I'm sure Soichiro would never have told her. What does she remember about that night when I rescued her? Probably not much.

We stood there and waited while the firemen did their work. I prayed and prayed for a miracle, but it didn't happen.

After a while, the firemen rolled out a gurney with a body bag on it.

Soichiro was dead.

It was then that my acute sense of hearing picked up a conversation between the firemen. The word "arson" was said a few times, along with "firebomb" and "homicide."

So it was murder.

And I was certain I knew who was responsible.

# 37
## Judy's Diary
### 1959

SEPTEMBER 10, 1959

It's 3:00 in the morning, I'm back in my apartment, and I'm lucky to be alive, dear diary. The Black Stiletto had quite an adventure tonight.

Carl Purdy lives in a brownstone, painted white, on West 130th Street, between 7th and Lenox Avenues. That seems to be a relatively affluent area in Harlem. Purdy's home is surprisingly pretty, I guess, not what I expected. Apparently he lives there with a wife and children. It's well guarded, though, and I don't think there's any way I could ever get in there. There are no buildings butting up against it, so he's got plenty of space. A wall surrounds the property on every side except the front. He's got men stationed all around.

I had gone out as the Stiletto to do my homework. What was the best way to get back at the gangster? As I studied his building from the shadows across the street, I realized I had to think of something else.

Almost on cue, Purdy and a couple of bodyguards came out of the house. A black Cadillac with fins on the back end pulled up and the men got inside. I desperately wanted to follow them; but there was no way I could grab a nonexistent taxi in the middle of the street, not to mention the fact that I was dressed as the Stiletto. But just before the car took off, a young Negro came out of the building and approached the passenger side of the car. He leaned in to talk to Purdy.

Then the Cadillac drove away, leaving the newcomer on the sidewalk.

I recognized him. He was the teenager Sonny, the cocky leader of that young street gang I encountered the night I busted up Purdy's bar, Good Spirits. So it didn't take long for him to be recruited into Purdy's organization. He was probably a low-level gofer who ran errands for the boss and other superiors. Sonny started walking east toward Lenox Avenue. If my intuition wasn't mistaken, I figured he'd just been given a task by the man himself. So I followed him.

There were more pedestrians out and about; it wasn't very late, maybe 11:30 or so. It was difficult flitting between dark alcoves without being seen, but I must have done all right. I heard no cries of, "Look, there's the Black Stiletto!" My outfit blended in with the night.

Sonny crossed 5th Avenue and then turned south, walking on the east side of the road. The avenue was more exposed, and I was reluctant to continue the pursuit. I huddled by a group of trash cans on the northeast corner of 5th and 130th and watched my prey. For some reason, at that point I noticed all the closed beauty shops on 5th Avenue. Now that I think of it, it seemed as if there was at least one beauty shop on every block of major streets in Harlem. Just about all Negro women straightened their hair. I know it's supposed to be a tedious and uncomfortable process because they have to use hot irons and chemicals that sometimes burn the scalp. Do they do it because they want to feel more "white"?

Sonny turned on East 129th Street, heading toward Madison Ave. I looked up to evaluate the risk of crossing 5th—the traffic was moderately heavy, and there were plenty of people on both sides.

*Aw, heck*, I thought. I just stood and darted across the avenue on a diagonal, dodging the cars and taxis. Someone honked at me. Pedestrians turned to look, but I quickly disappeared into the shadows of 129th. I crouched on the stoop of a brownstone, fingers crossed that no one had recognized me as the Stiletto. After a minute, I felt it was safe to keep going. I peered around the stoop's short wall and saw Sonny halfway down the block. In the dark he was just a silhouette, but my sharp eyesight picked him up.

He stopped and went inside a brownstone located halfway between 5th and Madison. I scooted across and down the street to get a better view of the place. It was a fairly decrepit five-story building with no fire escape in front. Lights were on in all the windows, and there were small barred terraces attached to those on higher floors. To get inside, I'd have to find a fire escape in the back of the building, which wasn't a pleasant notion. After creeping through the last Harlem alley, I swore I'd try to avoid doing that again.

The brownstone next door, however, did have a fire escape leading all the way to the roof. If I climbed up there and crossed over to Sonny's building, it shouldn't be too difficult lowering myself onto the terrace of a fifth-floor window. So that's what I did. Using my grappling hook and rope, I caught and pulled down the rung ladder from the neighboring fire escape and scampered up. I don't think the building was inhabited.

Once I was on the roof, I crossed over and leaned over the edge for a bird's-eye view of the fifth-floor terrace. A potted plant sat against the bars and light streamed out from inside. I heard music. The window was open! Actually I wasn't surprised, since it was a warm September night. It was about a ten-foot drop from the roof to the terrace. I could have jumped, but I wasn't sure about the terrace's stability. It looked safe to stand on, but not sturdy enough for the sudden impact of weight. Lacking a better plan, I secured the grappling hook on the edge of the roof and dropped a bit of rope to the terrace. The shimmy down took a few seconds. I decided to leave the rope and hook in place, and boy, am I glad I did.

The bedroom inside was empty. I climbed in the window and stood in a room that contained a bed, a dresser, and a radio that was tuned to WLIB, a station that catered to colored audiences.

The place looked just like the bedrooms that were in the 131st Street bordello I busted. I was sure I was in another of Purdy's dens of iniquity. The room smelled like an unmistakably familiar mixture of perfume and sweat.

I crept across to the door, which was ajar. Once again, I heard male and female voices floating up and down the floors, some of them talking and laughing, others in the act of you-know-what. To tell the truth, I really didn't want to be there. I'm still not sure why I thought I needed to go inside the building. I suppose I just wanted to find out what Purdy was up to. Seeing that teenager Sonny was also a motivation. I didn't like it that a teenager who probably wasn't yet 18 years old was now working with criminals.

Then I heard a woman scream. She shouted "No, no, no!" and a man hollered, "Shut up!" My mother-animal instincts kicked in, so I burst out of the room and ran in the direction of the voices. They were a floor below. I skirted down the stairs and was confronted by two Negro women standing outside a closed bedroom door. They shrieked when they saw me. I figured they were prostitutes, since they were dressed only in bathrobes. Before I showed up, I think they were concerned about what was going on behind the closed door.

"Out of the way!" I said, and pushed them aside. The woman's protests continued inside the room, so I turned the knob. Locked. Not letting that stop me, I stepped back and kicked the door in.

A colored man stood over a woman who was on the bed. In his hand was a recently used syringe. His jaw dropped in surprise. Before he could react, I moved forward and delivered a *tobi geri*—a jump kick—which, in hindsight, probably wasn't the best choice of maneuver. I ended up knocking the man on top of the woman. He dropped the syringe, though. I landed smoothly on my feet, reached for him, pulled him up, and gave him a powerful punch to the nose. He plummeted to his knees, grabbing my legs as he did so. I attempted to slam my elbows on his shoulders, but he managed to topple me midstrike. I fell on my back—hard. Before he could stand and attack, I performed a back roll, legs over head, and brought myself to standing position. By then he was coming at me with his fists. I blocked, parried, and smashed my *ippon ken*—one-finger fist—into his abdomen. That took the fight out of him for a second, so I pulled back and gave him an all-American roundhouse to the center of his face. He went down like a sack of potatoes.

I quickly went to the girl on the bed. Her bathrobe had come open, so I tugged it closed and then examined her face.

She was Ruby, one of the girls I'd met before. She was back doing the same old thing. Hadn't she learned something after her arrest? I guess she never made it through rehabilitation. Maybe this was the only life she knew. My heart bled for her.

I gently slapped her cheeks. She was pretty doped up. "Ruby? Ruby, can you hear me?"

She looked at me and her eyes widened. "You!"

"Yeah, it's me again. Why are you here, Ruby? You had a chance to get out and now you're back."

Tears welled in her eyes and her voice slurred. "I can't stop it. I need the fix. I gotta have the fix. It's the only way I can get it."

"What about the others I met? Angela? Sheila?"

She blinked and looked even more disoriented. "Angela dead. She OD'd. Sheila, I don't know, she stay away."

"Ruby, you could stay away, too, but your heart has to be in it. This life is gonna kill you if you don't do something about it." I don't know if she heard me.

By then I heard heavy footsteps running up the stairs. Company was coming. Since my only exit was blocked, I prepared for a scuffle. I turned just in time to see two colored men enter, one after the other. I immediately went into defensive mode, blocking blows from both sides. The room was just too small for me to maneuver properly; they had me at a disadvantage. One guy knocked me against the wall and started to pummel me. Then the other one joined in. I could barely block the blows.

"Stop!"

The booming voice came from the bedroom door. The men kept hitting me. I managed to ram my knee in a groin, causing the owner to back away, double over, and tumble to the floor.

"I said stop!"

I looked toward the voice, and there was Carl Purdy, pointing a gun at me. The other man stopped hitting me and turned to face his boss. At least three other men stood behind Purdy in the hallway.

*Oh my gosh, dear diary, one of them was Mike Washington!*

Purdy stepped aside and let them enter the room. "Take her to the basement," he ordered. "We'll deal with her there." To me he said, "Don't try anything or I'll just shoot you right now."

No one moved for a moment. Then, Sonny wormed his way into the room and helped Ruby off the bed. She was in tears and was moaning something awful. The poor girl collapsed to her knees and threw up on the floor.

"Goddammit! Get her upstairs to her room," Purdy commanded.

By now Ruby had passed out, so Sonny picked her up in his arms—she was so thin she probably weighed nearly nothing—and carried her out.

I knew if I didn't do something then and there, they would kill me. Washington and another guy came in the room to grab me. They each took an arm and marched me out toward the stairs. The gun still trained at me, Purdy and another guy strode behind us. As soon as we were standing at the top of the stairs, I resisted taking the first step. Washington and the other guy pulled on my arms as they started to descend. I quickly raised my leg and kicked the man on my right as hard as I could. I then turned, clasped Washington's arm, and threw him over my shoulder with a basic, never-fail *judo* maneuver. Both men tumbled down the stairs. Then, with lightning-fast precision, I swung around, ducked, and bull-rammed Purdy in the midsection, beneath his gun arm. The firearm went off and he dropped it as we crashed into the other guy behind him. All three of us crumpled in a heap. Whereas the men reflexively grappled with me there on the hallway floor, I was dead set on getting the heck out of that building. I leaped to my feet—my left boot smashing into Purdy's chest while doing so—and ran around the staircase to the steps leading up to the 5th floor.

"Get her!" Purdy shouted.

All this time the women were screaming and crying. I pushed past them and took three steps at once until I was on the top level. I heard the men scrambling to chase after me, but by then I was in the original bedroom. I wasn't alone.

Sonny stood bent over Ruby, who was sprawled out unconscious on the bed. Our eyes met and I could see he was concerned about the girl.

"She's not breathing," he said.

I almost stopped, but I knew I couldn't help her. Not then. As I started to slip out the window, he said, "She my sister."

I kept going. Outside on the terrace, I tugged on the rope to make sure the hook was snug, and then I climbed hand over hand to the roof. Just before I got there, one of the men slithered out the window in pursuit. Purdy leaned his head out behind him. "Get that bitch!"

Well, dear diary, I'm faster than they are and my clothing is dark. Up on those roofs I'm practically invisible. The rooftop levels along the street varied in height, but they were close enough that I didn't have to do any major climbing or jumping. I was all the way to 5th Avenue in less than a minute. I picked the closest fire escape connected to the top of a building, threw my leg over the edge, and ran down the steps until I was ten feet above the sidewalk. Rather than wasting time lowering the rung ladder, I jumped. Landing lightly on my feet, I immediately took off across 5th Avenue, darting in and out of traffic, and disappeared into the blackness.

# 38
## Martin

### THE PRESENT

When John Richardson opened his apartment door, I saw a tall, thin, good-looking elderly gentleman with white hair and blue eyes. He reminded me a little of James Stewart in his later years, except that Richardson had a much harder, no-nonsense demeanor. He was dressed casually in black trousers and a flannel shirt. It was difficult to guess his age. He was certainly older than my mom.

He looked me up and down and then held out his palm. "John Richardson." The voice was raspy but strong.

"I appreciate you seeing me," I said as I shook his hand. "Martin Talbot."

He held the door open wider so I could enter.

"Excuse the clutter. I've become less organized in my old age."

The apartment wasn't messy at all. Much of the furniture was arranged as my mom had described it, although I'm sure a lot of it had been replaced and updated since the fifties. The desk against the far wall, however, may have been the same. A computer dominated the top, and I doubted he still had a Dictaphone. I was dying to examine the many framed family photographs placed around the room, but I refrained.

"Can I get you anything? Coffee? Tea?"

Since I'd just eaten and had a huge cup of coffee already, I politely declined. He gestured to the sofa and waited for me to sit. Then he sat in a comfy chair at a right angle to the sofa. I suddenly found myself tongue-tied. He broke the ice for me.

"I was surprised to get your message. I wasn't sure how to respond, or even if I should."

"I can understand that."

"I have to ask, is Judy—is your mother—doing all right?"

At that moment I realized I hadn't thought this through, but I didn't see any harm in telling him the truth.

"Yes and no," I said. "She's alive and in relatively good health, but she has a serious case of Alzheimer's. Her memories are gone. She has the mind of a child. She lives in a nursing home."

"I'm sorry to hear that." He looked away, toward the bedroom. After a moment he turned back to me and asked, "How in the world did you find out about me?"

"My mother left behind some diaries. You play a large part in one of them."

Then he smiled. "I can imagine. So you've known for a long time that your mother was the Black Stiletto?"

"Not really. She kept it a secret my entire life. I just found out recently. And I want to keep her secret safe."

He nodded.

"I appreciate it that you've done the same," I said.

"It's the least I could do," he answered. He squinted and studied my face. "You know, I can see a resemblance. You have her eyes."

I shook my head. "I don't think I look like my mom at all. I'm short and pudgy, and she was tall and gorgeous."

"That she was. But I can tell you're her son. Perhaps it's the shape of your face. I know, because I've never forgotten hers."

That prompted another awkward moment of silence. I looked around the living room and asked, "I'm astonished that you're still here. Have you lived in this apartment all this time?"

"No. I got married in nineteen sixty-four. My wife and I moved to New Rochelle and raised two children, a boy and a girl. They're grown now. I lost my wife to cancer nearly ten years ago."

"Oh, I'm sorry."

"I kept the apartment, though. I own it outright. I knew it was a valuable asset, so I never sold it. My son Daniel lived here for many years. After my wife died, I couldn't stay in our house in New Rochelle. I sold it and moved back to the city. Manhattan's not the best place for an eighty-three-year-old man like me, but my health is good. I can still get around."

"Well, sir, you look remarkable for eighty-three. Congratulations."

"Thank you." He lightly knocked the wooden arm on his chair. "So, how can I help you, Martin? Why did you want to meet me? Was it just curiosity?"

"No. Actually, I came for some advice. I want to keep my mother's secret. Well, there's someone here in New York who's threatening to upset the apple cart."

I proceeded to tell him about Johnny Munroe, his father Jerry, the film, and the extortion scheme. When I was done, Richardson nodded.

"I know all about that film and Jerry Munroe. I was there when it went down. Jerry Munroe was a scumbag. I'm not surprised he kept a copy of that film hidden. I just wonder why he never did anything with it before now. Is he still alive?"

"No. His son Johnny said he found it in his dad's safety deposit box."

"That's puzzling. How long ago did he die?"

"I don't know."

"Well, the world's a better place without him. He was a child pornographer, you know. A real shit."

"So I've read. He served time in prison, right?"

"That he did. I think he served twenty years or so and got paroled. I don't know what he did with himself when he got out. I didn't know he had a son, or a wife, for that matter. How old is the son?"

"I don't know. From the looks of him on TV, he's maybe a little older than me."

"Must've been born before Munroe's arrest. It's ironic the father tried to extort your mother and now the son is doing the same to you."

"Mr. Richardson, as you can understand, I can't go to the police or the FBI. My mother's secret would come out if I did. Do you have any suggestions on how to stop this guy? I don't have the money to pay him off."

"You wouldn't even want to try. Extortion is a never-ending game. Once you paid him, he'd simply ask for more. And more. And more. That's the way it works. No, you have to eliminate the threat at the get-go."

"Can you help me do that?"

Richardson firmly grasped the arms of the chair, slowly stood, and then went to the kitchen. "Would you like some water?" he asked as he poured himself a glass.

"No, thanks."

He returned and set his water on a coffee table in front of us.

"Martin," he said, "your mother and I were . . . friends. But we lost touch and I never heard from her again. But I never forgot her, even after I was married."

I could tell I'd touched something deep within the man's spirit. It was obvious my mother's memory was a source of pain for him. I cleared my throat and said, "I'll understand if you'd rather not—"

He held up a hand. "No, I want to help. I owe your mother that much." Richardson leaned back in his chair and rubbed his chin. "You have Johnny Munroe's contact information, right?"

I nodded.

"And you think you can get him to meet you somewhere?"

"I'm sure of it."

"Do you think you could sit across from him in a public place and put him on the spot?"

"What do you mean?"

"Confront him. Accuse him of extortion."

"Sure, if that's what it takes."

"We'd need a public place where everyone feels comfortable."

"Like, over coffee?"

"That'd work."

The thought came to me quickly. "I know just the place, and so do you, Mr. Richardson."

He quickly figured it out, paused, and smiled. "The diner." He shook his head slightly and said, "I haven't been there in years."

"I saw it for the first time today myself. So will that work or not?"

The former FBI man considered it carefully and finally said, "It'll do." Then he leaned forward again. "All right. Here's the plan."

# 39
## Judy's Diary
### 1959

Mike Washington was missing in action from the gym until today. He walked in with a slight limp, probably due to taking that tumble down the stairs the other night. After he came out of the locker room, dressed for a workout, I asked, "You all right, Mike? You're limping."

He glared at me and said, "It's nothin'."

Gosh, I wonder if he knows about me. Surely not. How could he?

At least now I know why my danger senses go haywire when I'm around him. He emanates the lifestyle he's leading up in Harlem, working with Purdy and the Negro mob. I knew I should warn Freddie, but first I wanted more information.

It was cleaning day at the gym, a duty that fell on me. Washington had a regular workout routine—after using the wall pulleys, he'd box the speed bag and then spend time with the heavy bags. As soon as he started the pulleys, I knew I had a good half hour to "clean" the locker room. I had a little sandwich board I always put on the floor in front of the locker room door that said, "Caution—Cleaning in Progress." That alerted the men that a woman was inside. Only rarely was I interrupted by a guy wanting to shower and get dressed, so I took my chance.

Gym patrons check out a locker key at the front desk when they enter, or they rent one from us as part of their dues. Washington always checked out one and I knew which was his. With one of my Stiletto lockpicks, I easily unlocked the door and opened it. His street clothes were in a pile inside. I went through the pants and found his wallet. It was stuffed with cash. I didn't count it, but there was at least $200 in there. There was a state ID, no driver's license, and a business card. It was identical to the previous one I'd picked up at the Good Spirits bar—an advertisement for Harlem Delight, only this time the address was the newer establishment on East 129th Street.

That confirmed what I already knew. I quickly put everything back the way I found it, closed the locker door, and made sure it was locked. Then I hurried through actually cleaning the locker room to get the task out of the way.

Wayne and Corky, a couple of the regular guys, were waiting for me when I came out.

"'Bout time you finished in there, Judy!"

"Yeah, Corky has to take a dump!"

"Wanna wash my back while I shower, Judy?"

Har har har. They all talk like that around me. It's all in good fun; they don't mean anything by it. Everybody there practically treats me like one of the boys—except Washington.

I found Freddie at the front desk. Making sure no one was within hearing distance, I said, "Freddie, I have some bad news."

"What's that?"

"Mike Washington is involved with Harlem gangsters that deal narcotics and run prostitution houses."

"What?"

I told him how the Stiletto has been investigating the Harlem kingpin, Carl Purdy, and that I encountered Washington at the bordello the other night.

Freddie was shocked. "He can mess up his parole," he said.

"I'll say. And go straight back to jail."

"I can't believe it."

"Believe it, Freddie. No wonder I've been getting a bad feeling from him all this time."

He looked uneasy. "I don't see how I can ask him about it, Judy. I mean, I can't just go over there and accuse him. I can't tell him you told me."

"No, you can't."

"It would reveal how you know."

"That's right."

Freddie was silent for a moment. I could see he was mighty disappointed in his friend. "It just goes to show you never know someone like you think," he said. "So what do we do?"

I put my hand on his shoulder. "Try not to worry. Let's just act like nothing's wrong. We'll keep an eye on him. And so will the Stiletto."

"Judy, are you sure you know what you're doing? Those are dangerous people."

"I'll take care of it, Freddie. I just have to figure out how I'm gonna do it. But I will."


Freddie let me take off work for a while when Washington finished his workout. After the guy showered and dressed, he left the gym as if nothing was different. I followed him, in street clothes, of course, 'cause it was broad daylight. I did wrap a scarf around my head and wore sunglasses. I felt like Mata Hari, ha ha.

He walked through the East Village toward Astor Place and went down the subway steps to board the uptown East Side #6. I waited a few moments to make sure he was through the turnstile, and then I descended the steps to the station. A token got me on the platform. I quickly looked left and right and spotted Washington moving toward the southern end to board the back of the train. I stayed where I was but I backed against the wall in a huddle with other passengers so he wouldn't see me.

The train arrived after a few minutes. I watched Washington get on, and then I did. We were a car apart. Instead of sitting, I stood holding a pole and looked straight through the windows of the car between us. I could barely see him sitting on a bench. I figured he was going to Harlem—I'd never ridden the subway that far. The #6 train is a local, so it stops at every station. It would take a while to get all the way uptown. He never changed to an express.

The train became less crowded the farther uptown we went. Eventually we were past 86th Street. Then 96th, 103rd, 110th. Washington finally stood and stepped off the train at 125th Street. So did I.

Once again, I was struck by the shortage of white people. I must have really stuck out. Colored men and women gazed at me like I was the odd man out. I suppose that might have intimidated most white folks, but not me. I don't have a problem with it, never have and never will. We're all just people, for goodness sakes.

Washington went up the stairs to the street. I purposefully stopped at the station window to buy tokens in order to get a few steps ahead. Then, I scooted up the stairs and came face to face with—

Mike Washington.

"What you doin' followin' me?" he growled.

That scared the living daylights out of me. I was flustered.

"Uh, Mike! Hi! Fancy meeting you h—"

"Cut the crap, Judy, why you followin' me?"

"I . . . I'm not following you, Mike. I'm on my way to a thrift shop up here. I heard they have some good bargains on clothes." I knew it was lame when I said it.

"You gotta be kiddin' me. Did Freddie put you up to this?"

"Freddie? No! Mike, I wasn't following you."

"Go home, Judy. You ain't safe here."

"Mike, I—"

"Get outta here. You gonna mess everything up. Get back on the train and go home. This is Harlem. You don't belong here." And he turned and walked away.

I felt like a fool. Other people stared at me as they moved past.

Then it struck me. *You're gonna mess everything up.* What did he mean by that?

Puzzled and frustrated with myself, I boarded the downtown express train and went back to the East Village. To tell the truth, I don't think I'm any safer there than in Harlem.

# 40
## John
### Home Dictaphone Recording

Today is September 28, 1959.

My informant confirmed that Purdy gets the heroin in shipments from France. A Corsican syndicate is responsible. It's believed they get it from a region overlapping the East Asian countries of Burma, Laos, Thailand, and Vietnam. The Bureau calls this area the "Golden Triangle," because it's shaped like one. The opium plants are cultivated and processed into heroin in East Asia and then smuggled into Corsica by sea or air. It comes to America almost always by ship, hidden in everyday items such as furniture, automobiles, food crates, and the like. The traffickers constantly vary the methods of transport so that no pattern is detected.

It's also clear the Italian Cosa Nostra vies for the same product and is developing its own channels for smuggling the drugs into the country. However, their desire to do business with the Corsicans puts them in constant conflict with the Negro mob. We're all prepared for a blood bath sooner rather than later.

The good news is the informant believes a major heroin shipment is coming from France in November, but we don't know where the delivery will be yet. It's supposed to be such a large quantity that Purdy himself is handling the details rather than passing it off to lower-level lieutenants. I told the informant it's his top priority to find out the exact date, time, and location. It would be a coup to hit both the Negroes and the Corsicans at the same time.

As far as Judy Cooper is concerned, I haven't heard from her. I'm not surprised. She was pretty upset with me. There hasn't been any news in the papers concerning the Black Stiletto either, so maybe she's taking my advice and giving it up.

I went downtown to the diner a few times at the end of the summer but never saw Judy. Lucy, the waitress, was polite but I could tell she knew I had upset her friend somehow. Today I went again after a long absence. I saw Lucy and talked to her. I told her I really wanted to talk to Judy and asked where I could find her. Lucy naturally hesitated to give me any information, but I told her I wanted to make it up to Judy and apologize for "what went wrong." Lucy probably wanted to hear me say I was in love with Judy and couldn't live without her, but I wasn't about to say something foolish like that. Nevertheless, I must have convinced her I was sincere. She said I could find Judy if I looked in on the Second Avenue Gym at 2nd Street and Second Avenue, just a couple of blocks south. So I went down there, looked inside, but all I saw was a bunch of men working out and boxing in a ring. I couldn't imagine Judy being anywhere around there. A middle-aged man at the front counter asked me if he could help. I asked for Judy, and he said, "It's her day off. She's out." I asked, "Does she work here?" Then he got suspicious. I was wearing my Bureau "uniform" of a suit and hat—I probably smelled like a fed. The man didn't answer me; he just asked, "Who wants to know?"

I held up a hand and replied, "Just tell her John came by." Then I left.

I'm betting she won't call me, so I'll go back downtown again in a few days.

Now, whenever Haggerty asks me about her, I should say I know exactly where to find her, but I don't. But I suppose if it came down to saving my job—

# 41
# Judy's Diary
## 1959

John came to see me at the gym today. I kinda figured he would, cause Freddie told me a guy in a suit and a hat showed up last week to ask about me. "He looked like a fed," Freddie observed. I knew it had to be John. He'd found me. That did not make me happy.

I was working when he showed up. I didn't notice him at first because I was in the ring with Clark. My trainee had progressed to uppercuts and roundhouses. The young man was getting pretty good for a light-light-lightweight. Anyway, I looked up and there was John, standing at the front counter next to Freddie. I thought my stomach was going to upchuck. I told Clark to take a break, and then I climbed out of the ring.

Freddie said, "Judy, you have a visitor." The inflection in his voice questioned whether or not I really wanted to talk to the guy.

"Thanks, Freddie," I said, and then to John, "Let's go outside."

He followed me out of the gym and before he could open his mouth I turned on him.

"What are you doing here? What gives you the right to come down here and expose me in the place where I work? How dare you!"

"Judy," he said, "please don't be angry. I had to see you."

"Why? So you could arrest me?"

"No. I miss you." That shut me up. "There, I said it."

I didn't know what to say, but I was still livid.

"Judy, it's been months. Are you going to stay angry? Are we really finished? Is it over between us?"

"You're a smart Federal Special Agent, John, you should be able to figure that out."

"I thought . . . I thought since the Stiletto hasn't made the news in a while that you might have given her up."

"Not a chance. Just because I haven't made the news doesn't mean I've hung up the outfit. So your threat is still good? You'll arrest me if the Stiletto continues her work?"

"Judy, I was hoping you'd see reason."

I couldn't tell if I was mad or if I wanted to cry. Part of me wanted to scratch out his eyes. The other part felt like splitting open my chest, removing my broken heart, and handing it to him. I attempted to take a deep breath and calm myself. Then I said, "I thought there was something special between us, but you've broken the trust. You invaded my privacy. You've put me at great risk. Every day I wonder if the cops or the FBI are going to knock on my door and take me away."

"You honestly couldn't have expected us to have an honest relationship without me knowing your identity."

"That's the thing, John. You see, I know when someone is being honest or not. And I started to detect—don't ask me how, because I was born with this ability—I started to detect you weren't being straightforward with me, that you had ulterior motives for romancing me."

Dear diary, I hadn't realized that until I'd said it. It was true. I had felt John was hiding something from me when we were together. I'd refused to acknowledge it, but it's why I became so angry and distrustful of him last summer. Now it's all very clear to me.

"I'm sorry you feel that way," he said.

He lit a cigarette and offered me one. I shook my head. "I don't smoke, remember?"

"Right." We stood there a moment in silence, and then he said, "I saw that the Japanese martial arts instructor, the father of that girl you rescued, was killed."

"His name was Soichiro Tachikawa. His daughter Isuzu is living with another Japanese family now." That was true. I'd kept in touch with her after Soichiro's passing. Apparently her foster family was related—Soichiro's cousins or something like that.

"That's what I understand," John said. "You did know him, didn't you?"

"He was my teacher. My friend. He taught me *karate* and *judo*, and even how to fight wearing a blindfold. He was like a father to me."

"I'm sorry."

"Carl Purdy did it."

"We know. Unfortunately, no one can prove it. But the FBI will get him, Judy. I promise."

I glared at him and said, "Not if I get him first!"

"Judy—"

I put a hand up to stop him. "John, please respect my wishes. Don't come see me again. Leave me alone. I'm sorry. It's over. Arrest me if that's what you really want to do, but otherwise leave me be. I hope you'll do the right thing."

I left him on the street and went back inside.

OCTOBER 22, 1959

Dear diary, I haven't thought about John for almost two weeks! Until just now, of course. I've been spending time working, going to movies either alone or with Lucy, or reading. On Clark's recommendation, I did pick up *Invisible Man* by Ralph Ellison and am reading that. I like it. So it's good I haven't thought about him, isn't it?

I want to write down my impressions of the new Guggenheim Museum that opened yesterday uptown on 5th Avenue. Lucy and I went today—and it was packed. Peter was able to get us special tickets through his law firm so we didn't have to stand in line. What a marvelous building! The press has made such a big deal about it being designed by Frank Lloyd Wright, a famous architect who died last April. I wasn't very familiar with his work, but Lucy was. Even though Lucy's just a waitress and isn't a ritzy and sophisticated Madison Avenue female New Yorker, she's pretty smart. She likes art and we often visit the museums and stuff. Lucy explains things to me. Sometimes I'm interested and sometimes I'm not, but I enjoy the experience. Anyway, the Guggenheim is shaped like a top, sort of, with a descending spiral ramp on the inside. There're other parts of the building, too, but that's what you remember the most. The place also has a very peaceful atmosphere when you're there walking downward, as if you're in a kind of cathedral. I like the way voices echo.

I wanted to shout, "Black Stiletto," just to hear it go "Stiletto . . . Stiletto . . . Stiletto . . ."

OCTOBER 23, 1959

Oh my gosh, I saw Tony the Tank today!

It seems I've been getting a lot of unexpected visitors at the gym lately. He dropped by and asked if I wanted to have lunch with him. So we went up the street to the diner. Lucy was working. She knows Tony, of course, but isn't aware he's connected to the mob. She thinks he's in the fishery business, which I guess he is, but that's a front.

After giving us the menus, she asked me, "Judy, you coming over again Friday for *The Twilight Zone*?" That's a new show on TV that we *love*. Well, *I* love it. It scares Lucy, but she watches it with me. It just started a couple of weeks ago; there've been two episodes so far. I'm already addicted. I think it's gonna be better than *Alfred Hitchcock Presents*!

"I wouldn't miss it," I said.

The jukebox was playing Bobby Darin's "Mack the Knife,"

which is the big number-one hit these days. I got up, put some coins in the machine, and picked Santo and Johnny's "Sleep Walk," which I *adore*, and Ritchie Valens' "La Bamba" for old times' sake.

Once we had our sandwiches in front of us, Tony surprised me by saying, "Judy, I've come to see you to ask a favor."

"A favor of me? What?"

"Actually, it's for the don. *He* wants to ask you for a favor."

I almost choked on my Reuben. "Don DeLuca?"

"Yeah, he wants a meeting."

"With the Stiletto?"

"Yeah."

"Do they . . . do they know who I am?"

"No, no, nothing like that! I swear. But he put out the word to all the capos, you know, the lieutenants—"

"I know who they are, but how would he know how to find me?"

"Jerry Munroe."

I gasped. Had that slimy pornographer somehow got an unmasked picture of me to the mob?

"You see, Judy, Munroe was working for the family," Tony said. "This, um, photo and film business he was doing through mail order, well, that was using our distribution system. But the don was aware only of what we call 'straight' dirty pictures. You know what I mean. The don had no idea Munroe was dealing the child garbage. That deeply offended him. Normally, DeLuca would help out guys like Munroe with legal defense funds and an attorney who works for the family. But not Munroe. He's gonna let Munroe rot in prison for that filth."

"Good."

"But he found out how Munroe would contact you. You know, with the classified ad in the newspaper."

"Uh-huh?"

"DeLuca's running a series of ads in the classifieds right now in order to get your attention. Have you seen them?"

"No. I haven't looked."

"Better get hold of one. DeLuca wants you to call a number and set up a meeting."

"Tony, what for? They'll just kill me! Aren't I number one on the family's hit list?"

"You did the don a favor by exposing Munroe. He wants to thank you personally."

"I don't believe it."

"It's true. And he has a proposition to make."

"What kind of proposition?"

"I'm not sure of the details, but it has to do with Carl Purdy."

You coulda knocked me down with a feather. "If I agree to this meeting, how can I be sure I'll be safe?" I asked.

"If the don guarantees nothing will happen to you, then nothing will."

I told Tony I'd look at the paper and think about it. That was good enough for him.

Back home, I dug out the newspapers we hadn't thrown out, and sure enough, there it was in the classifieds—"To Munroe's Film Star for Urgent Meeting"—and a phone number to call.

What did I have to lose? I called the number and set up the meeting for Halloween night.

# 42
## *Martin*

### THE PRESENT

Gina was released from the hospital to her dorm room, where she would convalesce and heal. Juilliard graciously offered to refund the semester's tuition, but Gina wanted to continue going to class. I was against it, but of course, I was outvoted. I'd just as soon she come back to Chicago and go to Northwestern or somewhere close to her parents. But like her grandmother, Gina is stubborn. Through her wired jaw, she told me in no uncertain terms that she was staying in New York and remaining at Juilliard. Gina's roommates—both male and female, as I found out—were all very supportive. They agreed to help her out whenever they could.

I must say, Gina was doing remarkably well. She's still shaken and emotionally fragile, but her spirits were much more positive since that day we first saw her. The idea of getting back to her dorm room cheered her up immensely.

I briefly spoke to Detective Jordan this morning on the phone. They were still processing the DNA scraped from underneath Gina's fingernails. Hopefully they would get a match to someone who already had a police record. Otherwise, there wasn't much progress in catching Gina's attacker. That didn't make me happy.

Carol wanted to stick around another day. She asked me what my plans were and I told her I was "pursuing a job lead." So, once again, I left my darling daughter in my ex-wife's capable hands while I met with John Richardson to execute our plan.

*   *   *

Johnny Munroe agreed to meet me at the East Side Diner. I was already sitting at a booth when he walked in. I immediately recognized him from the TV show, although he appeared even heavier in person. He stood at the door and scanned the room. I raised my hand and he spotted me, after which he swaggered to the table as if he owned the joint. As we shook hands, he almost crushed mine.

"How ya doin'," he said, not asking a question.

I put Munroe to be in his early sixties. He was dressed in a suit but without a tie. The white shirt was unbuttoned to his breastbone, displaying a massive amount of gaudy gold chains around his neck. He reeked of cigarette smoke. Definitely an extra from *The Sopranos*.

When the waitress came over, all he ordered was a cup of coffee. "I ain't stayin' long," he said. I said I'd have the same. When she walked away, Munroe looked at me and asked, "You wired?"

"What?"

"Wired. You wearin' a wire? You recordin' this conversation?"

"No, of course not."

"You got a cell phone?"

"Yes."

"Hand it over."

"What for?"

"You can record our conversation with it."

I rolled my eyes, pulled out the phone, and placed it on the table. He took it, turned it off, and set it down in front of us.

"Okay, I'll trust you," he said. "You better not be recordin' this."

"I'm not."

"All right then."

I couldn't help but glance across the room where John Richardson was sitting at the counter, his back to us.

"So, you thought about my proposal?" Munroe asked.

"Yes, I have. I'll agree to your terms, but I want your assurance that this is a one-time payment and all prints and the negative will be destroyed."

"There ain't no negative."

"Are you sure?"

"Of course I'm sure! I'll give you the only copy of the film. Even exchange."

"Tell me again what you'd do if I don't pay you," I said.

"What?"

"I want to hear you say it to my face."

"I'll hand it over to *World Entertainment Television*. They'll give me half a million for it."

"You realize this is blackmail, or extortion, or whatever. That's a federal crime."

"Howzat?"

"You're saying if I don't pay you, you'll do something I don't want you to do."

His eyes narrowed as he leaned forward. With a menacing whisper, he asked, "You breakin' my balls?"

"What?"

"You heard me."

"No. I'm just saying—"

"Look, that's the deal, Talbot. It's a business transaction. I'm givin' you first refusal. Take it or leave it. Besides, you ain't gonna go to the cops if you want to protect the Stiletto's identity. You do that and everything comes out, whether you like it or not." He leaned back just as the waitress brought our coffee. Munroe took a few sips and then asked me, "So what's your angle, Talbot? How do you 'represent' the Stiletto's interests?"

I shrugged. "I just do."

"Is she alive?"

I lied. "No."

"Then what do you care?"

"Leave it, Munroe. I've agreed to your demands. With that comes no questions asked, all right?"

He rudely pointed a finger at me. "You don't tell me what I can or can't do." He sipped his coffee with loud slurps and then asked, "You got the money or what?"

"I have it, but not today. Not with me. We'll have to meet again here tomorrow. You hand over the film. I'll give you the money."

"Cash, right?"

"Cash."

"Make it unmarked one hundred dollar bills. That way you won't need a trunk to carry it all." He chuckled. "A suitcase maybe, but not a trunk."

I sighed. Funny guy. "I'll see what I can do."

"That's the only way I'll accept it."

"All right, then. We'll meet here."

"Same time?"

"If that's good for you."

"Sure." He swigged his coffee down and made as if to leave.

"Wait a second."

"What? Ain't we done here?"

"I'm just curious. About your father and the Stiletto. What's the story? How did he get the film? Why didn't he do anything with it?"

"My father was afraid of the Black Stiletto. He didn't tell me why, but I knew he was. She came up in conversation at some point. He said he'd met her and made this film as some kind of a promotional thing for her to use. I didn't know he had a copy until after he died. Like I told you, I found it in his safety deposit box. I think he left it for me to do with it whatever I wanted. As a legacy, sort of."

"I see."

"Now can I go? You done askin' your questions?"

"Yeah."

He got up and left without shaking hands or saying goodbye. What a prick.

Richardson waited a full ten minutes before he got off the stool and joined me at the booth.

"Did you get it?" I asked.

He nodded as he placed a mechanical device the size of a deck of cards on the table. He pushed a button and I heard Munroe's voice.

*"You wired?"*

And then mine. *"What?"*

*"Wired. You wearin' a wire? You recordin' this conversation?"*

*"No, of course not."*

*"You got a cell phone?"*

The first phase of Richardson's plan had worked. He picked up my phone from the table, slipped off the back panel covering the battery, and carefully removed the bug he'd placed in it earlier. The thing recorded the conversation regardless of whether or not the phone was on. Its signal went directly to Richardson's device in his pocket.

"So far, so good," he said. "Tomorrow will be the moment of truth."

# 43
# Judy's Diary

It's a few minutes before midnight and I've just come back from trick-or-treating, dear diary!

I met Don Franco DeLuca face-to-face a couple of hours ago. And believe it or not, it wasn't as scary as I thought it'd be. In fact, the guy was downright amiable. He was much more pleasant to me as the Stiletto than his brother Don Giorgio was to me as Judy Cooper.

Last week when I called the number in the classified ad, some guy with a heavy New York–Italian accent answered. I explained who I was and that I was calling about the ad. The guy sounded real surprised at first, but quickly got down to business. First he asked, "How do I know this is really the Stiletto?"

I replied, "Who else would know the meaning of that classified ad?" I didn't want to give Tony away so I asked, "So what's this all about and who am I speaking to?"

"I'm Guido Rossi. Don DeLuca would like a sit-down with you."

I remembered Guido. I met him a few times at social events when I was with Fiorello. Fiorello sometimes called him "Swordfish." He's pretty high up in the DeLuca family food chain.

It was my turn to pretend surprise. "Well, Mr. Rossi, I find that hard to believe. I thought he wanted to kill me."

"He does. Well, not really. That's what he wants to talk to you about."

"Why should I agree to meet him?"

"It could be mutually beneficial."

"How do I know I'd be safe?"

"The don guarantees it. Whenever the don guarantees—" Yeah, yeah, it was the same thing Tony said.

"When and where?"

He suggested a warehouse on the west side, on Horatio Street. That was close to the Meatpacking District, or maybe it was part of it, I didn't know. We agreed to 10:00 on Halloween night. I figured there would be a lot of Black Stilettos running around, ha ha; if I was seen on the street people might think I was just going to a costume party.

So tonight I went out in full regalia, zipped across town without an overcoat—it was unseasonably warm—and made it to the West Side without incident. I didn't see one other Black Stiletto, either! I don't know if I should be relieved or hurt!

I approached the building in the shadows, as usual. It was a large place, but there was no sign identifying what kind of warehouse it was. Whatever the business, it appeared to be closed down. Nevertheless, there were several cars parked in front. I guess Don DeLuca and his henchmen don't take the bus or walk. One goon stood outside the door, smoking a cigarette. I didn't know him.

Well, I was already on the edge of the frying pan, so I thought I might as well jump into the fire. I crept along the side of the building toward the back and found another entrance. It was locked, but my picks easily broke through that obstacle.

I stepped inside to something like the interior of a small airplane hangar. Vast emptiness. Eight men stood in the center of the floor, thirty feet away from me, and one sat in a chair—Don Franco

DeLuca. It was the first time I'd ever seen him in person. He was much younger than Don Giorgio, maybe in his fifties. He wasn't fat like his brother and still had a lot of dark color in his graying hair. One vacant chair faced him. The men were speaking in Italian or Sicilian, watching the front door, and hadn't noticed me at all. I stood there and listened for a moment, getting the lay of the land. There was a lot of space around them. Even if I got into a fight, I'd have lots of room. I felt comfortable with the situation. Then I saw that Tony was one of the eight standing men. That made me feel even better about it. So I said, "Hey."

They immediately shut up, turned to face me, and *drew guns*!

"Whoa!" I said. I raised my hands. "I thought you said I'd be safe!"

DeLuca said, "Put away your pieces, boys. This woman is our guest."

The men hesitated, but they did what the boss ordered. As soon as all weapons were in their holsters, DeLuca beckoned me with his hand. "Come forward, my dear, and sit down."

*My dear?* Geez.

I slowly moved around them toward the chair. Tony winked at me. He had drawn a gun on me, too, but I figured he was just playing his part. I kept a good fifteen feet, and the empty chair, between me and the group. "This is as close as I'm getting."

"You surprised us, my dear, we didn't hear you come in."

"I don't like to be predictable. What do you want, Don DeLuca?" I figured I might as well be polite and address him the correct way.

"I won't take too much of your time. I'm very busy, too." Yeah, he's busy smuggling drugs, racketeering, and murdering. Can't keep him away from his job, can I?

"I wanted to thank you personally for bringing the heinous activities of Jerry Munroe to my attention," he continued.

I played dumb. "Oh?"

"What he was doing is despicable in our eyes, a sin against nature and humanity. He will rot in hell. I am sorry we did business with him. Did you know we did business with him?"

"The papers alluded to it."

"At any rate, we wash our hands of him."

"Glad to be of service. I didn't do it for you." DeLuca smiled, but he probably wasn't used to being spoken to like that. Especially from a woman. "The guy on the phone said you had a proposition for me."

"That's right. Are you sure you won't sit down?"

"I'm fine right here."

"Very well." He put a cigarette in his mouth, and I swear—one of his sycophants *lit it for him*! Geez. "It seems we have a mutual enemy."

"We do?"

"Carl Purdy. He runs a Harlem outfit."

"I know who you mean."

"Yes." DeLuca took a long drag on his cigarette. "Mr. Purdy's interests conflict with ours. We'd like him to—vanish."

"So would I."

"Then our goals are the same."

"Hold on," I said. "Are you asking me to get rid of Carl Purdy for you?"

DeLuca shrugged. "For our part, we're doing what we can; but the violence is escalating between our people and his. It's unpleasant."

"You're talking about the narcotics business." DeLuca didn't respond. "Why should I help you? I despise it. You have a contract out on me. Your men have tried to kill me more than once."

"My dear, as you are well aware, I was never happy with what happened to my brother and to Vittorio Ranelli."

"I didn't kill your brother, Don DeLuca. He accidentally broke his neck."

For the first time, I detected venom in his voice. "While you were attacking him."

"Let's get back to the point. Why do you think I can help you with Purdy?"

"It seems you have an ability to get near him that we don't have."

I looked him in the eyes. Even from the several feet away from him, I could tell he was being honest with me. He really wanted my help.

"And what do I get in return?" I asked.

"The contract on you will be forgotten."

"I've done pretty well eluding your boys so far."

"That you have. But you'll always be looking over your shoulder. That becomes tiresome."

"I do that anyway. The cops and FBI are after me, too."

He shrugged again. "It's the best I can offer. You wouldn't have to worry about us anymore."

"Why don't you just go into another line of work?" I asked facetiously. "No one needs heroin. It's destroying lives. It's killing people. Why not give it up?"

He thought about his answer before he spoke. "The narcotics business is here to stay, whether we do it, or the niggers do it, or the French do it. It will become bigger than all of us. There is nothing you and I can do about that. I'm a businessman. It's good business for us. That's all I have to say about it."

You know, dear diary, I knew he was right. The narcotics plague would get bigger. It was only a matter of time before it was everywhere. If I took out one cog of the machine—Carl Purdy—would it really improve anything? Probably not. There would still be drugs. There would still be colored men and women struggling in poverty and getting addicted to the stuff. It wouldn't be long before it also became the scourge of white people. I knew it would happen sooner rather than later.

But maybe I could do one tiny part in the war against that evil blight. I've wanted to take out Purdy anyway, so why not agree to DeLuca's deal? It didn't mean I was gonna be the Mafia's friend or anything.

"All right, Don DeLuca," I said. "You have a deal. I'll see what I can do. But the contract on my head ends as of this moment."

"I don't have a problem with that. Can we agree on a time frame for your part?"

I didn't really think about it. I just threw something out. "Give me to the end of the year."

That seemed to satisfy him. He held out his hand. "Shall we shake on it, Miss Black Stiletto?"

I eyed the other guys and Tony and didn't detect a trick, so I walked forward and shook the crook's hand. Was it a deal with the devil? I'm trying not to think of it that way. Going after Purdy was on my own agenda, it was personal between him and me. If I could get the Italians off my back at the same time, then I suppose it couldn't hurt to shake DeLuca's hand.

I left through the front door after a single, "Goodbye."

NOVEMBER 4, 1959

Happy birthday to me, happy birthday to me, happy birthday dear Judy, happy birthday to me!

Wow. I'm 22!

Freddie gave me a beautiful winter coat this morning! He knew I needed a new one. It's cashmere with a mink fur collar. Beige. I couldn't believe it. Later I'm having lunch with Lucy and Peter at the 21 Club. I've never been there. Should be lovely!

Did I ever tell John when my birthday was? I can't remember. Oh well.

# 44
## John

Today is November 13, 1959. Friday the Thirteenth.

In just a few hours I'm going out on a risky surveillance operation.

If the informant is correct, Carl Purdy will receive a tremendous amount of heroin from Corsica tonight. The handoff will be at a machine shop in Harlem, near the East River. The shipment is coming by truck. We know the drugs were smuggled into the States by boat, but we don't know where the ship docked. Hopefully we can find out the smugglers' disembarkment location tonight.

The informant will wear a wire. I'll be outside the machine shop in my car, listening and recording the conversations. The plan is to get as much evidence as possible for an indictment. I asked Haggerty for a team to raid the shop, but at first he refused. Said I didn't have enough "cause" for the manpower. Then he reconsidered when he saw how much information I really did have, and decided to lead a backup team himself. I'm not particularly happy about that, but what could I say? Tonight's operation will go as planned.

Time to leave.

# 45
## Judy's Diary
### 1959

NOVEMBER 14, 1959

I slept late today because I was out all night on Friday the 13th, and let me tell you—the events were appropriate to the date. I'm lucky to be alive. For that I am thankful, but I also feel as if I've had my heart broken all over again. By John.

So much happened last night that I feel as if I could write an entire book about it. But I'll try to be brief.

It all started after work yesterday. Ever since Mike Washington caught me following him to Harlem, we've been avoiding each other. The few times we bumped into one another at the gym, it was awkward. He glared at me with hatred. Then, yesterday afternoon, I walked in and saw him in the ring with Clark. He was giving Clark boxing lessons. I don't know why, but this made me furious. Freddie wasn't around to stop me, so I stormed up into the ring and confronted him.

"What are you doing?"

"Just givin' Clark some tips," he replied.

"That's not your job. It's mine."

"There ain't no harm in me giving him tips, man to man."

I felt protective over Clark. Call it my mothering instincts or whatever, dear diary, but I wanted to scratch out Washington's eyes.

"He doesn't need your lessons," I snapped.

Shocked, Clark looked at me and said, "It's okay, Judy, Mike was just—"

"*No!*" Poor Clark jumped when I barked. I didn't mean to sound so harsh. "Go on down to the wall pulleys," I told him. "I'll be there in a minute." The young man looked back and forth at me and Washington, and then submissively climbed out of the ring.

"What's the matter with you?" Washington growled. "That boy needs a black man teaching him, not a white girl like you."

"What's the matter with *me*? What's the matter with *you*!" I turned on the guy, ready to go fist-to-fist with him right then and there. "Why do you hate me so much? What did I ever do to you? I know you're Freddie's friend, but I don't know why. You're the most disagreeable person I've ever met."

He raised his hand, ready to make a fist out of it, but then he hesitated. We locked eyes for a few seconds. I was itching for him to take a shot at me, but then he shook his head. "Aw, forget it," he said. Washington climbed out of the ring and headed toward the locker room. I stood there and attempted to calm down, but my heart pounded and adrenaline rushed through my body. Finally, after several minutes, I stepped down from the ring and went over to Clark. I apologized for breaking up his session with Mike. Clark did his best to say it was all right, but I knew he was disappointed in me.

I tried to forget what happened and went on with my job. Later, though, as Washington was leaving, he and Freddie chatted for a moment. I couldn't hear everything they said, but as Washington shook Freddie's hand to say goodbye, I overheard him say, "See you next week, if I don't die tonight." They laughed as if it was a joke, but I knew better. You know me, dear diary, I can sense when people lie or tell the truth. I *knew* Washington wasn't joking. Something was up.

And it had to do with Carl Purdy.

*

Later, after dark, I dressed as the Stiletto and wore the trench coat over my outfit. Without my mask, I hailed a taxi and took it to Harlem. I had the driver let me off on East 129th Street, a block away from the bordello I'd visited in September. Actually, I didn't know what the heck I was doing. I was acting on gut instinct. Would Washington be there? If my hunch was correct, something big was going to happen and he was involved. If I didn't see him after a while, I'd made up my mind to sneak in as I'd done before.

I put on my mask and hid across the street in the shadows next to a decrepit stoop. The building was in disrepair and smelled of garbage. Homeless people probably used it as a shelter. I held my nose and waited, watching the front door of Harlem Delight.

It wasn't surprising that Sonny, the colored teenager who thought he was a tough guy, was standing guard outside. He had on a heavy coat and tugged on a cigarette. I thought of his sister, Ruby, and wondered what became of her. Had he helped her as I'd suggested? Apparently Sonny was still entangled in Purdy's organization.

Looking back, I'm not sure if I was lucky or not that Washington soon emerged from the bordello. He was accompanied by two other men. They said something to Sonny, and then they laughed, talked low, and started to walk east on 129th. Sonny remained in front of the brothel. I followed the trio, dashing between dark spots along the street. They crossed Madison Avenue and kept going until they reached Park. I managed to stay in pursuit without being seen, despite a lot of pedestrian activity on Madison. Where were they headed? I'd soon find out, but at the time I was starting to get a little nervous. We were in an area of Harlem that was pretty run-down.

The trio turned right on Park Avenue and headed south for one block. Then they crossed Park and kept going east on 128th Street. Darting across the two-way Park Avenue was tricky, as it always is, but I did it without my prey noticing. It was at the other end of the street, close to Lexington Avenue, where they approached a large vacant building that appeared to be a warehouse of some kind. They went in through a door on its west side, but no lights were on in the windows. An old, rusted sign on the building read: L&S MACHINERY. I guess that meant it was once a machine shop, but now it was one of Purdy's many properties in Harlem.

Four cars were parked in front, including Purdy's black Cadillac with the fins. Interesting. Something was going on inside, and I was determined to find out what. I moved along the shadows, circling the building to map out my exit strategy. As before, there was a tiny alley in back that no one in his right mind would want to walk through. There were two "regular" doors—the side door the men went in and the 128th Street front door, which appeared to be locked and boarded, as well as a loading dock on the Lexington side of the building. Its steel rolling overhead door was all the way down. The building's windows were high with no fire escapes, so I figured the interior was one big space with a tall ceiling. Not good. There was only one way in or out.

As I crept along the wall on Lexington—where there was way too much light from streetlamps for my comfort—I saw a familiar black, 4-door Ford sedan parked on Lexington, between 127th and 128th. I couldn't believe it. My heart nearly jumped out of my chest.

John Richardson sat in the driver's seat. Cigarette smoke spiraled out his window, which was partway down.

*What was he doing there?*

For a moment, I completely forgot about Mike Washington and Carl Purdy. I strode right up to the car and tapped on the window. I scared the heck out of him!

"What the—?" he yelped. Dropped his cigarette, too!

"What are you doing here?" I demanded.

He immediately put a finger to his lips and shushed me. "Damn it, Judy, you're going to ruin it! Get out of here! I'm on a surveillance operation!"

"I'm not going anywhere! *You* get out of here. This is my deal."

He turned away from me, leaned over, and opened the passenger door. "Get in, quick!"

I didn't want to, but I did. After I closed the door, he said, "Judy, I can't tell you how dangerous this is for you. There's a major drug exchange going down tonight. The SAC, my boss, he's gonna show up soon and you can't be here."

I started to protest, but he shushed me and pointed to a device in his lap that looked like a tape recorder. A cord stretched from the machine it to a plug in his ear. "I have an informant inside who's wired up. I have to listen to everything that's being said, so be quiet."

"I will not be quiet. This is between—"

He quickly held up his hand as a worried expression crossed his face. The alarm in his eyes was enough to shut me up.

"Uh-oh," he said.

"What?"

"Shh."

He listened and then slammed his fist on the steering wheel. "Damn!"

"What is it, John?"

He checked his wristwatch and whispered urgently, "Things are going down a lot quicker than we planned. My informant's in trouble and my backup team isn't due for another fifteen minutes." He held up his hand again to keep me from talking as he listened. After a moment he winced.

"John? Tell me."

He looked at me and said, "Judy, I might need your help."

"What?"

"Listen to me. You know my informant."

"I do?"

"His name is Mike Washington."

You could've knocked me over with a peanut. "What?"

"I know he goes to that gym where you work."

Then I thought the worst. "Does he know—? About me? Did you send him to spy on me?"

"No. He doesn't know about you. At least, I don't think so. I've never told him. It's just a coincidence that he goes to the Second Avenue Gym, Judy. I swear. In fact, I was worried about that once I learned it's where you live and work."

"But how could he be working for you? He's an ex-con! He was in prison for killing a crooked boxing manager."

John's brow wrinkled. "What?"

"It's true. Freddie, you know, the manager of the gym—he told me. He was friends with Mike when they were boxers together back in the thirties and forties."

"He told you that?"

"Uh-huh."

"Well, it's not true, Judy. Mike served fifteen years in prison, all right, but it wasn't for manslaughter."

"It wasn't?"

"No. He was falsely accused of raping a white woman."

*"What?"*

"Frankly, he went to prison because of a racist white girl. Someone a lot like you, I'm afraid."

I was shocked. "I'm not a racist!"

"No, no, that's not what I meant. She was someone a lot like you physically. She could've been your twin sister. She looked just like you. Same age, same hair color, everything."

That gave me pause. "What happened?"

"She accused Mike of raping her, which was a goddamned lie. He never touched that woman. Never. He didn't look twice at her. It was in Central Park. She was put up to it by a bunch of white men who had it in their heads they were going to get themselves a 'nigger.'"

I hate that word, but I didn't say anything.

"It was 1942. Mike was minding his own business, walking through the park on his way home as he always did that time of evening. He heard a woman calling for help behind some trees. He ran over there, and the white woman was on the ground with her clothes pulled up and ruffled. Three white men were with her. Mike claims he heard one say, "There he is, right on time." Then one of the men clubbed Mike on the back of the head. When he woke up, he was in handcuffs, in police custody. The girl accused him of attempted rape, and the white men told police they rescued her. It was his word against four whites. Mike went to prison for fifteen years. If it had happened in the South, he'd have been lynched. Believe me, I thoroughly studied Mike's case before I hired him as an informant. It's the truth."

I was aghast. "How do you know all this?"

"My father was Mike's lawyer."

"Really?"

"Yeah. The incident happened in Poughkeepsie. He knew the truth, and I believe it."

I didn't know what to say. "Freddie said a crooked manager drugged him before a fight 'cause he wouldn't throw it, so Mike beat him up. The mob didn't retaliate 'cause the manager was cheating them."

"That actually did happen," John said. "But the police never knew Mike was the one who beat him up. He was never arrested for that. He was sent to prison by a lying, prejudiced white woman."

I felt terrible. It's no wonder Mike didn't trust me. Every time he looked at me, he saw *her*. I'd always thought the reason Mike didn't like me had something to do with my race. Now I know. He harbored a grudge against white women, and I have to say I can't blame him. As for Freddie covering up for his friend, my "lie detector" instincts didn't raise any flags when he told me Washington was in jail for manslaughter, because Mike really did beat up that manager. It just didn't happen in the way it was couched. Freddie hadn't lied, he just altered the truth.

John held up his hand again as he listened. "No. Oh, no. Mike's blown. Damn it! God, we have to do something. They'll kill him." He turned to me again and asked, "Will you help me?"

"Sure. What do you want me to do?"

"We have to get inside." He drew a gun from beneath his suit jacket, removed the magazine, checked it, and shoved it back in. "Let's go."

We got out of the car. I told him Mike had gone in with two other men on the other side of the building. As it was the only feasible entrance, that's where we headed. John opted to cross through the alley, though, rather than move in front of the building on 128th. Yuck.

At least the door on the west side of the building was in shadow. The light fixture above it was either burned out or broken. John drew his gun and held it with both hands, commando-style. Then, just as I was about to open the door, we heard two gunshots inside the building. I immediately cracked open the door to a small, darkened room with a low ceiling. We stepped inside, closed the door, and waited a moment to get our bearings. The space must have been a break room when the shop was operating. There was an old Coke vending machine that looked like it'd seen better years, a couple of chipped Formica tables and chairs, a sink, and a refrigerator that must have dated from the early '40s. A bathroom—the door was long gone—was in an alcove to the right. There was no seat on the toilet. Corridors led both left and right against the outer wall, and another door opened to the center of the building. Next to it, attached to the wall, was a fuse box. The switches were labeled— "Work Lights," "Loading Door," "Lunchroom," "Offices," and so on. I moved closer to the door while John checked the corridors in both directions.

"Clear," he whispered. "These hallways go around the circumference of the building, one to the front and one to the back."

I opened the door just a sliver and looked out. Just as I thought, the shop was a large, cavernous space. A few overhead work lights in the tall ceiling cast dim illumination on a horrific scene. I counted five colored men standing in the center, surrounded by broken-down machines—table saws, drill presses, and the like—still bolted to the concrete floor. One of the men was Carl Purdy. I thought I recognized a couple of the others as his bodyguards.

Mike Washington was on the floor, lying in a pool of blood and groaning in pain. Purdy had a gun in his hand. John's informant had just been shot in the legs, but he was still alive.

"Oh, God," I whispered. John joined me and peered through the slit and drew in a deep breath.

"What now?" I asked.

He studied the scene as the men spoke in low voices. "Look, there's the heroin," John whispered. I crouched beneath him so I could look, too.

Several stacks of bricklike packages, wrapped in plastic and tape, sat on the floor near the men. Each one was not quite the size of a shoebox. Behind them were pieces of smashed furniture—dressers, chests of drawers, and nightstands. An axe leaned up against one of the dressers.

"The drugs were already here," John said quietly. "They were hidden in that furniture. It must have been shipped by boat from France and then brought here by truck. Mike's information was slightly off. I wanted to catch them delivering the stuff, but I'll bet they're waiting for another truck. They'll load the heroin into it and distribute it to the far corners of the country. Or at least Harlem, but that's an ungodly amount of narcotics." He looked at his watch. "We have eight minutes before the cavalry arrives."

"Wait a second." I reached into my backpack and pulled out my camera. "I'll get some shots of this. You can use them as evidence." I snapped several pictures and then replaced the camera.

Then, suddenly, we heard a bell ring. One of the men said, "It's here," and went over to the loading dock rolling door. He pushed a button and the steel barrier began to rise.

John said, "We have to stop them. Keep them busy until Haggerty gets here."

I reached over to the power box and switched off the toggle marked "Loading Door." The rolling steel curtain stopped about a foot off the floor.

"What happened?" Purdy asked.

The man at the door pushed the button several times. "I don't know. Hold on." He fiddled with the controls and then said, "Must be the fuse box. I'll check it." Then he started walking our way.

"Here goes," I said. "You stand back. I'll take care of him."

John flattened himself against the inner wall by the door. I stood directly behind it, at the hinges, as I heard footsteps coming closer. The door swung open, blocking John and me from the gangster. I heard him mutter a curse word on the other side as he examined the fuse box. I gently pushed the door closed. He turned, saw me, and before he could shout an alarm, I punched him hard in the face. Surprisingly, he didn't go down. Dazed, he took a few steps back. I then had enough space to perform an *ushiro geri*—back kick. My boot slammed into his chest with such force that I'm sure his sternum cracked. Unfortunately, he reflexively reached out to one of the dining chairs that stood nearby, taking it down with him as he collapsed to the floor. The chair made a loud racket.

John and I looked at each other with concern. Then we heard the men inside the shop call out, "Walt! You trip over your left foot?" Laughter. I jerked my head toward the corridor, so John and I bolted. "You gonna fix the door or what?" Purdy shouted. We rushed into the dark hallway that led toward the back of the building. Along the sides were a couple of half-open doors, revealing empty offices. As we turned the corner, the corridor emptied into the larger area of the shop. I held John back and put a finger to my lips.

By now, one man was already on his way to the break room to check on "Walt." John checked his watch. "Six more minutes," he said. "If Haggerty's on time."

"I don't think we can stall any longer," I whispered.

The man entered the break room, took one look at the floor, and shouted back at Purdy and the others. "Walt's down! Someone's here!"

Immediately the other three men drew guns and went on alert, their eyes scanning the entire shop. The scout ran back to the group and also drew a weapon. Someone said, "Spread out, let's find 'em."

"No," said Purdy. "Stay where you are."

He walked over to Washington and aimed his gun at the man's head. Then he called out loudly, "You better show yourself or your rat gets his head blown off!" He reached into his pocket and pulled out a little box with wires on it. "I found this strapped to his chest, underneath his shirt. Come on out. You NYPD? FBI? I count to three and you better show yourselves with hands up."

"I have to go out there," John said.

"No. Let me do it."

"One!" Purdy called.

"It's too dangerous!" John whispered.

"Shut up!" I quickly evaluated the situation. The four men were twenty to thirty feet away from the corridor opening. There were a few big metal machines between us.

"Two!"

I stepped out of the corridor with hands up and said, "Here I am. Don't shoot."

The men whirled around and pointed their guns. It was just like what happened when I met Don DeLuca at that warehouse. The difference there, though, was that DeLuca ordered his men not to kill me. I had no idea what Purdy was going to do.

"Huh. So it's you," Purdy said. He smiled widely, revealing one gold tooth amongst shiny white ones. "You here by yourself, lady?"

"Of course," I answered.

He nodded and then said, "Kill her."

My reflexes saved me, dear diary. I immediately dropped and rolled to a position behind a machine I think was a lathe. At the same moment, the men unleashed a volley of bullets that ricocheted off the machine and concrete floor. I squeezed myself into as small a form as possible, fully protected by the steel object.

Then John went into action. He edged around the corridor corner and fired, hitting two men. The other two, including Purdy, leaped to the floor and crawled like madmen for cover behind other machinery. Once they were safe, they directed their aim toward the corridor entrance. I was trapped in the middle. One of the guys John hit wasn't dead, so he joined in the foray as he lay on the floor, holding his bloody gut. After a few seconds, the gangsters had emptied their handguns and were forced to reload. John took that opportunity to lean out from behind the wall and shoot again. This time he put the wounded man completely out of action. I jumped to my feet and ran toward Purdy and his buddy. Purdy was behind a dilapidated table saw; he saw me just as he finished feeding his weapon, and he aimed. Although I hadn't performed such a move since I was in gymnastics back in Odessa, I leaped for the table saw just as Purdy fired, barely missing me. With my palms on top of the machine, I managed to vault into a handspring. My legs soared up and over, and I collided feet first on top of Purdy! We tumbled to the floor and he dropped the gun. I swiveled on my right hip and kicked the weapon across the room.

The other gunman made the mistake of rising from his cover in order to shoot me. John picked him off with a carefully aimed round to the head.

Dear diary, I wasn't accustomed to this much gunplay. To tell you the God's truth, I was scared. Bullets had flown everywhere, and all I had with me were a couple of knives. For a few moments there, I was out in the open—and only now, as I sit in my bedroom and write this, do I realize how utterly vulnerable I was.

Anyway, there we were. It was just Purdy, John, and me. Purdy was unarmed and on the floor. So what did I do? I jumped on him. I wanted to make sure the guy wasn't going anywhere. I drew the stiletto and pressed the blade against Purdy's neck.

"Don't move. You know I mean it," I told him.

John approached, his gun still trained on Purdy. He went over to Washington, whom I thought had passed out. He kneeled and examined the bloody body.

"He was hit by a stray bullet," John said. "He's gone."

Before I could react to that news, I saw that John was wounded. Blood covered his right upper arm and he was holding the gun in his left hand.

I couldn't help it. I said his name. "John, you're hurt."

"It's all right," he said. "In two minutes backup will—"

And then a new voice boomed out, echoing in the cavernous machine shop. "Richardson! We'll take over here!"

A chubby guy in a suit stood in front of the break room; none of us had seen him. I didn't know who he was. Three other men in suits stood beside him. They were young, good-looking, and well-dressed—exactly how I always imagined what an FBI agent looked like. Obviously they were the chubby guy's inferiors but possibly more dangerous since they had guns aimed at us. Dear diary, for a single evening out as the Stiletto, I had a heck of a lot of guns pointed at me!

"Haggerty!" John said.

The fat guy was John's boss. I thought—*this doesn't look good.*

The three armed agents moved around us, the guns pointed mostly at Purdy and me. The man called Haggerty ordered me to drop my stiletto, which I did. Then he said, "Put away your weapon, Richardson, we're taking over. Two in one bag, not bad. Good work. Your little plan worked. You caught her. Lured her into the trap, just like you said you would."

*What did he say?* John's 'little plan' worked?

*Oh my God, dear diary.* I thought I couldn't bear the betrayal. I felt as if I'd been stabbed in the heart. I wanted to collapse on the floor and just start bawling. But I didn't.

John, said, "Haggerty, this wasn't—" As he lowered his gun, he looked at me and said, quietly, "I didn't, I swear—"

Haggerty addressed one of the armed male models. "Take Purdy out to the paddy wagon," and then spoke to a second, "Load the evidence in the truck. Don't open the loading door. Take it out the way we came in. I don't care how many trips it takes you!"

So one agent took hold of Purdy, got him on his feet, and walked him out through the break room. The other guy piled seven or eight wrapped "bricks" in his arms and followed his buddy outside.

Haggerty's remaining soldier continued to point his gun at me. I started to stand, but Haggerty barked, "Stay on your knees!"

I did. I even raised my hands. My stiletto was on the floor, two feet away from my right knee. The armed agent moved around and put the barrel of the gun against the back of my head.

"Cuff her," Haggerty ordered. The agent deftly swept handcuffs on my left wrist and twisted my arm down and behind my back. I didn't resist 'cause he did it with one hand—the other hand still held a gun to my skull. He then pulled down my right arm behind my back and locked the other cuff.

If you thought I was scared before, dear diary, I was *terrified* at this point.

Then Haggerty said, "It was a great plan, Richardson. Sleep with the Black Stiletto, get her to trust you, and coax the spider into the trap."

*Oh, my God.* I couldn't believe it. John had betrayed me in more ways than one. I was shocked, frightened, and angry. I thought my heart was going to shrivel and die.

Haggerty continued. "We gotta get you to the hospital. But first let's unmask this bitch, what do you say?"

It just gets worse, doesn't it, dear diary!

"No!" John said. "Let her go."

"Let her go? Don't tell me you actually fell for the slut, Richardson. I realize she must be pretty good in the sack, but she's the enemy."

The words I was hearing were the bullets that missed me earlier, dear diary.

Suddenly John raised his gun at the man behind me and *pulled the trigger*—but the gun clicked empty.

"Richardson, damn it," Haggerty said. "Why'd you have to go and do that? Now we gotta arrest you, too."

I could see that John was angry, confused, and in pain. "Are you mad?"

Even though I was still reeling from the sudden realization that John had betrayed me and the fact that I was on my knees and about to be unmasked, the situation struck me as awfully fishy. Haggerty had given the order to a single agent to escort Purdy out, and he was also confiscating the heroin. Was that FBI standard operating procedure? What was going on?

The agent doing the carrying came back for a second load.

"Before we cuff you, Richardson, we're gonna unmask her. Please continue, Agent Briggs."

Time stood still. I swear. I thought the Black Stiletto was finished. Over. Done.

And then John did something which at first I thought was puzzling, and then just plain cowardly. But it turned out to be neither. He bolted and staggered-ran back toward the corridor! Agent Briggs swung his gun to John, but Haggerty snapped, "Keep your weapon on *her*, Briggs." So he did. Then Haggerty shouted, "Where you going, Richardson? Don't you want to watch? You won't get far, you know."

I felt the agent's hand on the top of my head, grasping my hood. Could I fight back with my hands cuffed behind my back? Did I have a fighting chance if I attacked the agent with my head and shoulders? Would I be able to knock away his gun and avoid being killed?

Those questions were answered for me.

"Pull it off, Briggs," Haggerty commanded.

The agent tugged on my mask, removing it from my head—just as the work lights suddenly went out. The place went pitch black.

And I thought—*I can do this*. All that training while wearing a blindfold paid off. Soichiro did right by me. I propelled my body backward into the agent's legs. The gun went off above my head—it was terribly loud, but I also heard the bullet ricochet off the cement floor. Before Briggs could react, I mentally pictured where my stiletto was on the floor, grabbed it behind my back, and then rolled to the side, out of the agent's reach.

He couldn't see me. But I could *sense* him. I knew exactly where he stood. There in my mind's eye I saw the precise position of his head. So I breathed deeply, assumed the stance, and performed a back kick that struck the guy hard. I heard him drop, stunned and hurting. His gun recoiled again, but I had no idea where the bullet went that time. It was nowhere near me, that's for sure.

Once again I assumed position. Although my eyes saw nothing but a curtain of darkness, I mentally placed Briggs' body. He was on all fours, like a dog, trying to shake the stars out of his brain. A clean, short *mae geri*—front kick—to his noggin put him out of my misery for a while.

I then heard a scuffle in the break room. John and Haggerty. I can only guess John ran for the fuse box to protect my identity, but I was still very upset with the knowledge that romancing me was an FBI plot.

A gun went off in the break room. Then I heard sirens outside. The *real* FBI backup? The police?

I couldn't stick around. Even with my hands cuffed, I was a sitting duck. I tapped the floor with my right foot, searching for my mask. It took me a few seconds, but eventually I stepped on it. The only thing I could do to pick it up was sit on my rear end and grab it from behind. Then, with mask and stiletto in hand, I got up and ran toward the slightly open loading dock door. The light was better there.

I dropped to the floor and laid flat, parallel to the opening, and simply rolled outside. When I came to the edge of the loading dock, I swung my legs over and dropped to my feet.

Red-and-blue flashing lights illuminated 128th Street in front of the machine shop, but I was on the Lexington Avenue side. Cuffed and clutching my knife and mask behind me, I ran south and took a right turn on 127th.

# 46
# *Martin*
## THE PRESENT

After visiting with Gina in her dorm room, making a call back home to check on my mom, and seeing Carol off—she finally decided to return to Chicago and to her job—I made my way downtown to the East Side Diner for the scheduled appointment with Johnny Munroe.

Richardson told me he thought it best that I didn't know all the details of his plan. That way, I wouldn't unintentionally telegraph or anticipate anything to Munroe at our meeting. All I knew was that Richardson would be there with his recording device, and I'd once again have the bug planted in my cell phone.

He also supplied me with a leather money bag from a bank, stuffed with several stacks of crisp, new bills, all rubber-banded together. I don't know where he got them. He wouldn't say anything except, "I still have some connections." I asked him if it was really a million dollars and he said, "Sure," and then winked. I guess that meant they were phony.

All I could say was that I hoped he knew what he was doing.

Once again, I sat in the booth alone and waited. Richardson occupied his usual stool at the counter. He had a large brown paper bag from a grocery store with him. I didn't know what was in it. The place was moderately full, so I was lucky to get my spot. To my left was a group of elderly women. Sitting in the booth behind me were two very big young men in their twenties, one black and one white. I couldn't help but hear them discussing football; they looked like linebackers, but they were dressed incongruously in fancy suits.

Finally, Munroe walked in the diner. He was dressed the same, his gold chains glistening on his hairy chest. He carried a brown envelope. Without acknowledging me, he took the opposite seat at the table.

"Hi," I said. Munroe just grunted. He turned and caught the waitress's eye. We both placed orders for coffee. When she was gone, he got right down to business.

"You still got your cell phone?"

I took it out of my pocket, made a big show of turning it off, and setting it on the table.

"You got the money?"

I tapped the leather bag on the seat beside me. "Right here."

He nodded. "All of it?"

"All of it."

Then he smiled. "Good."

Our coffees came and we took a moment to doctor them and take a few sips. Then I asked, "You have the film?"

He held up the envelope. "It's right here, but I'm beginning to think I could sell it to some other outlet. *World Entertainment Television* didn't offer me enough. You convinced me it's worth more than a half million. Now I think it's worth more than a million. What do you think *Time* or *Newsweek* would pay for it? Or CNN?"

"Hey, we had a deal," I said. "I pay you a million, you hand over any and all copies of the film, and then you forget about it. Right?"

"I'm thinkin' I need to change the terms of the deal. Why don't you give me a down payment of a million today. I'll give you forty-eight hours to raise another mil. How's that sound?"

I just stared at the sleazeball. I wanted to strangle him, but he knew he had the advantage over me. He was bigger, tougher, and more experienced in breaking the law.

"That's not what we agreed on," I said.

"Agreements are made to be revised or broken," he said.

"Not if you want to keep doing business with people. You'll make a lot of enemies."

"Hey, Talbot, let's get one thing straight." He pointed a finger at me, jabbing the air for emphasis. "You ain't no friend of mine. I don't give a shit if you don't like my business practices. Now hand over the *down payment* or I'm walkin' out of here."

I was unsure what to do. This wasn't what we expected to happen. Surely Richardson was going to jump into action at any moment. If I didn't agree to Munroe's ultimatum, he was going to leave and I might not see him again. This was our only chance to get him.

"This isn't fair," I said, doing my best to appear affronted.

"Tough shit."

"If I agree to another million, I get the film now. Understood?"

"No way."

I drummed my fingers on the table, ran my hand through my hair, and put on a great show of being upset.

"Don't take all day," he said. "In five seconds, I'm gettin' up and leavin'."

Finally, I said, "All right, damn it. You win. But I want to see the film. Let me look at it."

He thought about it, shrugged, and pushed the envelope across the table at me. I opened it and pulled out a small roll of 8mm film. I then unthreaded a few feet, held it up to the glass window and the daylight outside, peered at the tiny frames, and verified it was indeed a copy of what I had at home. As I rolled it up and replaced the reel, I asked, "Munroe, do you swear on the soul of your father that this is the only copy?"

"Fuck you, Talbot," he said. "Not that it matters, but yeah, I swear it's the only copy."

I lifted the bank bag and handed it over the table to him. "Here's your blood money," I said.

He greedily snatched it out of my hands, placed it on the seat beside him, unzipped it, and glanced inside. His eyes bulged when he saw the stacks of bills.

"They're all unmarked hundreds," I added. "Just like you wanted."

To avoid being too conspicuous, he placed the bag in his lap; then he started to count one banded stack. It didn't take long for him to stop, blink, and wrinkle his brow.

"Hey, are you breakin' my balls? This money's fake!" He started to rise—but by that time, John Richardson was standing by his side.

"Sit down, Mr. Munroe."

"Who the fuck are you?"

Richardson whipped out a badge. "FBI."

Munroe's eyes went wild. He turned to me and growled, "Why you little motherf—"

"Can it, Munroe. Scoot over, I want to talk to you."

The blackmailer wasn't having it. "You ain't no FBI, unless they're recruiting at the old folks' home."

Richardson sat in the booth beside him anyway. "I'm retired."

"Then you can't do anything to me. Get out of my way, old man, I'm outta here."

"I'm retired, but Joe and Smithy aren't." He nodded to the booth behind me, where the two big guys in suits sat. They were busy chomping down on their lunch and talking about football, as if they were completely unaware of us. "All I have to do is say the word and they'll come over here and put you in handcuffs."

Munroe eyed the rhinoceroses wearing ties and then said, "You ain't got no evidence of anything. I ain't done nothin'."

Richardson pulled out his recording device and pressed a button. Munroe's voice came out loud and clear: *"I'm thinkin' I need to change the terms of the deal. Why don't you give me a down payment of a million today. I'll give you forty-eight hours to raise another mil. How's that sound?"*

Again, Munroe squinted at me. "You're wired, you piece of sh—"

"Mr. Munroe," Richardson interrupted, "you will be arrested on a federal charge of attempted blackmail if you don't do exactly as I say."

"Screw you."

Richardson pulled a white envelope from the inside of his jacket. He opened it, removed a piece of paper, and laid it on the table. He then took a pen from his shirt pocket and slapped it down as well.

"This is a legal affidavit. It says the film in your possession is indeed the only copy of it in existence, and that you have sold it to Mr. Talbot for the sum of one dollar. Furthermore, you agree to never speak of this transaction or of the film ever again, and you will never contact Mr. Talbot for any reason. Please sign and date it."

"One dollar? Are you out of your mind?"

Richardson ignored him. "*Is* this the only copy of the film?"

"Yes!"

"Then sign the paper."

"And if I don't?"

"Then Joe and Smithy will arrest you. A federal crime is serious, Mr. Munroe. You'd be looking at five to ten years. At your age, that's not so good. You're too old to defend yourself from the prison gangs and you're not old enough for them to leave you alone. You'd be somebody's bitch real quick."

That was enough to scare him. Munroe picked up the pen. Before he signed the paper, he gave me the most malevolent glare imaginable.

Richardson looked at me. "Do you have a dollar, Martin?"

"Oh! Sure." I removed my wallet and pulled out a dollar bill. I held it out to Munroe.

He looked at it as if was a scorpion. "Shove it up your ass, Talbot!"

"You don't want it?" I asked.

"No. Let me outta here."

Richardson stood and allowed Munroe to slide his bulk out of the booth. He did, however, snatch the dollar from my hand before he stormed out the diner door.

I couldn't believe it. I wanted to jump up and dance. "John! Holy smoke!"

Richardson sat again, folded the signed paper, put it in the en-velope, and handed it to me. "I don't think he'll ever bother you again."

"Thank you. Gosh. Thank you!"

Then Richardson called out to the two guys in suits behind me. "It's over, fellas."

"Joe and Smithy" stood. The white guy handed Richardson their bill and said, "Here you go, Grandpa. Did we do all right?"

"You did fine, Joe," Richardson said. "Martin, meet my grandson Joe and his good friend Smithy. Joe and Smithy play for the Co-lumbia Lions."

Dumbfounded, I shook their big strong hands. "They're not FBI agents?"

Joe loosened his tie and said, "I can't wait to get out of these clothes. I feel like I'm at church."

"You fellas go on," Richardson said. "Thanks for your help."

"No problem, Mr. Richardson," Smithy said.

Joe leaned over and gave Richardson an awkward hug. "See you, Grandpa," he said, and then they were gone.

"So we were bluffing the whole time," I said. "That was your big plan?"

"It worked, didn't it?" He handed me his grandson's lunch bill. "Here you go. A small price to pay, wouldn't you say?"

I laughed and took the check. Then he handed me the brown paper bag he was carrying.

"What's this?" I asked.

"Some old Dictaphone tapes I made, back when I knew your mother. I want you to have them."

"Why?"

He shrugged. "I've kept them all these years. I suppose they were a part of the source of conflict between your mother and me. You'll have to find an old Dictaphone to play them. I think you'll appreci-ate them more than I do now. And I know you'll keep them safe and secret."

I didn't know what to say, so I simply nodded, took the bag, and set it on the seat beside me.

"I'm going now, Martin," he said, starting to stand.

"Wait. Don't leave yet."

He shook his head. "I've done what I can. It's time for me to go."

"Can we . . . can we stay in touch?" I asked.

"You have my number."

"Do you . . . do you want to see my mom? You want to come to Chicago?"

Richardson pursed his lips for a moment and then said, "That's probably not a good idea. I'm too old and frail to travel that far."

"No, you're not!"

"Can't do it, Martin. Wouldn't be right. She wouldn't know me anyway." He gazed out the window at the pedestrians on the sidewalk. "I'm glad you contacted me, though. The way I treated your mother—well, let's just say this gave me a chance to make it up to her. Thank you for that."

"You're welcome. But it's me who should be thanking you."

He held out his hand and I shook it. Then he got up, took the bank bag, and left the diner.

I knew I'd never see him again.

# 47
## *Judy's Diary*
### 1959

LATER

I had to take a break and get a bite to eat, dear diary. I feel like I'm writing *War and Peace*, ha ha.

So where was I? Oh, yeah, I had my hands cuffed behind my back, I was unmasked but carrying the mask and my stiletto in one hand, and I was running west on 127th Street. I stopped in a shadowy alcove of a gutted brownstone to catch my breath and figure out what I wanted to do. I couldn't take the chance of anyone seeing me without my mask, and yet I either had to go the distance and pursue John's boss and Carl Purdy—'cause somehow I knew they were in cahoots—or I had to give up and make my way home.

I was too angry to surrender, so I headed toward Purdy's bordello on 129th Street between 5th and Madison. Part of me felt guilty that I didn't go back to the machine shop to help John. After all, he *did* help me. But I knew that would be suicide. An unmasked Black Stiletto was no match for all those cops or G-men, whatever they were. I couldn't think about poor Mike Washington, who turned out to be one of the good guys. And I couldn't worry about John. I was still upset about his treachery. How many people in the FBI knew he was sleeping with the Black Stiletto? I've heard of spies using sex to get information, dear diary, but I thought that was the stuff of pulp fiction. Of course, I suppose I did the same thing last year to that Cuban spy, Rafael Pulgarón, but I never imagined in a million years that tactic would be utilized against *me.*

Crossing Park Avenue was trickier than usual. Although it was pretty late, there was still a lot of traffic and pedestrians out. I felt so exposed without my mask. I finally just went for it and darted across the avenue with my head down. I must've looked like a chicken running across the road. I made it, though, and continued heading west until I reached Madison. As I moved north two blocks to 129th Street, I kept my head down again. I'm sure some folks saw me, but hopefully I was travelling so quickly that they couldn't focus on my face.

Sirens filled the air in the distance. It was impossible to determine where they were, but I knew they were close. Probably at the machine shop.

Finally, I made it to the brownstone. Sonny was still in front.

Could I trust him? Somehow, I thought I could. Call it that mothering instinct of mine. I was pretty sure I'd reached him before. Somewhere deep inside the young man was a good person that had been smothered by evil. No doubt he'd been promised a better life if he joined the gang. I had to appeal to the innocent teenager he once was.

I stepped out of the shadows about ten feet away from him.

"Sonny," I said softly.

He jumped and drew a gun from beneath his coat. When he realized who he was looking at, his mouth dropped and he lowered the weapon.

"I need your help," I said. "Please."

"I can't help you. Get out of here! They'll kill you if they see you! I'm supposed to be watchin' out. It's my job. Go away!"

"Sonny, is Ruby still here?"

The spark behind Sonny's eyes flickered. Something passed over his face, and I knew it was the specter of guilt and pain.

He shook his head. "She died."

"Was it the drugs?"

He hesitated and then shrugged.

"Sonny, you need to get out of this hellhole. This is a pit of wickedness. You're still young, Sonny. The cops don't know about you. You can walk away and leave it behind."

"I got nothin' else, lady. You're white. You don't know how it is."

"You're right. I'll never know what it's like for you or any other Negro in this country. But I think I understand it."

He didn't reply.

"Sonny, it was Carl Purdy who killed your sister. Not the drugs. You can't let him get away with it. I'm not gonna let him get away with it. Please help me. I trust you. You've seen my face."

"What do you want?"

I turned around. "Take my mask and put it on me."

Once again he faltered. Then, after a few seconds, he holstered his gun and approached. He took the hood out of my hand, reached up, and pulled it over my head. I turned to face him and let him adjust it. My hair was still sticking out the bottom and back of the mask, but I could fix that later.

"Now take my knife and put it in the sheath on my leg." He took the stiletto, examined it, felt its weight, and then stuck it in the small scabbard. "Great. Now open that pouch on my belt, the one by the flashlight." He did. "See that thing that looks like a key ring? Take it out." When that was done, I said, "Let's move into the shadows over here so no one will see us." We stepped into a dark spot, away from the light. "Now I need you to find the right pick that'll unlock these handcuffs. Start with the smallest one and then work your way to the larger ones. One of them should work." Sonny stuck the first one in the keyhole. Too small. "You need to jiggle it a little, and try to catch the pick on a latchlike thing inside the cuff. If it doesn't work or you don't feel any resistance, go to the next size up."

He quickly got the hang of it and tried the second lockpick. I thought that one would do the trick, but he couldn't trip the catch. "Try the next one," I prompted.

When he stuck it in, Sonny said, "I feel it." He twisted and turned the pick.

"Do it gently. Pretend you're working with very delicate parts of a watch, like a jeweler."

He worked the pick with a lighter touch. I could feel the object tugging on the mechanism inside the cuff.

"That's it! Now turn it sharply!"

Voilà! The right cuff was off!

"Bravo, Sonny! Thank you!" I took the picks from him and quickly undid the cuff on my left wrist. I returned the ring to the pouch, stuck the cuffs into my belt, and gave him a hug, which surprised him. Then I removed my mask again, bundled up my hair, and tucked it into the hood.

"I'm going inside now, Sonny. I hope you'll just go home. I have a feeling the police will be here in a little while. I don't want you to get in trouble."

He didn't say anything. Instead he just backed away, out of the shadows, and resumed his spot in front of the building.

Fine. I'd tried. Now it was time for a showdown.

But before I could make a move, a car with bright headlights pulled into the street, its tires screeching on the road. Whoever it was, they were in a hurry. I quickly hid in the shadows and waited. It was a 4-door black sedan, very similar to John's. The car squealed to a halt in front of the bordello.

The back doors opened. Carl Purdy stepped out on the sidewalk side. He wasn't cuffed or inhibited in any way. John's boss, Haggerty, got out on the other side. The driver was one of Haggerty's men I'd seen at the machine shop.

So my suspicion was correct!

"Help me get the stuff," Haggerty ordered as he unlocked the trunk. Purdy obeyed him, grabbing milk crates full of the wrapped bricks of heroin I'd seen earlier. Haggerty told the driver, "Wait here," and then the two men carried the drugs inside the building. Sonny held the door open for them.

How would I get in? Last time I used the fire escape on the building next door, climbed to the roof, and dropped down to the fifth-floor window terrace. That wasn't going to work this time, not in plain view of Mr. G-man behind the wheel of the idling sedan. Whatever I decided to do, I had to get rid of him.

I took the chance that he hadn't locked the car's back doors after the two men got out, so I simply emerged from the darkness, crept up behind the vehicle, squatted, and quickly opened the back door behind the driver. I jumped in before he could see me in the side mirror. Just as the man reacted, I leaned over the seat, reached around in front, and locked my arm around his neck. Soichiro had taught me a chokehold early in my training. It was not the ideal position with which to apply it; the hold was awkward to say the least, but I was able to apply the appropriate amount of pressure to his neck by forcing it back against the seat itself. My other arm locked around his chest and upper arms to prevent him from honking the horn. He struggled like all get-out, and for a few seconds I thought he was going to overpower me and break free. Darn, it took a long time for him to finally pass out—maybe a couple of minutes—but he finally did! I knew he wasn't dead and he'd probably regain consciousness in a few seconds, so I quickly got out of the car, opened his door, and pulled him out and onto the street. He started to stir, but I whipped his own handcuffs off his belt, pulled his arms behind his back, and locked his hands together.

Sonny had watched me the entire time without sounding the alert.

I still heard sirens in the distance. It seemed to me they were coming closer, but there were so many that it was difficult to tell.

"Where in the building do you think Purdy and that other man went?" I asked Sonny.

"Probably the office," the teen answered. "On the first floor."

"Where is it?"

"You go in and there's a hallway. Walk down the hall. To the left is a sittin' parlor and to the right is a closet. A little farther down the hall is another door on the right. That's the office."

"Thanks." I headed for the stoop.

"There'll be other men in there," Sonny warned. "With guns."

"I know. You should go now. I appreciate your help." He didn't move, so I went on with my business. I ran up the steps to the front door, put my ear against it, and listened. I heard men's voices, but they were distant. It was safe to continue, so I turned the knob and peered into the hallway. A man stood about twenty feet away, down at the end, next to the door Sonny identified as the office. His back was to me, thank goodness. The office door was open, and the voices I'd heard were coming from inside. Haggerty and Purdy.

I'm pretty good at creeping up behind someone without making a sound. I entered the building and ever so softly shut the door behind me. As long as the wooden floorboards didn't creak under my boots, I knew I could surprise the guy guarding his boss.

Step by step. One foot at a time. When I was about ten feet away from him, he shifted his weight, removed a cigarette pack from his jacket pocket, and tapped one out into his hand. He bent his head as he lit it.

*Now.*

I rushed to him and, using a *shuto*—sword hand—I walloped the man hard at the base of the head where it connected to his neck. A blow hard enough to break bones on this vital point would surely paralyze a person for life; however, using force conservatively could knock a guy out. That's what I did. I then caught him with my free arm before he made a lot of noise crumbling to the floor. He was heavy, but I managed to drag him back away from the door and laid him down in the hall.

I crept forward and listened beside the open door. Haggerty was talking.

"—because all hell will break loose. Give me the goddamned money now, Purdy! I saved your ass!"

"I know, I know. Where you gonna go?"

"Hell, I don't know. I may not have to go anywhere. It depends on if Richardson is dead or not."

When he said that, dear diary, I felt a twinge in my chest. As angry as I was at John, I certainly didn't want him to die. What happened back at the machine shop?

"You shot him," Purdy said. "He looked dead to me."

"I hope you're right. Even if he's not, he won't talk. Nobody would believe him. He has no evidence. His word against me and my boys. Now give me my cut and I'll get out of here. You hear the sirens. This place might be crawling with cops any minute. It won't take 'em long to figure out you got away."

"You realize how much product we lost? Your man picked up only a third of the shit."

"Shut up and just give me what you owe me."

I heard the flapping sound of money being counted.

"I'm gonna have to lay low, too. Maybe take a trip to Chicago or somethin'."

"Damn it, Purdy!"

"Okay, okay. Here's five hundred, a thousand, fifteen hundred, two thousand—"

Outside, the sirens grew closer. Now I was sure they were headed for the bordello. I had seconds to accomplish what I came to do.

I reached into the backpack and pulled out the Kodak Brownie. Making sure the film was wound and ready for a picture, I held it to my eye and moved in front of the open doorway. I snapped a shot of Purdy placing a stack of bills in Haggerty's open hand.

"Damn!" Haggerty shouted as he drew his gun from inside his suit jacket. "Get her!"

Without thinking, I delivered a back kick through the open door, striking Purdy in the side. He fell into Haggerty, who fired his gun at the ceiling. Money flew *everywhere*. Both men crashed against a desk, but I didn't stop there. I dropped the camera, leaped for Haggerty's gun arm, and slammed it against the desktop. He screamed in pain and released the weapon. Almost simultaneously, I performed a side kick at Purdy's ribcage, hopefully breaking a few of 'em. He fell to the floor and started to struggle for a gun holstered underneath *his* jacket. I stomped on his right shoulder with my boot. Purdy cried out, unable to complete the move. I wanted to break his collarbone. Ignoring Haggerty for the moment, I reached down, removed Purdy's handgun, and tossed it over by Haggerty's.

The sirens were now right outside the building. I heard men running down the stairs from the upper floors. Women screamed. I slammed the office door shut with my leg just before the men ran by.

Then the gunfire started. Purdy's men were stupidly shooting at the cops. Didn't they know that was the surest way to get killed?

At any rate, I had to get out of there. I pulled the FBI handcuffs off my belt, snapped one on Purdy's wrist, wrapped it around the desk leg, and locked the other cuff on Haggerty's wrist. Partners in crime, not quite joined at the hip, but almost.

I stood, picked up my camera, and noticed all that money on the floor. I thought *oh, what the heck?* I scooped up a handful of hundreds and opened the office door. The gunfire was deafening, but I didn't see a single soul. They were all at windows, engaging in a firefight with the law. I ran for the stairs and dashed to the second floor. A group of colored women huddled in terror, their hands over the ears. I kept going, up to the third floor, the fourth, and finally the fifth. I made my way to the room where I'd last seen Ruby. It was empty. I slammed the door shut, went to the window, and opened it. The gunfire continued outside, so I looked down to the street.

There were five police cars on the street along with Haggerty's sedan. A crowd of pedestrians was beginning to gather across the street and out of the way of the bullets. I saw bodies on the sidewalk. Uniformed officers scattered like bugs, taking cover behind their vehicles.

Then I saw him. Oh, my God, dear diary, poor Sonny. His young body was sprawled across the steps on the stoop. I wanted to scream.

If I hadn't been so desperate to escape, I would have started crying. It was such a tragedy. First his sister and now him, all because of Carl Purdy and his evil empire. For a moment I thought I should have killed Purdy when I had the chance. Somehow, though, I knew it wouldn't have done much good. Purdy would only be replaced by someone else. It was a mind-numbingly sad and vicious circle, indicative of the Negro's plight in our society.

I had to force myself to snap out of my despair. The shooting seemed to die down, and I heard shouts and screams through the closed door. I climbed out to the terrace, unlashed my grappling hook, and tossed it to the roof. It took me two tries to catch the edge. I prayed the cops wouldn't see me. They were busy already running inside the front door to raid the joint. They'd work their way up the stairs, arresting the women and whatever men were still alive. I climbed the rope hand over hand, swung my body over, and crouched on the roof. After pulling up my gear, I quickly moved west to the next building. I stopped there, laid flat on its roof, and stuck my head out just enough to watch the scene below. Voices were faint, but I could make out phrases here and there.

Haggerty came out of the building. He was no longer cuffed to Purdy. I heard him say, "—took me by gunpoint—got away—forced me to—gonna kill me—" That figured. Haggerty's story was the biggest tall tale I'd ever heard. Purdy kidnapped him. Sure he did. Then I heard, "Agent Richardson? He's alive?" I barely made out one of the officers answering him with something about a hospital.

Purdy came limping out next, handcuffed and surrounded by three policemen. He was all bent over, in pain. I guess I really did break a bone or two! Haggerty pointed at him and shouted, "He held a gun to my head and made me—!" They marched the gangster to a squad car and threw him in the back.

That was my cue to leave. I'd been lucky the cops hadn't seen me so far, so I wasn't going to tempt fate any longer. I made my way west toward 5th Avenue, climbed down a fire escape, and hit the street. In the shadows, I dressed in my trench coat and removed my mask. I hailed a taxi and, not surprisingly, the colored driver was astonished to see a white woman in Harlem at that hour. I had him take me to 3rd Avenue and 21st Street.

John's building.

After I paid the driver, I masked myself again and made my way up the fire escape to John's apartment window. Luckily, it was unlocked; it slid right up. I slipped inside and went to his desk.

I grabbed my camera and wound the film until it was at the end. I removed the roll and placed it on John's desk. I then searched the desk for pen and paper, and wrote a note explaining that the film contained evidence against Haggerty.

Then I noticed the Dictaphone and the box of tapes. Curiosity got the better of me, so I opened the box and examined the labels. I felt a shiver when I saw there was a group marked "Stiletto." I took one, placed it in the Dictaphone, and played it. The machine wasn't very complicated.

I sat in John's chair and listened. I spent an hour going through those wretched things. Everything I'd feared was proven correct. He *had* planned it all. He *had* seduced me just to get me to trust him. Haggerty knew all along. The boss wanted me caught, and John was going to oblige. He said this on the most recent tape: "—I should say I know exactly where to find her, but I don't. But I suppose if it came down to saving my job —" Then there's this juicy quote: "She trusts me more and more every day, which is exactly what I want." And this one: "I told Haggerty that the more confident she becomes, the easier it will be to lure her to a secluded spot from which she'd have no escape."

Once again my heart was ripped out of my chest and stomped on. I couldn't take anymore. I wrote a second note and left it for John to find when he came home from the hospital. In it, I said it was really over between us, that I had trusted him and he broke my heart, and that I hated him. I asked him not to contact me ever again. If he decided to reveal my identity to the world, then so be it; but if he did that, I said I was certain he had no soul. I then wrote, "Goodbye," and signed it "Judy."

Before I left, I found some of the booze he claimed to never drink and had a glass of wine. Then I walked out his apartment door, went down the stairs, and exited through the front door. It was very late when I finally got home.

My, the afternoon flew by as I wrote all this down.

I'm thankful I'm alive and unhurt, but I feel great sorrow for Sonny, and even a little for Mike Washington. As for John Richardson—well, I'll just have to purge him from my memory forever.

Good riddance.

# 48
## John

### Home Dictaphone Recording

Today is December 21, 1959.

It's a Monday before Christmas. My rehabilitation is going well, I'm back living in my apartment, and even though I haven't been to work since that night in Harlem, I've been promoted.

I've also been a damned fool. I'll get to that in a minute.

The bullet wound in my shoulder is healing nicely; it was the shot in the abdomen that was worrisome. I was lucky the bullet went all the way through, but my intestines were like mush. The three-week stay in the hospital was no piece of cake. But I'll live. Gotta take it easy for another two months, then I go back to work as a Special Agent in Charge.

Haggerty was indicted based on the evidence the Black Stiletto provided. The photo she took convinced a Grand Jury that the former SAC was guilty of corruption and drug trafficking. The police found the bullet that pierced my gut lodged in the wall of the machine shop break room. It was a match to Haggerty's weapon. Not sure when the trial will be, but I'm a star witness. It's troublesome to testify against a former boss, but everyone at the Bureau is behind me. They hated him, too. [Laugh.] Not only that, NYPD Chief Bruen has been indicted as an accomplice. The whole city is shocked by these revelations.

I was afraid Haggerty would reveal I slept with the Black

Stiletto. So far he hasn't. At first I thought he'd had *me* under surveillance and knew all about the trysts Judy and I had. I feared he had evidence tucked away somewhere. But when the D.A. confiscated all of Haggerty's files from his office and home, there was nothing linking me to the Stiletto. If there is, I haven't been told about it. So I assume Haggerty was bluffing at the machine shop. He made a lucky guess about the Stiletto and me. If he says anything, I'll just deny it. He can't prove anything.

As for Purdy, he'll be going to prison for a long time. He's been indicted for the murder of Mike Washington, racketeering, and drug trafficking. He's also been linked to a number of murders unrelated to the night he was arrested. For now, his operation is out of business. I'm sure, though, that someone else will step up to the plate and take over. The Bureau believes illegal narcotics trafficking is here to stay and will only get worse.

The Black Stiletto received a lot of credit in the papers for exposing the "Harlem Connection." I made sure of that, but I don't think it's going to alter the Bureau's attitude toward her. The NYPD isn't too happy with her, either. Nothing's going to change in that regard.

And then there's Judy herself. That's where I made a very big mistake and I suppose I should be man enough to admit it.

I saw her this afternoon at the gym. She wasn't happy to see me. We talked outside, as we did before. She didn't seem as angry now, but I know I disappointed her. I insisted no one at the Bureau had heard the Dictaphone tapes. They were personal. I also tried to convince her I was merely humoring Haggerty with the so-called plans to catch the Stiletto. At any rate, I will never reveal her identity.

I was in love with Judy, but I was too stubborn or stupid or whatever it was to tell her so. Instead, I did lead her on. I just didn't know how I was supposed to handle it. I was an FBI agent, and she was a wanted criminal. Now, in hindsight, I should have said, "Who cares?" She's a girl I could change careers for. But it's too late now.

Judy asked me to never contact her again. I'll respect those wishes. But maybe someday I'll be able to do something for her, and she'll forgive me.

That's all.

# 49
## Martin

### The Present

Gina returned to her dorm room after her first session of counseling. I met her there since her roommates were at classes. We sat in the living room as she sipped on a protein shake through a straw. I hated to see her jaw wired like that, but she was handling it well. The bruises were fading rapidly and she was beginning to look like her young beautiful self. You just couldn't see those straight, white teeth.

"I'm gonna go to class on Monday," she managed to say. Her speech had also improved. She'd gotten the hang of talking with her jaw closed.

"Are you sure you're ready for that?" I asked.

"I'm as ready as I'll ever be."

"What did your therapist say?"

"She said the sooner I try to make my life normal again, the better off I'll be. So that's what I'm gonna do."

It made sense. I just couldn't believe she could go through such a traumatic experience and bounce back like she's doing. I had the feeling she was covering up a lot of pain.

"Honey, you don't have to, you know," I said. "You can take all the time you need. The school said you could take the semester off."

"I'm not gonna do that! It's just a month into the term. I love my classes! I won't be able to take dance until next semester, but I'm not dropping out, Dad."

Before I could say my next sentence she interrupted with, "And don't even *think* about trying to get me to come back to Chicago. No way. I'm staying here."

"Okay, okay, I got that."

We were quiet a moment. She slurped her shake loudly and we both laughed. Then she asked, "When are you leaving?"

"My plane's at three. I have to go to LaGuardia in an hour."

She nodded, set her empty glass on the coffee table, sat back on the sofa, and folded her legs underneath her.

"Sorry I'll miss your birthday," she said. "Happy Birthday."

"Thanks, darling." To tell the truth, I'd forgotten it was coming up. On October thirteenth, I'll be forty-nine.

Another pause.

"I talked to Detective Jordan again this morning," I said. "They're still waiting for the DNA test results on your fingernail scrapings."

"They're not gonna catch him, Dad."

"Why do you say that?"

She shrugged. "If it's true he's the same guy who attacked those other women, then he's pretty good at getting away."

"But he's bound to make a mistake. That's how they catch those creeps."

She seemed to become pensive. Gina turned her head toward the window that faced Broadway and offered a nice view of the city. She and her roommates were lucky to get the suite.

"I'm starting to remember more," she said quietly. "The therapist said that would happen."

"That's why I wonder if it's still too soon for you to go back to classes."

She shook her head. "That won't make any difference. The memories and nightmares will be there no matter what."

"You're having nightmares?"

She hesitated and then nodded.

"Honey—"

"I was just walking home, Dad. Minding my own business. And

then he appeared out of nowhere. All I really saw was the glint of steel reflecting the streetlamp. It was a big knife."

"Gina, you don't have to—"

But she continued anyway. "He said, 'Don't make a sound or you're dead.' I remember a sudden rush of adrenaline and for a second I thought I could just run away from him. But he had a tight hand clasped around my arm and the knife pressed against my stomach. So I didn't do anything. Then he said, 'Come with me.'"

I really didn't want to hear this, but I let her talk anyway.

"He forced me off the lit sidewalk and into a dark spot surrounded by trees. And then . . . and then he *hit me*!"

"Honey—"

"I swear I saw stars, my head exploded in pain, and then I fought back with some kind of animal instinct. I must have scratched his face. But the next thing I knew, I was lying on the wet grass. That's all I remember until I woke up at the hospital."

"It's probably good you don't remember the rest," I said.

"Maybe. Maybe not. I do remember one thing, though."

"What's that?"

"I remember dreaming. In the hospital. They said I was out for a while."

"Nearly seven hours, Gina. You were unconscious for seven hours."

"Yeah. I had dreams. Vivid dreams. At least I think I did."

"What about?"

She looked at me with a curious expression on her face and she tried to smile. "Grandma," she answered. "I dreamed about Grandma Judy."

It was difficult leaving Gina, but I know she's a lot tougher than me. She would get through her ordeal. She admitted she was naïve about streetsmarts. What happened was an eye-opener. She promised me she'd be more careful in the big bad city. I know she will.

*

After arriving at O'Hare, I took a cab home, picked up my car, and drove to Woodlands to see Mom. I saw Dr. McDaniel standing at the nurses' station in the Alzheimer's Unit as I walked in.

"Mr. Talbot, how are you?"

"Fine, thanks."

She asked about my daughter and I gave her the scoop. Then I asked how Mom was doing.

"Pretty good," the doctor said. "She's been in good spirits. Nothing's really different, I suppose."

"Did she miss me?"

The doctor gave me a wry smile. "That's something we'll never know."

I started to walk away and then I got a crazy idea. I have no idea where it came from, but I acted on it.

"Say, Dr. McDaniel?"

"Yes?"

"Would you like to have coffee with me sometime?"

There was no doubt I found her extremely attractive, even though she often rubbed me the wrong way. Perhaps that's why I was interested.

She blinked twice, obviously just as surprised by the question as I was. Then she stunned me by answering, "That'd be nice, Martin. Thank you. I'm here on Mondays, Wednesdays, and Fridays."

"Okay. I'll see you one of those days."

And for the first time, she smiled at me.

"I'm gonna go see my mom now."

"You do that."

So I left her and walked through the common room, where I was suddenly struck by the ethnic mix of residents. I'd never really thought about it before, but reading Mom's 1959 diary has made me more aware of the whole racial *thing*. Had we as a population moved forward in our attitudes toward racism since then? In many ways, we had, of course, but a lot of work still needs to be done. Shoot, I'm guilty of unintentional racism. I jumped to conclusions about Gina's attacker, immediately believing he was some black guy. I said the wrong thing to the black detective. And I admit I'm not comfortable on the New York streets with so many African Americans around me. Why is that? What am I afraid of? I have no idea. My mother raised me correctly; there wasn't an ounce of prejudice in our home. Is bigotry inherent in our culture, even though we've taken huge steps to stamp it out? Will it ever be eradicated from human existence? I doubt it. These questions can't be answered with a simple "yes" or "no." Nothing is black and white, no pun intended. I'm beginning to see that this is something my mother learned in 1959.

She was happy to see me, that's for sure. Her eyes brightened and she gave me a big grin. I told her I'd been in New York to see Gina, and that her granddaughter sends her love.

"That's nice," she answered, as she always did.

Well, *I* think Mom missed me.

At that moment I was also struck by how much Gina is like my mother—stubborn, determined, and very independent.

So I sat with Mom for an hour or so. I read to her, told her how I still need to look for a job, and helped her with her dinner. I thought about mentioning I'd seen the East Side Diner and had met John Richardson, but figured it would either upset her or she'd have no idea what I was talking about. So I didn't.

At the end of the visit, I kissed her cheek, told her I loved her, and left Judy Talbot, née Cooper, alone in her room.

I'd see her again tomorrow.

# 50
## *Judy's Diary*
### 1959

**DECEMBER 31, 1959 — NEW YEAR'S EVE!**

Our annual party's going strong downstairs, dear diary. I popped up to my room to change clothes. The new pedal pushers I was wearing just aren't fancy enough. I decided to put on one of the evening dresses I used to wear when I was out on the town with Fiorello. It's much more glamorous. I thought maybe it'd make me feel more spirited. Then I saw you sitting there on the table and figured I should go ahead and write a quick entry before I get too drunk, ha ha! After all, it's time for what I've decided will be my regular end-of-the-year look back. Gosh, I can't believe we're starting a new decade. I don't remember when 1950 rolled in. I was 12 then, but I don't recall anyone noting the event with any special attention.

You're wondering why I haven't written in over a month. Well, I was in the dumps for a while after that night in Harlem. I still am. You know why. Then with all the Christmas madness, and throwing myself into work, I just didn't get around to it. Besides, nothing of note has happened.

Freddie closed the gym for the four days surrounding Christmas weekend and the four days surrounding New Year's. Good idea! Today he was my date to finally go see *Ben-Hur*, the movie everyone in the world is raving about. I thought it was fabulous! The chariot race was so exciting I nearly peed. I've been going to a lot of movies lately. Last week Lucy and I went to an Elvis double bill at the Waverly—*Jailhouse Rock* and *King Creole*. Heaven! I heard he's coming back from the army in the spring, and I can't wait for some new music. Oh, and golly, Lucy and I watched *The Wizard of Oz* on television a couple of weeks ago. I've *never* seen it before! I think it's been on TV only one other time, but I didn't see it then. What a *great, great, great* movie! I loved it so much. I wish I could see it in a theater on a big screen.

The party started an hour ago. Everyone is here—Jimmy and Louis and Wayne and Paul and Corky and Freddie and Lucy and Peter. Even Isuzu is here. I tracked her down and invited her, even though she's too young to drink. I'll keep a watch on her, though, won't I? Ha ha. She's doing very well, all things considered. She misses her father, of course, but she's happy his killer is behind bars. I miss Soichiro, too. It's like a hole in my heart.

Clark is here, too. I gave him a big hug when I saw him, which I think surprised him a little. What a nice, intelligent young man. For his sake, I hope the Negroes get what they want in all this civil rights fuss. I have a feeling, though, it won't happen overnight. It's gonna be years. Clark thinks calling his race "Negroes" will go out of style in this country. One day, he said, he'll be called an "African American." I like that. It has a nice ring to it. I often think about Ruby and Sonny and Angela and Sheila—and even Mike Washington. They were innocent souls caught up in something dreadful. One thing I learned this year is that anyone can be a good person or a bad person; it doesn't matter what the color of his or her skin is. I believe most of the African Americans up in Harlem are good people. They've just been handed a raw deal and they have to somehow find a way to make it better. Maybe that Dr. King will help. Times are changing.

I do still think about John. It didn't help that he came to see me a few days before Christmas. He'd been injured pretty badly. Shot twice. I told him I was glad he's all right. John apologized and tried to explain his actions. I told him once again: it was over between us.

I said I enjoyed our time together—when we *were* together—but that it's best we not see each other again. I believe that, dear diary. I don't think the Black Stiletto and law enforcement boyfriends mix very well. So I shook his hand and asked him not to contact me anymore. I watched him limp away, and then he hailed a taxi. When I finally went inside the gym, he was long gone.

I better get downstairs. There's champagne to be had! Yep, I think I'll really tie one on tonight. I deserve it. I've been so unhappy lately. Even if I end up bawling like a baby and feeling sorry for myself, it'll be a nice catharsis. I could use a good cry.

As the 1960s begin, what will become of me? All this melancholy is a result of the Black Stiletto. On one hand, she's been a life-altering release for me; on the other, she's a millstone, a huge weight on my shoulders.

I wonder if it's time to give her up.

Well, as they say, tomorrow is another day. Another year, actually.

I'll think about it then.

Happy New Year!

# ABOUT THE AUTHOR

Between 1996 and 2002, Raymond Benson was commissioned by the James Bond literary copyright holders to take over writing the 007 novels. In total he penned and published worldwide six original 007 novels, three film novelizations, and three short stories. An anthology of his 007 work, *The Union Trilogy*, was published in the fall of 2008, and a second anthology, *Choice of Weapons*, appeared in the summer of 2010. His book *The James Bond Bedside Companion*, an encyclopedic work on the 007 phenomenon, was first published in 1984, and was nominated for an Edgar Allan Poe Award by Mystery Writers of America for Best Biographical/Critical Work. Using the pseudonym "David Michaels," Raymond authored the *New York Times* best-selling books *Tom Clancy's Splinter Cell* and its sequel *Tom Clancy's Splinter Cell: Operation Barracuda*. Raymond's original suspense novels include *Evil Hours*, *Face Blind*, *Sweetie's Diamonds* (which won the Readers' Choice Award for Best Thriller of 2006 at the Love is Murder Conference for Authors, Readers and Publishers), *Torment*, and *Artifact Of Evil*. *A Hard Day's Death*, the first in a series of "rock 'n' roll thrillers," was published in 2008, and its sequel, the Shamus Award-nominated *Dark Side of the Morgue* was published in 2009. Other recent works include the 2008 and 2009 novelizations of the popular videogame, *Metal Gear Solid* and its sequel, *Metal Gear Solid 2: Sons of Liberty*, and *Homefront: The Voice of Freedom*, cowritten with John Milius.

The first book in the Black Stiletto series was published in 2011.

Raymond has taught courses in film genres and history at New York's New School for Social Research; Harper College in Palatine, Illinois; College of DuPage in Glen Ellyn, Illinois; and currently presents Film Studies lectures with *Daily Herald* movie critic Dann Gire. Raymond has been honored in Naoshima, Japan, with the erection of a permanent museum dedicated to one of his novels, and he is also an Ambassador for Japan's Kagawa Prefecture. Raymond is an active member of International Thriller Writers Inc., Mystery Writers of America, the International Association of Media Tie-In Writers, is a full member of ASCAP, and served on the Board of Directors of The Ian Fleming Foundation for sixteen years. He is based in the Chicago area.

www.raymondbenson.com